SCARRED FOR LIFE

Kerry Wilkinson's debut, *Locked In*, the first title in the detective Jessica Daniel series, was written as a challenge to himself and went on to become a UK Number One Kindle bestseller within three months of release.

Since then, his Jessica Daniel series has sold over three-quarters of a million copies and he became the first formerly self-published British author to have an ebook Number One and reach the top 20 of the UK paperback chart.

Scarred for Life is the ninth title in the Jessica Daniel series.

Kerry is an occasional sports journalist and can frequently be spotted cycling the hills of Lancashire while trying not to be knocked off. Please drive safely around him. He was born in Somerset but now lives in Lancashire.

For more information about Kerry and his books visit:

www.kerrywilkinson.com or
www.panmacmillan.com

Twitter: twitter.com/kerrywk

Facebook: www.facebook.com/JessicaDanielBooks

Or you can email Kerry at kerrywilkinson@live.com

By Kerry Wilkinson

The Jessica Daniel series

LOCKED IN

VIGILANTE

THE WOMAN IN BLACK

THINK OF THE CHILDREN

PLAYING WITH FIRE

THICKER THAN WATER

BEHIND CLOSED DOORS

CROSSING THE LINE

SCARRED FOR LIFE

The Andrew Hunter series

SOMETHING WICKED

The Silver Blackthorn Trilogy

RECKONING

KERRY WILKINSON

SCARRED
FOR LIFE

PAN BOOKS

First published 2015 by Pan Books
an imprint of Pan Macmillan, a division of Macmillan Publishers Limited
Pan Macmillan, 20 New Wharf Road, London N1 9RR
Basingstoke and Oxford
Associated companies throughout the world
www.panmacmillan.com

ISBN 978-1-4472-4789-0

1 3 5 7 9 8 6 4 2

A CIP catalogue record for this book is available from the British Library.

Typeset by Ellipsis Digital Limited, Glasgow
Printed and bound by CPI Group (UK) Ltd, Croydon, CR0 4YY

SCARRED FOR LIFE

1

Adam Compton undid his top button and tugged at the collar of his shirt.

The tut came almost instantly as Jessica Daniel nudged him in the ribs. 'Stop fidgeting – we're supposed to be incognito, not looking shiftier than a used-car salesman taking a lie-detector test.'

'It's itchy.'

'Stop moaning and keep walking with me.'

Jessica stretched out and took his hand in hers, giving him a squeeze and leading him around a set of benches.

'I still don't get why I had to dress up?' Adam complained.

'You're only wearing black trousers and a shirt – it's hardly a tux. Besides, it's because you're out with me – not slumming it around the house watching children's cartoons in your underwear. I've even got heels on for the first time this year.'

Adam glanced down as if he didn't believe her, even though he had driven because she didn't fancy chancing her feet on the car's pedals while wearing them. 'We're at a railway station – it's hardly dinner at the Ritz,' he said.

Before she could reply, a public address announcement boomed around Manchester's Piccadilly Station reminding everyone to keep their bags with them. Jessica continued to scan the crowd as they ambled past the main departure board for the fourth time, before stopping close to the exit and turning to look at the times on display.

Small groups of people mooched past, clinging onto their bags and squinting at the digital display board before pointing and heading off to their platforms. Men and women in business suits, children climbing over large cases as their parents scanned for the next train to the airport, scallies with their caps pulled down and hands jammed in pockets, City fans, United fans, teenagers – Jessica searched them all but no one stood out. At least not in the way she wanted.

Adam was fidgeting again. She couldn't remember the last time she had seen him in anything other than a pair of jeans and a T-shirt. Even when he went to his job at Manchester Metropolitan University, he got away with it by putting a jacket over the top.

The scruffy git.

He freed his hand from hers and tugged at his hair. She knew he was wishing it was long again, having caved in to her relentless nagging and had it sliced down to ear-length.

'You're not looking posh enough,' Jessica said.

'How do posh people look?'

'They stand straighter and don't pull at their hair.'

Adam pushed himself up onto the tips of his toes and cricked his back. 'Do they stand near open doorways doing nothing as the wind howls through?'

'We're here for a reason.'

'What reason?'

Jessica took his hand again and started to lead him

across the concourse. Her heels clip-clopped awkwardly as she had to think her way through every step. This used to be easier when she was seventeen and sneaking off with her friend Caroline trying to get into pubs. Heel-toe, heel-toe, don't step in the cracks between the tiles. Noise echoed around the enclosed area: footsteps, chatter, a child wailing, the whoosh of an espresso machine, ding-dong: 'For security reasons, passengers are reminded to keep their bags with them at all times.'

All right, sod off, we get the message.

Jessica continued to peer at the crowd as she led Adam to an area close to the women's toilets and turned to face a different departure board.

'So . . . ?' Adam said.

Jessica replied without facing him, still people-watching. 'There are a few blank spots in the CCTV – where we were by the doors, here, over by the far tables at the coffee shop and a few other places.'

'Are we trying to stay out of view?'

'We're trying to appear enticing. You're failing.'

'Enticing to who?'

Jessica spotted a teenage boy, fourteen or fifteen, squeezing between two people hauling suitcases behind them. He took a phone out of his pocket and stopped in front of a rotating advertising board to make a call. His slanted spiky hair pointed high to the heavens and he looked the type to have covered himself in half a can of deodorant that morning. Earring, arse hanging out of his trousers, shiny white trainers, fake gold bracelet, swagger: not who she was looking for.

As the board clicked over to 18.16, Jessica double-checked the catch on the small handbag hanging over her shoulder. That, the heels and the long dress weren't just beginning to feel uncomfortable, they had been since the moment she'd tarted herself up. Not that she could tell Adam that after ticking him off for complaining. In many ways, it was a shame that the first time they'd got dressed up to go out in months involved them hanging around a train station. The fact it was for work purposes pretty much summed up their relationship.

'There've been a series of pickpocketings here in the past month,' Jessica said. 'We've had people going over the CCTV but there's never anything on there. The victims are always in the camera's blind spots and dressed like we are: people who have come in to the city to go to a show, the Opera House, or for a swanky swingers' party. Whoever our thief is knows the layout and how to get in and out without being seen. Every time we've had police down here, they make it so obvious they're our lot that nothing ever happens. The security guards and transport police are as much use as sun cream in Manchester, so I told the guv I'd try something different.'

'And that involves me?'

'The victims are always part of a couple, so yes. Just stand there, gaze at the board and put on that innocent look you always have when I come downstairs late at night and you're pretending you've not just wiped the laptop's Internet history.'

Adam huffed in a way he probably thought was outrage but it only made him sound guiltier. Jessica nudged him gently and they started to loop around the station again, passing the escalator and the platform exits before heading towards the main doors. Jessica found a spot close to the hot-dog stall and tried not to wince as the scent of burnt onions wafted across. Even she was a better cook than that.

A Goth couple; a lone woman in higher heels than Jessica's running as if the laws of gravity and physics didn't apply; an old man with a walking stick and tattered brown coat; a student type in shorts and a T-shirt even though it was dark and November; a blonde girl no older than sixteen on her mobile phone: 'No, I only snogged him, like . . . Get lost, you cheeky bitch, I don't care what he says, I didn't shag him.' A pause to tug at an oversized hoop earring. 'Oh, *that* time. Well, yeah, but it was only the once and I didn't know he was going out with her. It didn't last long anyway.'

Jessica zoned out of the conversation, continuing to watch the crowd. She didn't fancy coming back here every night until something happened. Six separate pickpocket cases in five weeks. It wasn't the crime of the century but Jessica liked being out and doing something, instead of cooped up in her office at the station, filling in paperwork, signing things off and generally boring herself. DCI Jack Cole had given her the same shrug she'd seen a lot recently when she had suggested going to the train station with Adam. If she wanted to do something pro-active in her spare time then so be it.

'Can you see the board from here?' Adam asked.

'Why wouldn't I be able to?'

'Because it was only a couple of months ago some bloke

5

was lasering your eyes. I didn't know if it had any other effects.'

'Like what?'

Adam mumbled something under his breath but he must really be bored if he was back to talking about her eyes again. Jessica had eventually gone for laser eye treatment, having spent months constantly losing her glasses. At the time, he'd gone on about how it would give her superpowers – some sort of laser projectile out of *Star Wars*, *Star Trek* or some other geeky thing she couldn't care less about. He really was a nerd sometimes. If someone had told her sixteen-year-old self she was going to end up engaged to a person who, in most circumstances, would've been suitable for an intimate relationship only with his own hand then she would've told them to sod off. She tried to remember the name of the boy she lusted after in college; the one whose name she wrote in love hearts and blathered on to Caroline about over cheap cider. Was it Jez? Jeremy? Had there ever been anyone fanciable called Jeremy? She couldn't remember. Maybe it was Jeff? No, that was worse than Jeremy. Definitely a J in there somewhere.

Ding-dong: 'For security reasons, passengers are reminded to keep their bags with them at all times.'

The voice reverberated around the station again, as Jessica wondered if anyone had ever kept hold of a bag because of it.

Her mind was wandering annoyingly from the crowd she was meant to be watching back towards work, as ever. Adam took her by surprise as he leant in and spoke softly: 'What are we going to do later?'

'I'm not keeping the heels on just for you, if that's what you're asking.'

He stifled a smile, mind firmly read.

'We need to get some milk,' Jessica added. 'There's that twenty-four-hour place on the way home. Hopefully we'll hit that sweet spot where all the sandwiches and meat have been reduced but before everyone else piles in and only leaves the egg ones.'

Adam sniggered. 'What rock-and-roll lifestyles we live: a night out at the train station and reduced-price sandwiches on the way home.'

'You won't be moaning if we get a reduced pack of cookies or muffins.'

Adam started to reply but his words dissolved into a saliva-filled 'Mmmm'.

So easy to please.

A man in a suit hurried past, phone clamped to his ear, other hand readjusting his crotch. 'Who authorised twenty per cent?' he said too loudly. 'I'm not going out to Stockholm to sort it again.' He glanced up to see Jessica watching him, finishing playing with himself and scowling at the same time: a piece of multitasking she wouldn't have thought him capable of. He told whoever he was moaning to that he'd call them back and then stomped into the nearby coffee shop.

Jessica was just thinking about how unsociable mobile phones made everyone when she felt hers begin to vibrate in her bag. With Adam standing next to her, it meant there were only two candidates – either her mother or someone from the station. If not them, then someone trying to sell her any number of financial products she definitely didn't want.

She fumbled in the bag, tugging the phone out before realising that the contents were a lot less compacted than when she'd left the house.

'Something wrong?' Adam asked, as Jessica emptied her bag onto the top of a newspaper dispenser.

'Shite.'

'What?'

'Someone's nicked my purse.'

2

She may have lost her wallet but Jessica eventually answered her phone on the third ring. There must have been a quiz show on television distracting her mother because it wasn't her. Jessica had left a pair of jeans, warm top and sensible shoes on the back seat of the car and got changed in the shadows of the multi-storey car park. Poor old Adam had been ditched for work again, left to catch the bus or tram home. One day she would make it all up to him. Or, at the very least, she would keep telling herself that.

With the rush-hour traffic long gone, Jessica headed along Oxford Street, over the river and into Salford. As she passed the university buildings and made the turn into Peel Park, the familiar blue haze lit up the car park, spinning blue bulbs on top of police cars eating into the darkness and signalling some poor sod hadn't had a good day. Aside from a breeze whipping off the water and through the park, the evening was surprisingly mild. Jessica headed towards the group of silhouettes massing close to one of the bridges which crossed the River Irwell. Cigarette smoke and northern accents drifted into the air, joined by the sound of activity somewhere close to the river.

The shadows dissolved into a handful of uniformed officers, with the cigarette smoke coming from a man muttering to himself in an Eastern European-sounding accent.

In the mix of the orange glow from the street lights above and the blue rotating lights of the police cars, the scene looked like the type of disco where no one ended up going home alone.

One of the detective constables was taking notes but stopped to peer up as Jessica arrived. 'I thought you'd knocked off for the day,' he said.

Jessica shrugged – it was no wonder she always got the call: she was always the one stupid enough to drop everything and attend. 'They told me there was a body,' she said.

The DC nodded backwards. 'Scene of Crime are there now.' With a slight sideways motion, he indicated the man with the cigarette. 'This is Pavel. He found the body.'

Jessica looked the man up and down: muddy jeans, walking boots, and a thin dark jacket. His eyes darted sideways catching the orange light, his pointed nose and stubbly chin making him look like a startled rabbit.

'*Kto?*' he said, his accent sounding thicker than before.

Jessica stepped a few metres away, gesturing for the officer to join her. 'How's his English?'

'Better than my Polish.'

'What did he say?'

The DC lowered his voice, even though they couldn't be overheard. 'He does agency work for some cleaning company in the city. A few people called in sick, so they've been behind all day. There's a university rowing club-house down by the river they're contracted to do once a week – but he only got here as it was getting dark. He was

10

mumbling something about striking bin men and everything being messed up.'

'What did he find?'

'You're better off seeing for yourself. SOCO are going to be there for a while.'

Jessica nodded, heading past the officers, down a slope towards the water's edge. Away from the blue and orange lights, the moon gave the river an unearthly glow, black ripples serenely rolling towards the bank. Jessica watched them for a few moments, breathing the night air, knowing this was going to be another late one, followed by an early morning tomorrow and then who knew what else. She held the cool air in her lungs and then turned to face the large building behind her. At its front was an elaborate arched doorway, with wooden decking sloping down towards the water. Three boat landings stretched into the water, waves lapping at the struts that plunged into the dark depths. The whitewashed facade had some sort of cross-paddle logo painted on it that she couldn't entirely make out in the dim light.

At the back of the building, bright white lights seared through the night, illuminating the grass verge that surrounded it. Jessica followed the light until the all-too-familiar shapes of the paper-suited Scene of Crime officers came into view. One of them was leaning into a tall metal wheelie bin, its once blue sides scratched grey, as another ducked into a translucent white tent.

Jessica didn't need to go any closer to figure out what had happened. 'Was the body actually in the bin?' she called across.

One of the female SOCOs she recognised but didn't know the name of eyed her suspiciously, until Jessica stepped into the light and revealed herself. 'Thrown out like an old takeaway tub,' the officer replied grimly.

'Is the bin full?'

The woman shrugged, not knowing why it mattered, but she nodded anyway. It took Jessica a moment to remember which day it was: one of the curses of age.

Thursday, definitely Thursday.

With the bin full, it seemed likely that today was collection day – or would have been if the bin men weren't on strike. It had been on the lunchtime news that they'd walked out that morning, protesting at a colleague's suspension. She wondered if the killer knew the routine, assuming the body would be landfill by now. If it wasn't for the industrial dispute, it probably would have been.

Jessica scanned the rest of the alleyway without edging any closer; the days of inspectors trampling on crime scenes were long gone. The wheelie bin was next to another, both pressed against a red-brick wall close to a fire exit. Above, a steep grass bank sloped down from the park towards a rough patch of concrete. Aside from a stray crisp packet blowing from side to side and the Scene of Crime gear, the alley was clear.

Sometimes you wanted to see more but occasionally the setting was enough, knowing that a person had been tossed away like they were nothing. Jessica would wait for the photographs and report.

She felt the wind bite, whistling between the verge and the clubhouse as she turned and headed back up the slope towards the other officers. Jessica approached the constable from before, who was standing by himself tapping something into his phone.

'Any clue on the identity?' she asked.

He looked up, nodding. 'There was a wallet in his pocket. They've bagged it but there was a student ID in there. Some kid named Damon Potter; nineteen years old, local by the looks of it. We did an informal ID from the photo on the card and someone's on the way to see his parents so they can make it official. Paperwork's already being sorted. Poor sods. I'm surprised they called you down.'

At least the evening crew knew what they were doing, which was more than could be said for the new recruits on day shift. Jessica wouldn't trust some of them to tie their own shoelaces.

With the SOCO team doing their jobs, the initial admin in hand, and not much more likely to be confirmed until morning, the handful of officers had begun to drift away, cleaner Pavel in tow. They were either heading for the patrol cars to go back to the station, or they'd felt the siren's call from the kebab shop around the corner. Jessica knew where her money lay.

As she started digging for her car keys, Jessica noticed someone hurrying towards them: a tall, slender frame with large shoulders illuminated in the mishmash of light. The DC gave Jessica his best 'no idea' shrug as they waited. As he got closer, Jessica could see that the man was in his early twenties, athletic, with eyes that were darting past them towards the slope that led down to the boathouse.

His tan was apparent even in the faded light, tufty sand-coloured hair topping off the beach-bum look.

Ignoring Jessica, he went straight to the constable, standing a good four inches taller than him and introducing himself as Holden Wyatt, student president of the university rowing club. Even before she heard the accent – gently northern but with the harsher twang coached away – Jessica knew the type. He'd ignored her because he'd automatically assumed a man would be in charge.

'I got a call from campus security,' Holden said.

'Do you know Damon Potter?' Jessica asked.

He spun to face her, realising his mistake and weighing Jessica up in an instant by running his eyes up and down her. He was seemingly used to being in charge of situations and followed with a short, assertive nod, before pushing himself up onto the tips of his toes, ensuring he towered over her. 'Who are you?'

Jessica took her identification from her pocket and held it in the light for him to see. 'De-tect-ive In-spec-tor.' The words rolled around Holden's mouth, as if he didn't quite believe them. 'Why have I been called down?' he added.

Jessica didn't actually know but she wasn't going to show him that. 'I tend to ask the questions. That's where the whole "detective" bit comes from. Anyway: Damon Potter – who is he?'

Holden's nose twitched and he looked skywards, biting his bottom lip as if trying to remember. It was a show entirely for her benefit as there was recognition in his eyes.

'I think he's one of our members. Perhaps a first year?

The newbies only join in September or sometimes October, so I don't know everyone yet.'

'How many members do you have?'

'Active? Eighty or so – I'm not sure. We have a membership secretary. Then there are life members, alumni, the president and so on.'

'And you're affiliated to the university?'

Holden's head bobbed from side to side before he nodded. 'Traditionally, yes, but we have our own constitution. Members must come from the university but we're not a part of the students' union, or the university itself.'

'Do you get funding from them?'

'A little.'

'And how do you get to become student president?'

Holden glanced at the constable, wondering why he was being questioned. 'Look, it's getting late. I thought there'd been a break-in, or something. Is there a problem with the club? Or Damon?'

Jessica checked her watch, making the point that it wasn't *that* late, and then nodded. 'It's not been confirmed but Damon's body was found dumped in one of the bins at the back of your clubhouse.'

For a moment, Holden stared at her. She could almost see the cogs whirring in his head. 'He's dead?'

'Yes.'

'How?'

'We don't know yet. When did you last see him?'

Holden ran his hand through his thin mop of curls and noisily blew out through his mouth. A thin stream of breath spiralled into the air, making Jessica realise that it was now colder than it had been. 'I'm not sure – we have a lot of new members at this time of year. Most of the first years row in their own teams because we already have established line-ups. I'm in the final year of my master's and don't necessarily know everyone. We have our own schedules for practising and so on.'

Jessica took a business card from her pocket and told him to call her if he remembered anything else about Damon. He asked if he could check the club over but she told him not until their search teams had picked through everything. After his previous confidence, Holden now seemed distracted, scratching his head and rocking back on his heels, losing an inch or so of height. He read the details on Jessica's card before pocketing it and turning to walk back the way he'd come. They would need to talk again properly but she wanted to know her facts before she went eyeball to chest with him again – she was certain he hadn't told her the entire truth.

As Jessica was about to call the station to find out where the search team was, the first drops of rain began to clatter onto the path. She felt sure that whoever had left the body knew what they were doing and wouldn't have trampled across the grass at the back of the club – but an evening of rain wasn't going to help.

Welcome to Manchester: mild one minute, chilly the next, pouring down moments later.

For now, the late team could deal with things but tomorrow someone was going to have to dig through the contents of both bins. Jessica knew just the people for the job.

3

The lights flickered in the newly refurbished incident room at Longsight Police Station. After a temporary spell upstairs without heating but with an increased risk of everything from asbestos poisoning to Legionnaires' disease, everyone was allowed to work in the basement again. Well, 'work' being a subjective term considering the electricity had been on the blink since they'd moved back the previous month. That was combined with the fact that it still reeked of fresh paint.

Jessica scowled upwards as the white strip bulb chuntered angrily before deciding it wasn't going to douse them in darkness. Below, the mix of uniformed officers and CID officers rabbited to each other.

Quieting them with her trademark 'all right, shut it, you lot', Jessica glanced at the scrawl of notes she'd made. Her handwriting really was appalling. Behind her on a whiteboard, images had been pinned up of the area at the back of the rowing club, alongside a large photograph of Damon Potter in his rowing uniform. He had a physique much like Holden's the night before – tall and lean but with strong shoulders. His dark hair was cut short, determined brown eyes staring out into the room atop a chiselled jawline.

'Okay, so we have an official ID on the body of Damon

Potter from last night,' Jessica said. 'We should have cause of death back later but there were no obvious bruises on his body and no signs he was attacked. Regardless, he didn't just fall into the bin – so someone knows what happened to him. I've got things to do today, so I want you lot doing the digging here. Who does he hang around with? Does he have a girlfriend or boyfriend? Where does he live? Who are his family? Is he a cat or dog person? All that sort of stuff. The night boys have started but nothing was open.' Jessica nodded towards DS Louise Cornish, a middle-aged, slightly frumpy woman who was staring past her towards the board. 'Louise will sort things at this end. Damon was a member of the rowing club, so I want details on that too – who are the main people involved? What do they get up to when they're not dinghy-racing, or whatever it is they do? Those of you with Iz already know what you're doing; those on bin duty are already on site – everyone else with Louise.'

Chairs scraped and tea was slurped as the assembled officers slowly started to move. Jessica nodded at Acting Detective Sergeant Izzy Diamond, indicating an unoccupied desk near the front of the room.

Izzy looked tired, blinking rapidly and pushing a loose strand of long brown hair behind her ear. 'I know what you're doing,' she said, peering at Jessica, eyebrows raised.

Jessica tried to sound as if she didn't know what her friend was talking about. 'What?'

Izzy's half-laugh wasn't convincing. 'You should've pulled my people to investigate your body in the bin.'

'We've got enough officers.'

Izzy shook her head, not complaining. Jessica slid a photo out from under the keyboard on the desk. It was a still frame taken from a CCTV camera at an off-licence, showing a balaclava-wearing man pointing a serrated-edged knife in the direction of a cashier.

'Any luck with the tattoo?' Jessica asked, pointing at the complex shapes on the robber's bare wrist.

Izzy shook her head. 'That picture from Monday is the clearest. The marks are distinctive but we've not had anyone coming forward to say they know someone with tattoos like that. We've been around the city's tattoo places and identified them as some sort of African tribal patterns but if our guy got it done in Manchester then no one's saying anything.'

Four off-licences robbed after dark around the city, thousands of pounds taken, with the only clue being the tattoo. Jessica stared at the figure again. Not particularly fat or thin, dark short-sleeved top, jeans from George at Asda, size nine or ten workman's boots, balaclava covering his face. It wasn't an original outfit but it did the job.

Izzy had recently been promoted from constable to sergeant on a temporary six-month basis. This was the first proper case she had been assigned. Jessica knew the fact she hadn't solved it quickly was annoying her.

'How's Amber?' Jessica asked, referring to the sergeant's young daughter.

'Growing,' Izzy replied, not wanting the subject to be changed and lowering her voice to a whisper. 'I really need to get the job permanently. Mal's had his hours cut and the extra money . . .'

'They're not going to deny you that because there's some tattoo we've not been able to find.'

'It's not going to help – especially if this guy keeps holding up shops.'

Jessica couldn't argue; if the attacks continued then someone higher up the chain would take over the case anyway – likely her. She was about to offer some sort of encouragement and head off when Izzy added: 'Has the guv still got the arse with you?'

Jessica tried to brush the remark off with a shrug but Izzy wasn't going to let it go. 'Did you ever figure out what's up with him? It's been going on for months now – ever since that Scott Dewhurst guy was shot.'

Even the sound of his name made the back of Jessica's neck prickle. That bald head, the thick fingers and his vice-like grip. If she closed her eyes, she would still be able to see him.

'I don't think it's that,' Jessica replied. 'Anyway, it's not just me. I think he's just getting grumpy in his old age.'

It was true: Detective Chief Inspector Jack Cole *had* been off with her ever since Dewhurst was shot. It wasn't that he'd said anything specific, more that his replies were always short and that he went out of his way to avoid meetings involving her that weren't absolutely necessary. Jessica didn't mind that as such – anything that got rid of extra paperwork and what she considered time-wasting was fine by her – but the fact other people had noticed proved it wasn't just in her mind. As for why, Jessica didn't know. She was up with all of her targets and, despite the tattoo robberies, there wasn't much on their unsolved pile.

20

Izzy caught Jessica's eye, nodding towards the door with a knowing grin. 'Here's your sidekick.'

Jessica turned to see Detective Constable Archie Davey swaggering towards her. There was no other way to describe the way he walked: knees bent outwards, chest pumped forward, shoulders back. It would be laughable but for the fact that he actually had the presence to pull it off. After being short-staffed for longer than Jessica could remember, Greater Manchester Police had finally got around to hiring some new constables and Archie had been the first face through the door six weeks previously. At barely five foot eight, he was hardly the stereotypical police officer but he had served his dues working for uniform in the Southern district of Manchester.

'All right?'

Archie's thick Mancunian accent rarely failed to make Jessica smile. In another life, he would have been the exact type of lad about town they spent half their days trying to catch. With the raise of an eyebrow, he could turn from being a happy-go-lucky constable to looking like he wanted to tear a person's lower intestine out. He probably could as well. The product of a Stretford council estate, Archie knew the city as well as anyone but had chosen the right side of the criminal fence. On the odd occasion she had seen him in action, Jessica had been surprised at how far a local-sounding voice could get them on Manchester's estates. He was the perfect appointment. Even at twenty-seven, he sounded like more of a scally, chav or whatever else they were called nowadays, than half the people they arrested. His dark tight curls were gelled back, which, combined with his cocky smirk, had contributed to a few of the females around the station noticing him. His ladies' man reputation preceded him.

'You're with me today,' Jessica told him.

'Wanna brew first?'

He really was the perfect appointment.

Jessica nodded. 'Make Izzy one too and see if the canteen's got any fried bread on the go. We've got a busy day.'

Archie pushed out his bottom lip, spinning to head back the way he'd come. 'Sorted. They had some barms on yesterday.'

For a moment, Jessica thought he was going to add 'luv' but he just about clung onto the final word. During his first fortnight, he'd managed to get himself into trouble by calling almost everyone – male, female, sergeant, inspector and everyone else alike – 'luv'. It was part of the vocabulary where he'd grown up and he'd kept hold of it through his days in uniform. It didn't go down quite so well when he told the chief inspector that he'd 'be there in a minute, luv'. After apologising, when it was just him and Jessica, he blamed the guv for not being up on Mancunian dialect.

Izzy was smiling as Jessica turned back to her. 'He's going to get himself into trouble one of these days.'

'He's all right.'

'Only because we know him. Dave's got a man-crush on him.'

It was Jessica's turn to smile. Detective Constable David Rowlands had spent the past few weeks barely concealing his admiration for the new DC. Jessica figured it was because Dave believed Archie was a younger version of him. The difference was that, with Archie, the casual boasts about girlfriends were actually confirmed by other officers. With Dave, even when he'd been younger, they had always been questionable to say the least.

'Where is Dave?' Izzy asked.

'Bin duty with Jane and a couple of the others.'

'Joy Bag?'

Jessica nodded. Jane's unfortunate nickname was also something that preceded her around the station, a product of finding a pile of used condoms under a flower pot during another fingertip search.

'She's going to have it in for you even more than before,' Izzy said. 'Still, "Bin Boy" and "Joy Bag" have quite the ring to them.'

'If you have no luck catching our tattooed robber, you have my permission to spend the day trying to get that to stick.'

Izzy laughed. 'What happened with your pickpocket thing?'

Jessica had almost forgotten about it. The crimes were so minor that they weren't high on their unsolved list. She shrugged. 'No luck – it was only a long shot. Adam moaned all evening about having to dress up.'

'You should've taken Archie – he's up for anything that gets him out in public where there might be girls.'

That was true – but Jessica hadn't exactly treated the Piccadilly stake-out seriously. 'Did I ever tell you the first thing Arch said to me?'

'No.'

Jessica grinned. 'Someone had just introduced me as an

inspector, so he shakes my hand, looks me in the eye and goes, "Are you a red or a blue?"'

'What did you say?'

'I thought he was talking about politics and said I don't vote for any of those bastards. He looked at me as if he'd just eaten lasagne from the canteen, then said, "I meant footy. City or United?" I sort of shrugged and said I wasn't into football. For a moment he seemed confused, as if he couldn't believe it, then he nodded and said: "At least you're not a bitter." That's a Man City fan, apparently. The next week, he was asking if I could swing the rota so he was off for a United game.'

'I said he was going to get himself into trouble.'

As Izzy finished speaking, Archie waltzed through the door again, carrying a grease-soaked paper bag and three polystyrene cups with steam seeping through the lids. Jessica wanted to disagree but from the way Archie nodded towards the car park, she couldn't help but feel that it was only a matter of time before he was too casual with the wrong person.

Manchester's weather was continuing to be predictably unpredictable. After the coldest May and wettest July on record, this November was unseasonably warm. Jessica skirted through the streets of the city in a creaky pool car as Archie glanced through the passenger's side window at various women wearing low-cut tops.

'Will you stop doing that?' Jessica said.

'What?'

'Doing an impression of the Exorcist girl every time we pass a woman.'

'It's not my fault the sun's out. I'm only looking. There are blokes for you, too.'

Jessica glanced across to where Archie was pointing. An overweight man wearing jeans and muddy boots had his shirt off and tucked into his back pocket. 'Are you joking? He's got bigger boobs than me.'

Archie puffed between his teeth dismissively. 'What I don't get,' he said, 'is why this Damon kid was at Salford Uni. His parents live out in Wilmslow, so they must have a few quid about them. He could've gone anywhere but he chose Salford. One of the *Manchester* ones, maybe, but *Salford*?'

Jessica wasn't sure if his annoyance was due to his Manchester bias and the fact that Salford was a separate city, but he had a point. Salford wasn't a bad university – but if you had money and a choice, it probably wouldn't be the first one.

They got their answer fairly quickly after meeting Damon's father. Francis Potter had made his money building up a haulage firm and was a director for four other companies – all based locally, all full of cash. Not that his large house and three cars on the driveway made up for the loss of his son. Francis, clearly devastated, told them that Damon had gone to the University of Salford to study Business and Management because their family was committed to the area. He had an accent more profound than Archie's. The plan had been for Damon to complete his degree, work for a master's, and then to set up his own company with his father's help. From everything Francis said, his son's career path had long been mapped out, with grades less important than the fact that Damon was studying locally.

He answered the rest of their questions but didn't seem to know much about his son's current life, perhaps not a surprise as Damon had chosen to live in student accommodation rather than at home.

Jessica and Archie left the house knowing little more than they did before arriving. As they were heading for Salford, her phone rang with the cause of death. Damon had choked on his own vomit and had cocaine and high levels of alcohol in his system. From the initial examination, there was no sign of a struggle but it had likely happened sixteen to twenty hours before his body had been found.

It seemed such a waste. He wasn't the first young person to die in such a way and wouldn't be the last – but if it was simply a case of an accidental overdose, then why would someone go to the hassle of dumping the body in a bin?

4

Jessica and Archie's next visit was to the head of Business and Management at the University of Salford – a thrilling job that someone had to do. Professor Robert Harper was what Jessica considered to be a stereotypical lecturer: cord jacket, elbow patches, balding, barmy. The strands of what was left of his hair appeared to be independent of each other, jutting off at unrelated angles like the straws in a game of KerPlunk. His office made Jessica's look as if there was actually order to it. Hers might have files, papers, crisp packets and who knew what else strewn around the floor and desk but his had the contents of at least one rainforest. Books were piled on top of each other, covering an entire wall, with extra shelves running around the rest of the space overflowing with more tomes. The computer keyboard on his desk was buried under a pile of papers, with a printer burring in the corner, spitting page after page into a plastic tray.

After insisting they call him 'Bob', Robert invited Jessica and Archie into his office, muttering about how awful everything was regarding Damon's death. The body find had led the local news that morning, even though the exact details of the location hadn't been revealed. Officers would be flooding the campus that morning to talk to classmates and anyone else who might have known Damon – but Jessica wanted to talk to a few key people herself.

'Very bright, very bright,' was the professor's first assessment after being asked what he thought of the dead student.

'How long have you been teaching here?' Jessica asked, taking a seat but being careful not to move too much in case it brought the nearby tower of books crashing down upon her. Death by hardback would be one unforgettable way to go.

Call Me Bob sucked on his teeth and glanced up to the ceiling. 'Let me think . . . I was at City, then I did two years at John Moores, then I came here, so that's eight, nine, twelve years here; a bit over twenty in total.'

The printer in the corner finally stopped spitting pages out, leaving a moment of silence before Jessica filled it: 'Roughly how many students do you teach a year?'

Apparently unaware of the meaning of 'roughly', Call Me Bob started hunting through the papers on the keyboard, holding up the lists of students before giving Jessica an exact number, then explaining that he didn't teach all of them, simply that he was head of department. Jessica could feel Archie tensing next to her; she didn't think down-to-earth Mancunians and erratic university lecturers would ever be the best of bed-fellows.

As she glanced across to him, Archie caught Jessica's eye, leaning in and whispering into her ear behind the back of his hand. 'Who the fook's called Bob nowadays?'

Jessica nodded knowingly, as if he'd raised a good point.

In many ways he had but she still wondered what he was up to.

Call Me Bob's eyes flickered between the two of them, wondering what had been said.

'If you don't teach all of the students,' Jessica said, peering back at the professor, 'how come you know who Damon is?'

Leaning back into his chair, Call Me Bob stroked his chin. 'When you're head of course, you tend to know the students at the very top and very bottom. Those who do exceptionally are the ones the staff always talk about, of course, but there are also the students who miss classes, deadlines, or end up dropping out. The others, who turn up regularly and get middle-of-the-range grades, are the ones you tend to gloss over and perhaps don't know the details of.'

'Was Damon at the top or the bottom?'

The professor nodded enthusiastically. 'Oh, the top, definitely. His father is well known in business circles around the city, so it was a name that jumped out when I saw this year's admissions list. He was immediately one of the exceptional students, though. I was getting reports back straight away to say he was one to watch. I teach the introduction module – something to keep my eye in each year. All the students take a test in their first fortnight. It's nothing too serious and has no bearing on their final mark; it's more to assess their initial knowledge. He had one of the highest scores since we brought the test in.'

'And Damon continued in the same vein?'

'Yes. I don't think he missed a class in the couple of

months he was here. His work was always on time and the marks were consistently in the top two or three in the year. In the introductory class, whenever I asked a question, his hand would usually be in the air.'

'Did you notice any changes in him in recent weeks?'

Call Me Bob shook his head, hair flapping wildly in a breeze Jessica couldn't feel. 'I took a class with him on Tuesday and he was the same as ever – hand in the air, taking notes and so on. If anything, he seemed more enthusiastic than usual.'

Archie leant in again, whispering into Jessica's ear behind his hand. 'Is it me or is this guy's head on upside down?'

Jessica's eyes flickered up towards the professor. Now Archie had mentioned it, the flapping strands of hair on his head would have made more sense as a beard. She nodded thoughtfully and made a 'hmm' sound as Archie leant back. Call Me Bob peered from one officer to the other but said nothing.

'Is that attentiveness unusual?' Jessica asked.

Call Me Bob tried to flatten his hair but only succeeded in making it more static, then he scratched his shoulder. 'When I first got into teaching, all the students were interested and wanted to learn. Now everyone goes to university. Tuition fees slowed things down a little but there was a period where courses were accepting any old body – people with Ds and Es at A-level, just to make the numbers up and keep government funding. Then you have all these offshoot, new-fangled courses – herbology, hairdressing and who knows what else. It's not like the old days, so it's nice when you have students who want to learn.'

Jessica clarified a few further points, taking the names of the other lecturers who taught Damon. At some point they would need to be spoken to, but someone else could do that. As they were standing to leave, the professor stood too. 'Do you think you'll find out what happened to him?' he asked.

She began to answer but was interrupted as Archie sent a pile of papers tumbling from the desk. 'Shite, oops, sorry mate,' he said, hunching to help pick things up. Together, they tidied everything back into a stack but Jessica couldn't help but notice the metal hip flask which had previously been hidden. Still, if she had to spend every day surrounded by hormone-riddled teenagers, she'd probably have a sly drink every now and then too.

Jessica told Bob that they'd do their best to find out why Damon had died – as if she could say anything else – and then they headed along the student-filled corridors in silence, following signs to the cafe.

'You're buying,' she told Archie, sitting in a low-backed wooden chair, taking in the room. Compared to the greasy spoon places round her way and most of the cafes in the surrounding Salford area, the university one could have been built for a king. Clean tables were a start but there was also a spiral staircase linking two floors of the teaching building, with bright stainless steel coffee machines behind the counter whooshing intermittently as a line of students queued for their skinny lattes. Archie might well have fitted in with the locals but he couldn't stop himself standing out among the student population. His posturing and pigeon chest made him look like a particularly short students' union bouncer.

He arrived at the table with two cups of tea and a scowl. 'Fooking students,' he complained. 'Girl behind the counter tried to serve me some shite with peppermint in it.'

Jessica sipped from her cup. 'Is camomile more your thing?'

Archie was about to spit out a 'no' when he caught Jessica's eye and grinned instead. 'Aye, and that green shite.'

'What was going on upstairs with you whispering to me behind your hand?'

He shrugged slightly. 'Dunno, he seemed a bit iffy. I was seeing how he'd react. Did you see the flask on his desk?'

Jessica was surprised Archie had spotted it. 'Yes.'

'I saw it early on but thought I'd knock those papers off in case you hadn't. Then there's the books.'

'I was afraid to move in case they came tumbling down.'

Archie blew into his cup. 'Not that; there were all these textbooks but then he had these general poetry books at the back.'

'So?'

'He's a business professor – not even English professors read poetry.'

'Perhaps he likes poetry?'

'Leave it out – there's no way he's read everything in there. It's all bobbins – all for show. Give me Cooper Clarke any day.'

'Who?'

'John Cooper Clarke – punk and poet. Manc lad – well, Salford, but you can forgive him that.'

'You're into poetry?'

Archie finished swilling tea in his mouth and swallowed. 'Not really, but I know someone trying it on when I see it. Takes one to know one.'

Jessica took a mouthful of her own drink, wondering if he was right. In her younger days she might have been the one storming in to put the proverbial up people just to see how they'd react. Now she was supposed to be sensible and clamping down on it. The hip flask was likely doing no harm; still, if Archie had spotted it before her and had bothered to scan the spines of the books – something she hadn't done – then perhaps he wasn't just the Manc loudmouth everyone thought.

5

Tea drunk and students slagged off, Jessica double-checked the address with Izzy at the station and then headed half a mile down the road to a bright red-bricked student accommodation block. When Jessica's friend Caroline had been a student in Manchester, it was all rundown houses covered in blankets and bean bags, reeking of stale cigarette smoke and spilled alcohol; now it was custom-built flats and studio apartments, with free WiFi and coffee shops on the ground floor. Archie's 'tsk' as they rang the buzzer made his feelings clear too.

Damon's roommate, Alistair, buzzed the door open and then met both officers on the stairs. He took two or three steps at a time, his gangly legs getting him to the third floor just as Jessica was rounding the corner from the second. As he waited in the doorway of a flat, she could see the blankness in his face. He was tall and thin but appeared cowed, having discovered Damon's fate. He pushed open the unlocked front door and let both officers in without a word, leading them into a living room that had two leather sofas, a large flatscreen television fixed to the wall, a games console on the floor and any number of other expensive-looking electrical devices at intervals around the room.

Jessica and Archie sat next to each other, with Alistair slumped on the other sofa, elbows on knees, staring at the floor. 'When the police came round last night, I thought they were joking,' he said. 'Well, not joking, but you know what I mean. I couldn't take it in.'

'When did you first meet Damon?' Jessica asked.

'September. These are private halls – they do anywhere between two and five people per flat, then you share a kitchen, living room and bathroom.'

'But this flat was just you and Damon?'

'Yes, you pay an extra tenner a week but you get more space, so it's worth it. The company who owns this place puts lads with lads and girls with girls, unless you're moving in with people you know. There's this complicated form. I ended up with Damon but we didn't know each other before that.'

'Did you get on?'

Alistair looked up from the floor, glancing between Jessica and Archie. 'Pretty much from the moment we met. Do you know his dad?'

'Yes.'

'So you know he's got a few quid, then – except you'd never know by being around him. I didn't find out until we'd been hanging out for a couple of weeks, then we were at a pub and a girl from his course was there. She made some remark about it and he ended up telling me that his dad ran a company and so on. Apparently he was ready to go away and start a business when his course was over.'

'Was he happy about that?'

Alistair seemed surprised: 'Why wouldn't he be?'

'Some people don't like the feeling that their life is

already mapped out. They want the freedom to make their own choices.'

'If he was unhappy then he never said. He was only in year one but was already talking about how the final project for year three was to create a viable business plan. He had a few ideas because that's what he wanted to go and do afterwards.'

'Were you his best friend at university?'

Alistair shrugged. 'Dunno. He hung around with a few lads from his course, and liked going rowing, of course.'

Jessica had been waiting for Alistair to steer the conversation round to the rowing club so that it felt more like a natural topic of conversation. 'How often did he go?'

'Three or four times a week, depending on the weather. He tried to get me into it but it's not my thing.' He sighed, pursing his lips. 'To be honest, I'm not sure it was his either. He liked the competitive thing and said he was decent at it – but he would never have put it before his course.'

'Do you know any of the people at the club he was friends with?'

'No, I think it was more of a social thing for some of them but he actually wanted to race. That was pretty much the only thing he ever said about it. He was always exhausted when he got back from practice – we'd sit in front of the TV and have a drink.'

'Was he a big beer drinker?'

Alistair shook his head. 'Not really.' Jessica raised her eyebrows but he didn't wilt. 'Well, sometimes we'd go out and have a few but it was never ridiculous. Beer wasn't his thing anyway. He might have a cider but was more into spirits.'

'Drugs?'

The reply was instant: 'No.'

'There were substances in his system when his body was found . . .'

Alistair gulped, peering between her and Archie, weighing them up: 'Okay, we sometimes do a little bit of weed, but it's less harmful than cigarettes, isn't it? It's only the odd rollie now and again, I'm not a druggie – neither was he if that's what you're asking.'

Jessica waited, wondering if there was anything else. When Alistair didn't reply, she added: 'Ever done anything harder?'

'No – honestly.'

'What about Damon?'

'No . . . well, I don't think so. If he has, he never said and we never did anything like that together. He was into his studies – we only had the odd joint to relax at the end of the day. I don't think he would've wanted to do anything that would risk his place on the course.' Alistair peered down at the floor again. 'I'm not in trouble, am I? It's only a bit of weed.'

He sounded more pathetic than aggressive.

'Where does the cannabis come from?'

'Er . . .'

'I'm asking because if someone was dealing drugs to Damon then he could've been into something more serious than you knew. If you tell the truth, you won't be in trouble.'

37

Alistair's head popped back up again, eyes showing slightly more clarity after being told he wasn't about to get nicked. 'It's someone I know, he's, er, some lad—'

'All right,' Jessica interrupted, 'let's not go digging any holes. If you can assure me it's just some small-time arrangement between you and a mate, we'll pretend this part of the conversation didn't happen.'

'It is.'

'Fine.'

The truth was, Jessica didn't have the time, manpower or inclination to pick up some small-time campus cannabis dealer when he'd be back out in twenty-four hours, fresh with an eighty-five-quid fine and a criminal record that would likely get him kicked out of university.

'Did Damon have any enemies?' Jessica asked. 'Anyone he'd fallen out with?'

A shake of the head.

'Girlfriend?'

'Not as such.'

'And what's he been like this past week or so?'

'Fine, if anything, he's been happier. He was getting up earlier to go rowing.'

Call Me Bob had said something similar.

'Any idea what he was happy about?'

Another shake of the head. 'No idea. We'd have a drink and go out now and then but we didn't really talk about too much . . . y'know . . . girly stuff.'

Jessica had to stop her eyes rolling – presumably that meant relationships. She glanced sideways towards Archie, who almost imperceptibly raised an eyebrow. In an instant, it was gone again and Jessica knew what he meant, as if she had read his mind.

'I need the toilet, then I'll brew up,' Jessica said, getting to her feet.

'Tea bags are—'

'Yeah, under the sink, over the sink, in a cupboard somewhere. I'll find them. Be right back.'

Archie had wanted a few minutes alone with Alistair. Although the student didn't seem the blokey type, sometimes men were happier talking to other men. Archie would turn on the lad-about-town charm, bang on about a few of the better clubs and pubs in the centre, and then see if he could get some real information out of Alistair. Meanwhile, Jessica went for a poke-around.

She went through the kitchen into the hallway, leaving herself three doors to choose from. After finding the toilet at the first attempt, Jessica closed the door quietly and moved on to the next one.

The police's search team had been in the night before and cleared anything from Damon's bedroom that could be classed as evidence, leaving the space eerily empty. The bed had been stripped, exposing a plain blue mattress. Wardrobe doors were hanging open, coat hangers limply clinging to the rail, while there was a dusty patch on the desk in front of her from where a computer had been taken. At this very moment, someone at the forensics base in Bradford Park would be picking over the hard drive. Damon's mobile phone records would be checked, and everything in the room would be examined meticulously in case there was a clue. Occasionally they'd come up with something; usually it was a lot of work for no reward.

Jessica tried the final door, Alistair's room, and was hit by the toxic whiff of aftershave. She hadn't noticed it on him in the living room but it was as if he bathed in the stuff, the rampant pong almost making her sneeze. Taking a breath of cleanish air from the hallway, Jessica crept into the bedroom.

Above the unmade bed, a large poster of a barely clothed model with breasts the size of her head was pinned to the wall. Jessica lifted the duvet onto the mattress and used her phone to light the space underneath the bed.

Dust, fluff, a crusty tissue – ick – some football magazines, a pair of trainers marginally less stinky than the aftershave, and a bong.

Jessica sniffed it but could only get the faint whiff of marijuana. Putting it back where she'd found it, she next tried the bottom drawer of the cabinet next to the bed.

Socks, boxer shorts, a jock-strap – ick – a mucky mag – double ick, didn't they have the Internet for that nowadays? – a flattened baseball cap.

Middle drawer: pyjamas, red checked lounge pants, a toilet roll, a Mars bar, packet of chewing gum.

Top drawer: more boxer shorts, a belt, two ties, a paperback *Kama Sutra* – seriously? – the back panel of a mobile phone, some batteries, and a small polythene bag containing black, vaguely green, flakes.

Jessica had a sniff and finished checking through the drawer just in case. She then had a poke around the dressing table and wardrobe before convincing herself that the hardest drugs on the premises were as Alistair claimed. She had believed him anyway but it was worth the search.

Back in the kitchen, Jessica could hear Archie's and Alistair's voices drifting from the living room. She couldn't make out the words but they seemed to be having a back-and-forth conversation. In the cupboards were packets of couscous, dried risotto and some fancy seasoning. It was all a far cry from baked beans, Cup-a-Soups and noodles.

Jessica gave it a few moments and then returned to the living room, holding her phone in the air. 'We've got to go,' she said, looking at Archie. 'Sorry, Alistair, unless there's anything else, we need to be elsewhere.'

Alistair exchanged a glance with Archie and then shrugged. 'I've told you everything.'

Back in the car Archie was swaggering as per usual. 'Come on then,' Jessica said.

'He reckons Damon had a girl or two on the go – nothing serious, just a Friday-night fumble. Lucky sod.'

'He's not that lucky . . .'

'Oh right, yes, er, sorry . . .'

'Any names?' Jessica asked.

'I can pass them on to Louise at the station. It didn't sound like much.'

'Anything else?'

'He reckons Damon was popular because he had money and would buy drinks on a night out. It doesn't feel like he was killed for money, though, does it? If he'd been coked up and robbed, they'd only be able to steal what he had on him because everything else is in his dad's name or in a bank account. At most they'd have got a few hundred quid, perhaps a thousand if we're pushing it.'

Jessica agreed – Damon's financial situation was worth keeping in mind but it didn't seem like it was a legitimate motive, plus it would be a strange way to kill someone if it was a straight robbery. Why go to the hassle of dumping him at the back of the rowing club?

'Did you find out why he's apparently been happier in the past week?'

'No idea,' Archie replied with a barely concealed smirk.

'What?' Jessica asked.

'I did find out what he was up to the night before last.'

'The night he died?'

'Aye – those rowing jessies were all getting bevvied at that club of theirs.'

6

The rowing club looked significantly different in daylight compared to the night before. What had appeared to be gentle black waves from the river lapping at the shore was in fact a browny liquid clattering into the rocks, with empty beer cans bobbing on the far side of the bank. The grass surrounding the building was muddy and soft, the white front of the clubhouse greyer and dirtier. The bins and their contents had been taken somewhere else for Rowlands, Joy Bag Jane and the rest of the fingertip team to check over. There were wheel marks on the ground where they had been pushed up the slope.

Jessica and Archie headed across the decking towards the front of the clubhouse for her second meeting with the student president.

'Afternoon, Holden,' she said, entering the clubhouse and making him spin with such surprise that he almost fell off the stool. As he composed himself, she took a moment to take in the enormous room. Aside from a wall at the far end with one door marked 'changing rooms', another labelled 'office', and the small bar area in the far corner, the rest of the giant area was given over to a single hall.

'Nice of you to leave the door open,' Jessica added, walking towards the bar. Above it was a row of plaques, trophies, medals and certificates. On the wall to the side

43

was a roll of honour, with a list of competitions the club had won.

Holden got up and glanced between Jessica and Archie, waiting for an introduction that she didn't provide. He had been alone in the large room, using the bar as a table and working on a laptop.

'There was a bit of cleaning up to do here,' he said.

Jessica was about to reply when her phone buzzed. It was a text message from Rowlands: 'The bastards are calling me Bin Boy. Joy Bag's furious too.'

She could feel Holden watching but Jessica took the time to reply: 'She's not going to get any happier if you keep calling her Joy Bag, is she? Stop moaning and find something.'

'Sorry,' Jessica said, peering up. 'Important police business. I arranged to meet you here because I wanted to ask a few more questions about the club's hierarchy. You're student president, so what does that let you do?'

Holden's brow furrowed as he stared at Jessica. His hair was fairer than she'd thought the night before. 'Am I under arrest?'

'Why would you be?'

He nodded gently, weighing up the situation. If he wanted to be awkward, then Jessica would happily take him down to the station and caution him. 'It means I sit on the committee. We decide the competitions we're going to enter each year, plus deal with various things relating to how we spend our funds. We had to renovate the changing rooms over the winter, plus get a new rowing machine. It's only a twelve-month position. You take over in June each

44

year, at the end of the summer term. It's almost always someone doing a post-graduate course.'

'What are you studying?'

'An MSc in global management.'

'Did you do your undergraduate degree here?'

'Yes.'

'And you've been a member of the club since your first year?'

Holden nodded as Jessica gave Archie a nudge, letting him know he was up.

He peered at the honours board and then addressed Holden. 'If you're *student* president, that implies there's a real president.'

'There's a life president, he's on the committee too. There are ten positions, all voted for except life president.'

'Who does that role?'

'James Jefferies.'

Archie shrugged. 'Who's that?'

Holden pointed towards a photograph on the wall that showed a slightly wrinkled man next to a boat holding something she couldn't quite make out. Next to him, Jessica recognised Holden.

'He won an Olympic bronze medal thirty years ago,' the student said, grinning.

Archie was having none of it: 'Bronze medal, eh? Did he fall in or something?'

'Huh?'

'Well, if he only won a bronze, what was he doing? Rowing backwards?'

Holden spluttered, eyes wide, staring at Archie. 'It's

really hard just to qualify for the Olympics, let alone win a medal.'

'Bollocks is it. I'd be ashamed to come home with anything other than gold.'

Archie wandered up to the honours board and brushed away a speck of dust as Jessica stifled a grin. In the old days, the softening up would've been her job. He was like a little pitbull she could let off the leash as and when she chose. Usually, she wouldn't go in so strong, but given the information Holden had opted not to tell her the previous night, she wasn't in the best of moods.

'When you sit on the committee, do you talk about upcoming social events?' Jessica asked before he could compose himself.

Holden turned back to Jessica, wondering what was going on. 'I suppose.'

'And what's your memory usually like? Can you remember what you had for breakfast earlier?'

'I didn't have breakfast.'

'Aah, but you remember that – and if you recall that, then why didn't you tell me last night that you, Damon and all the other members of the rowing club were here for a giant piss-up two nights ago?'

As Holden's eyebrows rose, Jessica could see the penny dropping. 'It was a busy night,' he replied, trying to stay cool. 'I didn't know if Damon had been at the party and didn't want to give you wrong information.'

His cheeks puffed out, a sigh of relief that he'd come up with that on the spot.

'So, was he here or not?' Jessica snapped.

46

'When the news came out about his body this morning, everyone was in shock. Some of the lads were saying that it was only Wednesday night that we saw him last. That jogged my mind.'

Holden smiled unconvincingly. He'd known full well Damon had been at the rowing club's party on the night he died. When Jessica had seen him the previous evening, she'd known he was holding something back; now his evasion had given her every reason to arrest him.

Jessica peered across to Archie. 'What is it we usually call this?'

'Being a knob head?'

'I was thinking more "obstructing a police officer".'

Holden was even more confused than before, glancing between Jessica and Archie, trying to work out what was going on. Good, Jessica wanted him sweating. 'I wasn't trying to obstruct anything,' he protested. 'I'd just forgotten; there were a lot of people here.'

'How many?'

'Most of our eighty members, plus some partners, alumni, the committee – at least a hundred and fifty.'

'Do you have a list of attendees?'

'Our membership secretary might.'

'Good – I'm going to need those details.'

'Right, I can—'

'What do you remember about seeing Damon on Wednesday night?'

Sometimes silence worked, making the witness or suspect fill the awkward gaps, but Holden was too calculating; the best method was to keep firing questions at him.

'Not much. It was a big black-tie thing – suits and cocktail dresses. We hold one every November because that's when our membership has settled with the new recruits – once they've decided they're committed. We hold another one at the end of the university year.'

'That's not what I asked.'

'Right, right, I . . . I assume he was looking smart. We all were.'

That tallied with the shirt and dark trousers in which his body was found, so Holden wasn't lying about everything.

'Was he here with anyone?'

'I'm not sure. I don't think so. A lot of the rowing teams tend to keep to themselves – I didn't spend any time with him. People started drifting away after a couple of hours. I think he left.'

'Did he or didn't he?'

'I'm not sure. Some of the others might know. I was here all night.'

Archie jumped in without being asked: 'I suppose you've got witnesses? Someone who'll tell us you spent the evening knocking back girly cocktails?'

'Well . . .'

'This is quite a big club,' Jessica said. 'What else do you do here? It can't just be rowing and posh parties?'

'We hire it out now and then—'

'I was thinking more about the two separate date rape allegations against club members from the past eighteen months.'

Holden's eyes narrowed and he glanced around nervously at the empty surroundings. He was shrinking in front of her, clearly wishing he'd got out while he could. 'Both of those were unproven with the charges dropped.'

Jessica turned to Archie, who had taken a sheaf of papers from a cardboard wallet and was sorting through them. 'Aye, but what about the three call-outs for public disorder in the past three years?'

'I wasn't president for any of those. We've been adhering to rules about noise and sticking to the curfew.'

Archie moved to the next sheet. 'One of your members ended up in hospital with hypothermia last year.'

'He was training on his own on the water! How were we supposed to know?'

Archie moved to the next sheet but Jessica cut him off. 'The fact is, Mr Wyatt, there's a disturbing pattern here: complaints about noise and mess, a serious medical incident, date rape allegations and now a murder. All apparent accidents, all connected to the club you're running. Things are spiralling out of control, aren't they?'

Holden opened his mouth to reply and then stopped, drawing himself back up to his full height. Archie puffed his chest out and splayed his legs slightly, as if gearing up for a good old-fashioned ruck on Deansgate. Jessica looked from one man to the other, feeling the testosterone. Holden towered over the constable but Jessica wouldn't have wanted to guess who'd come out on top if it ever came to it. Not that it would.

'None of those earlier things happened while I was president,' Holden said calmly. 'Whatever happened to

Damon is unfortunate – but I was here and I'm pretty sure he left halfway through the evening. I don't know what happened after that. If you're unsure then perhaps you should go and do some *proper* police work.'

Jessica let the silence hang for a moment, hoping Archie wouldn't jump in. When he didn't, she felt even more confident that he really did know what he was doing. She stared at Holden, who held her gaze defiantly. 'I'm going to need a full list of all current and former members of this club,' she eventually said.

Holden shook his head. 'Those details don't exist.'

'I thought you said the membership secretary would know who was at the party?'

'That was different – it was a ticketed event, so we would have kept track. We'll have the current members but nothing other than that. I think you'll find there are data protection laws anyway.'

He rocked back on his heels, the hesitation of before now gone. The smug bastard.

Archie started flicking through the folder again and handed Jessica a printout without her having to look at him.

'One of my colleagues found this on the university website this morning,' she said, beginning to read. '"For clubs to be able to use the official university seal, or to be eligible for loans, bursaries or grants, they must securely keep full membership lists of all current and former members for a minimum of ten years, or for the length of time the club has been in operation. Said details must be provided to the university upon written request within seventy-two hours."' Jessica looked back up at Holden, wide-eyed and innocent. 'Didn't you tell me last night that some of your funding came from the university?'

Archie rolled his shoulders forward and snorted quietly.

'A little . . .' Holden replied, trying not to look at either of them.

'And there's a university crest underneath the logo with oars on it out the front as well . . .'

'Yes.'

'It'd be a shame if you lost all of that because someone had been careless with the records. That doesn't seem the type of thing that a well-run place like this would risk happening . . .'

'I did say there was a membership secretary, perhaps he'd have a better idea—'

Jessica pointed towards the door in the far corner. 'How about you go into that office back there and do whatever it is you have to do in order to get me what I need. There might be data protection laws but then there's also telling porkies to an officer.' She turned back to Archie. 'What is it we call it again?'

'Being a knob head?'

'Obstructing a police officer.'

Jessica gave him her best glare and Holden shook his head slightly, scarpering in the direction of the office.

'He's a lying little rich kid, isn't he?' Archie said when they were alone.

'Not so little.'

'Whatever – we should do him for something anyway.'

'Nah, I'd rather he was out here shitting himself. If need be, we'll keep an eye on him. He'll be off talking to all his chums later on, getting their stories straight. I want them all nervous; that's when one of them will say something stupid.'

'You think he was involved?'

Jessica blew out through her clenched teeth. 'Dunno. Even if it was some sort of drinking accident, why would he leave the body in the bin out the back? Dumping it in the river would be better – it might've been dragged down stream and ended up in the canal. He might be a slippery little shite but he's not stupid. I still don't think he's telling us everything.'

Peering up at the walls, Jessica took in the rest of the surroundings. There was a large upturned boat hanging from the ceiling that was snared to the walls, as well as half-a-dozen crossed oars.

'What do you know about initiations?' Jessica asked quietly.

'When I was playing footy as a kid, they made us do a lap of the field before we could start. Do you think they've got the new recruits giving them handjobs in the shower or something?'

Jessica shrugged. 'It was the way he said they always hold this function at this time of year, after the new recruits have decided they want to commit. It's odd having a party in November – why wouldn't they do it at Christmas instead? They'd still have the same number of members. "Committed" was a very odd choice of word. Plus people keep saying they thought Damon was looking forward to something – perhaps it was becoming a full member here.'

'Posh twats beating up other posh twats . . .'

Jessica replied sternly. 'Someone's died.'

Archie sighed, letting her know it was just a front. 'Aye, I know. I was only arsing around.' He breathed in deeply through his nose. 'What shall we do?'

'When we're done with him, how about you look through his membership lists and make a few phone calls? See if you can find a pissed-off former member. If they have been hazing people, there must be someone who'll blab.'

Before she could say anything else, Holden hurried out from the office on the far side of the room carrying a handful of papers. He gave them to Jessica and then stood tall, refusing to meet either of their eyes. 'If that's everything, I've got things to do.'

'For now,' Jessica replied. 'But the next time we have a word, it'll be under caution at the station. That way, if you try to lie again, we'll have it on tape. I don't like people looking me in the eye and feeding me a pile of shite.'

His expression didn't change. 'Fine, I'll bring a solicitor too.'

'You do that – see you soon.'

Jessica slowed as she walked, allowing her footsteps to echo around the deserted building. Archie followed suit until they were outside, where drizzle had replaced the earlier mildness.

'Do you think we'll see him again?' Archie asked.

'Definitely.'

'What are you doing later?'

The question took Jessica so much by surprise that she answered without thinking: 'I've got someone to meet tonight, then I'm off for the weekend.'

7

Jessica sat alone in the late-night greasy spoon drumming her fingers on the sticky once-white table. Fry-ups for breakfast were one thing but she was definitely getting too old to be eating this late, let alone putting away something this unhealthy. She had deliberately chosen a cafe just off the Northern Quarter, easily within walking distance of anywhere in the city centre. It was a place in which Friday-evening drunks and after-dark regulars would sit in silence and pile through solidified fat on a plate before or after sloshing down some ale from around the corner.

This really was living the dream.

She peered at the clock over the door, where a brown film of grime covered the vaguely transparent face. Nine o'clock on the dot – another evening away from Adam, another evening of doing things vaguely related to work. Each time he'd smile and nod, saying he understood and that he wanted to watch something geeky on television anyway. Either that, or he'd go to his sister's flat and they'd sit and chat about whatever it was they talked about when Jessica wasn't there. Probably her, or was that being paranoid?

One minute past nine: the person she was hoping for wasn't coming.

Jessica should've known it. She'd tried to be clever but,

as ever, she was being too smart for her own good. Who wanted to spend Friday night in a place like this? She should've been at home, wrapped up in a blanket watching reality television in what she and Adam both pretended was an ironic way, even though they each secretly enjoyed it. Actually, she should've been out on the town, drink in hand, enjoying herself: she wasn't that old, for God's sake. Thirty . . . something. Definitely not the big four-oh.

Ugh.

Two minutes past nine.

Jessica wiped the remaining streak of egg yolk from her plate with her finger and held it in her mouth. Why had Archie asked what she was doing that night? Was he asking her out? Or trying to be a mate? They didn't really know each other but there was undoubtedly a spark there, like when you're on a train or a plane, or stuck in a waiting room somewhere and something funny happens that you're not sure anyone else has noticed. You exchange a knowing look with a stranger, a mere flicker of the eyes or a slightly raised eyebrow, and suddenly you know exactly what they're thinking. For the tiniest of split seconds, you have a window into their soul and it feels fabulous. You might never see them again, never know their name, perhaps not even speak, but just for a moment you understand what being human is all about. She had that with Archie. They worked on the same wavelength and yet she'd gone from being the apprentice kept on a leash to being the handler allowing the new recruit to do his thing. She'd gone from being Darth Vader to Emperor Palpatine, she'd . . . hang on a minute, was that from *Star*

Wars? Bloody hell, it was. *Star Wars*! Christ, going out with Adam and hanging around with Dave Rowlands had rubbed off on her so badly, she now knew the names of people in geeky sci-fi films. This was a new low.

Three minutes past nine.

The depressed-looking man behind the counter of the cafe leant forward onto his elbows and yawned, peering up at the relic of a television perched precariously on a mount above Jessica's head. In the days of flatscreens, 3D, digital, plasma, LCD and who knew what else, this was a square box out of the dark ages. Either that or the 1970s, one or the other. There was a socket high on the wall, with the yellowing grungy plug practically welded into position. Jessica doubted it had been moved since the day it had been installed. It was on silent and there was a boxing match on. Jessica peered up at the clock again.

Four minutes past nine.

The time on her phone said the same. How long should she wait? She'd said nine, yet she didn't know what the other person's time-keeping might be like, let alone if they were coming at all. Five past nine? Ten past?

Jangle, jangle.

Jessica looked up to see a rake of a girl push her way through the door, a stringy mess of tangled black hair whipped backwards by the breeze as she peered from side to side, taking in the surroundings. She couldn't have been any older than seventeen at the most. Her face was thin, her skin almost white; her eyes skimmed across the two men sitting at the back of the dining area before settling on Jessica. When their eyes met, Jessica gave a gentle nod, knowing this was the girl.

The young woman stepped quickly and soundlessly across the cafe, moving like a trained ballet dancer on the tips of her toes but without the grace. She was wearing a pair of skinny jeans that seemed loose, betraying the stick-like legs underneath, with a padding of tops and a thin-looking dark fleece covering her upper half. On her hands she had half-fingered gloves with a hole in the left palm. Through her nose there was a small silver ring.

Jessica tried to hold her stare but the girl clearly wasn't comfortable, looking everywhere except directly at her, before sliding into the chair opposite. Without a word, she reached into her pocket and tugged out a small leather purse, plopping it on the table between them.

'I suppose you want this back,' she said, staring at the table.

Her tone made her sound even younger than she looked, even though it had an edge.

Jessica picked the purse up and opened it, unfolding the note she had left inside before going to Piccadilly Station the night before.

'Thanks for stealing my purse. Sorry there's no money in here but if you'd like a free meal and twenty quid, then come to Rav's Cafe in the Northern Quarter at 9 p.m. tomorrow.'

'What would you like to eat?' Jessica asked.

The girl glanced at the menu on the wall over the top of the counter. 'You police or something?'

'Let's say "something". What do you want, or shall I get you the all-dayer?'

For a moment there was no reply. Jessica could hear the young woman breathing in, wondering what she should do. Eventually, the answer came: 'That sounds good.'

Jessica picked up her plate and empty mug, returning it to the counter and asking the bored man if he could sort out a second all-day breakfast, a rack of toast, and two mugs of tea. She gave him a tenner, told him to keep the change and then sat back down opposite the girl.

'What's your name?' Jessica asked.

The girl still wouldn't look up. 'What's it to you?'

'If I'm going to buy someone tea, it's nice to know what to call them.'

'I only came for my twenty quid.'

'Fair enough.'

'You're Old Bill, aren't you?'

'I think "Old" is a bit harsh. I'm still in my thirties.' The girl didn't laugh. 'All right,' Jessica added. 'I'm police but it's just me on my own: no big flashing lights parade, no army of clowns in uniform with truncheons – they're all over by the Printworks waiting for Tiger Tiger to kick out later. It's like a bloody zoo down there on a Friday night.'

Not even a smile. 'Am I in trouble?' the girl whispered.

This time it was Jessica's turn to pause. 'No.'

There was a moment of silence punctured by the scraping of forks on plates from the two men at the back. In the kitchen, there was a sudden sizzle, making the girl jump. Her eyes darted from side to side as her chair slid back.

'It's just a pan,' Jessica said.

The girl righted herself, picking at the hole in her glove. 'Bex.'

'Is that short for Rebecca?'

'What does it matter?'

'Fair enough, Bex. Nice to meet you. I'm Jessica.'

Jessica held out her hand for Bex to shake but the young woman simply stared at it, unmoving. Jessica put her palms back into her lap. More silence.

'How old are you?' Jessica asked softly.

'Old enough.'

'Do you have somewhere to live? Parents?'

Jessica already knew the answer, even though it didn't come. She sat listening to the plates being scraped behind her and the various clatters from the kitchen.

Fourteen minutes past nine.

The man from behind the counter sloped across to the table and plonked a plate in front of Bex loaded with three rashers of fat-laden bacon, two sausages, fried bread, two fried eggs with orange juicy-looking yolks, two slices of crusty black pudding, a mound of chopped tomatoes and a large dollop of baked beans.

Not bad for three pounds fifty.

Bex didn't hang around, grabbing the bottle of brown sauce, giving everything a liberal coating, and then diving in with her fork. Slop, slop, crunch, squish, swallow, mmmm . . . and then it was on to the toast.

Jessica cradled her tea, watching the waif of a girl demolish the meal in under five minutes and then use the final slice of toast to wipe every last drop of sauce and egg yolk from the plate.

'Do you want anything else?' Jessica asked.

Bex's eyes flickered hungrily towards the menu. 'You some sort of do-gooder?'

'I wouldn't say that.'

'You're not a lezzer, are you?'

'No.'

The door jangled again, three men stumbling through, bouncing off each other drunkenly before collapsing into a booth three tables away from the one Jessica and Bex were sitting at. The biggest one – a fat bloke wearing a T-shirt two sizes too small – shouted that they wanted three all-dayers 'chop chop' and then collapsed into a fit of laughter along with his boorish mates.

Jessica turned back to Bex, who had shrunken into herself, knees up to her chest, arms wrapped around her legs.

The fat man caught Jessica's eye. 'All right, love?'

'Oi, dickhead, shut up, yeah?'

He smiled and nudged the friend next to him. 'Steady on, darling, what is it, your time of the month or something?'

Jessica pulled her identification out of her pocket, striding across the floor and thrusting it under his nose. 'Fancy repeating that down the station on a D and D charge? If not, then pipe down and shut your pair of monkeys up too.' She jabbed a finger at the other two men and then returned to her seat. Behind, the other two men had stopped scraping at their plates and hurried towards the exit. The man behind the counter said nothing.

Bex had finally looked up from the table and was staring at Jessica. She dropped her feet back to the floor as Jessica handed over her ID.

'You're a detective inspector?' she asked quietly, passing the card back.

'Yes.'

'But you're not going to arrest me?'

'No.'

'I'm sorry for stealing your purse.'

'Did you steal all six wallets and purses over the past month?'

Bex eyed her feet. 'Maybe.'

'How old are you?'

'Seventeen.'

'And you live rough?'

She shrugged: 'Some nights I get into the shelter.'

'Parents?'

A shake of the head.

'Y'know, I can probably—'

'It's fine.'

Bex pulled her gloves off, putting them next to the clean plate and balling her fists. Jessica could see the scrapes along her knuckles and a separate scab on the back of her right hand.

'I only pinch from people who have a few quid.'

'I'm not that rich.'

'You looked it.'

'Exactly – and maybe it was like that for the other people you stole from too. Some people just make an effort one day a month, or a year, because they come into the city to watch a show. They might save for months, might have children at home with a babysitter they can barely afford to pay. It might be their only treat.'

Bex said nothing for a little while, though her fists were still clenched. 'I don't have the money to give back if that's what you're asking.'

'I'm not – I'm just pointing out that people aren't always what they seem.'

A pause. 'Like you?'

'Maybe.'

'What are you going to do?'

Jessica reached into her pocket and took out a twenty-pound note, placing it on top of Bex's gloves. 'A deal's a deal, but you have to stop nicking. There are cameras all over the city and it's only a matter of time until someone snags you. Plus I'm a police officer; I should be taking you in.'

'Why aren't you?'

Jessica finished the rest of her tea and put the mug down, shooting a glance towards the still-silent trio of men in the booth. 'There was this guy I knew who lived on the streets for years. He finally got clean a few months ago but I've been thinking about him, wondering if I should've done more to help earlier.'

Bex stared at the money but didn't pick it up. 'So you're helping me?'

'I don't know . . . perhaps. The pickpocket could've been anyone.'

In a flash, Bex snatched the twenty-pound note and whipped it into her pocket. She rolled her sleeves up and wrapped her hands around the tea mug.

'Nice tattoo.'

Bex glanced down at the spidery patterned web on her arm and then rolled her sleeve down again. 'Thanks.'

'What does it mean?'

'No idea. I just liked the pattern. Some guy in town did it for free . . . well, not exactly "free" but . . .'

'Perhaps you can help me with something?' Jessica delved into the bag by her chair and pulled out a copy of the same photograph she'd been looking at with Izzy earlier – the robber with the tattoo on his wrist. 'What do you think of this?' she asked, passing the picture across.

Bex held it at arm's length. 'I don't know who it is.'

'I meant what do you think of the tattoo.'

Bex narrowed her eyes and stared at Jessica, wondering if there was some sort of trick being played. Eventually she brought the photo nearer and narrowed her eyes. 'It's nice – some sort of tribal thing. Samoan or Hawaiian? Maybe African? It's intricate. The artist is good.'

'Have you ever seen anything like it on a person before?'

'No.' Bex moved the photo even closer until it was directly in front of her face, and then handed it back. 'It's not finished.'

'What?'

'The tattoo. Look at the bit that loops under his wrist.'

Jessica stared closely at the picture. It wasn't that they'd missed the discrepancy when they'd examined it, more that they'd thought it was a glitch in the quality of the CCTV footage. The scythe shape wrapped around the robber's wrist, interlocking with a thick dark line, but there was a spot where they joined that looked as if the tattoo-ist's needle had slipped. It was almost smudged. It could still be problem with the camera but the more Jessica looked at it, the more she thought Bex was right. For something so permanent, it was a strange mistake for a person to carry around on their body.

Jessica put the picture back into her bag as the younger girl started to put her gloves back on.

'Where are you sleeping tonight?' Jessica asked.

'Don't worry about it.'

Jessica took a business card out of her pocket and a pen from her bag, turning the card over and scribbling her address on it. 'I'm out in Swinton if you need a roof. We've got a spare room . . .'

Bex snatched the card away, pocketing it without looking at it. She glanced across to the men in the booth and then back at Jessica, top lip curling into a snarl. 'I told you I'm not a fucking lezzer, right? Now piss off.'

Jangle, jangle, and she was gone into the night.

8

'Buster, will you come back here? Buster! Buster!'

The cold air set Philip Raymond off coughing. Bloody Manchester weather: cold one day, warm the next. Frosty, misty, rainy, icy. What the hell was wrong with this place? And where had the sodding dog gone?

'Buster!'

Philip pulled his coat tighter and zipped it up, setting off in the direction in which the dog had disappeared. On a nice day, it was a lovely stroll through the woods that separated Ellesmere Golf Course and the M60. The previous day, it had been warm enough for people to be walking around with their tops off. Well, the men, anyway. Now his breath corkscrewed into the sky and his sodden feet slid across the muddy slope as he tried to up his pace. It must have rained overnight. For a change. This really was an ungodly time to be up on a Saturday morning.

Philip dug the toecaps of his boots into the soft ground and kicked his way up the slope towards the tree-line.

'Buster!'

Bloody dog. It wasn't even his. Emily had promised she'd do all the feeding and walking if only she could have a puppy for Christmas. Eleven months on and it was exactly as he had predicted. Emily spent half her time in her room on the computer and the other half chatting on her phone to her friends. At least it had better be her friends. She wasn't old enough for boys yet. He tried to remember what he was like at thirteen. Was he into girls then? He didn't think so; it was all football down the park with his mates. But then kids were different today, weren't they? It wasn't just football down the park, it was shooting heroin in the playground and sending naked pictures to each other on their phones. That's what it said in the papers anyway. They grew up so quickly. One minute you could hold them in the palm of your hand, the next they're telling you they hate you, slamming doors and refusing to be seen in public with you.

'Buster!'

And they couldn't look after their own pets.

Philip stood on his tiptoes, peering through the darkened gaps between the trees. In the distance he heard something scurrying but it was as likely a squirrel as it was Buster. He walked the long way around a thickly packed hedge and quickened his pace. This happened every time he let the dog off his lead. Buster would spot a critter somewhere, get his shaggy head down and tear off.

The truth was, whether Buster was his daughter's dog or not, Philip liked getting out of the house on a weekend morning to go for a walk. He preferred it when it was warm but at least it wasn't raining today, even if the ground was sodden. The cool air helped to clear his head and at least it got him away from his wife's snoring. It was like a pneumatic drill boring into a concrete block. Philip dreaded to think how many hours of sleep he'd lost over the years lying awake, hoping she'd shut up sometime soon. Rolling her over, pulling the covers away, poking her in the back, holding a pillow over her face for ten minutes . . . well, threatening it at least: none of it made any difference.

Yap, yap, yap.

Somewhere over the next ridge, Buster was barking. He'd either caught whatever he was chasing, or, far more likely, had got scared by something small and quick and was now hoping to be picked up and taken home for a bath. The little softie.

Philip slurped his way across the thick mud, up a short ridge and through a gap between hedges. He could see Buster sitting on the ground at the bottom, lower half caked with mud, tail tucked between his legs.

'What's wrong, boy?' Philip called, steadily making his way down the slope. Thick tree roots weaved their way in and out of the earth, with mulched remains of autumn leaves mashed into the ground from where other walkers had been out and about.

Buster tucked his legs under himself and lay on the floor, nose-down, peering at a spot under the ridge Philip was trying to descend. As the animal let out a gentle moan, Philip quickened his pace, worrying what was wrong. He already felt as if his legs were travelling too quickly for him when his foot snagged on one of the roots, sending him sprawling forward, arms flailing uselessly. With a thump, Philip hit the ground chest-first, the wind coughing out of his lungs. As he struggled to breathe, his legs cricked over his head, sending him into a roll. Something slammed into the back of his neck, with an unseen branch snagging his trousers, ripping them above the knee and slicing into his skin. Philip tried to grab something, anything, to stop himself but it only made things worse, vines and roots tearing at his skin. He yelped in pain, bump, bump, bumping his way to the bottom until eventually coming to rest next to Buster.

Ouch.

The dog crept forward and began licking Philip's face apologetically. Batting him away but at least appreciating the gesture, Philip rolled onto his back and groaned. His eyes felt better closed but he was going to have to pick himself up at some point. Slowly, he opened an eyelid, and then hauled himself into a sitting position. His hands were covered in a mixture of mud and blood, waterlogged trousers sticking to his legs as more blood sluiced from the cut. He reached out and patted Buster gently with his fingers, making sure not to use his aching palms.

'Silly dog, what did you see?'

Philip followed his pet's gaze. A mound of leaves, tree bark and twigs had been shoved backwards into the gully but that wasn't what his eyes were drawn to. Poking through the undergrowth was a pale, lifeless human arm.

9

So much for a day off.

Jessica sloshed her way through the woods until she came to the area that had been covered with white tents. Body suit, over-shoe covers and hair net in place, she allowed the SOCO officer to lead her through the site. In contrast to the scene at the rowing club, Jessica knew the queasy looks on the faces of the other attending officers meant this was something she should see for herself. Not that she wanted to.

Small piles of leaves, twigs and dirt had been moved to the side, exposing the washed-out limp body of a young strawberry blonde. Without wanting to step any closer than the doorway of the tent, Jessica felt the twinge in her stomach. 'She was probably strangled,' the officer said softly.

Jessica remained silent, listening to the rest of the details. It was so easy to become desensitised to the things witnessed every day, but every now and then something would hit you. As well as the marks around her neck, the index finger on the woman's right hand had been sliced off, along with part of her ear. Both cuts were likely made after death because of the lack of blood but Jessica found it hard to tell where the slits began and ended because she had been so brutally beaten too. The woman's torso, especially her breasts, was peppered with bruises, the remaining fingers jutting off at unnatural angles. Across the small of her back, there was a spiky tattoo weaving its way towards her hips. From the state of the injuries, the officer said it was likely the body had been there for longer than a day, less than two.

With the photographs taken and initial assumptions reached, it was time for the body to be taken for autopsy. Jessica and the other officers watched in a calm reverence as it was carried away through the woods, and then it was to business. Officers had been called in from days off, with others lent from surrounding districts. With the woods a popular spot for walkers, at least a third of those were needed to keep the place as untouched as possible. Jessica separated the rest into teams ready to pick through the area centimetre by devastatingly slow centimetre.

That was all well and good but they all knew the real damage had already been done. Even with the area surrounded by tent and tape, Jessica had seen the footsteps and paw prints all around the body. With everyone off doing something, she walked back to the parked cars and approached a man resting on the bonnet of a muddy Range Rover. At his feet lay a dog, covered with grime, head nestled between the man's feet.

'Are you Philip?' she asked.

The man was middle-aged, bundled up in any number of coats and tops, which made him look chunkier than he actually was. His jeans had ripped and blood was beginning to dry into the material. His lived-in fatherly face was partially obscured by a mud-spattered, skewed deerstalker. He looked at Jessica, nodding, but his eyes were empty.

She pointed towards the wound in his leg: 'Someone should look at that.'

He held up his hand to show where the ring finger on his left hand was missing the very tip. 'I've had worse.'

'How did you manage that?'

'Accident with a forklift a few years back. To be honest, filling in all the accident forms hurt way worse than losing the finger.' He chuckled humourlessly but Jessica knew what he meant: if someone stubbed their toe around the station then she'd have three dozen forms to fill out in triplicate. No wonder things didn't get done.

'I messed up, didn't I?' he said, more quietly than before.

'How?'

'With the body. You're supposed to stay clear and not touch anything, aren't you? That's what they say. I went and fell on my bloody arse, then the dog was sniffing around.' He hunched and ruffled the dog's ears.

'What's his name?'

'Buster. Stupid bloody name. Some kids' TV show, I think. My daughter named him.'

The dog rolled onto his side, still nuzzling against Philip's shoes.

'It's not your fault,' Jessica said, touching him on the upper arm. 'Our scene was screwed the moment it started raining. The body had been out there for more than twenty-four hours anyway. By the time you found it, pretty much anything useful we were going to get had been washed away.'

That wasn't strictly true and Philip's tumble around the body certainly hadn't helped – but there was no point in making him feel any worse than he already did.

'Your girl who interviewed me said I could go home but I don't think I can face it yet. I called my wife to say I was going to be late. I didn't tell her about the body, not over the phone, I just said I'd gone for a longer walk. She asked if I could pick up some milk on the way home. I don't know why but it made me laugh, not because it was funny – it was just one of those things. I was thinking, "Milk, bloody hell, there's some poor girl that's been cut up and I've got to worry about nipping by the corner shop on my way home."'

Jessica wanted to say something soothing but what was there? It was always the normal things that got you.

'Who was she?' Philip asked.

'We're not sure yet.'

'Bloody waste, though, isn't it? Some young girl like that. Can't be any older than twenty-one, twenty-two. Christ, my Emily's only thirteen. You think they've got their whole lives ahead of them and then you see something like that.'

Jessica didn't reply for a few moments, allowing the gentle breeze to skim between them. 'We can have someone take you home if you want, plus we have people you can talk to.'

'Aye, I know, love. Your other woman told me. I'll be all

right. I've seen a few things in my time, not like that but, y'know . . .'

Back at Longsight Station the usual Saturday morning chaos was fully in evidence. The regular array of Friday-night drunks were being processed, the quieter ones sent on their way after a telling-off, the ones with the big gobs left downstairs in their cells to stew for a few hours longer. Some people never learned that shouting their mouths off at the police got them nowhere.

A pair of constables was pulling together a list of missing people who could potentially be their victim, so Jessica went to her office and flicked through the messages on top of her keyboard. Something about pensions, a note from Fat Pat about forgetting to sign cars back in, notification of some all-department briefing, blah blah blah. If they filed these things straight into her bin, it would save her the hassle.

Jessica picked up her desk phone and called Archie. One ring, two rings, five rings: 'Can't you pick up on the first ring?' she said.

The familiar Manc twang: 'Jess?'

'Yes, y'lazy sod. What are you doing?'

'Give over – it's my day off, it's Saturday.'

'I know what day it is and it's my day off too. They found some body out Walkden way, just off the East Lancs Road. Some poor girl.'

'I've not had the news on. Do you need me in?'

'No, I was wondering how you'd got on sniffing around the rowing club.'

'Well, it smells like shite, that's for sure. I went through those membership lists and started to get together a few potential names. They have a website that tallies all of their results going back years, so I've been cross-reffing. I don't want to start phoning everyone because then the word will get around, so I'm trying to find a certain type of member. The ones who row in the main teams are going to be quieter than a City fan after derby day, so I'm trying to find people who were members of the club but not mentioned. There's bound to be someone who's annoyed at being left out.'

'Find anyone yet?'

'I only started yesterday afternoon?'

'So what are you doing taking days off then?'

'All right, bloody hell, they told me you were a nightmare.'

'Who told you?'

Archie's muffled cough revealed nothing. 'You know . . . *they.*'

Jessica let it go. 'When are you back in?'

'Tuesday.'

'Are you working part-time?'

'Ha ha, very funny. United are playing this afternoon, so I—'

'Whatever, just get something sorted and we'll talk on Monday.'

Jessica hung up just as Archie's muttered protests were getting abusive. She knew it was harsh but that was the way things were. The fact that she was turning into one of the inspectors she used to complain about wasn't lost on her either. What a cow.

With that sorted, her notes filed in the bin and a cheeky Hobnob from her desk drawer devoured, Jessica went through to the stupidly named sergeants' station, where Izzy was having an agitated phone conversation with her other half. She swiped a pile of cardboard document folders away from the space in front of her and offered an apologetic smile as Jessica sat and waited on the corner of the desk. As Izzy lowered her voice to use a very rude word, Jessica picked up the tattoo robbery case file and started shuffling through the information. The original version of the photograph she'd shown to Bex was at the front and she stared at the tattoo, knowing that if it had been etched onto her body, then she would have done whatever she could to get rid of such an obvious glitch.

Izzy soon hung up and turned to Jessica. 'Sorry – you'd think I somehow managed to have Amber by myself, like some sort of immaculate conception.' She sighed. 'Anyway, aren't you off?'

'I'm always hanging around.'

'Like a bad smell?'

'Something like that. I wanted to go through these photos. How closely did our guys look at this?' Jessica pointed to the fuzzy part of the tattoo on the robber's wrist.

Izzy took the photo and looked at it again. 'I flagged it up straight away but they had already seen it. They said it had to be a problem with the camera footage because the tattoo doesn't look like that on the other pictures.'

Izzy slid out the images they had from the other robberies and showed Jessica what she meant. In those, the scythe shape on the robber's lower arm connected perfectly with the dark line as it reached his wrist. Jessica took each photo and peered at them closely. She had only had the single photograph the evening before, which she'd taken on a whim. Neither Jessica nor Adam had tattoos but one of Adam's friends at the university where he worked had a keen interest in them. She'd hoped he might have something useful to add but had forgotten to take it out of her bag, only remembering when she met Bex.

She thought back to that morning: the tattoo on the dead woman's back and the sodden conditions. Jessica held up the most recent photo again. 'What day was this taken?'

'Monday.'

'What was the weather like?'

Izzy shrugged. 'Probably raining. It usually is.'

Jessica tried to remember. Monday had been her last day off and she'd celebrated by going to Tesco and then sitting at home watching daytime television. It definitely had rained because she'd got wet lugging the shopping bags back to the car. She also remembered watching the news the previous night with Adam where the weatherman had promised it was going to be a dry day. The fact that most of their advance forecasting seemed to involve looking up and guessing was beside the point.

'Why?' Izzy added.

Jessica chewed on her bottom lip, thinking. 'Is there somewhere we can find out what the weather's been like for each day there was a robbery?'

Izzy peered at Jessica for a few moments but didn't ask the obvious question; sometimes it was best to let potentially mad ideas run their course.

Between them, they found a website that contained an archive of weather for the region. After cross-checking the details with the dates of the first three off-licence thefts, Jessica picked up the final photo again, staring at the same smudge as before.

'What are you thinking?' Izzy asked.

'The first three robberies were committed when it was dry. On Monday, it was due to be clear but it rained. When we saw the very first photo of the robber, we thought this would be one of the simplest cases ever, didn't we?'

Izzy nodded. 'Yes, because the robber was clearly stupid – if you had markings so distinctive, you'd do everything you could to cover them up.'

'When we put these pictures out, we thought we'd get a call from at least one member of the public. The few we did have were from the usual nutters and well-meaning people who'd got things wrong. We wondered how no one could have noticed such an intricate mark on someone's wrist – but what if it's not a proper tattoo? What if someone drew that onto themselves and then deliberately left their sleeves up to throw us off?'

Izzy thought for a moment and then a half-smile crept across her face. 'It would have to be non-permanent, otherwise it'd be noticed the same as a normal tattoo. So when it rained unexpectedly, it smudged slightly?'

'Exactly.'

10

Although Jessica now had a theory about Izzy's tattoo robbery case, they didn't have the officers to start working on it. Identifying the body in the woods had been simpler than it could have been and, instead of spending a day or two waiting for a positive ID, officers were now busy delving into the victim's background.

While Jessica was at the rowing club on Thursday night, trying to figure out what had happened to Damon Potter, Cassie Edmonds had gone out. When she hadn't returned home, her boyfriend, Carl, assumed she'd stayed at a friend's house and then gone straight to work the next day. On Friday evening, he'd gone out with his mates, got back to their shared flat late and guessed she'd gone out too. By the time he'd woken up hung-over on Saturday morning, the realisation that she hadn't replied to any of the text messages he had sent and wasn't answering her phone had hit. He called her friends, only to be told that none of them had seen her since Thursday evening. That was when he'd called the police and, after being asked about any distinctive features she might have, he'd described the tattoo on her back.

That was his story and, at least for now, they had no reason to doubt it. Well, no proof anyway – doubt was always the first thought.

With someone dispatched to formally take the boy-friend's statement, and a couple more officers trying to confirm his alibi, Jessica's day off that wasn't stretched into the afternoon.

By the time she arrived at the dead woman's flat, Cassie's best friend Jade was helping the police while trying to avoid going to pieces. She invited Jessica in, streaks of mascara lining the area around her eyes and red raw rings in the bags underneath from where she'd been rubbing her skin. She held the door open, sniffing and trying to suppress more sobs, then led Jessica into her living room. Celebrity magazines were scattered on a table and some dance tune thump-thump-thumped from a set of speakers in the corner.

'This was our song,' Jade said, failing to stop her voice cracking. 'We used to play it when we were getting ready to go out.'

The poor neighbours.

Tea and tissues at the ready, Jade settled on her sofa opposite Jessica. 'She was my best mate,' Jade said, just about holding herself together as she twiddled the large hooped earring in her right ear.

'And you were out with her on Thursday?'

'We were at this place just off Tib Street for one of our other friend's birthdays. It was supposed to be a quiet night – Italian and a few drinks – but we'd ended up staying out a bit later, even though we both had work the next day.'

Jessica took the details of the other friends who were there, as well as the places they had visited. 'How was the evening?' she asked.

'It was good, a bit like the old days. We've all known each other since school and have been going out since then. We used to get dressed up and head to town to try to get into places. Some would serve you, some wouldn't . . . although . . . I probably shouldn't tell you that, should I?'

Jessica smiled, remembering her own youth. 'I was young once too.'

Jade coughed a sombre smile through the still-near tears. 'Right, so you know what it's like?'

'Too much make-up, shoes you can't walk in, push-up bra, try not to make too much eye contact, in you go.'

'Exactly – you have the best time of your life . . . well, you tell yourself that at the time. Back then, you scrape together a few quid and go out when you can, then get one of your dads to come and pick you up if you don't have enough left for a taxi. Things begin to catch up with you, though, because you get jobs and boyfriends – two of our old mates, Jane and Vee, have little girls – slowly you drift away.'

'But you'd stayed friends with Cassie?'

Jade let go of her earring and blew her nose loudly. 'She was my best mate.'

Jessica thought of her friend Caroline and the relationship they had now. Since first meeting as teenagers all those years ago, they'd travelled together, lived together, drifted apart, back together and then, to a degree, apart again. Life did that. On some level, they'd always be a part of each other's lives. In different circumstances, this could have been her giving the interview.

'How often did you see each other?'

'Once or twice a week? She worked at this office near the Printworks and I'm at a tanning salon in the centre. We'd go for lunch now and then. Even if we didn't have time, we'd text all the time.'

'How frequently would you all go out?'

Another sad smile slipped onto Jade's face. 'Not often enough. Once a month? Maybe not even that. If one of us had a birthday, we'd try to make an effort. Yasmine was turning twenty-three and we'd managed to get everyone together for the first time in ages. Even Jane and Vee were there.'

'Talk me through the evening.'

'We'd arranged to meet at the Italian place for eight but Cassie, me and Yasmine had gone to this pub around the corner first.'

'What time did you get there?'

'Seven. It was pretty busy – a load of lads in suits out after work. It's always like that.'

'Did anyone show any particular interest in you?'

Jade curled her feet up on the chair and shook her head. 'I don't think so; we had a booth in the corner and shared a bottle of wine. We were talking about work and TV – the usual things – having a laugh.'

'Was she happy at work?'

A shrug: 'You're never that pleased at work, are you? It's just what you do to get a few quid. I don't think she was unhappy.'

'What time did you leave?'

'Just after eight. We were laughing because I'm always

late for things and this time it wasn't even my fault. We were just chatting and lost track of the time.'

'What was the restaurant like?'

'Normal – everyone was waiting for us. We had more wine in the bar bit while we were ordering, then we ate.'

'Was there anything unusual?'

'Only that the food came out really quickly. We chatted and laughed. Zoe fell off her stool because she was so pissed. It was one of those evenings. The waiters are friendly but that's just because they're after a tip, isn't it.'

Jessica was making notes on the places that had been visited. She knew the area and it was only a few hundred metres from the pub to the restaurant. There would be CCTV cameras nearby, hopefully inside the places too. When she'd finished with Jade, she'd get someone onto tracking it all down. Officers would interview the people behind the bar in the pub and the waiters at the restaurant. No one would remember anything; they never did.

'What time did you finish eating?'

'I don't know but because the food had come out so quickly, some of us were up for going on somewhere else. We all paid and said our goodbyes, then Cass, Zoe, me and Vee went on to this cocktail bar across the road. They have a little dance floor.'

'Was it busy?'

'Sort of – not packed but not empty. It's nice going out in the week because there's a good atmosphere but you can still move around. They were playing some good tunes and the barman was giving Zoe the eye.'

'What about Cassie?'

Jade stopped to dry her eyes again but only succeeded in making a bigger mess of the mascara that had already smeared across her face. 'I should've let her go.'

'What do you mean?'

'She wanted to go home to Carl after the restaurant but I persuaded her to stay out for one more. Then it was two more. If I'd let her go in the first place then . . .'

What an awful thing to live with.

'You can't blame yourself.'

Jade closed her eyes but there were tears again. She waved a hand dramatically in front of her face, whispering: 'It wasn't just that.'

Jessica reached across the pile of celebrity magazines and grabbed the box of tissues, joining Jade on the sofa. 'Someone did this. I want to find out who.'

Jade pulled out three tissues and dabbed at her face again; the result made her look like a painting of a panda that someone had spilled a mug of coffee over.

'What happened next?' Jessica asked.

Jade slowly composed herself. 'There's a taxi rank on the main road, so we decided we'd all go together and then split it. I took my shoes off because they were bloody hurting and I was feeling a bit pissed. Zoe was just giggling.'

'What was Cassie like?'

'I think she wanted to go home.'

'What happened?'

Jade gulped deeply. 'I'm seeing this lad, Ben. He's a dick. I know he's a dick, Cassie knew he was a dick, the other girls know he's a dick. I know he's only using me for . . . well, y'know . . . but sometimes you don't care, do you? I know I should but I'm getting stuff out of the relationship too – if you can call it that. It's not as if I'm going to be settling down with him.'

'Cassie didn't approve?'

A shake of the head sent rogue tears splattering onto Jessica's arm. 'She's my mate, so of course not. She was always saying he wasn't good enough for me and that I should dump him for someone better. It's not as if I disagreed but I guess I was so drunk that it touched a nerve.'

'So you had an argument?'

The reply was so quiet that Jessica almost missed it, even though she was next to the other woman. 'Yes.'

'What happened?'

'We were right next to the taxi rank. Vee said something about wanting to get home because her lovely boyfriend would be there. She reckoned he always waited up and that she was going to jump him. Zoe was saying she might go back to see if she could cop off with the barman and Cassie was smiling. She really loved Carl – they were beginning to think about getting married and the like. Usually, that would make me happy, but just for a moment I felt so angry. It was like I was someone else, I was so furious. I was thinking, "You bitch". How dare she be so happy when I was stuck with that prick Ben. It must have been the booze, I'm not usually like that, honest.'

Jessica waited for Jade to blow her nose again.

When she continued, she couldn't face Jessica. 'I had my shoe in my hand and felt this rage, like I wanted to kill her. I don't even remember it properly – Vee and Zoe were holding me back and I was shouting and going crazy. It was like I was watching myself.'

'Did you hit her?'

'I don't think so, I just threatened to.'

'What did she do?'

'Nothing. She looked at me and said she was sorry for whatever it was she'd done. I knew she hadn't done anything but I was still furious. I was screaming, "Go on, fuck off" – and she did.'

'She started walking?'

'Our taxi turned up a minute or two later and she was already out of sight. When I woke up the next morning I didn't even remember at first, then I was having flashbacks. I texted her about ten times. When I didn't get a reply, I assumed she was still annoyed – which was fair enough. I was going to go round later today to say sorry in person but then Carl called me this morning, asking if I'd seen her. I phoned the other girls and none of them had – then I realised that no one had seen her since the argument . . .'

At that, Jade finally lost it, doubling over and sobbing into her hands. Jessica rested a hand gently on her back but there wasn't a lot she could say. It wasn't likely you'd forget the day you argued with your best mate and never saw her again.

11

After spending Sunday at home, taking and making calls, replying to emails and generally working in a not-working kind of way, Jessica found herself standing in front of the chattering, biscuit-eating, tea-drinking masses in the incident room of Longsight Police Station the following morning, trying to stifle a yawn. Even DCI Cole had come down from his high horse, or upstairs office as it was better known, to see the proceedings.

'All right, all right,' Jessica said loudly. 'It's too early, I've got a headache and if you can't all shut up then I'm going to confiscate the biscuits.'

An outraged hush descended as Jessica turned to the pair of whiteboards behind her. On one, there was a large photo of Damon Potter, with Cassie Edmonds on the other.

'Damon died on Wednesday, Cassie on Thursday evening – one murdered, the other we're not sure,' Jessica said. 'There's no obvious connection from one to the other but the fact we've got them both to investigate means numbers are tight, so it's all hands on deck, to the pump, or however the saying goes.'

Jessica paused to have a sip of her tea: 'At around half eleven on Thursday night, Cassie had an argument with her friend as they were waiting for a taxi. We have CCTV of her walking along Great Ancoats Street and then turning onto Oldham Road but that was the last anyone saw of her until a dog-walker discovered her body in the woods close to Ellesmere Golf Course on Saturday morning. Forensics say she was likely dumped in the early hours of Friday morning, meaning she was killed relatively quickly after disappearing. Her boyfriend has an airtight alibi and we don't have any obvious suspects.'

A hand: 'Was she assaulted?'

'Not sexually, which means we don't have a motive either. But she was beaten very badly.'

Izzy was operating the laptop connected to the projector and Jessica asked her to flash through the photographs of the body. Any murmurings around the room quickly stopped as the horror dawned.

'Our crime scene was a bit of a mess,' Jessica continued. 'For one, the weather was at its usual welcoming best and then our dog-walker had a bit of an accident. Forensics did what they could but they're mainly relying on what they can get from the body, not what was at the scene. Because Cassie was dumped on the night she disappeared, they're not sure if she was killed in the woods, or elsewhere. Either way, the killer couldn't have gone far with her. We've been looking at tyre tracks around the car parks close to the golf course but we've not helped by parking there ourselves. Because it's in a fiddly spot close to the motorway and there are a few smaller roads underneath, we've had no luck tracking number plates either.'

Another sip of tea: 'Our search teams spent an unproductive weekend trawling through the woods, ending up doing little more than litter-picking. We've got a mass of discarded crisp packets and old carrier bags but not much else. Cassie was strangled and we're still trying to see if we can get anything from the indentations in her neck, although I was told not to hold my breath – an unfortunate choice of words.'

Jessica continued to tell the officers about the few things they did have, namely a vague description of what the killer was like based upon the injuries inflicted – male, taller than the victim, wide fingers, right-handed, the usual kind of thing. Then she moved on to the profile that had been commissioned, which was more of the same. The cuts on the body apparently showed that the male had a deep-seated hatred of women, possibly his own mother or partner. The beating indicated the killer had an anger problem, as if murdering someone in the first place wasn't enough of a clue. Blah, blah, blah.

Drawing on a mixture of the profile and the forensic work, an unfortunate group of officers had spent their Sunday cross-checking the details against everyone with a history of violence in the north-west of England. An initial 'short' list of five hundred potential names had been narrowed to a mere seventy who required further investigation. It was the standard type of thing they'd do for any major case that didn't have a natural suspect, but it didn't feel right to Jessica. The people listed had beaten up their wives or had a fight in the street. It was a big step up from that to strangling and beating someone to death and then cutting parts from their body.

Photos of the victim had gone out to the media over

the weekend but it had already been eclipsed in a tale of two blondes.

One: a pretty young *Coronation Street* actress had announced she was pregnant via her Premier League footballer boyfriend.

Two: a pretty young receptionist had disappeared and turned up dead in the woods a day later.

They were almost the same age, had gone to school a mile apart and had similar looks, except that Cassie's nose was slightly crooked and her teeth weren't as straight. One of them was splashed over seven pages of the local newspaper, and between three and five of the national tabloids; the other was worth a few paragraphs at the bottom of a page.

In the battle of blonde versus blonde, there was only one winner. If you were on telly, you were a someone; if not, you were a no one. Even in death, nobody would know who Cassie Edmonds was.

DC Archie Davey answered his phone with an agitated: 'All right, I'm doing it!'

'Good morning to you too,' Jessica replied. 'Here I was giving you a friendly Monday call to find out if you'd had a nice weekend at the football and I don't even get a hello.'

'Yeah, my arse were you. Anyway, I'm still trying to find the right former rowing club member to talk to. I've spoken to a couple but don't have anything yet. How's it going there?'

'As you'd expect – we've interviewed the people who were at the rowing club party the other night and everyone says the same as Holden. Damon left midway through the evening. No one actually saw him go, of course, let alone saw him leave with anyone. They've all got the same story.'

'There's a surprise.'

'Exactly. There are no cameras in the park and his flat-mate says he didn't go home afterwards.'

'So he drank himself to death and put himself in the bin?'

'Apparently so. We're doing what we can – all we need is someone to say there were drugs at the party, or they saw him drinking to excess. Everyone there either didn't see him, didn't know who he was, or only saw him briefly. We've not even got confirmation that anyone saw him drinking. We didn't find anything at the scene either. For now it's a stand-off. Someone knows more than they're letting on.'

'We should nick the lot of them and sling 'em down-stairs until someone talks.'

Jessica sighed. 'Don't think I haven't thought about it. I'll call you later, okay?'

'Am I allowed to say "no"?'

'Yes, I'll still call but . . .' Jessica paused, wondering how best to phrase it. In the end, she settled for the simplest way. '. . . thanks for working on your days off.'

Archie didn't reply for a moment but when he did, he was laughing. 'Stop being so soft or I'll have to tell every-one you're not such a cow after all.'

12

Now they had CCTV footage of Cassie from Thursday night, Jessica, Izzy and DC Dave Rowlands headed into the centre of the city for a poke-around. After a period where the three of them seemed to work together on everything, it was rare that happened nowadays. Part of that was down to Jessica's promotion, but because of a scandal over policing standards that had been brewing through the summer, and a report that was due early the next year, anything that looked like it could be a clique suddenly seemed a dangerous thing. For once, Jessica thought 'sod it' and decided she wanted to surround herself with people she trusted.

Following the usual bickering over who was driving, Dave's protestations that everyone was calling him Bin Boy, and Izzy's explanation of how she hadn't had time to look into non-permanent tattoos, they parked and walked the route Cassie and her friends had taken. After heading along Tib Street, they crossed to the cocktail bar and then made their way onto Great Ancoats Street, where Jade and Cassie had argued close to the taxis. The last image of the murdered girl had been crossing the road next to the comedy club and heading onto Oldham Road. The theory was that, with her Failsworth flat three miles down the road, Cassie had decided to walk.

Jessica tried to take in as much of the surroundings as she could: initially a row of slightly rundown shops and takeaways on the right and an elaborate Chinese on the left, then, a little further down, an elaborate six-storey red-brick building on the right, an Oriental supermarket on the left and roadworks.

In the centre of the road, red and white signs read 'road ahead closed', as if the row of knocked-over orange traffic cones, horizontal striped barriers and the hole in the ground stretching across four lanes didn't give it away. Still, some drivers would likely try to follow their sat navs straight through the makeshift obstruction into the ditch.

On one side, there was a stretch of three boarded-up shops next to a billboard and a covered-over bus-stop sign, with a long red-brick building on the other. Mustard-yellow boards signalled a diversion, with an arrow pointing into one of the side streets. At night, the whole area would have looked particularly bleak, even for Manchester.

With it being a little after ten in the morning, Jessica wasn't entirely surprised to see a group of workmen in bright jackets standing around chatting, drinking tea, flicking through newspapers and looking at their phones. They must have been working for at least half an hour, so it was time for a break, after all. Give it an hour and they'd be off for lunch.

Jessica left Izzy and Dave taking photographs and approached the one who looked like he was in charge – or, in other words, the fattest one. He was just starting to tuck into a sausage roll fresh from a Greggs paper bag when she interrupted him mid-bite. 'Are you in charge?'

'Mmmf,' he replied, straightening up as flaked pastry tumbled from his lips. She waited as he continued to chew, squidges of pale pink sausage oozing between his teeth and sticking there. 'Sorry, darling, we'll be right back on it. Just a quick five-minute rest. Back-breaking stuff, this.'

Jessica held up her identification for him to see. 'I'm from the police.'

A look of relief flashed across his face. 'Oh, right, sorry – I thought you were from the council.'

'How long have these roadworks being going on?'

Before answering, he took another bite of his sausage roll, whirring a hand close to his face as he chewed. Somehow a scrap of pastry had found its way into his nostril and it fluttered distractingly as he spoke. 'This is the start of week three. We're resurfacing the entire stretch.'

'And what sort of hours do you work?'

9 a.m.: Arrive and chat.

9.30 a.m.: Unload equipment from van.

10 a.m.: Morning break.

10.30 a.m.: Start digging as long as it isn't too rainy, windy, snowy, sunny, warm or cold.

11.30 a.m.: Lunch.

1 p.m.: Continue digging as long as it isn't too rainy, windy, snowy, sunny, warm or cold.

2.30 p.m.: Afternoon break.

3.30 p.m.: Start packing up.

4 p.m.: Knock-off.

'We normally start at around seven,' the foreman claimed.

'What about finishing?'

'Six? Sometimes seven?'

'Is there any night-working at all – say after ten?'

He spluttered: 'You're 'avin' a laugh, luv. Council don't want to pay for that.'

'Weekends?'

Another munch of the sausage roll: 'Nah, you've gotta have some time to yourself.'

'So between six in the evening and seven in the morning, there's no one here?'

'Right.'

Jessica suspected that it was more likely between around four in the afternoon and nine in the morning but it didn't make much difference – the key thing was that this area would have been unoccupied at the time Cassie walked past it late on Thursday. With all the shadows created by the boarded-up shops and surrounding barriers for the roadworks, it would have left multiple places where someone could have hidden before grabbing her. From where she was standing Jessica could see at least half-a-dozen spots. She thanked the man for his time and then returned to Dave and Izzy, who had reached much the same conclusion as she had. Behind and in front of them, there were bright street lights, through traffic, flats and shops; here it was gloomy and shaded.

Although they might never have it confirmed, as the workmen laughed at a joke she hadn't heard, Jessica knew instinctively that this was the spot from which Cassie had been abducted.

*

With a narrow width of tarmac, Tib Street was a one-way, third-of-a-mile-long throughway connecting the centre of Manchester with the main road leading in and out. Tall buildings created long shadows and with boarded-up shops, graffiti, small bars, a chippy and a hydroponics shop that definitely didn't sell wacky baccy, it was the type of place that chain stores didn't want to be a part of, while entrepreneurs smelled the chance for an opening into a big city. A complex web of small side streets linked it to the Northern Quarter on one side and a shortcut to the Manchester Arena and Printworks cinema and restaurant complex on the other.

Metal-shuttered cubbies and an array of cheap flats provided the perfect haven for artistic types, meaning that as the three officers weaved their way back towards the car, they passed a pair of tattoo shops within a couple of hundred metres. By the time they reached the third, Jessica couldn't resist the lure any longer, stopping and turning to Izzy. 'Which one do you want to go in?'

'What for?'

'You know why. Pick one – there's a bunch right here.'

'What if I didn't bring the photo of the robber with me?'

'I know you did. If I had to guess, you've got half-a-dozen copies in the car just in case.'

Dave laughed as Izzy admitted that was the exact number.

'Why don't we pick a shop each?' Dave suggested. 'We can ask about non-permanent tattoos and what someone might have used to create something that can be rubbed off. If they seem like they know what they're on about, we can show the photo.'

'We've already had someone down here going into all the shops,' Izzy said.

'Yes, but that was to ask if they knew anyone they'd tattooed with that design – this is different,' Jessica said. 'It's more about asking what techniques someone could use and then jogging their memory about the picture we do have.' Jessica slipped her phone out of her pocket. 'Anyway, Bin Boy, first roll up your sleeve.'

Dave glanced from Izzy to Jessica. 'Why?'

'Just do it.'

He narrowed his eyes but did it anyway. Jessica focused the camera on her phone and snapped a photo of the tattoo on his inner forearm.

'What are you going to do with that?' he asked.

'I'm going to ask the guy in the shop what those symbols actually mean.'

Dave looked down at the Chinese lettering on his arm, scowled, then rolled his sleeve back down. 'I told you years ago, they mean "warrior".'

Izzy giggled: 'Ten quid says they don't.'

'I want in on that too,' Jessica added.

Thrusting his hands into his pockets, Dave muttered something about not having any money on him and how he didn't gamble anyway.

Five minutes later, photos in hand, and they were back. Jessica naturally picked the dingiest-looking tattoo parlour, Izzy chose the one that had an impressive if slightly pornographic-looking drawing of a barely clad woman in the window, which left Dave with the shop that had a vast mural at the front containing images of straight swords, scimitars, a kilij, assorted knives, throwing stars and any number of other weapons. Jessica assured Dave he was unlikely to get himself stabbed, but if he did then he should keep the noise down because this was a quiet area.

The shop that Jessica had chosen looked far nicer on the inside than it did on the outside. Compared to the half-closed shutters that had 'rachal takes it up the arse' graffitied onto them in admittedly fancy letters, the bright cream of the interior and spotless floor was a surprising change. Lining the walls were row after row of artwork ranging from small black and white letters up to elaborate prints of safari animals. There were two doors at the back, with a bored-looking slim woman resting against a desk near the front. Her long, straight black hair and bright red lips were offset against extravagant red and green tattoos winding the entire length of both arms.

Jessica didn't ask but mentally named the woman 'Rose' because it was etched onto her shoulder.

'How can I help you, luv?' Rose asked.

'Do you actually do the tattoos?'

'Not yet – only piercings.' Without missing a beat, she screeched the word 'Bones!' so shrilly that it made Jessica wince.

From one of the rooms at the back a man emerged wearing an apron. Average height, average weight, mid-thirties, half-smile: everything about Bones seemed perfectly normal – except for the fact that his entire bald head was tattooed with an intricate, inter-connecting pattern of shapes, lines and symbols. Around his eyes there were crescent moons, with ripple-like markings stretching out to his ears. At least half-a-dozen small rings were pinned into his right nostril, with some sort of spike poking out from the other side. As he walked towards her, Bones interlocked his fingers, cracking his knuckles and showing off his bare arms.

'A'ight?' he asked, with a slight hint of a local accent.

Jessica showed him her ID and asked if he could spare a few minutes. With a shrug he said it was okay if she was quick. Considering his shop was teeming with hordes of invisible people, Jessica thought it was fair enough.

'How much do you know about temporary tattoos?' she asked.

'I don't do henna,' Bones replied.

'I'm not sure that's what I mean. Is there any sort of ink you use that's particularly easy to clear away? Perhaps in the shower? Something like that?'

'Why?'

'It's something we're working on.'

'I think she means ballpoints,' Rose called across.

Jessica turned to Rose, who hadn't looked up, and then back to Bones. 'Like a biro?' she asked.

Bones shook his head. 'It depends on the artist. Generally, you'd use a regular tattoo gun that was slightly modified. You'd be putting the ink onto the surface of the skin, rather than puncturing it. I've heard of some lads who do it with an actual pen but you'd have to really know what you were doing – and trust whoever was inking you.'

Jessica thought of the tattoos she'd seen on a few prisoners over the years who had used needles or blades and a biro. They were nothing like the intricate markings on the arm of their robber.

'How elaborate can a ballpoint tattoo be?' she asked.

Bones shrugged, indicating the images on the walls around the room. 'You could turn any of these into a ball-point tattoo if you wanted – it'd cost you a lot, though.'

'Is the ink expensive?'

He scratched his head, just below a wide arc that dipped towards his eyebrows, and glanced towards Rose. 'It's the time. It takes the same length to create as a real one but only lasts a few days.'

Jessica was confused. 'So why would you get one?'

'People rarely do. Perhaps if you were in a play or on television, something like that. If you're doing a movie with a huge budget, then the cost doesn't matter.'

She paused for a moment, thinking that it would be a lot of expense if you were simply going to hold up a few off-licences. Jessica took the folded photograph out of her pocket and showed it to Bones, asking what he thought of it.

He stared closely and shrugged. 'One of your lot came around asking about this the other day.'

'I know, but we believed it was a real tattoo then. Now I'm thinking it could be one of your ballpoint ones.'

Bones took another look but shook his head. 'Not my thing. There are a few places around here, perhaps try them?'

Jessica was about to ask how long it might take to create when Bones started scratching at his crotch. 'Sorry, I really need a slash. Been on the water all morning.'

Charming.

As he scurried into the back room, Jessica approached Rose again. 'Have you ever seen anything like this?' she asked, holding out the photo.

The woman took it. 'Not as something temporary but it's fairly common stuff. If you were good, you'd be drawing lines like those pretty much every day.'

'How long would it take to come off?'

Rose shrugged and handed the photo back. 'If you did nothing to it, it could be there four or five days, maybe longer. But you could make it really temporary by washing it off yourself.'

'Could you smudge it by accident?'

'Maybe. The ink's on the skin so I suppose.'

Interesting.

Jessica put the photo away and then remembered Dave's arm. She held up her phone, showing the photograph. 'Any idea what this says?' she asked.

Rose peered closely. 'Is that Mandarin?'

'No idea. He claims it says "warrior".'

With a smile, Rose climbed off the stool and led Jessica to the far wall. 'People always come in wanting things like that – "king", "general", "prince", "ninja", any old shite.' She pointed to a string of Far-Eastern-looking characters. 'That's Mandarin for "warrior". We have some steroid-freak in every few weeks asking for it.'

Jessica compared the characters on the wall to the ones on her phone. Although the design seemed similar, the exact characters were completely different. Jessica grinned: if only she could find out what the tattoo actually said.

She packed her phone away, ready to give Dave the good news, when she had one final thought. Showing Rose the photo of the robber again, Jessica asked: 'If the ball-point tattoos cost roughly the same as a regular tattoo, how much would this be?'

'A few hundred?'

Definitely not worth it just to hold up an off-licence then.

Rose chewed on her tongue for a moment, before adding: 'Well, unless you did it yourself, of course.'

Jessica glanced down at the photo, taking in the scene: balaclava, bare arms except for the drawn-on tattoo, normal height, normal weight . . .

Oh. Shite.

13

'He's got to be bloody somewhere,' Jessica yelled into her phone, trying to run at the same time. 'His head's covered in tattoos – it's not like he's going to be sitting on a park bench twiddling his thumbs. I only saw him two minutes ago.'

She reached the end of the alleyway at the back of the row of shops and looked both ways. Aside from a short man shuffling along with a bin bag, there was no sign of anyone.

'There's no one out here.' Dave puffed back from the other end of the alley, trying not to sound out of breath.

'All right, keep looking; call Iz.'

Jessica hung up. This would've been a lot simpler if they'd had their radios with them; easier still if Jessica had noticed the signs around Bones a couple of minutes earlier. She continued out of the alley into the street, heading towards the man with the bin bag. 'Did you see a bloke with his head tattooed come this way?' she asked.

It was hard to tell if the man was homeless or simply taking his rubbish out because his glazed stare gave him the look of someone who had spent more than a bit of cash at the hydroponics shop. 'What's the tattoo of?' he asked, gazing through Jessica.

'I don't know; it's all sort of squiggles, suns and moons. You'd know it if you saw it.'

The man dropped his bag and scratched his head. 'Why would you tattoo your head?'

Not bothering to answer, Jessica spun in a circle, hoping for any sign of Bones, just as her phone rang: Izzy hadn't seen him either – and with that, their chief suspect for the shop robberies was gone.

With a name like 'Dougie Harrison', it was perhaps no surprise that the tattooist chose to call himself Bones. Rose told them where he lived and Jessica, Dave, Izzy and her piled into the pool car and barrelled across the city. Izzy requested a tactical entry team, uniformed officers and anything else she thought she might be able to get her hands on. For a moment, Jessica thought she was going to ask for a helicopter.

While that was going on, Rose told them that Bones owned the shop, but with the abundance of competition nearby, he'd been complaining about money for a while. The previous week he had laid off the third person who worked in the shop, with Rose claiming the only reason he'd kept her on was because 'he liked looking at my tits'.

Whoever Izzy had threatened at the station had got their act together because, as they pulled up outside a grungy-looking semi-detached around the corner from the Belle Vue speedway stadium, a van full of suited and booted tactical entry officers screeched to a halt too. Some went around the back, the others around the front; one, two, three – go, go, go. Bang, slam, crunch.

When it was clear their man wasn't home, Jessica left Rowlands with Rose in the car, giving him the raised eyebrow treatment about not chatting up a witness – even though she'd probably eat him for breakfast – and then headed into the house with Izzy. The first sign that Bones' house was going to be a shrine to motorbikes should have been the rusting engine in the garden. If that wasn't enough of a clue, then the bus-stop-sized Harley Davidson logo pinned to the back of the first door on the right as the officers poured in definitely gave it away.

In the living room, there was an impressive airbrushed mural of a biker riding into a sunset along a road so straight that it could only be in America. It certainly wasn't Manchester – for one thing the sun was out, secondly you'd be lucky to drive a few hundred metres in the city without having multiple sets of red traffic lights.

Officers hauled away electrical equipment to be checked over as Jessica and Izzy picked through anything that looked remotely interesting.

'At least you know who your robber is,' Jessica said, trying to sound optimistic.

'Not much good if we can't find him, is it?'

'His head looks like someone's been trying to fill in a crossword with a crayon – there can't be too many places he'll be able to hide without being spotted.'

'If it gets out we'd already visited him once, then we'll be a laughing stock. That's before the fact that we were confused by a fake tattoo.'

'Anyone could've been taken in by that. I've never heard of ballpoint tattoos. Besides, I wouldn't worry too much – there are too many pregnant soap stars out there for anyone to pay attention.'

Aside from the motorcycling keepsakes there wasn't much else to see downstairs, so Jessica and Izzy headed upstairs. Inside the first door, they were greeted by a black carpet, deep red walls and thick dark curtains they had to open in order to see anything.

Bones' bed had a pair of handlebars in place of a headboard, with an impressive, if rather creepy, skull that Jessica hoped wasn't human in the centre that stared into the room.

'Imagine coming back here after a first date,' Izzy said.

'Do you often go back to blokes' houses after a first date?'

'Only the ones who don't have their entire heads tattooed.'

'No wonder he needed a few quid – between running the shop and collecting all this stuff, you're talking thousands.'

As Izzy headed for the bedside table, Jessica opened up the wardrobe. Underneath a set of outfits more suited to a night out on Canal Street, she spotted a battered white shoebox. As she crouched to remove the lid, all Jessica could think was: 'Surely it's not . . .' Except that it was: bundles of ten- and twenty-pound notes had been neatly stacked into thousand-pound bundles. For someone who had cleverly planned the tattoo side of the scam, Bones really was as stupid a criminal as so many others. Now they just had to find him.

Back at the station the investigation into Cassie's murder was ticking along as well as could be expected considering the lack of evidence at the crime scene. Rose gave them a statement about Bones and his apparent financial problems, while Dave hadn't taken the news that his tattoo definitely didn't say what he thought it did particularly well.

All of that by midday – not bad for a morning's work – which is why Jessica phoned Archie to start annoying him.

'I'm busy,' he said by way of answering his phone.

'Good, what have you got?'

'Some local lad, a good ol' Urmston boy – worked his balls off to make the Salford team for the national rowing finals, then it all went to cock when he got dropped for some Yank. I had a word this morning. He has nothing to do with any of them now. He didn't want to say anything at first but we got chatting about United and he invited me over.'

'When are you going?'

'Soon.'

'Want some company?'

Archie laughed. 'Haven't you got other things to be doing?'

'I was thinking he might want a sympathetic female ear.'

It was nonsense and they both knew it – Jessica had a stack of things to be signing off but she wanted to be doing something. In the old days, she might have been narrowing down the list of people who had a history of violence against women for the Cassie case, or handling the interview with Rose for the tattoo robbery one. Now she was supposed to take an overview of it all. If she ended up sitting around the station for much longer, she'd end up being called into a meeting before she knew it.

Perhaps picking up on the hint of desperation in her voice, or maybe because he didn't want to annoy her, Archie replied with a not entirely convincing: 'Aye, perhaps he might appreciate a woman being there; don't want too much of a testosterone overload.'

After initial apprehension, Liam Withe turned out to be the exact kind of person they were looking for. Archie turned on the Manc charm, spending ten minutes talking Manchester United and how they were going to win the league that year – or, at the absolute least, finish above the 'bitters' and 'bin-dippers' – then he gradually brought him around to the topic of being a student and part of the rowing club.

Liam told them that when it came to the elite races, culminating in the national championships in which they raced against other universities, the teams were almost always dominated by post-graduate students. He'd studied for three years doing a finance undergraduate degree, before staying on for an extra year for the post-grad course specifically because he wanted to take part in those races. After working his way through the fourth-, third- and second-string teams, over the course of three years, he'd been eagerly awaiting his chance with the elite squad. He had rowed in some of the preliminary races but was then dropped for an American third-year student who was only going to be there for nine months.

'And he was called fooking Corey,' Liam fumed. Despite

the fact he was an apparently successful sole trader working from home, it still enraged him.

After Archie had brought Liam's annoyance to the fore, it was Jessica's turn to steer the conversation. Given the conspiracy of silence from the rest of the club members, this might be their only chance for an insight into what really went on when the clubhouse doors were closed.

'I suppose you read about the death of Damon Potter,' Jessica said.

Liam was tall and lean with short dark hair, dressed casually in loose jeans and a shirt. On the arm of his chair was perched a laptop that he kept checking, saying it was for his trading job.

He nodded without looking up.

'We've been having increasing problems with the club in the past few years: rape allegations, public disorder complaints, someone ended up in hospital with hypothermia . . .'

A hint of a knowing smile crept across Liam's face but he still didn't look up. 'Training accident, was it?'

'So we were told. I realise almost all of this comes after your time, but I couldn't help but notice that when you were in your final year with the university, the person who is now student president was in his first year.'

'Holden Wyatt?'

Jessica made a show of checking her notes to ensure she didn't seem quite so keen on him as she was. 'Do you know him?'

'There were always one or two a year – first years who already knew people. Sometimes their parents had been to the university, or perhaps they were keen sportsmen. For some, the social side of university and joining the club is far more important than what you study.'

'Was it like that for you?'

Liam finally looked up from his laptop, fixing Jessica with his bright blue eyes. 'I just liked being fit and it seemed fun. I'd never even been on the water before university.'

'But Holden was different?'

A knowing laugh: 'He'd been doing it since he was a kid but wasn't good enough to get into Oxford or Cambridge, either for rowing or academically. I think his dad knew a few of the Salford alumni and they come from somewhere around here. From day one, he was in with the post-grad students and the elite team. Usually when that happened, they'd get slapped down – but he had something about him.'

'Did you ever talk to him?'

'Not really. As soon as you drop off the team, suddenly the younger lads aren't interested in you any longer.'

'When I brought up the hypothermia, you seemed to indicate that perhaps it wasn't an accident . . .'

Liam glanced down at his laptop and tapped on the tracker pad but the atmosphere had changed. 'I suppose what happened to that Damon kid was only going to be a matter of time . . .'

'How do you mean?'

At first, Liam didn't reply, tapping away at his computer before sighing and finally closing the lid. When he looked at Jessica again, his eyes had lost some of their blue. 'Obviously I don't know for certain, but . . .'

Jessica said nothing, hoping Archie wouldn't fill the silence either. He didn't, and Liam was left to do so himself. 'The big November party they have is more of a congratulations to the students left standing who still want to be members after "hell week".'

'Hell week?'

Liam took a deep breath, perhaps wondering if he'd said too much but there was no going back now: 'It happens in the final week of October leading up to Halloween. If you're a first year and want to become a full member, then you have to have a series of tests. It's usually only the elite lads involved after-dark in the clubhouse. At first it's something simple, like drink a few pints in a row, but the tasks get more intense as the week goes on.'

He shivered slightly and Jessica felt it catching as a chill rippled along her spine. 'It can move on to things like taking a beating from the team. They'll hit you with paddles but every time you take it, the next day it's worse.'

'What happened to you?'

'When I was a first year, it wasn't too bad. I think it comes down to who the student president is. I had to do some drinking, late-night swimming in the water – I'll bet that's how your other lad got hypothermia – and this game where you had to do a lap of the park, then drink, then more laps, more drinking. I was sick a few times and took my beating on the final day but that's as bad as it got.'

'What might've gone wrong with Damon?'

Liam now seemed resigned to spilling everything. 'I don't know for sure – I don't talk to anyone there – but things were beginning to get out of hand when it was my final year. We had this real sicko student president. Night one was swimming a width of the river, doing shots and pints, then going again over and over. People were collapsing and everyone else was uneasy. I mean I was there but . . .'

He didn't need to finish the sentence – he hadn't spoken up because he didn't want to be kicked off the team.

'The week got worse. On night two it was beatings, night three they had these eating challenges.'

'Who could eat the most?' Archie asked.

Liam shook his head. 'Not how much, *what* could they eat. At first it was these awful meat products: offal, I don't even know what that is. Then they'd have to drink milk really quickly, so people were vomiting. But because they were being sick, the president was saying that was cheating as they weren't keeping it down, so he made them . . . well, you can guess . . .'

Ugh.

'By day four, some people hadn't come back and it kept getting worse. You might be surprised – but all the first years knew what hell week was, so they didn't even bother starting it unless they thought they could do it. There's a code of silence about it, too. What happens in the club stays in the club – that sort of thing. It was pretty grim but everyone from my year got through. I never heard of anyone pulling out until that year.'

'And that was the year Holden was a first year?' Jessica asked.

'Exactly – but he was the one person who never flinched. I know you might not believe me but I never went in for any of that; it was only ever a few of the guys. That's why student president is an odd position – it's more social and organisational. The best athletes just want to row. It's more of a tradition but certain people take it more seriously than others.'

'Like Holden?'

'Yes. I didn't know he was student president until I read it but I'm not surprised. He wasn't the best of athletes but he wanted to be a part of everything. If you get to student president, you've got to really want it – but also have to do some crazy things to get there.'

'What sort of things?'

Liam glanced between the two officers and then turned away. 'For a start you need the kind of mind to come up with things for hell week.'

'Didn't anyone ever say anything?' Jessica asked.

A shrug: 'I know it sounds bad . . . it was bad . . . but it was also part of this weird bonding thing. Especially if you weren't popular, it gave you a chance to get in with the cool kids. When you first signed up, you'd start to hear the whispers, then you'd be told to get ready for hell week. If you chose to walk away, that was that – but no one would ever have told the lecturers or faculty. It would have been denied and there would have been a long line of people to call you a liar. Then you'd have all the pressure from the people who *were* into it. Ultimately you're there to study, so it's not worth it.'

That pretty much tallied with everyone they'd interviewed who might have seen Damon on the night he died. Some admitted they had spotted him but that he'd left the party early, others said they hadn't seen him at all. The one thing they had in common was that nobody said anything to criticise Holden's version.

'Did things like hell week ever happen after Halloween?' Jessica asked.

Liam shook his head. 'Not that I ever saw. The party signalled the end of all that – if you got that far, then you'd earned everyone's respect and you got on with it.'

Jessica had nothing left to ask, and from the look on Archie's face neither did he. They'd have to speak to Holden again, perhaps even charge him with assault if they could make someone speak – but if any hazing Damon had had to go through was over by Halloween, then what had happened to him on the November night he died?

14

Jessica called the station when they got back to the car. The media appeal for information about Cassie's death had barely got off the ground because of the lack of interest. They were following up a few lines of inquiry but nothing that had anyone excited. As for the list of seventy locals with a previous history of violence, all but nine had been eliminated as definitely being somewhere else, being in prison or, in one case, having died the year before.

That's what you called an alibi.

She told the officers to arrange for all nine to be brought in for interview later that afternoon. Even if it was nothing to do with them, there was a chance they mixed in the circles where someone might know something. It was desperation tactics already.

With that sorted, it was time to talk to Holden again: this time with a tape recorder and video camera running. Considering it was his day off, Archie seemed particularly in the mood for round two with 'posh boy'. After first trying his flat, a swanky studio apartment overlooking Salford Quays, they found him at the rowing clubhouse. Jessica knew something was different the moment they walked in. Instead of the athletic gear from before, Holden was wearing a smart suit with a tie and recently shined shoes. He was chatting to someone on his phone but hung up when he saw them, acknowledging Jessica with a clipped nod and 'Inspector'.

'What's with the get-up?' Jessica asked, as Holden led them across to the bar area where there was a circular table that had three chairs placed around it.

He took a seat, leaving them standing as he replied. 'I thought it was time for a change.'

'To the untrained eye, it could seem as if you were waiting for us.'

'What exactly do you want?'

'We've been speaking to a few of your members – current and former. We've heard some very interesting stories about things that go on here.'

'Like what?'

'Hell week, for one.'

Holden shrugged dismissively.

'Don't you have anything to say?' Jessica added.

'I think I'll call my lawyer.'

On arriving at Longsight Police Station, Holden had gone downstairs to meet with his solicitor. Jessica hung around upstairs asking where her nine 'people of interest' for Cassie's murder were as officers hurried around making excuses. When it was clear she was going to have to wait regardless, she ushered Archie into her office and closed the door.

'Enjoying your day off?' she asked.

'I was hoping posh boy was going to be a little unhappier about coming in for interview.'

'Hmm, I wouldn't say "hoping" but I wasn't expecting

him to cooperate either. Somewhere along the line, news of your phone calls to current and former club members has got back to him.'

After Holden had had an hour with his solicitor, Jessica finally got into interview room one, with her and Archie on one side of the table, Holden and the legal representative on the other. The student's suit was marginally sharper than his solicitor's but there wasn't much in it as the pair sat impassively opposite them, looking somehow resigned and defiant at the same time.

Jessica told them she had first-hand witness testimony that the rowing club hazed new members, leaving it slightly woolly that she had no proof about what had happened to that year's intake, specifically Damon.

As it was, Jessica didn't even have to let Archie loose before Holden started telling them what they wanted to know.

'It's not what you think,' he said, not looking up as his solicitor watched on silently.

'What do I think?'

'Damon's death was nothing to do with me.'

'Let's go backwards. Tell me about hell week.'

Holden glanced at his solicitor and then up at the camera high in the corner recording everything he said. 'It's a silly tradition.'

'Something you're in charge of as student president?'

He looked at Jessica properly for the first time but there was no focus to his gaze. 'To a degree.'

'Did Damon Potter take part in hell week?'

There was a pause punctuated by a sideways glance towards his solicitor. 'Yes.'

Holden gave the names of the other half-dozen first-year students involved but refused to implicate any of the other senior members in whatever had gone on. Jessica didn't know if the loyalty should go in his favour considering he was apparently the ring-leader, or if he was trying to cover up for others. For now, it didn't matter.

'What did you force the new members to do?' Jessica asked.

'It was their decision – nobody coerced anyone to do anything.'

'But they wouldn't have been allowed to join your club if they didn't undertake your challenges – so the pressure to take part came from you, didn't it?'

Another glance at his solicitor: 'I suppose. Everyone wants to be wanted, don't they? It's about feeling a part of something.'

Jessica paused for a moment: he couldn't have said a truer thing. 'What did you do to them?'

'Immature things: drinking, exercising, eating things.'

'Did you beat them?'

'Yes.'

'I need to know specifics.'

And so he gave them, talking for half an hour about the tasks he had set for the new members. Detail after detail of activities meant to degrade and humiliate. It wasn't so much the individual aspects that Jessica found disturbing, more the fact that someone could speak so matter-of-factly about thinking them up. She had interviewed serial murderers and psychos in the past who would hurt and kill for their own gratification but Jessica didn't get the sense that Holden had enjoyed any of it – more that he saw hell week as a custom it was his duty to maintain.

The one thing she did get the sense of was that, if Damon was looking happier in the few days before he died, it was likely because he had got to the end of hell week unscathed.

Holden's solicitor was silent throughout, listening and making the odd note but never interrupting. By the time his client had finished, Jessica knew they could definitely charge the student with actual bodily harm and sexual assault at the minimum. Depending on how the Crown Prosecution Service read things, it could even be revised up to grievous bodily harm if any of the victims made statements. Even without that, his own confessions would condemn him – and in any normal situation, his solicitor would have stopped him from implicating himself.

Something was definitely going on but she still had a couple of key questions.

'How much does James Jefferies know?' Jessica asked.

The question surprised Holden, who reeled back in his seat. 'James?'

'He's your life president, isn't he?'

'Yes . . . but that's more of a figurehead position. He might come to the odd practice and big race day but that's about it. The guy's in a wheelchair.'

That was something Jessica didn't know. Why hadn't anyone told her?

'What about the night Damon died?' she added.

This time, Holden looked at her directly, holding his arms out to the side. 'I really don't know anything about that. After hell week, that's it – we get on with the rest of the year. We hold elections for the new student president in March or April and I would have been graduating. I don't know anything about his death. Everything I told you is true – I didn't see him after around an hour of the party. I think he left.'

'There were drink and drugs in his system. What if we've been speaking to someone who's told us they came from you?'

Finally, Holden's solicitor cut in: 'You don't have to answer that.'

His client responded anyway: 'They'd be lying because I didn't. I don't know what happened to him. It was just a party and I had things to organise on the night.'

'I want the names of the other people involved in the assaults.'

Holden shook his head in a show of baffling loyalty.

Jessica waited for a moment, wondering what to say. It wasn't often she was lost for words but eventually they came: 'Why have you told us all of this?'

'It's the truth.'

'Okay, say it is. We've heard these sorts of allegations from at least one other club member and I'm pretty sure we'd have got evidence soon enough about everything that went on behind closed doors at your club. Chances are, we'd have ended up in this room anyway and I would've been putting all these allegations to you. But it wouldn't have happened today, perhaps not even tomorrow. So why admit to everything now?'

Holden's eyes flickered to his solicitor and Jessica knew that this was a question the legal representative had asked himself. When Holden peered back, he held Jessica's gaze. 'Because I know how it looks but it wasn't me who killed him, dumped him, or did anything else. James Jefferies called me, asking if I knew anything about Damon. He said that if I did, then I should step forward.'

'Why did he tell you that?'

'He's probably seen things on the news and wants to protect the club. I might've done a few silly things but I didn't do that.'

'Do you know who did?'

'No.'

'Could it have been any of the other members who didn't realise the hazing was over?'

'No.'

With that, there was little else to say. Jessica called for one of the officers to take him back to the cells downstairs while they decided what to do with him.

Jessica led Archie back to her office while she tried to clarify her thoughts. By the time they sat down, he beat her to it: 'What do you think?'

It was the kind of thing she would have asked a supervising officer when she was a gobby young pup. 'How about you tell me what you think?' she responded.

'He might be a snooty, toffee-nosed tosser but I think he's telling the truth. The job would be a lot easier if everyone took responsibility for the things they did. It sort of makes sense – I spoke to a few people, so someone would've told him. Plus he looks up to that Jefferies Olympic guy. There's no way he would have been able to keep everyone quiet, and the minute one breaks, they all would. We'd have had him strung up by the bollocks sooner or later.'

Quite.

'What else?' Jessica asked.

'He's not an idiot. If he killed Damon, even accidentally, why would he have dumped the body in the bin outside the place where he'd get asked about it? He could've lumped it in the river and it would have floated down stream. Or buried it somewhere else in the park. Or taken it anywhere.'

'Perhaps because he knew the bins were supposed to be emptied the next day? The only reason they weren't was because of the strike.'

'Pfft. He also knew the cleaners would come the next day. He might have done all those other things but I don't think he knew anything about our lad ending up in that bin.'

Archie raised an eyebrow, wondering what Jessica thought, but her tight smile said it all: she agreed with him completely.

15

Before they decided whether to charge Holden with any-thing now, or bail him to return to the station in a few days, Jessica knew she needed to get some advice. She also had nine local scroats apparently on their way in to the station to deal with too, plus a colleague who'd been with her all afternoon who wasn't actually on duty.

Out in reception, the desk sergeant, Patrick – or Fat Pat to everyone who knew him – was two-thirds of the way through a family-sized packet of steak-flavoured crisps, barely concealed under the counter.

'Let's have one then,' Jessica said.

Frowning, Pat reluctantly pulled the bag out and offered it to her, gripping the bottom half tightly so she couldn't go delving. As soon as her hand was withdrawn with a broken crisp, he snatched the bag away again, returning it to the hiding place.

'What are you doing in?' he asked, nodding at Archie.

'He's helping me,' Jessica interrupted with her mouth full. 'Don't worry, I'll sort the overtime. Now there should be nine scumbags hanging around here somewhere. Where are they?'

Pat's eyebrows curved downwards into one long cater-pillar. 'Haven't you heard?'

'Heard what?'

He grinned in the way he always did when he knew things others didn't. 'Loads of officers have been moved away from investigating the Cassie Edmonds death so we've got enough people to interview the rowing-club members.'

Pat reached for another crisp, eyebrows leaping into two separate entities again, apparently in surprise that she didn't know.

'We've already spoken to the rowing lot once.'

He shrugged and munched at the same time. 'Dnt sk mmf.'

'What?'

He finished chomping his way through the crisp. 'New priorities – don't ask me.'

'Who authorised it?'

Pat raised his index finger skywards, indicating DCI Jack Cole. 'Who do you think?'

After telling Archie to wait for her, Jessica headed for the stairs, trying not to make it seem so obvious that she hadn't known anything about it. The chief inspector had every right to make such a decision – but it would be rare for that to happen without a discussion involving her, or a word in her ear at the very least.

Through the glass front of his office, Jessica could see Cole sitting behind his desk talking to someone on the phone. She knocked gently but he held a hand up, indicating for her to wait. It wasn't necessarily untoward – there was every chance he was on a private or confidential phone call – but it left Jessica standing by herself in the corridor, leaning on the wall opposite staring at a mixture of her own reflection and Cole's silent conversation. As he spoke, he glanced up towards her, catching her eye for the merest fraction of a second and then quickly looking away again. He had aged dramatically over the past couple of years, with the break-up of his marriage, shared custody of the children and pressures of his role taking their toll.

Then there was their own relationship.

Izzy had been right: Cole had seemed to have some sort of problem with her over recent months but had never told her specifically what it was. He was the reason she had returned to the force when she wasn't sure if that was what she wanted to do with her life. It was he who was instrumental in her promotion, and in getting Izzy the detective sergeant's job on a trial basis. It wasn't as if he didn't know the way she worked – he'd been out on jobs with her enough – so why now?

Jessica watched him spin in his chair until he was facing the wall away from her, the light catching the bald spot on his head.

Check phone, put it away again. Run fingers through hair – why is it always knotty in that same area at the back? Straighten trousers. Trace the line of bricks in the wall – is there meant to be a crack there? Wonder what might be for tea tonight. Has it always been so quiet up here? You can't even hear the bustle of everyone downstairs; perhaps this isn't such a bad spot to work after all—

'Jessica . . .'

Jessica was so surprised at Cole's voice that she literally jumped and took a second to compose herself. 'Sorry, er . . .'

Cole was peering along the corridor, as opposed to actually at her. 'Did you want to see me?'

'Shall I come in, or . . . ?'

Cole held his office door open but everything felt so awkward. When he took his seat behind the desk, the DCI still didn't look at her, instead picking up a cardboard folder from his desk and examining the papers inside.

Jessica began hesitantly, wanting to be diplomatic: 'After Cassie Edmonds was found, we put together a list of people with a history of violence against women around here. I know it was a bit of a long shot but we'd got it down to nine men without alibis who we thought we might be able to put some pressure on. I know it was a bit of desperation but we've done far worse in the past. I was expecting them to be brought in this afternoon, but . . .'

Cole didn't look up. 'But what?'

'But Pat said those nine weren't being brought in yet because you wanted all the members of the rowing club spoken to again . . .'

'Correct.'

This was torturous – he really did want to make her squirm. 'I was wondering why . . . ?'

Cole sighed, dropping the documents on the desk and finally looking at her with a frown. 'I don't need to explain everything that happens around here to you.'

'I know, Sir, it was just that we'd had people working on those lists most of the weekend . . .'

'Word has come down from above to get the Potter case sorted.'

'At the expense of Cassie Edmonds . . . ?' The words

blurted out with far more of an edge than Jessica intended.

Cole's eyelid twitched and for a moment she could almost see a fire in him that had rarely been there before. He'd always been known for being laid-back but now he seemed like a different person. When he replied, his tone was level but there was no warmth. 'Not "at the expense of" – this is just the priority for now. We're going to charge Holden Wyatt with GBH and aggravated sexual assault—'

'Aggravated?'

'Yes. Do you have a problem?'

'No, I just hadn't realised anyone had been watching the interview – or that it had been discussed. That was the other reason I was coming up here.'

'Things have been moving quickly while you were in the interview room. A few of the other club members have come forward to say their recollections of the party might have been incorrect.'

'Why didn't anyone say something?'

'I didn't want to interrupt your flow – besides, everything was in hand.'

Jessica didn't know if she was confused or annoyed – probably both. What on earth was going on? 'What have they changed their story to?'

'One of the members said they thought they were mistaken at seeing Holden in the later parts of the evening. They couldn't say for sure they'd seen Damon and Holden leave together, just that they hadn't seen them after a certain point in the evening.'

'And they just so happened to change their stories at

the exact time Holden was admitting to the initiation ceremonies?'

'Perhaps that was why he came clean? He knew other members were going to turn on him, so he got in first.'

'He didn't admit to murder – or dumping a body.'

'We've got a confession that he assaulted Damon Potter on numerous occasions, now we have witness statements to say both Holden and our victim disappeared at around the same time on the evening Damon died. We have people talking to the other witnesses to clarify what they saw—'

'Clarify?'

'Yes, *clarify*. Do you have a problem?'

'No, it's just—'

'Holden Wyatt is our prime, indeed only, suspect in the death of Damon Potter – be it accidental death, manslaughter or murder. While he's in custody for the assaults he has admitted to, we have the opportunity to find out exactly what happened.'

I might've done a few silly things but I didn't do that.

It wasn't that what Cole was saying didn't make sense; Jessica's issue was that she didn't believe Holden was their man. She didn't think he'd confessed to the assaults to cover up for anything else but she also didn't sense he'd had any inkling the other club members would blow apart his alibi.

'You said word had come down from above . . .' she stammered.

'Your point?'

'Does that mean there's someone trying to make sure this case gets closed?'

Cole's lips barely moved as he replied, teeth gritted, stare fixed. 'Don't question me, Inspector.'

He always called her 'Jess'.

'I'm not questioning you—'

'Good, then you can go and interview James Jefferies.'

'Why?'

'He's in a wheelchair and you know what the ramps are like around here, so we're going to him. You can call me when you're done.'

Archie seemed to have learned without being told when it was a good time to ask what was up with Jessica and when it was a good time to say nothing. The journey to James Jefferies' house was definitely a say-nothing ride, with Jessica fuming silently at everything from pedestrians having the audacity to cross the road when she wanted to drive on it, to the way certain places seemed to be sign-posted only from the opposite direction to the one in which she was travelling.

Not to mention lorry drivers, of course. That was a given. And people who owned BMWs.

And DCI Cole. What an arse.

James Jefferies lived in a small detached bungalow just outside Leigh to the west of the city, part-way towards Liverpool. When Jessica rang his doorbell, she heard a crotchety, 'All right, blimmin' 'eck, gimme a minute', even though she'd only pressed the button once.

The door was heaved open to reveal a wrinkled man in

129

a wheelchair, still wearing pyjamas. His hair was thinning, arms and legs stick-thin, betraying no sign of the Olympian he had once been. The only evidence that he wasn't as old as his frame indicated was his eyes, which darted suspiciously between Jessica and Archie but with the verve of someone around fifty, instead of seventy. Across his lap was a blanket and a walking stick, which he kept one hand on, as if to defend himself in case either of them tried anything.

'You lot,' he said. 'You better come in.'

James' bungalow had been custom-fitted to allow for the fact that he was in a wheelchair, with lower handles on the doors and wider passageways to accommodate his condition – which Jessica didn't ask about. The kitchen was both terrific and strange at the same time, containing everything you might expect to see in any other house – but eighteen inches lower. It was a disorienting experience because most homes were set up with surfaces and objects at roughly the same height. Here, Jessica was left feeling taller than she actually was. For someone who had to live their life in a wheelchair, this must be a godsend.

James wheeled himself through the kitchen into a wide conservatory. Even though the skies were grey, the natural light was a little dazzling, making Jessica squint awkwardly as she sat on the sofa next to Archie, who had apparently accepted the fact that his day off was anything but.

'What is it then?' James asked.

Jessica was on the back foot, partly because of his abrupt tone but also, she suspected, because she was literally talking down to him. 'I understand you're the life president of the university rowing club.'

'Yes.'

'What exactly does that entail?'

'Why do you want to know?'

People didn't usually ask that.

'We've been investigating the death of one of the members – Damon Potter. His body was discovered in one of the bins at the back of the club last week . . .'

'I heard.'

Jessica decided to try her original line: 'Perhaps you could tell us what being the life president means?'

James sighed loudly, a deliberate act to make it apparent he was going out of his way to help them. 'They wheel me out a few times a year, mainly at the bigger events towards the end of the season. I bring along my medal and smile for the camera, they feed me something fancy and then I'm back here again.'

'Do you have anything to do with organising things?'

'Not really.'

'We were told you had a position on the committee.'

The reply snapped back instantly: 'What do you think that means?'

This was tough work.

'That's what I was hoping you could tell us . . .'

'I'll tell you what it means – it don't mean shit. I'm an old man with a round piece of metal – these kids don't want anything to do with me nowadays.'

'We met the student president, Holden, and he seemed impressed by your achievements.'

'Pah, these kids are all the same – they see an old fella in one of these chairs and think, "What does he know?" I know what it's like – I only do these things because it's a day out at the river in the sun and a free meal. Some of the girls are all right too, if you get what I mean.'

He winked at Jessica and she knew exactly what he meant.

'We've heard disturbing reports about initiation ceremonies for new recruits,' Jessica said. 'What do you know about that?'

'Nothing.'

'You've never heard any rumours?'

James fixed Jessica with a fearsome stare, the type she'd rarely seen since the days when her dad had caught her up to no good. He didn't need to say 'are you questioning my honesty' because everything about his gaze already said it.

'You understand why I have to ask,' Jessica added.

'I told you I don't know anything.'

'How well do you know Holden Wyatt?'

'I know the name – they have a new president every year. It's nothing to do with me. I shake a few hands, turn up when I'm asked, and make a few phone calls now and then.'

'Phone calls?'

James frowned, as if this was something he shouldn't be questioned about. 'Just because I'm in a chair, it doesn't mean I can't use a phone.'

'Holden said that you called him and said that he should tell the police anything he knew about Damon's death.'

'Did he now . . . ? Was that the wrong thing to do?'

'That's not what I meant,' Jessica replied. 'I wondered which of the students you were calling – and why.'

Jessica suddenly found herself in a staring contest, locked in a battle of wills with a man in a wheelchair, neither of them wanting to give ground.

Unexpectedly, Archie's was the voice of reason: 'Can I see your medal?'

The man's eyes snapped from Jessica to Archie, giving her the window to look away herself. A moment later, she could feel James searching for her gaze again but she refused to acknowledge it, even if she did still want an answer.

'An Olympic bronze is impressive,' Archie added. 'I've never seen a medal before.'

James wheeled himself across to a cabinet, making sure his back shielded what he was doing. After a bit of fiddling, there was an electronic-sounding whirr and a pop, then he wheeled himself to the side, revealing what looked like the interior of a safe. Because it was inside a wooden cabinet, it was disguised from the outside by its innocuousness. He waved Archie across with a flick of his wrist and held out a brown-grey medal on a dark ribbon.

Considering the way he had asked Holden whether James had 'fallen in' because he'd only won bronze, Archie did a good job of portraying someone transfixed by what he was holding. Even Jessica didn't know if the aggression towards Holden had been the act, or if this was one now. Either way, Archie knew what he was doing. With Holden, he had known who to be: off the leash, aggressive, intimidating. Here, he was respectful and interested. He asked about the year that James had won it, making a crude joke about the host nation that would've been entirely inappropriate anywhere else – except that James cracked and laughed himself. Suddenly, they were like grandfather and grandson, sharing stories and gags. All the time, Archie kept his hands on the medal, showing the reverence it was clear its owner thought it deserved.

Eventually, Archie handed it back. 'Thank you,' he said, as James returned it to the case. 'I wish I'd tried a bit harder at things now. I can't even imagine the amount of work that must have gone into winning that.'

James closed the cabinet and batted Archie away with a 'bah!' and a grin.

'What I think my colleague was trying to establish,' Archie said, 'was how much contact you have with members of the club. You said you make the odd phone call . . .'

This time, James replied instantly. 'Sometimes a few of them need a little encouragement, especially ahead of the big races. I have a word in their ears. I don't remember the names half the time but they just need someone to tell them they can do it. It's always better if it's someone who's been there and seen things.'

Jessica couldn't help but wonder exactly which type of things he might have seen.

'I thought you said he must've fallen in if he'd only won bronze,' Jessica said as Archie drove – a privilege she rarely allowed anyone if she was in the car too.

'I was hardly going to say that to him.'

'So what do you really feel? Were you actually impressed by the medal?'

Archie kept one hand on the steering wheel and glanced sideways at her, grinning. 'You do what you have to.'

That didn't answer her question but Jessica let it go. 'What do you think of him?'

'He doesn't seem to know much. I doubt he knew Damon's name and he barely seemed to know Holden. He's just someone they wheel out a few times a year – literally and figuratively. He probably likes the attention but doesn't want to admit it, while they like being able to mention his name because he's actually done something and most of them haven't.'

Jessica agreed: it was an uncomfortable marriage of convenience.

As they headed back to the station, Jessica called Cole. He answered on the fourth ring, then asked her to wait. The line sounded dead as he put her on hold until, eventually, he returned with: 'How was he?'

Jessica explained that James had told them very little.

'As expected,' Cole replied.

'Is anything else going on?'

'The other members of the rowing club have had a slight change of heart. When they've been asked specifically to remember when they saw Mr Wyatt on the night of the party, most can only say for certain that he was there at the beginning.'

In other words, they'd all subtly changed their stories.

'Does that mean Holden no longer has an alibi for the night Damon was killed?'

'That's how it seems.'

'How can we accept that a whole group of people have changed their statements at the same time?'

'Before, we had a lot of people to interview in a short period. Now we're asking very specific questions about timings and who saw what and when.'

Jessica knew that was how a lawyer might dress things up but it was nonsense. The students had previously told them that Holden had been present for the whole party. Now they were saying differently.

'Some have said they'd heard rumours that Damon was going to go public about the hazing activities,' Cole added. 'That would give a motive.'

Jessica couldn't hold back: 'More like they've changed their stories because they're all worried about their own roles in the initiations and they'll say anything that gets them off the hook.'

'Weren't you the one who brought Holden in for questioning because you thought he knew more about the death than he was letting on?'

'Yes, but—'

'But what? This is only confirming what you were speculating about. Results have started to come back from everything that was found in the bin. There's a trace of Holden on at least two separate items.'

'Of course there is – he was at the club, no one's disputing his whereabouts.'

'That may be the case but, alongside his confession earlier and the statements from other club members, it's all painting a picture.'

'Are you saying Holden killed Damon and dumped the body in the bin at the back of the one place where it would be linked back to him?'

Cole coughed. 'I'm not saying anything – that's for you to figure out.'

Jessica had to think carefully about what to say next but there was no easy way. 'It sounds like we're fitting him up for this.'

For a few moments, it was as if everything had stopped. Archie came to a halt at a set of traffic lights and his head flicked towards her. Jessica felt a tingle along her back in the moment of silence. The investigation into events surrounding the arrest and conviction of the Stretford Slasher twenty-five years ago was still going on, with the report due in the new year. 'Fitted up' were two words they simply didn't use together.

'You're on very thin ice, Inspector.'

'Sir, I—'

'You nothing. Do *not* continue to question the decisions that are made around here. You've been on a loose chain for a very long time – something I blame myself for. If the message hasn't yet got through then I'll make myself very clear: this is the end of the road for not doing things properly. Now do your job and get the rest of the evidence against Holden Wyatt.'

The reply stuck in Jessica's throat before she finally coughed it out. By the time she'd mumbled an apology she didn't feel was deserved, he had already hung up.

Another say-nothing ride.

*

Back at the station, it was almost the end of shift and Jessica didn't want to talk to anyone anyway. She mumbled a 'see you tomorrow' to Archie, strode through to her office, grabbed her stuff, and then marched back out again, ignoring Fat Pat complaining that she hadn't yet signed something she was supposed to.

She turned the radio off in her car and drove home in the usual stop-start-stop-stop-stop-stop-stop-stop-stop-start traffic, alone with her thoughts. For once, the commute didn't bother her because she didn't feel anything. Cole had been her friend – without him she wouldn't be at work. Now he was just another colleague. Something really had changed.

Slowly she manoeuvred her way back to Swinton as if on autopilot, remembering nothing of the journey. She pulled onto the driveway of the house she shared with Adam at the same time as the sun dipped over the horizon for the day. The area was bathed in a strange mix of daylight and night, orange street lights and white headlamps, and yet Jessica was out of the car, key in hand, reaching for the front door before she noticed Bex sitting on her doorstep, subdued smile on her face.

'You did say you had a spare room . . .'

16

For a young woman thinner than most children, Bex really could eat. In the yellowy glow of Jessica's kitchen, the teenager wolfed down anything put in front of her. Her black hair was balled underneath a woollen bobble hat, with only a few wisps dangling around her face. Jessica was struck by how pale the girl was, even though there were no obvious signs she was ill in any way other than being under-nourished. Bex kept her canvas rucksack underneath her feet protectively, not wanting to take her fleece off either. Jessica understood that living on the streets meant that looking after your possessions was imperative, so it was no real surprise.

'Do you want anything else?' Jessica asked, having already turned six slices of bread into cheese and pickle toasties, which Bex had topped off with two bags of cheesy Wotsits (Adam's), a pork pie (Adam's), a sausage roll (Adam's), half a packet of sliced ham (theirs), a bowl of Coco Pops (Adam's), a beef and tomato Pot Noodle (hers, although there were loads more), an apple (Adam's), two nectarines (Adam's) and half a box of fish fingers (theirs).

Jessica half-hoped Bex hadn't spotted the Cadbury's caramel bars (Jessica's), chocolate biscuits (Jessica's), non-chocolate biscuits (Jessica's), Chunky Monkey Ben & Jerry's (Jessica's), or bag of doughnuts shoved to the back of the bread bin (Jessica's), and might instead go for the low-fat, low-taste, girly yoghurts in the door of the fridge (Adam's).

Bex fiddled with her nose ring and patted her tiny frame which had defeated all physiological laws by packing so much into it. 'Maybe in a bit?'

She grinned and it changed everything about her, even if it didn't seem to come entirely naturally.

'If you've got any dirty clothes, I can put a wash on?' Jessica said.

Bex glanced away from her towards the door, shaking her head. 'I shouldn't have come . . .'

'I wouldn't have given you my address if you weren't welcome. We can get the lezzer stuff out of the way later.'

They caught each other's gaze and Jessica dissolved into a childish fit of giggles. Bex smiled but there were delicate dimples in her cheeks, matching the one in her chin and offering a wonderful sense of fun. That was until she stopped grinning; then her eyes showed her youth and vulnerability.

'Are you really a police officer?' she asked.

'Yes.'

'You don't seem like one.'

'What do you think a police officer should be like?'

'The ones out at night are usually right twats.'

A perfectly accurate description of a select few of Jessica's colleagues.

'Some of us are normal people.'

Jessica took the dirty plates and moved them to the sink (Adam's). 'Do you want the tour?'

'I only need a place for tonight. Last night was really cold and—'

'Stay for as long as you want. It's almost winter and we live in the north. The weather's always shite anyway.'

Bex didn't reply but she hoiked her backpack over her shoulders as Jessica led them into the living room. 'This is where we waste our lives in front of the TV.'

'We?'

'My boyfriend and me. Well, fiancé. Well, sort of, it's complicated.'

Bex's eyes darted left to right and she took a step backwards towards the hallway. 'I, er, didn't realise.'

'It's fine, why would you?' Bex mumbled something about not wanting to be a burden but Jessica cut across her. 'Honestly, it's fine. He's called Adam. He's cool, he's normal. Well, he's into sci-fi but everyone seems to be nowadays. At least it's not slasher porn.'

Jessica tried to make a joke of it but Bex was backing further out of the room and Jessica had to stride quickly to catch her before she was at the door. She put a hand on the teenager's shoulder but the girl flinched away.

'Sorry,' Jessica said.

'It's fine; I think I should go.'

'You don't have to. Honestly, Adam's fine – no one's going to harm you here.'

'I know, I—'

'Bex, I'm a police officer – do you really think I'd be living with some nutter? I've got enough of them at work.'

Jessica placed her hands on the girl's shoulders again

and this time Bex didn't flinch. Slowly she tilted her head upwards until they were looking at each other. 'Okay.'

'Shall we have a look around upstairs?'

'All right.'

Jessica first showed her the bedroom she shared with Adam and even got a smile as Bex asked why one half was strewn with clothes, shoes, books, a television remote control and an empty plate while the other was spotless. Jessica's reasoning was identical to the explanation she had given her mother after being scolded.

1) The bed wasn't quite in the centre of the room, which created a subtle optical illusion that she and Adam had equal space. The truth was that he had approximately four centimetres more space on his side of the bed, which, multiplied by the length of the room, meant that she had correspondingly less room to store her stuff.

2) Adam wore, essentially, the same clothes to work as he wore around the house, meaning he had far fewer items to pack away. She, on the other hand, needed an increasingly more complex choice of clothing to accommodate many different scenarios, meaning there was no sensible way she could be expected to neatly fold, or hang, everything she owned.

3) Adam slept on the window side of the bed, meaning there was marginally less light on her side of the room. Because of that, when she got dressed in the mornings, it was often advantageous to have clothes nearby – even if that meant them being on the floor.

4) There was a complex system of organisation on show that was far too understated for most human eyes to appreciate. Items were sorted by cleanliness, colour, appropriateness for work and by how much she liked them. That occasionally meant that a few things ended up on the floor, rather than in drawers or the wardrobe. Because of the multifaceted nature of the system, there was no way she could explain it in anything approaching a dumbed-down way that people could understand.

Jessica never got to 5) because Bex cut her off: 'Basically, you're a bit messy.'

'That too – but if you ever tell Adam, then you're out on your arse.'

Bex smiled and Jessica was laughing again too. After her day at work and the way Cole had been with her, this wasn't at all what she'd expected.

Jessica showed Bex the smallest upstairs room, which was filled with a handful of boxes they hadn't yet unpacked and an exercise bike she had bought, used once, and then never gone near again. In the bathroom, Jessica picked up the wet towel from the floor which she'd forgotten about that morning, telling Bex that Adam must have left it by accident, then she led the teenager into the final bedroom.

'This is where you can sleep,' Jessica said.

Bex stood in the doorway, peering at the space. 'It's really nice . . .'

'It was going to be a nursery but then . . . well, it didn't happen. We did it up as a guest bedroom.'

'It's got a double bed.'

'I know.'

Bex sat on it, bouncing gently, dropping her bag behind her. 'I've never slept in a double bed before.'

'Make the most of it. I sleep in a double bed but I've got some skinny string bean next to me who spreads out like a drunken spider. Half the time I wake up with an elbow in my eye.'

From below, the sound of the door opening and a loud 'I'm home' echoed through the house. Bex froze again but Jessica touched her gently on the arm. 'It's just Adam – let's go and meet him.'

Bex instinctively reached for her bag but Jessica gripped her delicately. 'It'll be fine here. No one will touch it.' Bex hesitated for a moment and then nodded. 'As long as you stay here, I won't even come into this room if you don't want me to,' Jessica added.

'You don't have to do that. It's your house – it's only one night.'

Jessica led Bex down the stairs into the kitchen, where Adam was standing at the sink. His hair was messier than usual at the back, blown all ways by the wind on his walk from the bus stop to the house. He didn't look around. 'Christ, Jess, how much did you bloody eat?' He turned to see the two women standing in the doorway. 'Oh, er, sorry, I didn't realise . . . I'm Adam.'

He stretched out a hand for Bex to shake but ended up holding it there uncomfortably as Bex almost hid behind Jessica.

'Look at the state of you,' Jessica said breezily, 'she

doesn't want to shake your hand – you bloody stink. Go and have a shower and then maybe she'll go within three feet of you.'

She caught Adam's eye, telling him without words to let it pass. He sniffed his own armpits, grinned and apologised with a smile.

He really was good.

After pecking Jessica on the cheek, he was away, running up the stairs like a child on Christmas morning.

'He seems nice,' Bex said, emerging from behind Jessica.

'He is. There are a lot of wankers out there but he's all right. I don't hang around with dickheads. Well, except the ones at work.'

'I shouldn't have been rude to him.'

'It's fine – if we're really lucky, he might cook for us when he's had a shower. That's if you're hungry yet.'

Bex grinned again.

In the living room, she asked where she was allowed to sit but Jessica said she could have her pick. She opted against the sofa (Jessica's), instead choosing the recliner (Adam's). Jessica even showed her where the catch was to make the seat slide backwards and footrest pop out. Suddenly, Bex's dimples and grin were fixed.

'It's really nice in here,' Bex said.

'We were in a fire. A lot of our stuff was lost, so we had to replace it all. Almost everything is new – or newish. It's nice but it takes more than that to make it a home.' Jessica stood and crossed to the shelf underneath the television, picking up a pair of silver candlesticks. 'Look at these – they belonged to Adam's grandmother and survived the fire. We keep them on display to remind us that all this stuff might look nice but, ultimately, it only takes one stray match, one burst pipe, and it's all gone. For whatever reason, these survived the fire – and so did Adam and I.'

Bex nodded, understanding.

Jessica persuaded Adam to make them tea by whispering in his ear that she'd do something for him that she hadn't done in months. He then spent ten minutes telling them over lasagne and homemade chips exactly who the ThunderCats were because Bex had never heard of them. Jessica had listened to it all before and spent the entire lecture thinking he was inadvertently doing his best to talk himself out of partaking in that particular act after all. Somehow, after all that, Bex still managed to eat her way through a bagel (Adam's) and, thankfully, a yoghurt (Adam's).

The three of them spent the rest of the evening in front of the television watching a soap that Jessica *definitely* wasn't secretly into and *definitely* didn't know anything about, a documentary about animals, a quiz show and the news. Bex didn't say a word throughout, she simply watched, knees to her chest, arms wrapped around herself. Once or twice, Jessica caught her eye and they exchanged a half-smile. There were so many questions she should ask – the girl was a stranger – and yet this wasn't the time.

Jessica was resting on Adam's shoulder feeling tired, when she felt her head being jarred and realised she had drifted off. 'Jess,' Adam whispered.

'Uhnf, sorry.' Jessica sat herself up, blinking, trying to wake up.

'Bex is asleep.' Jessica glanced across to the recliner where Bex had curled herself up like a cat and was wedged into the seat. 'Shall I wake her?' he added.

Jessica grabbed his arm as he started to move. 'Not you. Go to bed and I'll see you there.' She kissed him on the forehead and waited until his footsteps finished clumping on the stairs, then she gently stroked Bex's hair away from her face. The girl awoke with a jolt, a hand flashing out and grabbing Jessica's wrist roughly.

'Ow,' Jessica said, grimacing.

Bex took a second to release her, eyes half-open. 'Sorry, I thought . . .'

'It's bedtime.'

Bex uncurled herself, stretching her legs and stifling a yawn. 'I can't believe I fell asleep here.'

'It's comfy.'

'I know but I'm usually so careful. You've got to be when—'

'I get it.'

'Are you going to be here in the morning?'

'It depends what time you wake up.' Jessica stood and crossed towards the shelf where the candlesticks were. She picked up a monkey ornament and turned it upside down, emptying a key into her hand. She gave it to Bex. 'If you only want to stay one night, that's up to you – but please don't sleep on the streets again. That room is yours as long as you want it. Eat what you want, have a shower when you want. Adam and I have jobs so we won't be here all the time but you're a sensible girl – I know you are. If you

147

know how to use a washer, then you can sort your clothes out. If not, there's a basket in our bedroom. Just drop your things in there.'

Bex stared at the key in her palm for a couple of seconds before squeezing it into her pocket. 'What do you want from me?'

Jessica shrugged, not having an answer.

They said goodnight at the top of the stairs and went their separate ways, Jessica sliding under the covers next to Adam and then fighting for what she claimed was her share of them – roughly two-thirds, according to him.

'What's her real name?' Adam whispered, cradling an arm around her.

'I don't know; I assume Rebecca.'

'Who is she?'

Jessica pushed herself up until she was sitting, messing the covers up again. 'I know I shouldn't just invite people here – it's your house too – but . . .'

'I trust you.'

'. . . when we were at Piccadilly last week and you were busy moaning, I had my purse nicked.'

'I remember.'

'I wasn't exactly honest with you. I was hoping to be robbed and left a note for the pickpocket.'

'That was her?'

'Yes – she's homeless and that's all she had to live on. Everyone assumes this kind of crime is done by gangs but the type of people they use would usually stand out in a train station. I figured it was somebody else doing it for a reason. I suppose I—'

'You wanted to help.'

'I guess.'

'Do you know what you're doing?'

'No.'

Adam snorted and reached out to pull Jessica towards him again. Together they slid back down underneath the covers. 'How old is she?'

'She says seventeen – I don't know.'

'Is there someone you should call – social services or someone?'

'If I do that, she'll run. She's not technically a child anyway.'

'What do you want to happen?'

Jessica breathed deeply, cradling her head into his chest. 'I really don't know . . . sometimes it's just nice not to be a bitch for a day.'

17

Jessica was awoken by Manchester's usual soundtrack: it was pissing down. The rain clattered against the glass of their bedroom window, thundering off the roof, the pavement, driveway, car, everything – a melody that might as well be trademarked by the north-west of England. Adam's sister, Georgia, had moved up from the south not too long ago. After a month, she'd asked Jessica if the weather was always this bad. That was during a particularly mild spell. If God truly had attempted to wipe humans from the face of the earth after giving Noah a cheeky tip-off, then it was as if he was still trying with Manchester.

Through the slit in between the door and the frame of their spare room, Jessica could see Bex folded up like origami on top of the covers, breathing deeply. Thank goodness she hadn't been out in this overnight. Jessica was interrupted, jumping when Adam delicately touched the base of her back.

'How is she?' he whispered.

'Sleeping.'

'Good.'

Downstairs, they went about their business slightly more quietly than they did usually. Jessica clicked the toaster on and then checked the news on her phone.

First the BBC: some bollocks about London, as if everyone in the UK lived there; an article about the weather, because looking out of the window didn't suffice; a yawn-fest about why people are living for longer. Is this what she paid a licence fee for?

The *Guardian*: something about politics; more about politics; something about America; more about America; a celebrity banging on about some cause. Boring.

The *Daily Mail*: a girl barely eighteen with her top off; an overweight woman berated for being too fat; someone else having the piss taken for being too thin; a photo of a monkey – isn't that cute?; the royal family leeching their way around some colony Britain had once owned, grinning as the locals wondered who they were; something about why women hate themselves. Probably because they're constantly having people point out that they're too fat or thin, or having long-lens photographs of themselves without a top on being printed. Too depressing for this time of the morning.

The *Manchester Morning Herald*: oh shite.

Jessica sat in the supermarket cafe sipping orange juice and thinking about how soulless the place was. The clientele was a mixture of pensioners picking up their four-quid full-English breakfasts and single mums catching a quiet cappuccino before the chaos of their day kicked in again. The staff bustled between the tables, cleaning up and taking orders in their uncomfortable-looking uniforms. It wasn't the people themselves Jessica found depressing, it was the fact that nobody really wanted to be there.

Or perhaps she was simply in a bad mood.

Garry Ashford slid into the seat across the table from her and plopped a copy of the *Manchester Morning Herald* in between them. 'You buying?' he asked.

'You probably earn more than me.'

He grinned. 'Shall we have an argument about whether journalists or police officers are paid the worst?'

Jessica stood and gave him an awkward half-hug. Were they mates? People who knew each other? Enemies? To a degree they were all three. She was a detective inspector, he was the *Herald*'s news editor. They shouldn't really know, or like, each other – but they frequently seemed to be inexorably drawn to each other. If she was ever pinned down and waterboarded, Jessica might even admit that she liked him. Sort of.

'Every time I see you, you've got different hair,' Jessica said. On the last occasion she'd seen him, he'd been unshaven and his hair had grown scraggily to his ears. Now it was short again, sensible. He was even dressed quite smartly in a suit that almost fitted him, not the retro cords he usually wore. 'Oh, I get it,' Jessica added. 'Mrs Ashford's been on your case, hasn't she? The wedding's coming up and she doesn't want you looking as scruffy as you usually do. Sensible woman; she's growing on me.'

'It was my choice actually – and as I keep telling you, she's not *Mrs* Ashford. Well, not yet.' He paused, before adding: 'Come on then, let's have it.'

'What?'

'The usual cracks – something about her having cataracts or a mental disorder because that's the only reason she would be interested in me.'

'Pfft, as if I'd still be recycling all the same jokes. Who do you think you're talking to?'

Garry raised his eyebrows and nodded at the newspaper between them. 'I know who I'm talking to.'

'Fine – but I hope you appreciate this one, I spent the entire car journey here thinking of it.'

'Let's hear it then.'

'You told me before you've invited over a hundred people to the wedding, but how are you going to fit them all into the venue?'

'What do you mean?'

'Well, if you've got her chained in the basement, there can't be much room . . .'

Garry rolled his eyes. 'Your jokes are getting worse – and I use the word "jokes" loosely.' He paused to pick through the menu and then went to the counter to order himself a sausage sandwich.

When he sat again, he opened out the paper, showing the large 'AUTUMN HAZE' headline.

'You do know it's winter, don't you?' Jessica said, pointing at it.

'November's one of those months – a bit of autumn, a bit of winter. Besides, I think the "haze" word is the more important one.'

Jessica had read it on her phone before asking Garry out for breakfast. The article was chapter and verse on Holden Wyatt – how he had initiated the new members, the things he'd admitted to in the interview with her, insinuations that the death of Damon Potter could be linked to hell week, as could the hypothermia case from the previous year.

'You said you had new information,' Garry added.

'You could say that . . .'

'Oh . . . you've not brought me here to try to bollock me again, have you? It's a solid story.'

'You must know it's going to prejudice his trial?'

'The lawyers said it was fine – he's not been charged yet.'

Initially, Jessica had thought Holden would be in court this morning, charged with the assaults. Cole had even told her as much – but the decision had been made by someone to keep him in custody and continue questioning him about Damon's death, then they could talk to the CPS about what to charge him with. Jessica was out of the loop either way.

'Oh, well, that's all right then,' Jessica shot back. 'A prick in a suit signs it off and some lad ends up going down for something he's not done.'

'Are you saying he didn't take part in any of those initiation rituals?'

Jessica didn't have time to reply before the waitress came over with Garry's sandwich. He squeezed three packets' worth of brown sauce – good choice – onto it and took a bite.

'I'm going to tell you something here I shouldn't,' Jessica said, watching him eat. 'Everything you've printed is true.'

Garry's eyes widened – he hadn't expected that. 'Are you praising something we did?' he asked.

'Let's not go that far. My point isn't that any of it is wrong; it's that people are going to put two and two together and get five. Yes, he admitted to those initiations – although I'm not confirming that on the record – but that doesn't mean he had anything to do with Damon's death. Maybe he did, maybe he didn't – that's what we're going to spend our time trying to figure out. You've put the two side by side and made it look like they're connected – he's not been charged with the assaults yet, let alone anything else.'

'A story's a story, Jess. This is what we do. You said it yourself: everything we've written is true.'

'Someone's trying to stitch him up.'

'Are you on the record?'

'Of course I'm bloody not.'

'Why are we here then?'

Jessica looked around the setting again; it certainly wasn't the type of place they'd been to together before, nor was it the type of place she'd usually go to. All the more reason for it to be here.

'If anyone bothered to notice where I was going, they'd think I was doing the weekly shop.'

'Why would anyone be watching where you were going?'

Jessica suddenly felt a little silly, exposed in front of someone she didn't even know if she was friends with. 'It's complicated – things are different at work. Everything moved really quickly yesterday with this Potter case. One minute we had found Cassie Edmonds' body and were looking into that, the next it was all systems go on nailing Holden.'

Garry finished chewing his next mouthful, leaving a

smear of brown sauce on his chin. 'Why are you telling me this?'

'Because there's something going on at the station that I can't figure out.'

'You said that.'

Jessica sighed, knowing she wasn't getting herself across very well, largely because she wasn't entirely sure what she was doing either. She finished the rest of the orange juice in her near-empty cup. 'Your story was written by a name I didn't recognise.'

'He's one of the newer guys – we've hardly got any staff nowadays but he's not long out of uni.'

'Did he tell you who he got the story from?'

'Yes. I'm news editor – I wouldn't have run it otherwise.'

'Who was it?'

Garry took another bite of his sandwich and shook his head. 'You know a reporter's source is protected.'

'Perhaps I'm asking because there's something bigger going on?'

'Is there?'

'I don't know.'

'I can't tell you anyway.'

'Did whoever leaked it tell you that a lot of the other club members altered their stories? At first they said they'd seen Holden all evening on the night Damon died, then they changed their minds. That's why you were able to link the initiation ceremonies to the actual death.'

'Is that on the record?'

Jessica crunched the paper cup into the table. 'Will you sod off with your "on the record" shite?'

'I'm a journalist, what do you expect?'

'Well, it's not on the record. I'm telling you because I want you to know the full story if anything else gets leaked. If and when this ever goes to court, people are going to remember the rich kid who shoved things up new recruits' arses. It's only a short step from that to believing he forced some other kid to drink himself to death, or hid the body at the absolute least – he'll never get a fair trial.'

'That's probably what his lawyer will argue.'

'We both know that never works.'

Garry took the final bite of his sandwich and leant back into his chair with his cup of tea. 'What do you want me to do?'

'If you won't tell me the source, then nothing, I suppose. I just wanted you to know this stuff.'

'Perhaps you should talk to your chief inspector?'

Jessica mocked surprise. 'Well, why didn't I think of that? Whatever's going on involves him – even if it's some-one above him putting pressure on.'

'Fine. I'll keep an ear out and let you know if I get any-where.'

'Thanks.'

'And you're still invited to my wedding, by the way. You've not returned the invitation yet.'

Jessica motioned to stand then stopped herself. 'Hang on a minute, are you going through this whole ritual – bribing a girl to marry you and inviting a bunch of people – just to get me into a dress?'

Garry stood and winked. 'Got me.'

*

At Longsight Police Station, there was a strange atmosphere. Everyone was so busy that no one had a moment to stop. To Jessica it was as if people were avoiding her but then she knew she was feeling paranoid anyway and there was every chance it was in her imagination. Fat Pat did slide his bag of crisps further under the desk when he spotted her, so at least he'd noticed her.

In her office, Jessica read through the notes of everything that had happened overnight, which only made her feel more marginalised. She dialled Izzy's extension and waited for the sergeant to pick up.

'. . . No, I don't bloody have it,' Izzy's voice shouted away from the speaker. 'Tell him to check his own bloody desk then. Hello.'

'Busy morning?'

'Aren't they always?'

'Have you got five minutes?'

'Yeah, I'll come to you.'

A few minutes later, Izzy sighed her way into Jessica's office, looking particularly bedraggled. She screeched a chair around until she was next to Jessica's desk and then slumped on it. 'We really do work with morons.'

Jessica nodded at her hair. 'What happened to you?'

'We were staying at Mal's mum's house last night. I looked at the weather forecast before we left and it said dry, so I only had my regular clothes with me. I got this wet walking across the car park this morning, then it's been dip-shit day in here today. It's like there's a convention on.'

'Did you see this?' Jessica said, pointing at her monitor.

Izzy nudged the Post-it note stuck to the side with her fingernail. 'The Samaritans' phone number?'

'No, I think Dave left that there for a laugh. I meant the fact that they brought in all nine of the people I wanted to talk to about Cassie Edmonds last night.'

Izzy peered in closely at the screen, reading the information for herself. 'Since when do they let the night team do things like that?'

Jessica shrugged. 'I have no idea. When I left last night, I thought we'd be charging Holden with GBH and sexual assault and that he'd be in court this morning. Instead, they interviewed him again first thing this morning before I got in.'

'What's going on?'

Another shrug – what else was there to do? 'I read the report – Holden says he knows nothing about Damon's death but they've been hammering him on it. He had the exact same story as he told Archie and me and was surprised when they told him his alibi had fallen apart. He kept saying he was at the party for the entire evening and that his friends must be mistaken. That's what he kept calling them – "my friends"; he didn't even know they'd stitched him up.'

'Have they charged him yet?'

'No one would likely tell me if they had – it was only my case in the first place because I got called out. It could have been another inspector on call. It'll only be a matter of time – if they don't do him for manslaughter, they'll get him for the assaults, and see if they can dig anything else up while he's in custody.'

'You don't think he'll get bail.'

Jessica snatched the Post-it note with the Samaritans' number on and balled it up. 'Why do you think all that stuff got leaked to the papers this morning? All the magistrates around here would've seen that. Our lot will take him to court this afternoon and they'll remember the name. Who's going to let him out when they've already heard the story? Someone's been very clever.'

Izzy lowered her voice: 'The guv?'

Jessica launched the Post-it note at the bin and missed – as usual. She shook her head. 'He's acting like a dick but this isn't his style. Someone else.' Before Izzy could add anything, Jessica changed the subject. 'Any luck finding Bones?'

Izzy ran a hand through her sodden hair. 'You'd think that if you had your head tattooed, then it might be hard to go incognito, but we've not had a single sighting – plus we can't get anything on the news because they're obsessed with the hazing thing and that knocked-up soap star. The only place we've got his picture out is on the force's website and no one looks at that.'

'I'm sure you'll find him.'

'He's probably in the Maldives by now. Anyway, don't think I didn't notice you changing the subject. What are you going to do about everything going on around here?'

'Keep acting as if everything's fine and everyone can walk all over me.'

Izzy tilted her head to the side, unconvinced. 'What are you *really* going to do?'

Jessica winked at her friend. 'I'll think of something.'

18

As it was, Jessica didn't have much time to think of anything because everything around the station went into meltdown when the call came through that another body had been found. Whoever had killed Cassie Edmonds hadn't stopped with just her. The killing of Grace Savage lived up to the young woman's surname. She had been dumped in a ditch in Little Hurst Wood, barely half a mile from where Cassie had been found. The crime scene was in a marginally better state given that it had been discovered by two kids skiving off school, as opposed to a clumsy dog-walker, but the torrent of the night before had done little to preserve the site.

The bad news didn't end there: because they were almost certain Grace had been murdered the night before, the nine people of interest they'd brought in in relation to Cassie's death were being interviewed at the station at the time Grace was killed, meaning that they were off the hook. It had been a long shot anyway; now, alongside a second victim, they officially had no suspects. As well as the beating her body had been given, the killer had again used a knife to nick away small parts of her body post mortem. It was yet to be confirmed but there was no obvious sexual motive, with the fingertip search in the rain throwing up nothing other than a lot of tired, wet, muddy officers.

A deep-seated hatred of women and an anger problem indeed.

Grace's husband, Nick, had already been notified but someone had to take a formal statement. Feeling left out of the Potter case and as useless as she had done in years, Jessica went to do the dirty work. She arrived at the Moston house sopping wet, Izzy in tow, both of them nursing bruised egos – not that any of that compared to what Nick was going through.

A liaison officer let them into the house and then scuttled off to make some tea. If there was one thing you had to be able to do well when you were a liaison officer, it was make tea. Jessica assumed that the first week of the course was spent figuring out the exact amount of milk it took to make a perfect brew and stirring techniques. Week two would be the application of sugar, whether brown was better than white, and how to ensure there was no sludge in the bottom of the mug.

Then they'd move on to how to talk to a man whose wife had been beaten, murdered and sliced to pieces.

Nick was sitting in an armchair, legs curled under him, staring into the nothingness of the wall in front of him. In his hand an empty mug dangled, perilously close to slipping onto the floor.

Jessica introduced herself and sat with Izzy on the sofa. The sergeant had her notebook and pen out; just like the old days, before station politics and arseholes took over the asylum. Well, there were always arseholes – they just hadn't always been in charge.

'Can you talk me through yesterday evening?' Jessica asked.

Nick had an earring in each ear, a stud through his nose and a ring through his lip. Above him, there was a wedding photograph on the wall, him with his bald head atop a grey suit, Grace looking every inch the perfect bride: her hair in long dark ringlets, beautiful smile, glint in her eye. Nick clucked his tongue into the lip ring and closed his eyes. 'She goes to yoga every Monday.'

'Where?'

'This place near the Arndale – she works in the centre, so it's easier for her to be a member of a gym there and then come home after rush hour. You know what the traffic's like. I can't remember the name of it but I've got the details somewhere.'

He motioned to stand but Jessica stopped him – they'd already checked those details after identifying her by cross-checking the missing persons reports. They had the CCTV from outside the fitness studio of her leaving on foot. It was only a quarter of a mile away from the spot from where Cassie had disappeared.

Before Jessica could ask anything else, the liaison officer entered with the brews, with Jessica's as perfect as she expected it to be. As Nick swapped his empty mug for a full one, cupping his fingers around it for warmth, Jessica couldn't help but feel England really was a ridiculous place. For all the prejudged ideas those from overseas had about Brits thinking a cup of tea made everything better, people really did everything to live up to the cliché. She had definitely become worse as she'd got older.

'Did your wife usually walk home from the gym?' Jessica asked.

Nick shook his head. 'Occasionally in the summer, never in the dark.'

She wanted him to finish the story without her having to ask but he stopped to have another sip of his drink and then sat in a dazed silence.

'It was dark yesterday . . .'

'I know. It's bloody November.'

'What happened?'

'Our car's bollocksed – this piece of shit Peugeot. The bloody thing's always breaking down. We were at the Trafford Centre this weekend, mooching around looking for Christmas presents, like you do. The place was heaving: kids screaming, people with huge bags, all sorts trying to get you into their shops. It was a nightmare, then we got outside and the car wouldn't start. We had to sit there waiting for the AA to turn up and tow us home. Grace was always going on about what a shit-heap it was – well, she didn't put it like that . . .'

Nick's voice cracked and he stopped for another drink. Jessica knew exactly what it was like to have a car like that. There had been more than one occasion where she'd had to be towed home, although her old Fiat had now reached a sort of beatified state in her mind where she only remembered the good old days of strong-arming it around a corner while crunching through the gears. If she really, really tried, Jessica could recall all the times she'd cursed it and threatened any number of despicable acts upon it for not starting.

When he had settled, Nick continued. 'Grace had a bit of time off work ill at the end of the summer, so there was no way she could take any more. I phoned in sick yesterday, then spent the day trying to get the car into a garage. She took the bus to work, even though she hates it. I normally give her a lift in because the bus is always overcrowded and you have to stand. Then it's full of window-lickers too.' He glanced up at Jessica. 'I suppose you drive everywhere?'

'I've been on my fair share of buses and trains.'

'You know what it's like then.'

'Yes.'

'The plan was for me to get the car fixed, then pick her up after yoga.' He delved into his pocket, taking out his mobile phone and pressing the screen, then tossing it across to Jessica. 'Look.'

Jessica turned the screen around and read:

Nick: 'Sorry hun. Car's still shite. Shall I meet you?'
Grace: 'Don't worry babez. I'll get the bus.'

Jessica stood and passed the phone back to him.

'That was the last I heard from her,' Nick said. 'That stupid heap of shite car . . . we've only been married for four months. She was talking about little wee bairns . . .'

Jessica finished getting the rest of the details as Nick chain-drank his way through mugs of tea. Cassie and Grace had gone missing from a similar spot within days of each other.

When they were done, Jessica and Izzy got back into

the car ready to head back to the station and swap cars. Their shifts had finished more than an hour ago.

'I know that look,' Izzy said from the passenger's seat.

'What?'

'Cogs whirring, hamster wheels turning.'

'It's probably nothing.'

'If you don't want to trust anyone else at the station, you can tell me.'

Jessica flicked the headlights on and pulled onto the road. 'It's not that – I just don't want to be wrong. Not now; I feel like there are people waiting for me to fail.'

'All the more reason to run things past me.'

'You, me and Dave walked along Oldham Road but it's all blocked off. Did you know that before we went?'

'No.'

'Me neither – and you can only see the "road closed" signs when the barriers are already in view.'

'Okay . . .'

'So it's not been well advertised and it's not well sign-posted. Let's assume most people don't know that the road's closed, even if they know the area. Cassie lived in Failsworth, Grace in Moston – the areas are right next to each other; they probably live a five- or ten-minute drive apart and they'd take a similar route home.'

'That's still a big area for them to go missing from.'

'I know; too big to have everyone out on the streets checking every small side street they could have cut through. When we were in that area with the roadworks, I thought then that it was where Cassie disappeared from; I had this feeling.'

'You think Grace was taken from around there too?'

'Maybe . . . it was something Nick said. Have you ever been out in town late and you're the last one standing? You've only got a few quid left, not enough for a taxi but just enough for the late bus. He called people "window-lickers", which I nearly laughed at, but it means the people who are catching that last bus home. Most of them are either pissed, high, horny, or all three. Perhaps when Cassie was walking along the road, she thought she'd get the bus. Grace texted Nick to say she was either going to walk or get the bus. She might have started walking and then realised it was too far and that she'd get the bus instead. They'd have both been catching it from the same road.'

Jessica indicated to turn onto the main road but she could sense Izzy figuring it out herself. 'When we were by those roadworks, there was a cover over the bus-stop sign.'

'Exactly – and if there were no buses running along that route, who do you think might have been hanging around?'

'Taxis.'

'Bingo.'

Izzy didn't reply for a moment. Jessica thought it was because she was thinking how brilliant her friend was, but the response was far more devastating than that: '"*Bingo?*" You've been hanging around with Archie for way too long.'

Despite her reservations about Jessica's choice of words, Izzy did agree that it was something worth looking into.

Without making too much of a fuss, she asked one of the night-crew constables who she claimed 'wasn't a total dick' to see what they could come up with.

Jessica arrived home to a smell she didn't recognise: cleanliness. She went into the living room, where Adam was sitting in his chair with his feet up watching television. 'What's going on?' she asked.

Adam nodded towards the kitchen and smiled. Jessica walked through the hallway into the kitchen to find Bex sitting at the table reading a magazine. She glanced at Jessica and instantly apologised. 'Sorry, I found this in the other room. You can have it back.'

Jessica batted it away. 'It's just some celebrity shite, which means it's Adam's.'

'Oh.'

'Why does it smell funny in here?'

'I, er, don't know . . . I cleaned . . .'

'You cleaned?'

Bex peered at her feet, cradling her knees into herself again. She was so tiny, arms nearly as thin as the mop handle resting against the wall behind her. 'Sorry, I wanted to do something to help.'

'Don't apologise, it's just . . . *I've* never cleaned in here.'

'I did the bathroom too.'

'Whoa!'

'Sorry . . .'

'Stop saying sorry. It's a good thing . . . well, sort of. You don't have to clean up after us.'

'I thought because you were both working hard and I was sitting around, that I should do something to help.'

Jessica sat on the chair next to her and rested a hand on the girl's knee. 'It was very kind of you. I hope you spent the day looking after yourself, too.'

That grin spread across Bex's face again. 'I had a bath.'

'Did you enjoy it?'

'I don't think I've ever had a bath before. It was amazing.'

'Good.'

The smile shrank to its minimum once more. 'I don't want to be a burden.'

'You're not.'

'Adam . . . ?'

'He's happy for you to be here.'

'He told me off for cleaning.'

'That's because he's an old woman who likes to do it himself.' They swapped grins as Bex reached across the table and picked up a letter. 'This came for you, by the way.'

The only items of mail Jessica usually got were bills (Adam's), junk (the bin's), bank statements (Adam's), or vouchers for the booze shop around the corner (Jessica's).

Jessica took the letter but it was different from the type of thing that generally came through the door – the envelope was padded but thin. On the front, her first name was written in block capital letters but there was no last name and no address – this had been hand-delivered.

She was about to flip it over to open it when she noticed a small, sketched symbol in the top-right corner. It was a fork shape, with three prongs: one curling to the left, one straight up, one curling to the right. Holding them together was a loop at the bottom, making it look like some sort of

169

sheaf. Jessica tried to place it, but wasn't sure if she had ever seen it before.

Jessica could already feel the tension beginning to slink along the top of her neck as she ran a finger under the flap and opened it. Reaching in, she pulled out a single sheet of thin card with five words written on it in the same handwriting that had put her name on the envelope. Jessica read them three times then returned the card to the envelope before Bex asked about it. She wouldn't be forgetting them any time soon though because, assuming the words referred to Holden, they were telling her what she already knew.

'You've got the wrong man.'

19

Jessica's first thought was to hand in the envelope and note – but that would have been what she'd have done when she thought she could trust people around the station. She spent a partially sleepless night wondering who else the words could relate to if it wasn't Holden, but there was no one. She already believed that someone, somewhere, was trying to put pressure on them to make sure Damon's death was pinned on Holden and now this note seemed to confirm that. Not only was there a person trying to make that happen, there was now somebody else trying to make sure that she was the one who stopped it.

Somebody who knew where she lived.

In the end, her Wednesday morning didn't begin in the way she thought it would – it began in the way her Tuesday morning had: supermarket cafe, pensioners, single mums, bored-looking waitresses, orange juice, sausages in a bap, brown sauce, newspaper on the table and Garry Bloody Ashford. This time it was at his request.

Jessica peered around at the surroundings, wondering if this was what her life had come down to: the faint smell of coffee and the wafting aroma of fried egg, together with intermittent public address announcements for Janice to go to the front of the store.

'So you couldn't quite get enough of me,' Jessica said,

watching Garry cover his chin in brown sauce again. There really was no elegant way to eat a sausage sandwich. Still, if you were the one with the sausage sandwich then you were winning anyway.

Garry rolled his eyes. 'Yes, I'm here to declare my undying love for you and this is the best place I could come up with.'

'What do you really want?'

Garry wiped his lips and nodded at the paper in front of him, which showed a photograph of Holden being led into court the previous afternoon. As she had predicted, he hadn't been given bail.

Jessica glanced across the page and shrugged. 'Didn't we talk about this yesterday?'

Garry shook his head. 'This wasn't supposed to happen. When the story came in on the wires that you'd found that second girl's body out at Little Hurst, we started pulling things together about the fact two young women's bodies had been found a few days apart. No one at your end was giving details but we got a camera down there and were trying to get a name.'

'We couldn't have told you before we told the victim's family.'

'I know; that's not the issue. The point is that we'd cobbled something together anyway. Admittedly it mainly went over the first body find – Cassie Edmonds' – but we had something. It was all lined up ready for the front page when the editor was called out of conference. Usually, he refuses to take calls when we're in those meetings but his secretary told him it was important and he left the room.

A few minutes later, he came back and everything had changed. Suddenly, he was saying we didn't have enough to run the young-women-being-killed story properly and that we'd lead on Holden. Within a few minutes, your press office was on giving us every tiny detail we might possibly want about the decision to charge Holden Wyatt. We'd normally have to coax each morsel out, but we were given it all on a plate.'

'So your main story was changed?'

'Yes – it was the same on the radio and TV this morning. They might not have had the same call but the fact you were so cooperative with details for Holden meant that story was always going to be the easiest to run.'

'Who's your editor?'

'You won't know him. He's been in place for about a year. The old one was making too much money, so the parent company made him redundant and parachuted in some guy from down south. He doesn't know the area but no one in management really cares about that, as long as the paper comes out and the ads get sold.'

'Do you know who called him?'

'No. The old editor would do things like that all the time – decide what he wanted, then blow his top at anyone that disagreed – it's just the way he was. But the new bloke is different. We all know he's the management's guy, there to make a few cuts. He usually leaves the news order to those of us who've been there a while and know the area. He doesn't get angry because he's got nothing to be angry about. Half the time, he's itching to get back outside and have another fag. Yesterday was different, though. When he said we should change the order, one of the lads asked if he was sure and he totally lost it. He was going on about people questioning his authority, asking if unemployment was an attractive prospect and so on. Everyone sat in silence because he's usually so passive.'

'What was he like before he took the phone call?'

'The same as ever; slumped in his seat fiddling with his phone. I thought you were just moaning yesterday but—'

'"Moaning"?'

Garry hid behind the final mouthful of his sandwich. 'You're always going on about something.'

'Justifiably!'

'Either way, there's something going on. I'll see what I can find out and give you a call if I come up with anything.'

'"Moaning"? You're back on my shit list.'

At the station, results were beginning to come in from Grace Savage's body but it was a similar story to everything that had been found on Cassie Edmonds'. Neither had been sexually assaulted, both had broken ribs from the beating their upper torsos had taken, and both had had a finger and part of an ear cut off. The rain had washed away much of the evidence at both scenes, with the fingertip search a waste of time too. They hadn't been able to find anything to link the two victims, other than their age and the fact they lived in roughly similar areas.

As Jessica waded through her overnight emails and memos, Izzy knocked and entered her office with a sheaf of printouts. 'This is your list of registered black cab drivers,' she said.

'What about people who drive pre-booked taxis?'

'Shite, I didn't think of that. I'll get someone to do it. Everyone's got to be registered with the city council, so it's not too hard to pull it all together.'

'Get Archie to contact all the companies and find out who was on duty that night. I know a driver could've gone out anyway but it'll give us somewhere to start – and let's start running the plates through ANPR. Even if we haven't got CCTV, we've got enough number-plate cameras along the main road to look for a match from one database to the other.'

Izzy nodded and headed out of Jessica's office just as DCI Cole stormed in, making the door bang against the frame. Jessica was so taken by surprise that she bashed her knee against her desk, sending a cardboard folder flying off the edge, which created a domino effect of things collapsing around the floor. Her office really was a tip.

Cole had one hand on his hip, the other clinging onto a printout. 'What's going on with Holden Wyatt?'

'I don't know.'

'You're supposed to be one of my inspectors and you don't know?'

'I didn't even know you'd charged him! You can't expect me to know every aspect of a case if you tell me one day you're charging him, then you hold off and continue questioning him about something else, then he ends up getting charged for the first thing. I went to see Grace Savage's husband last night and we're trying to sort a possible link to taxi drivers this morning. I—'

'You've what? Last week it was trying to catch a pick-pocket but I don't have a name for that. A knife robber is on the loose because you or one of your team let him go. His head is covered in tattoos – why's it so hard to find him? You had a student dumped in a bin but you've not been able to pin that on anyone either. Now there are two dead girls and the best you've got is something to do with taxis. What exactly is it you're doing down here?'

Jessica had two words for him but narrowly managed to bite her tongue. 'You're forgetting everything else that we have sorted out.'

Cole removed his hand from his hip, so he looked a little less like a teapot and more like the dumpy man he had become. He ran a hand through what was left of his hair. 'There's no use living off past glories – you know there's a big report into the effectiveness of this force coming at the start of next year. What we don't want is a host of unsolved cases.'

'Isn't trying to rush things what got us into this mess in the first place? Well, that and fabricating evidence but we're definitely *not* trying to fit up Holden Wyatt, are we?'

Jessica glared defiantly at the DCI but knew she'd gone too far.

Cole's lips were pursed, eyes fixed: 'What exactly are you trying to say?'

'Nothing, *Sir*.'

'Good – then do your job and let's start moving some of these unsolved cases into the non-incompetence pile, shall we?'

'Yes, *Sir*.'

Cole gave Jessica one final hand-on-hip stare and then he was gone, back into the corridor to act like a dick in front of someone else.

Jessica sat for a few moments, running through everything he'd said to her. What. An. Arse. She picked up some of the items that had clattered to the floor and then headed through the station to the main floor, where she found Rowlands frantically bashing away at his keyboard.

'Is this another letter to the problem pages?' Jessica teased, nudging him in the shoulder as she perched on the desk in front of him. '"Dear agony aunt, my right wrist is so completely swollen compared to the left one that my entire body leans to one side. If that's not enough, then I smell a bit like a bin . . ."'

'Haven't you got better things to do than hang around here trying to be funny?'

'I never *try* to be funny – I *am* funny. Anyway, let's go for a walk. You can practise trying not to lean to one side.'

Jessica led him through the corridors until they were back at her office. Once inside, she locked the door. Dave spun round at the sound of the click.

'All right, calm down,' Jessica said, pressing herself against the door. 'Go to my desk and open the top drawer. Inside the top envelope is another one.'

Rowlands shrugged but crossed the room and opened the drawer, pulling out a blank white envelope and reaching in to take out the one inside with her name written on it. He held it up. 'Where did this come from?'

'Someone put it through my door at home yesterday. Look inside.'

Rowlands read the card. 'Who's the wrong man?'

'I presume Holden Wyatt – I don't know who else it could be talking about.'

'Who sent it?'

'No idea.'

After reading the card again, then turning it over to check the back and returning it to the envelope, Rowlands noticed the sketch in the top-right corner. 'What's this?'

'I was hoping you might be able to look into it. I would . . . but things are awkward around here and I've got people on my shoulder the whole time.'

Jessica was about to add something else when there was a large bang from the other side of the door, followed by a female-sounding 'Ow'. Jessica unlocked the door and opened it to find Izzy rubbing the side of her face and blinking rapidly.

'Your door was locked,' she said, pointing out the obvious.

'I know; people usually knock.'

Izzy continued rubbing her head and looked a little woozy, glancing conspiratorially between Jessica and Dave. 'Sorry – I was in a rush and thought you might want to come along. We've had a sighting of Bones.'

20

Jessica watched from the passenger seat of an unmarked car as either end of the road was blocked off by officers as conspicuous as someone wearing a fluorescent top at a funeral.

'I don't remember your operations being this chaotic,' Izzy said from the driver's seat, anxiously. Jessica should really have been doing the heavy lifting but it had been Izzy's case throughout and the sergeant was more than capable. Jessica was only there to take the flak if things went badly. She was in enough people's bad books as it was, so one more balls-up wouldn't make much difference.

Jessica nodded towards an officer at the far end of the street arguing with a driver who was trying to make their way along the road. 'Where did we hire this new lot from? He looks like a duck that's been sniffing glue.'

The officer started whirring his hand in the air, the universal sign for 'turn the car around, love', and then reached for his pocket when the driver began arguing.

'He's not going for the pepper spray, is he?' Izzy said, one hand on the radio.

Luckily it was just his identification which, in fairness to the driver, Jessica would've been asking for if she'd been asked to turn around by someone who looked like they belonged on a farm.

With the obvious escape routes blocked, the tactical

entry team scurried into place around the rundown semi. The Eccles estate wasn't the prettiest at the best of times. If tourists had been taken around the area and told it had been deliberately left as it was to provide a snapshot of war-torn, bombed-out 1940s Britain, then their cameras would've had plenty to snap at. There were the once red-brick houses now stained with black soot, even though Jessica doubted there was a coal fire anywhere nearby. There were the inexplicable mud piles in front gardens, the pot holes in the road, the random heaps of scrap dotted around, the upturned sofa on the side of the road with yellow foam spilling out, the smashed-up bus stop with the words 'arse on toast' graffitied onto it. What was it with spray-painters and the word 'arse'? Not to mention the fact that Jessica had no idea what the toast reference was about. Perhaps it was some gang thing? Bloody hell, she was getting old.

Even among all that, the house Bones was apparently hiding in stood out as being a dump. The windows and doors across the lower floor were boarded up, with yet more graffiti shining out like a beacon. If your name was Sharon and you lived on this estate, then you certainly seemed to have a varied sexual appetite. Upstairs, the windows were just about in place – well, the frames were. Some of the single-glazed panes had been smashed, with all manner of stone-shaped holes adorning those that were left. Even for an estate agent, this would be a hard sell: 'The downstairs can be a little dark, while you get the odd draught upstairs. Overall, though, it's still a bargain . . .'

Luckily for them, a little old lady across the road had

spotted someone with a tattooed head sneaking inside earlier. Most people on this estate wouldn't bat an eyelid but thank goodness for little old ladies.

Behind the tactical entry squad, armed officers primed themselves, looking like a pack of beetles with their rounded black armour and shiny helmets. Across their fronts, their MP5s hung.

'Christ, I hope they don't shoot anyone,' Izzy said.

'They're more likely to shoot each other than they are Bones,' Dave chipped in from the back seat, unhelpfully.

'If you count the officers with guns,' Jessica added, 'we've probably doubled the number of automatic weapons on this estate, at least temporarily.'

'Will the pair of you shut up,' Izzy snipped, not taking her eyes from the house.

Jessica and Dave exchanged chastened looks like a pair of naughty schoolchildren, but they did at least pipe down. Jessica peered around the rest of the area. There were a few faces in windows and the inevitable camera phones taking pictures to try to sell to the news channels. From where they were parked, they had a clear view of the front and side doors of the rundown house, plus a hint of the over-grown rear garden. Jessica wondered what the people who lived next door must think. That house was admittedly in a little better state, with a frail-looking once-red wooden front door and cracked window frames that hadn't seen paint in the last decade or three, but the windows were at least intact.

Confirmation came over the radio that everyone was in

place and Jessica turned to Izzy for the passing of the baton. 'Go on then,' she said.

Izzy looked at both officers, then the house, and then she gave the order: 'Go, go, go.' It might be a cliché – but it was a bloody cool one.

Thunk, crash, fwoosh: the boarded-up door splintered in an instant as the tactical entry team jumped to one side and allowed the tactical firearm squad to thunder into the building. Jessica wondered if her department could be rechristened the 'tactical figuring-stuff-out crew'. Adding 'tactical' to the front of anything instantly made them sound better.

'Please don't shoot anyone,' Izzy whispered to herself.

All they could hear over the radio was the doof-doof-doof as boots clattered around the property. Jessica was about to suggest they have a word with the little old lady when her eye was caught by the house next door. The front door was now open a fraction, with the unmistakeable tattooed head of Bones peering out. He took one look at the back of the tactical entry team, now standing around awkwardly, and then tiptoed out like a cartoon baddie who had just been discovered. Before Jessica could say anything, he was running away from their roadblocks towards a patch of grass.

'Shiiiiiiiiiiiiiiiite,' Jessica shouted, opening the car door. It might not have been the most informative of instructions but Dave took the hint, half-leaping, half-falling out of the back seat and following her as she set off after their suspect.

The first few metres were definitely the worst. Jessica

felt something tighten in her stomach and then the cold air hit her lungs. Was it always this hard to breathe? Her only consolation was that Bones was clearly suffering too. He had at least a hundred metres on her but glanced over his shoulder and stumbled as his hand shot up to his chest. He was wearing jeans, heavy work boots and a thick coat, which must be even worse for running in than her suit was. As he reached the green, Jessica could see Bones was heading for a dingy-looking alley. When they'd rolled in to block the ways off the estate, the overgrown hedges shielding the cut-through had looked like someone's garden gone out of control; now there was clearly a pathway. Jessica peered over her shoulder and held an arm out, pointing Dave towards the nearby cul de sac and hoping he got the message that there was hopefully a cut-through there too. Meanwhile, she put her head down and ran.

She was definitely faster than Bones but had no idea what type of shape he was in – short bursts of speed she could just about handle; endurance, she didn't really want to find out . . .

The grass was muddy and Jessica slid for the final metre before regaining her footing on the cracked concrete of the alley. She ducked under the overgrown hedge, batted away a dangling branch and then kicked on again, trying to ignore the building pain in her thighs, stomach, calves and back.

The alley curved right around someone's back garden and then left again. If Bones had gone over the top of one of the fences, he'd be out of sight already but Jessica stuck to the path until she reached another small grassy area.

Large heavy footprints were embedded in the muddy sludge and Jessica followed the long stride pattern into another ginnel.

Run, run, run.

As she rounded another corner, she finally saw a glimpse of Bones. He was leaning against a gatepost, puffing even more heavily than she was. At the sound of her footsteps, he glanced over his shoulder and then set off again, barrelling straight ahead without looking and sprawling over the bottom half of an overturned wheelie bin.

Dave Rowlands emerged from around the corner, looking more surprised than Jessica was. 'It was all I could find,' he said apologetically, kneeling and telling Bones to hold his wrists behind his back.

Jessica felt light-headed and leant against the closest fence, hands on her knees, wanting someone to take her home and put her to bed.

'What is it with you and bloody bins?' she gasped.

'He's twice the size of me! It was outside someone's back gate and I thought it could be some sort of obstacle if he came this way.'

The only way Bones was twice the size of Rowlands was if you took his padded coat into account but Jessica had neither the breath, strength nor willpower to point it out.

Slowly, she made her way over to the crossroads where Bones was sitting on the ground, hands cuffed behind his back, blood streaming from his bottom lip. 'Morning, Dougie,' Jessica said, trying her best not to sound as if she felt close to a premature death.

When he realised she was the same officer he had run from previously, his eyes widened in recognition. 'You do deals, don't you?'

'What?'

'I've seen it on telly – they have all these lawyer blokes who get people off if they know something about something else.'

Jessica rolled her eyes. 'You're thinking of the Yanks. We don't do deals here.'

'I know something about your case.'

'Cassie Edmonds?'

Bones licked away the blood from his lip and shook his head. 'That Potter kid.'

21

Bones spent the best part of an hour in the basement room of Longsight Police Station with the duty solicitor, presumably being told that British police forces do not do deals. Jessica sat in her office with Izzy, trying to pretend that she wasn't aching in places she'd forgotten existed, feeling particularly smug that this was one investigation that could be crossed off DCI Cole's list of things that hadn't yet been solved. The series of pickpocketings was always going to remain unsolved – from the moment the teenager had entered the cafe, Jessica had known she was never going to turn Bex in.

After an interminable wait, there was a delicate knock on Jessica's office door and the rather defeated figure of the duty solicitor stood in the doorway. He was a familiar face around the station, often dealing with the Friday- and Saturday-night drunks who refused to believe they'd done anything wrong by puking in the street and starting a fight with a stranger. 'It's just a bit of bants, innit,' was the motto of half the morons they booted out the morning after with a slap on the wrist and directions to the nearest bus stop.

Jessica couldn't stop herself from grinning as the solicitor caught her eye. 'You did tell him we don't do deals, didn't you?' she said.

The solicitor let himself into the room and closed the door behind him, taking a seat on the edge of the empty desk. His suit was a fraction too big for him and he looked as if he could do with a good night's sleep.

'Are we all right to talk in here?' he mumbled.

Jessica shrugged. 'I'm not being bugged by MI5 if that's what you're asking. Well, not that I know of.' She peered up to the corners of the room, wondering.

He glanced towards Izzy. 'Off the record?'

'Whatever you want,' Jessica said. 'Sergeant Diamond is sound. Well, she's a bit slow at getting out of cars when there's a chase on but she's fine apart from that.'

Izzy scowled. 'Hey!'

The solicitor perked up, lowering his voice and grinning in a way that didn't suit him. 'You really know how to find them around here, don't you? I've been looking to do some work up in Lancashire because they only get half the wankers you get down here.'

'Is that your professional legal opinion?'

'Something like that. Anyway, Mr, er, Harrison—'

'Bones.'

'Yes, him. He claims to have information about the death of Damon Potter. He won't tell me what it is, so it's not that I can even give you a steer . . . not that I would . . .'

'I get it,' Jessica replied. 'Did you tell him we don't do deals?'

'I told him, but he's seen it on television.'

'So what? Godzilla was stomping around New York City on television the other week; it doesn't mean it's true.'

187

'You know that and I know that – but he's insistent.'

'Tell him to sod off – he held up four off-licences with a knife and we found the money at his house. Then he went on the run and left me doubled over like someone twice my age. Believe it or not, I don't have that much sympathy for anyone that makes me run, especially not in this weather. I could've ended up on my arse – did he think of that?'

Another grin flickered across the solicitor's face before disappearing again. 'It doesn't matter to me what he knows and what he doesn't. He knows you've got him bang to rights and he'll probably tell you as much. He's hardly the shy and retiring type. I'm trying to help you – if you can give him something, anything, he'll tell you what he knows. Either way, he knows he's going down for this, he just wants an olive branch.'

Jessica sighed and exchanged a brief glance with Izzy. Bloody TV shows and the bloody idiots that watch them. 'I could probably swing it for him to get a Twix? Perhaps a KitKat? That would even be out of my own pocket – and you know what's happening to the price of chocolate nowadays. In my day you could get a Freddo for ten pence. They're probably a quid now.'

The solicitor shook his head. 'Perhaps if I bring him up in fifteen minutes, you might be able to think of some-thing?'

Jessica thanked him for the tip and then waited for him to leave before turning to Izzy. 'Any ideas?'

Izzy screwed up her bottom lip. 'Actually I do . . . but I'm not sure you're going to like it . . .'

*

Jessica sat on one side of the interview room with Izzy, watching Bones on the other next to his solicitor. He glared down at the Twix and KitKat and then glanced sideways. 'I'm not telling them for that.'

'Bollocks.' Jessica swept the chocolate bars off the table and pocketed them. 'So what do you want, Mr, er, Bones?'

Bones nodded at the solicitor. 'I told 'im – I want a reduction in whatever sentence I'm going to get.'

'How about half a mil in used notes and forty virgins in your cell too?'

'Really?'

'No, of course not really!'

With his piercings removed, it was hard for Jessica to look anywhere other than Bones' hanging flap of skin and large round hole through his nose. It was as if he had an extra nostril. She sighed and leant back in her seat. 'Look, whatever sentence you get is nothing to do with us. We investigate, we hand the evidence over to the Crown Prosecution Service, they take you to court, we might give evidence, and then a jury decides if you're guilty. It sounds as if you're going to confess, so it won't even get that far. A judge will give you a sentence, then they'll give you a third off for pleading guilty. That's it – if I'm really lucky, I'll be sunning myself on a beach by then.'

'There must be something you can do?'

Jessica glanced at Izzy. Always with the clever ideas.

'All right – first, you tell us everything about the robberies, and then I'll see what I can do before we discuss anything you might or might not know about Damon Potter.'

189

Bones looked at his solicitor, who gave a small nod, and then he was away, regaling them with the shoddy financial situation of his business. He'd come up with the idea of the temporary tattoo and, at least for a while, thought he'd got away with it. He'd been caught out by the Manchester rain, of course.

With his shop leaking money, his main point of contention was he didn't want to prove his mum correct by having to shut it down. Apparently, she'd always said he was going to be a failure, and going out of business would show she was right. Quite what she'd think about having a son in prison for a series of knife robberies wasn't exactly certain. The truth was, they didn't need his confession because they had all the necessary evidence, but it did make things a little clearer. Jessica clarified a few details of the timings and dates, plus queried what had happened to the small amount of cash they hadn't accounted for – 'I spent it, dint I?' – and then that was one more case officially moved from the unsolved side of the whiteboard to the solved side. Well, if anyone could be bothered to find the pen.

Jessica terminated the interview, stopped the tape and waited until the recording light on the video camera in the top corner of the room had gone off, which she pointed out to Bones.

'Why have you done that?' he asked.

'Because there's one thing we didn't mention in interview. We can either include it in our reports, or selectively leave it off. DS Diamond here has a shocking memory and I'm not much better. That whole incident with you running off and hiding for a few days, not to mention scarpering this morning, could be conveniently omitted from our paperwork – or it could be written in big fat red capital letters. You might think that doesn't mean much but judges take a very dim view of people who try to evade justice. If we can drag them out of the lunch room for long enough, they tend to plonk another six months or so onto a sentence for things like that.'

Bones scratched the hole in his nose and glanced at his solicitor, who nodded a fraction. 'It's not necessarily six months,' he said, 'but you'd likely get something. Plus it stays on your record forever. After you're released, if you're ever arrested again, there's very little chance of you getting bail because they'd consider you a flight risk.'

'It's up to you,' Jessica said. 'Personally I don't care either way, but after all this arsing around, you'd better have something interesting for me.'

'Can I have the Twix, too?'

Jessica delved into her pocket and slid the chocolate bar across the table. 'Right, get talking, I haven't got all day.'

'On the news, they were showing the photo of the dead kid who was dumped in the bin.'

'Damon Potter.'

'I recognised him straight away because he'd been in my shop.'

'When?'

Bones started counting on his stubby fingers. 'Sorry, I've lost track of days. When did you find him?'

'Thursday night.'

'So he would've been on the news on Friday?'

'Right.'

'It would've been Wednesday then.'

Jessica was about to ask why he hadn't come forward if he'd seen Damon on the day the teenager died but it was a stupid question considering the last thing Bones wanted to do was attract the attention of the police.

'There weren't any tattoos on his body,' she said.

Bones nodded. 'Rose was off for the morning and I was by myself. He was a nervous kid anyway but I was probably a bit much for him.' He indicated unnecessarily towards his head.

'So he didn't go through with it?'

'He said he might come back another time, but you get a lot of people who change their minds when they realise you actually have to use a needle on them.'

'Did you talk to him about anything?'

'He knew what he wanted, so I was all ready to go. When you've got nervous people, you usually try to calm them. You ask about their lives, what they're into, that kind of thing. He said he was part of some rowing club and studying business. I thought it was a strange mix but you never know with kids today.'

'Did he seem worried about anything other than the tattoo?'

Bones stuck out his bottom lip, exposing another gaping hole from where he'd had his piercings taken. 'He seemed happy enough until the needle came out.'

'He wasn't worried when talking about the rowing club?'

'Nope.'

He couldn't have been that worried about Holden then . . .

'You said he knew what he wanted . . . ?'

Bones nodded enthusiastically. 'He had a picture of it – some sort of three-pronged thing.'

Jessica felt that chill again. It couldn't be. She delved into her pocket and took out a notebook and pen, sliding it across the desk. 'Can you draw it?'

Bones' penwork was as crisp and clear as the tattoos on his head. When he turned the pad around and slid it back, there was no doubt what he had drawn: it was an exact match of the logo someone had etched on the top right of the envelope that had been delivered through Jessica's door.

22

Jessica managed to hide her recognition of the symbol from Bones, the solicitor and Izzy. Somebody knew her address and wanted her to believe that Holden Wyatt was innocent. They'd even drawn a symbol on the envelope that, for whatever reason, Damon Potter had wanted tattooed onto himself hours before he died.

Couldn't they have picked someone else?

After the interview was over, Jessica found a quiet moment to talk Rowlands through what Bones had drawn. The fact that it was now a part of an official case meant he didn't have to be quite so quiet about investigating it – even if Jessica did tell him to be as discreet as he could. She didn't want news getting back to Cole about what she was looking into. If he wanted to trawl through the logs to find it then he could but there was no need to make it obvious.

With Bones dealt with and ready for his court appearance, which he seemed surprisingly chipper about given the circumstances, Jessica was back to investigating the deaths of Cassie and Grace. Forensic results were now officially in for Grace, and endorsed many of the initial indications. The killer of the two women was almost certainly the same person: taller, male, right-handed, thick fingers, comfortable with a knife, and so on. It didn't add much because that was who they were already looking for.

Just as she was about to go and find him, Archie came hurrying out of the corridor that led to Jessica's office, Post-it pad in hand, grin on his face. 'I've been looking for you,' he said.

'Is that why you're dribbling?'

Archie wiped the non-existent saliva from his face, grin disappearing. 'I've been wading through your taxi list. There's an ANPR camera a quarter of a mile along the road from where Cassie disappeared. We checked it at the time but it hadn't thrown up anything unusual. When I ran the list of taxi number plates, there were a few but all on duty, all easy to account for because the offices know where their drivers are. There's one exception.'

He couldn't stop himself from grinning. Trawling through endless lists of numbers and names might not seem like *real* police work but it was how most crimes were solved. For a new constable like him, getting things to move on was as good as it got.

'Go on,' Jessica said, suppressing a smile, letting him have his moment.

'I've got a plate registered to a black cab that was definitely *off*-duty. The driver went past that camera on the night Cassie went missing and the night Grace disappeared, too.'

'Is there a picture of the driver?'

'No, the angle's shite, but we've got the name and the plate.'

He was bouncing on his heels, waiting for the metaphorical pat on the head. Jessica gave him a literal one instead.

'Good boy,' Jessica said. 'Now let's go get a bad guy.'

Linking the cab to Hamish Pendlebury had been the easy bit – finding him was not proving quite so straightforward. He wasn't at home, and although he was technically supposed to be at work, he couldn't be raised on his mobile phone, while there was some sort of problem with the radio system that connected the cab office to the vehicle. Officers were keeping an eye on ANPR cameras around the city in case he did pop up anywhere but there was every chance he'd nicked into the offy for his break and was currently sat in a park somewhere having a fag. Or doing whatever else it was taxi drivers did when they weren't taking the long way round the ring road to get a few more quid from unsuspecting punters.

It was almost dark by the time Jessica, Archie, Rowlands and a uniformed PC – brought along because he looked like he worked out a bit – arrived at the taxi office. It had taken them almost half an hour of driving and walking around to find the place, before realising the door marked 'Benny's Lunchtime Supplies' was actually 'Tim's Taxis'.

Jessica eased the frosted-glass door open and entered the reception area. Maroon velvet chairs lined a small room with peeling cream wallpaper and an overall smell of stale shoes. It was what seasoned observers might call 'a bit of a hole', with décor that harked back to the types of working men's clubs that used to be so prevalent in the area. When she'd been in uniform, Jessica once had to visit one on the outskirts of the city. The older members had stuck a piece of white tape across the floor which they insisted females weren't allowed to cross. When a pair of students had popped in for a cheap drink, the woman had naturally refused to abide by what she saw as an archaic law. After taking a seat on the 'wrong' side of the tape, all hell had broken loose, with threats of physical violence, allegations of sexual assault because they'd physically lifted the chair she was in, a riot squad, and two dozen other officers sent in to enforce the peace. When the police had pointed out that the club wasn't allowed to segregate in the way it had, members had gone to the papers saying it was political correctness gone mad. Within four months, the whole place had shut down.

Jessica was about to stride through to the office at the back when a woman's voice bellowed: 'It's not my fault you've not changed the sodding sign.'

A man's voice shouted back: 'All right, keep your bloody hair on.'

'Don't you fucking swear at me, you dickhead. It's not my fault the bastard radios aren't working either – I told you not to buy such cheap shite but it's always about saving money with you, isn't it?'

'If you didn't spend so much getting your hair done—'

'What is it with you and my hair? Christ's sake, you're fucking obsessed.'

'Oh, shove it up your arse – there's enough room up there. Jesus, what is it, your time of the month again?'

Wallop.

'Ow,' the man's voice shouted. 'Fucking hell, you psycho bitch.'

Wallop.

Jessica opened the door again and slammed it this time. For a second there was silence and then a couple emerged sheepishly into the main waiting room. They were not what Jessica had expected: the woman with the big gob was shorter than she was, thin, tottering on heels, clutching an enormous bag and, in fairness to the man, it did look as if quite a lot of time, effort and backcombing had gone into her hair. The man, who Jessica assumed was 'Tim' of 'Tim's Taxis' fame, was a hulk – over six foot tall, nearly as wide as the woman was tall, with long hair down his back that wouldn't have been amiss in a biker gang. If this wasn't proof that opposites attract then nothing was.

The woman glanced between the four officers and smiled sweetly. 'Can you deal with this, Tim, hon?'

Tim had his teeth gritted. 'Yes, sweetie, you go and get your nails done. I'll see you at home later.'

A quick peck on the cheek and she was away, somehow managing to keep her balance in heels that would be classed as weapons in some countries.

Tim rubbed his upper arms as Jessica could sense Dave and Archie suppressing giggles.

'I think someone's already spoken to you,' Jessica said. 'We're trying to find Hamish Pendlebury.'

With a frustrated toss of his hands skywards, Tim sighed. 'Our radios have been on the blink. We've had to stop taking pre-bookings because I can't get hold of any-one.'

'But you also manage black cabs?'

The distinction was important because Hamish drove a black cab – a Hackney cab – which was legally allowed to cruise around looking for business and did not have to keep track of all the bookings it took. The private-hire taxis could only be pre-booked and full records had to be kept of all journeys.

'We do a bit of both,' Tim replied. 'Nowadays you've got to dabble where you can.'

'And Hamish is out in a black cab now?'

'Right, but I don't know where. Our system is down. I bought it in second-hand and the guy who fitted it reck-oned it was as-new. Can you do anything about that?'

'I think you're after trading standards. Do you have any other way of contacting him?'

'No, it's not the first time it's happened. Our private guys have to hang around waiting – either that or we call their mobiles. The Hackney lot go off and do their own thing until we can get in contact.'

'I know you've gone over this on the phone but I need access to your tracking records of who's on shift and when.'

Tim led them into the back but there was barely space for two of them, so Archie, Dave and the uniformed officer returned to the maroon room and took a seat. Tim showed Jessica how the computer worked and, after she'd wedged herself behind the desk, started fishing for information. 'Is it, er, serious . . . ?' he added.

'Is what serious?'

'The reason you're looking for Hamish.'

'I can't tell you.'

'But you think he might be in trouble?'

'I can't tell you.'

'Right . . . is there anything else I can help you with?'

'Getting your radios working would be a good start. If you've got a kettle, then I'm sure that lot out there would appreciate it. I think we're all white without.'

Tim opened the filing cabinet behind Jessica and took out a kettle, heading into a smaller side room, filling it with water and then putting it on top of the cabinet, jamming it into a socket that already had eight different plugs slotted into various extension adapters, which Jessica felt sure was a fire hazard. He hovered behind her, making her feel uncomfortable, mainly because he was so much taller than she was as she sat.

'Any luck with the radios or trackers?' she prompted.

'Oh, aye, yeah.' Tim edged around the desk and picked up a large metal box with a few speaker holes on the front. He unplugged a cable, turned it upside down, looked at the bottom, and then plugged it in again. 'Hmm . . .'

Obviously a technical genius at work. Well, at least one on a par with the plonkers they employed to fix – or not – the computers at Longsight.

'Any better?' Jessica asked.

'No . . . I think it might be a loose connection.'

Apparently at a loss how to fix it, Tim dropped to the floor and started to shuffle under the desk, cracking his head on the corner with a solid thwack.

'Are you okay?'

Tim squealed slightly. 'Fine. Just a little tap.'

Jessica continued looking through the logs. As they had been told, Hamish was definitely off work on the nights Cassie and Grace had disappeared, yet the number plate of his black cab had shown up very close to the area Jessica suspected both women went missing from. It was enough to arrest him.

Crack!

Tim's head crunched off the table again as he tried to manoeuvre himself out.

'Do you need me to move?' Jessica asked.

Tim creakily emerged, rubbing his head. 'I'm fine. I've disconnected everything under there and tried again.' He pressed a button on the desk but nothing happened. 'Stupid piece of shite . . .' He paused. ''Scuse the language, like.'

'It's fine.'

Still at a loss, Tim leant forward and smashed his hand on the top of the box with such force that the entire desk shook. There was a crackle, a pop and then static.

'Does that mean it's working?' Jessica asked.

Tim shrugged. 'I suppose so.'

'Try radioing Hamish.'

Tim checked his lists and then put the call out. Seconds later the reply buzzed back from a gruff Scottish accent. 'I'm here, son. Is your radio on the blink again? My phone's out of charge, else I would've called in.'

Jessica grabbed a pen from the desk and wrote, 'Where is he?' on the pad between her and Tim.

'Where are you, mate?' Tim asked breezily.

'Just picked someone up from the Tesco on Oxford Road. I'm on my way out to Longsight. I'll call in when I'm done.'

23

'Better put your seatbelt on, mate,' Dave warned the uniformed officer as the four of them packed into the marked police car. Jessica had taken the driver's seat before anyone could complain and screeched them away into rush-hour traffic, sirens blazing, blue lights spinning, heart pumping.

'Fuuuuuuuuuuuuuuuuuuuuuuuck,' Archie wailed from the passenger seat as his head thudded into the window.

'Stop whingeing,' Jessica barked, slamming the car into fourth and blazing around a bus. 'Call the station and get backup.'

Archie wound down the window an inch, saying he felt a little woozy, and Jessica half-turned in the seat towards Rowlands. 'Have you still got Tim on the phone?'

'Yes, can you watch the road, please?'

Jessica accelerated into a speed bump and felt the suspension bounce as the car took off and landed with a metallic thud. She rounded a corner in third just as their radio blazed to life.

'Answer it, then,' Jessica ordered Archie.

'I think I'm going to be sick.'

'Stop being wet.' Jessica punched the dashboard. 'What is it?'

'We've just caught your cab on ANPR,' an officer chirped.

'Thanks for the help but we're already on our way.'

The tyres howled as Jessica undertook a lorry, swerved right and overtook a mini, before breezing through a set of red traffic lights.

'I really think I might be sick,' Archie said groggily, winding down the window even further.

'Will you put that back up?' Jessica said. 'It's bloody freezing in here.'

She was so busy bellowing at Archie that she almost missed the ramp from Mancunian Way onto Stockport Road. Not wanting to double back, Jessica stamped on the brake, spun the steering wheel hard left and hoped for the best. With a crunch of metal, the rear bumper clipped the concrete barrier but she gripped the steering wheel tightly and righted the front, accelerating at the same time and racing down the incline in one smooth-ish movement. Well, that was how it felt in her head.

'I hope you've packed some clean pants,' Dave told the uniformed officer in the back seat.

'I've been in a rally car and that was nothing like this.'

Jessica eased off the pedal as she reached the bottom, had a quick glance right, and then steamed onto the A6. 'Will you two girls stop bitching in the back? This is how an expert does it.'

In the front, Archie slumped towards the open window, making an unhealthy-sounding combination of gurgles and groans. Jessica slid the car into fifth as she accelerated again.

'Find out from Tim where his mate is now,' Jessica shouted.

Dave asked the question and replied moments later: 'That estate out the back of Levenshulme train station. Second right after the station, first left.'

'Gotcha.'

A motorbike swerved to turn across her and then thought better of it when the rider realised how quickly she was going. Jessica swore under her breath, weaving around a car coming in the opposite direction as Archie groaned again.

'You're really putting me off,' Jessica said.

'Hnnnnnfhh.'

Jessica skidded around the turn towards the train station, second right, first left. *Screeeeeeeeeeeech.*

Blue flashing lights already filled the road, with the black cab stopped in the centre, two police cars ahead of it, one behind. Jessica slotted in next to the one at the rear and wrenched the door open. Her heart was pounding from the adrenaline as she bounded forward.

Close to the stopped cab was an officer talking into his radio. When he spotted Jessica, he waved her across. 'We only got here thirty seconds ago. We've been waiting for you.' Behind her, Archie, Dave and the uniformed officer staggered across, out of breath. Even in the dim light from the street lamps, Archie looked green. 'What happened to you three?' the officer added. 'You look like you've shat yourselves.'

'I nearly did,' Dave replied, trying to catch his breath.

The officer passed Jessica a bulletproof vest. 'We've got armed officers on the way,' he said.

'Sod that, I've already bailed them out once today.'

Jessica marched across to the cab and knocked on the driver's side window, taking a step backwards as the rear door opened. Out stepped a dumpy woman, hands up, Tesco bag for life in the air. 'It was only a pack of choc ices!' she shouted, eyes wide in fear. 'I thought I'd only picked up one box but there are two. I'll pay the difference.'

Jessica ignored her, opening the driver's door, crouching and telling Hamish Pendlebury he was under arrest.

Archie sat in Jessica's office cradling a chipped mug of tea. 'I don't think I'm going to sleep tonight,' he said, voice still trembling.

Dave laughed. 'I've seen way worse than that.'

Jessica scowled at the pair of them, Rowlands in particular. 'Aren't you done for the day?'

'I just need an hour or two for my heart rate to return to normal, then I'll nick off,' Dave replied.

'You have been on the advanced driving course, haven't you?' Archie asked.

'Pfft, I should be teaching that,' Jessica replied.

Neither of them seemed convinced. 'Is that why you took a chunk out of the back bumper?' Dave asked.

Jessica nodded at Archie. 'That was *his* fault – if he hadn't been squealing like a trapped mouse, I would've been able to concentrate.'

Archie sipped his drink but his eyes were blinking rapidly. 'That guy in uniform's gone home for the day. It wouldn't surprise me if he's off on the sick for six months now. Poor bastard.'

'Will you two stop moaning about my driving? I got

us there, didn't I? We're all in one piece – you should be thanking me.'

'What for?' Dave asked.

'Showing you how to multi-task. There you were crying like a baby abandoned in a box, while I was driving, answering radios, navigating—'

'Scaring the shite out of cyclists,' Dave added.

'Bah, they should get a car.'

There was a knock on the door, with a PC poking his head around to say that Hamish Pendlebury and his solicitor were now ready. Jessica was already past the end of her shift – again.

'Go home,' she said, nodding at Dave and then turning to Archie. 'Right then, brown pants, you did the legwork, so you can ask the questions if you can keep your lunch down for a few minutes.'

Archie perked up, sitting straighter in his chair and then standing. 'Really?'

'Yes, just splash some water on your face first – you look like you've got chronic bowel syndrome. Meet me at the interview rooms.'

Hamish Pendlebury was a big man. His studded leather jacket had been confiscated but he was still wearing jeans and a scruffy black skull and crossbones T-shirt full of creases. His hair wasn't as long as Tim's but they could have been members of the same biker gang, and he had a long grey beard which had been clumped into a point. His solicitor was the complete opposite: small, well decked out, expensive leather satchel, cocky. Hamish was looking fairly confident too, his steady gaze sweeping across Jessica and Archie, which wasn't a good sign.

Before Archie had said a word, Jessica had a sinking feeling. When both the suspect and his solicitor were looking conceited in the interview room, it was because they knew something the officers in front of them didn't. There was a definite smugness about the pair of them. A smuggy smugness that they weren't even attempting to conceal with their smug grins and smug posture. Even the satchel had a smug look about it, as if the solicitor had spent an hour in Marrakech bartering some poor kid down from thirty quid until he'd managed to buy it for fifty pence – and then put it on expenses when he got home. The smug bastard.

Archie didn't seem to notice. The only sound in the interview room was the tapping of his foot on the floor as he curled his top lip aggressively.

'I suppose you think you're clever, don't you,' he said, glaring at Hamish.

That hint of a Scottish accent again. 'Not really.'

'Two young girls – what was it, you couldn't get a shag so you took it out on them?'

The solicitor tutted but didn't say anything. Jessica knew he was going to cut in when they'd made big enough idiots of themselves. She was going to at least let Archie show her what he had.

'I'll bet you were well chuffed after the first girl, weren't you,' Archie added, laying the accent on thick. 'You thought you had it all worked out – go cruising close to the closed bus stop for any girls unfortunate enough to be looking for a lift home. But it all went to cock, didn't it?'

No reply.

'No offence, mate, but you've even got the name for it, haven't you? I mean, if I was called "Hamish", I'd be out there trying to cop off with anything that moved. I've only heard of one Hamish in my life and he was a right paedo, he—'

Another tut from the solicitor. This was going badly.

'All right,' Jessica cut in. 'How about we go back to last Thursday night. We know you weren't on shift at the taxi place, so what were you doing?'

'No comment.'

Oh, for God's sake. He was one of *those*.

'You do know that if you don't talk to us, then it can go against you?'

Hamish's solicitor cut in. 'My client isn't saying he won't *ever* answer your questions, simply that it's difficult to answer that exact one.'

It seemed to be the week for Jessica not quite grasping what was going on. At a loss, she nudged Archie with her knee.

He began tapping his foot again. 'Hmm, Hamish, Hamish, Hamish . . . I think you *do* remember what you were up to last Thursday. I'm guessing you knocked off work at around five or six. Went home, had a couple of crispy pancakes, watched a few cartoons on television, perhaps even got excited by that one who presents the news.' He turned to Jessica. 'What's her name?' Without waiting for a reply, he continued. 'Never mind. Anyway, after that, you spent a while looking at questionable material on the Internet. I know, I've been there myself after a long day.

The difference is that I don't currently have officers poring through my search history. What do you think they're going to find on there? Horse sex?'

Hamish peeped sideways at his solicitor and motioned him to stand.

'Whoa there, big fella,' Archie said, not moving.

'I went out on Thursday night,' Hamish said, sitting again.

'Well, hal-le-lu-jah – he speaks,' Archie added mockingly.

'I left my cab at home and I walked to this place a few streets over from mine.'

'What place?' Archie asked.

A hint of a smile slid across the cabbie's features. 'It's called Sandra's.'

Jessica and Archie exchanged a look and mouthed the same word simultaneously. 'Shite.'

24

Jessica stood outside the unassuming doorway in the gap between street lights and turned to Archie. 'Ever been here before?'

'No!'

'I won't hold it against you if you have.'

'Sod off – I don't have to pay for it.'

'Some men like the seedy nature of paying for sex . . . apparently.'

'How do you know, is your boyfriend a fan?'

Jessica saw Archie's simmering grin and let it go. 'I went on some vice course a couple of years ago. A lot of it was about people smuggling but then it took us a day or so just to figure out what the laws are. Half of what I thought was illegal is perfectly fine. It's a bloody minefield.'

'All that to get a quick shag off a prostitute.'

Archie motioned to step towards the doorway but Jessica pulled him to one side, deeper into the shadows. 'We need a quick word first.'

'What?'

'About the interview room – what were you doing?'

In the gloom, she could just about make out his shrug. 'I dunno, trying to get a reaction. I thought that if I acted like a knob head, then you could jump in and be the sensible one.'

'Bloody hell, I've never been called that before.'

'Is there a problem?'

Jessica started to reply and then stopped herself. He reminded her far too much of what she was like when she was younger – stupid, brash, gobby, trying to get under people's skins. Sometimes she still felt like that now, but here he was, a decade younger than her, figuring it all out for himself. She could hardly give him a hard time when she had done far worse things than he was likely to.

'No, just . . . try to think a little more before you speak. You're going to get yourself into trouble.'

'Aye, fair enough. Now can we go scare the shite out of a few punters?'

'Lead the way.'

The only markings on the dark door were the number thirty-one and a buzzer. Archie pushed it open and headed up the stairs with Jessica behind. He led the way through a second door at the top into a small waiting room. On one side was a counter like the reception desk in any office, except that the woman behind it had approximately forty per cent more cleavage on show. Directly across from the door was a flatscreen television fixed to the wall displaying a porn star mid-act, while underneath two men sat, staring at the floor and definitely not at each other. A scattering of pornographic magazines was on the coffee table in front of them.

When Jessica entered, the two men looked up in unison, eyebrows arched in mutual confusion about why the fully dressed woman in a suit was there. The receptionist knew instantly.

'Are you Sandra?' Jessica asked.

The woman was somewhere in her early forties but had definitely kept her looks – and chest. She nodded. 'Feck off, will ya – all my accounts are in order; the girls are all healthy, all tested, all English, all willingly here. There's no trafficked European girls here. Oh, and before you ask, I'm not a madam and I'm not running a brothel either. I'm an employee the same as anyone else. You can ask any of the girls.'

One of the men got slowly to his feet, desperately re-arranging the crotch area of his trousers. 'Is, er, everything, er, okay?'

Jessica slipped her hand into her jacket pocket and took out her identification, showing it to both men and then Sandra. Before she could turn back, both men had dashed for the exit, stumbling their way down the stairs and slamming the door at the bottom.

'Feck's sake, there was no need for that,' Sandra said.

'Aren't you chilly?' Jessica asked.

'Ha ha, aren't you the funny one.' She nodded at Archie. 'And you can stop looking at my tits too.'

'Where else am I supposed to look?' he shot back. 'They take up half the room.'

Jessica put her ID away. 'Look, we'll leave quietly – we just need you to tell us something.' She reached into her pocket and pulled out the printout, folding it flat on the counter until Hamish Pendlebury's features were clear. 'Do you know who this is?'

Sandra picked up the sheet and glanced at it, before returning it to the desk, pursing her lips, and rearranging her cleavage. 'Everyone has confidentiality when they come in here.'

'You're not a sodding doctor's surgery.'

'Too bloody right we're not. For one thing, we don't have a three-month waiting list; for another, our clients always leave satisfied.'

'If you don't tell us, then we'll have people coming here all day every day – hanging around, asking questions. Interviewing all the girls individually, going through your accounts with a fine-tooth comb.'

'Knowing you bastards, you probably would as well.' She winked at Archie. 'Don't think we don't have your off-duty lot popping in for a quick in and out anyway. You're all dirty bastards, you've gotta be to hang around with paedos and weirdos all day long.'

'Yeah, yeah,' Jessica replied. 'And that's just the super-intendent and his mates. Anyway – do you know this guy or not? Believe me, whatever confidentiality you think you're offering, he'd be grateful for an alibi.'

A grin spread across Sandra's face as she picked up the sheet again. Somewhere in a back room a woman's moaning reached what was either a genuine peak, or she was nailed on for some sort of acting award. Sandra nodded at Archie again. 'That's Holly – she'd like you.'

'Do. You. Know. Him?' Jessica snapped.

'Fine! He's one of our regulars. He's in here at least once a week – you can't forget that hair. I think he lives nearby.'

'What days did you work last week?'

Another heave of the bra: 'Christ, you're not enforcing working time directive, are you?'

'Do you ever answer a question?'

'All right, bloody hell . . . I did daytimes Monday and Tuesday, then evenings Thursday to Saturday.'

'What about this week?'

'I've been on lates all week.'

Jessica pointed at the picture. 'What days was he in?'

Sandra demonstrated an impressive set of lungs as she exhaled thoughtfully. 'He always comes in to see Arianna – so that's Wednesday and Friday last week and Monday this week.'

'Is there any proof – a credit-card transaction, a cheque . . .'

'What do you think we're running here? We're not bloody Asda.'

'So it's cash only?'

'Obviously.'

'But you're absolutely, one hundred per cent positive he was here on those three evenings.'

Sandra folded up the photograph and handed it back. 'Darling, when someone with a beard like that starts wanting to do the types of thing he does with Arianna, believe me, us girls talk about it.'

25

Jessica rolled over and fell onto the floor. She thought she was being nice after sneaking in late, not disturbing Adam and instead sleeping on the sofa. The result was that she'd barely slept at all, huddling under a thick blanket and twisting herself around it into such knots that she wasn't sure what was blanket and what was clothing. Once again, she'd managed to work the entire day and most of the evening. The only thing she had done after getting home was creep up the stairs and peer through the crack that Bex left between the door and the frame to make sure that the teenager was still there. Jessica didn't know why she felt so protective of Bex, but there was something there, something . . . motherly. No, not that. Sisterly? She couldn't explain it because she'd never had those instincts before. Her younger self would have nicked Bex for the thieving and then spent the rest of the day congratulating herself for being so clever. Now . . . she didn't know.

Jessica clawed her way onto the sofa again and started trying to straighten the blanket when the door creaked open. She spun to see the painfully thin outline of Bex standing in a vest top and pair of shorts. Her legs looked like a frog's, thin with bandy knees, while her arms were wrapped around her midriff as they so often were. 'Sorry,' she whispered. 'I borrowed your stuff. Adam said—'

'It's fine, you can wear what you want. I don't use half of it anyway. We'll go through my wardrobe if you like.'

'I couldn't sleep – I was worried about you getting home. Adam said you're always late but I was thinking about you being a police officer and . . .'

'I didn't want to disturb anyone, so I slept down here.'

Bex bobbed awkwardly from one foot to the other.

'Are you cold?' Jessica asked.

'A bit.'

'Hungry?'

She suppressed a smile. 'A bit.'

Jessica picked up the blanket and draped it around Bex's shoulders. 'Let's see what's left in the kitchen.'

Bex sat shivering at the table under the blanket as Jessica began picking items out of the fridge. 'I'm not really in the mood for a sandwich,' she yawned, peering around the door at Bex. 'You?'

'I don't mind.'

'It's too early to cook and the microwave's too noisy, so we can't really have anything warm. All the sausage rolls are in the freezer, so they're off the menu.'

'Honestly, don't put yourself out.'

'I don't know why we have so much healthy shite in here. This is what happens when you let Adam do the shopping – it's all bloody fruit and yoghurt. Oh sod this.' Jessica opened the cupboard, lifted out the tins of baked beans and a packet of cream crackers, and then poked around for her secret stash of chocolate-coated chocolate chip cookies. She placed them on the table in front of Bex and then put the kettle on. 'Nothing beats a brew and a biscuit – especially at three in the morning.'

With a tremor and a pop, the kettle finished boiling, so Jessica and Bex decamped back to the comfort of the living room, shivering under the blanket together and dunking their way through Jessica's biscuits.

'Are you sure you don't mind me being here?' Bex asked.

'This place is too big for Adam and me.'

Bex pressed the mug to her chin, breathing in the warm fumes. 'Does that mean . . . ?'

Jessica hated the question – it was what she always got from her mother and why she tried to avoid her phone calls. Kids: it always came down to bloody kids.

Bex must have sensed she'd asked the wrong thing. 'Sorry . . .'

'No, it's . . .' Jessica stopped, remembering – as if the name was ever out of her mind. '. . . I lost a baby and now they don't think I can get pregnant again.'

'Oh . . .'

'We were thinking about adopting or fostering, but it's awkward with the job . . .'

'So you have to choose between one or the other?'

It was an honest question – a natural one – but Jessica suddenly felt that itch at the back of her throat as if tears were near. She'd tried to block out the fact that the choice was as simple as that. Izzy combined the two, as did so many others, and yet Jessica knew that wasn't her. As with anything in her life, it was all or nothing.

You're either living life at 100 m.p.h., or you're not living at all.

Jessica just didn't know which of the two camps she was in.

'Sorry,' Bex said.

Jessica shielded herself behind half a biscuit. 'Don't be.'

Bex drew her mug up in front of her face and began to speak. 'I didn't know my dad – never met him, never knew his name. I was brought up by my mum in Hulme. My first memory is of waking up early in the morning, a bit like this I suppose. I was maybe five or six and it was cold, so I got up to see if I could find my mum. It was only this little two-bed place and her room was next to mine but there was no one in her bed. I heard voices downstairs, so I crept down into the living room and she was there with two blokes. I thought . . . well, I didn't know what I thought then. It's obvious now – it all is.'

Bex pulled the blanket tighter under her chin, leaving one bony arm sticking out, clutching her mug. 'I used to think she was ill because there were needles everywhere. She'd say they were because she was feeling poorly but you don't know any differently when you're a kid. If I ever asked about my dad, she'd get furious, saying he was no good and that I shouldn't worry about him. Then I'd have all these "uncles". There was always someone there.'

She paused, then added: 'When you're a kid, you think normal is what's in front of you.'

So young, so wise.

'How long have you been on the streets?'

'I don't really know – a couple of years, maybe? When I

was a kid I really enjoyed school but there was never any pressure from home to do well and when I got a bit older I started hanging around with the wrong people. We'd bunk off, smoke in the park, see if we could get some booze. No one said anything, so we just kept doing it. Then Mum started seeing this bloke named Stu. By then, I pretty much knew what was going on with the needles and so on but it was normal. I was still sleeping at home and this one night I woke up and he was just *there* at the bottom of my bed, watching.'

Jessica gurgled a noise of revulsion, not knowing what to say.

'He didn't say anything but he was . . . well, you can guess.'

'How old were you?'

'Fourteen.'

'And how old are you now?'

'Seventeen.'

'What did you do?'

'I started screaming at him, telling him to get away.'

'Did he?'

'He turned around and walked out of my room as if nothing was wrong but I'd woken up my mum by shouting. She came stumbling in from her room, screaming back – wanting to know why I'd woken her up. I was telling her what Stu was doing at the bottom of my bed but she shrugged and asked what the problem was.'

Jessica couldn't stop herself: 'No . . .'

Bex took another biscuit and crunched into it. 'I spent the rest of the night sleeping up against the door and then the next day I packed all the clothes I had into a bag and left. I knew the parks pretty well and there was usually an unlocked toilet or a pagoda somewhere. During the summer, it's not too bad . . . well, it's not great but it's not the worst. But then it was winter.'

'What did you do?'

'You get into the hostel where you can. Sometimes the woman on the desk lets you in but other times, when they have a bunch of people in, you have to pay. When you need eight quid a day for a roof, you become pretty good at figuring out the types of people who are a bit careless with their wallets.'

'You did that for two years?'

Bex finished the biscuit and put her mug on the floor, curling herself up entirely under the blanket and edging closer to Jessica. She seemed more childlike than ever. 'More or less. There are always blokes saying they'll do this or that to help you but it's pretty easy to figure out what they actually want.'

Jessica felt the need to defend Adam. 'Not everyone's like that.'

'Maybe . . .'

'Why did you decide to come here?'

Bex yawned widely. 'I don't know – why did you invite me?'

The yawn was infectious and Jessica found herself trying, and failing, to stifle one herself. 'I don't know . . . instinct.'

Bex indicated the sofa and Jessica's sleeping arrangement: 'Are you and Adam going to be okay?'

'Yes; it's just the job.'

'Are you going to have to choose between being a police officer, Adam, and children?'

Jessica couldn't look her in the eye. 'Not yet.'

26

Jessica and DC Archie Davey spent the morning trapped in what would have looked to outsiders like an elaborate yawning competition. Jessica didn't want to spend time in her office in case DCI Cole came looking for her, so, instead, they holed up in the back corner of the canteen – somewhere neither he, nor anyone with intestinal problems or taste buds, would go anywhere near. Archie complained that the job was taking a toll on his social life but Jessica could do little other than laugh and yawn. 'Get used to that,' she advised.

Hamish had been kept in overnight while his story was checked out. The first-hand sighting at the massage parlour was as much of an alibi as they were going to get and there wasn't much desire to haul all the girls in for interview. Sandra had likely been right about one thing – off-duty officers *would* be known faces at some of those establishments, and in a model of mutually assured destruction conducted through the media, the police would come off worse if they caused too many problems.

For the most part, the massage parlours weren't the problem anyway – the girls who worked there knew what they were doing and the blokes who lumbered in on the way home from work knew what they were paying for. Sandra knew that too: if she and her girls didn't create a

223

problem, then they wouldn't get one, even if the books might struggle to hold up to the closest scrutiny. It was the people-smuggling that GMP's Serious Crime Division was desperate to get a handle on – mainly of Eastern European girls – but if they were going to close that down, then leaving a safe alternative was probably for the best too. It was on the borderline of legality but it served most people's interests to leave it be. Well, unless you lived next door to one – and then you were screwed either way. Literally, if that was your thing.

That left Jessica with a problem, because if Hamish wasn't driving his cab in the area Cassie and Grace had disappeared from, then who was? He insisted it had been left on his driveway while he'd gone for a walk to Sandra's. He'd spent two hours – and a hefty chunk of change, no doubt – at the parlour and then headed home. Because of the shift Arianna worked, Sandra had practically been able to give them a clocking-in and -out time for Hamish's appearances, ruling him out of killing either woman. He said that his cab was exactly where he'd left it when he got home and that, although he hadn't checked in the evenings, the keys were still on the table where he'd left them by the next morning.

That left them with two options:

1) Someone had broken into Hamish's house, stolen his keys, stolen the cab, picked up both women, beaten, killed, cut up and dumped them – all without making a mess in the vehicle, then returned the taxi and keys

unnoticed, possibly simultaneously inventing a time machine; or

2) Somebody had cloned his number plate.

Option one was unlikely; option two left them trying to track down all the black cabs in the city, close to the city and possibly any others that had been bought second-hand and stored in a garage for what could have been years. For now, as the full list of anyone with a licensed Hackney cab within a fifty-mile radius was put together, they could do little else other than hope their number plate recognition system flagged up that particular plate in a place where it wasn't Hamish going about his daily business.

After deciding there was nowhere in the station she could get away with catching half an hour's sleep, Jessica found Rowlands on the main floor.

'Any luck with that symbol?' she asked.

Dave started typing on his keyboard and then pointed to the screen.

'Why are you showing me rugby players' thighs?' Jessica asked, peering closely at the screen. 'I'm not complaining – I just didn't realise this was what you spent your days looking at.'

'This is the Wales rugby team,' Dave replied.

'That guy looks like he sleeps in a ditch,' Jessica said, pointing at one of the hairier players.

'I thought you might be more interested in the badge.'

Dave zoomed in on one of the players' jerseys until the image appeared of three feathers arching in a similar pattern to the one on the corner of Jessica's envelope.

Jessica stared closely at the screen but shook her head. 'That's not it.'

'I know. When you first showed me it, I thought it reminded me of something but I was wrong – it was only this. This is the Prince of Wales' crest – it's close but not the same.'

'If the Prince of Wales is stalking me, he can sod right off.'

Before Jessica could start to list the ways the royal family annoyed her, her phone rang with an unregistered number. She quickly thanked Dave and hurried towards the corner, phone at her ear.

'If this is double glazing, then I'm not interested.'

There was a confused male voice at the other end: 'Huh?'

'I said . . . forget it. Hello.'

'Jess?'

'Yes, who's calling?'

'It's Garry. Can we meet – usual place as soon as you can?'

Jessica checked her watch: ten past eleven. Early lunch it was.

For the third day in a row, Jessica surveyed the scene of the supermarket cafe. Pensioners: yep. Single parents: yep. Bored-looking assistants: yep. Half-asleep copper and journalist who looked like he'd had a near-death experience huddled around a table looking sorry for themselves: yep.

Jessica had gone for three espressos, with a Danish and vanilla slice on the side. Added to the chocolate biscuits at three in the morning, this was a new high for sugar intake before midday. As she returned to the table, Garry groaned, closing his eyes and turning to stare out of the window.

'What's wrong with you?' Jessica asked.

'I can't even look at food this morning.'

Jessica dangled the pecan Danish in front of his face. 'Sure you don't want a bite?'

'Bleugh. I knew I shouldn't have come out this early.'

'Did Mrs Ashford keep you up with her arthritis?'

Garry turned back to Jessica, almost focusing on her but not quite. 'One day, you're going to meet her and then you're going to have to take all this back.'

Jessica downed the first espresso and took a bite of the cake. 'Whatever – why are we here for a third day running? The staff are going to think we're having an affair. That might be something that raises you in their eyes but what about my reputation? They're going to think I'm having a breakdown.'

'I was on the lash last night.'

'You called me here to tell me that?'

Garry shook his head but his bottom lip was hanging limply and his eyes were slits. 'I'm too old for this. I remember being at uni and we'd go out through the night, sleep for two hours and then roll up to lectures as if nothing was wrong. Now I can barely get through the afternoon without needing a kip.'

'You're younger than me!'

'Ugh. Anyway, I went out with the editor last night. Like I said, he's been brought in from down south and doesn't really know anyone. Everyone's been saying for months that someone should make friends with him – actually go out with him, find out what he's all about – that kind of thing.'

'So the pair of you were out and about in town, being turned down by numerous women – then what happened?'

Garry didn't even have the good grace to smile. 'It wasn't like that. I didn't want to risk being out with the boss, so we went to this dive out Eccles way.'

'Bloody hell, what were you thinking?'

'Evidently I *wasn't* thinking. I've been in some rough places when I was a student in Liverpool but they were nothing. The barmaid had a baby in one arm and was pulling pints with the other, there was a fight on the other side of the bar, and I'm pretty sure the stain on the carpet by my feet was blood, not red wine.'

Jessica nodded in agreement. 'It's not really a red wine kind of area. Why did you go there?'

'For you! You had me thinking there was something going on and I knew the only way I'd be able to get the editor talking was if I got him laryxed. I didn't want to be seen dead with him in the city centre and if I was going to be buying drinks all night, then it had to be somewhere cheap – so we had a quick half down this side street off Deansgate, where I didn't think anyone would notice, then we got a bus.'

'Aww, and you got hammered just for me? You're so sweet.'

'Anyway, for every pint of cheap lager I had, I was ordering him a pint of this local ale that's about eight per cent. After three drinks, he could barely say his own name.

Mind you, I wasn't much better – I can't remember the last time I was on the beer.'

'Were you at least sober enough to ask him who phoned and asked him to change the front page?'

'I'm getting to that.'

Garry paused to wipe strands of sweat-drenched hair away from his forehead.

Jessica downed her second espresso. 'You really don't look well.'

'Moonlighting as a doctor, are we?'

'I've had the odd alcoholic beverage in my time.'

Garry downed the rest of a glass of water – the only thing he'd attempted to eat or drink – and then rubbed his eyes. When he spoke again, his tone was lower, more serious. 'This is a big thing for me.'

'What is?'

'I've never broken a source. It's one of the biggest things in this job, like a doctor or a lawyer with their confidentiality – you have to keep your sources.'

'Anything you tell me will stay between us.'

'Promise?'

'Of course.'

'The person who called to talk about our front page is the same person who leaked the initial story about Holden Wyatt to our reporter. I asked what was talked about but the editor said there were no threats, just that he was told we'd get a lot more cooperation on all sorts of fronts if we could do a favour.'

'Do you do many favours?'

Garry shrugged. 'More than you might think – usually

it involves PR companies who ask if we can be nice about something in return for access to a celebrity or two. Sometimes the council tries to get a bit smart. It shouldn't really happen but it's hard to stop. You and me have had *agreements* in the past, haven't we?'

That was one way to put it.

'Who made the call?'

Garry reached across and touched Jessica's third and final espresso. 'Can I have this?'

'Go for it.'

Garry drank the coffee in one go and breathed out deeply. 'I need to know you're going to look after me if it comes down to it – I'm getting married; I've got a life.'

'You can trust me.'

Garry gulped and then finally said the name. 'It was Graham Pomeroy.'

Jessica paused, breathing through her nose, repeating the name in her mind. '. . . As in *Assistant Chief Constable* Graham Pomeroy?'

'Yes.'

'As in *Porky* Pomeroy – one of my bosses?'

Garry plonked the cup back down on the table and nodded. 'Yep.'

27

To say the structure of Greater Manchester Police was complicated would be underestimating quite how convoluted the whole thing was. As well as being split into CID and uniform divisions, everything was then carved up into regions – North, South, East, West and Metropolitan. Individual stations then housed officers based loosely upon geography, so Jessica worked for Manchester Metropolitan CID, based at Longsight, with DCI Jack Cole as the highest-ranking officer permanently on site, and Detective Superintendent William Aylesbury overseeing half-a-dozen stations.

So far, so simple – sort of.

Above that were two chief superintendents, five assistant chief constables, a deputy chief constable and the overall chief constable.

No one Jessica spoke to ever seemed to know quite what the chief constables actually did. Clearly it involved rolling up at civic functions in a suit, quaffing champagne, and guffawing every time the council leader told a rubbish joke. There was definitely an element of turning up if anyone important was in town, or flouncing off to London for a glass of rosé with other chief constables a few times a year. If you were really lucky, you might even get a knighthood if you brown-nosed the right person. What you definitely *did not* do was head into the city centre on a Friday night to help pack drunken revellers into the back of a riot van while simultaneously trying not to get puked on. Not that Jessica did that either, but that wasn't the point.

Admittedly, she rarely spoke to anyone who wasn't Izzy, Dave, Archie or, in the old days, DCI Cole, but that wasn't the point either.

All that could be put to one side, however, because the fact was that Graham Pomeroy was a significant name in the Greater Manchester Police force.

Jessica wasn't sure what to say and couldn't get past her first question: 'Why would he be getting involved in day-to-day police work?'

Garry was looking slightly perkier after the coffee. 'I thought you might know.'

'Usually you can't get that lot off the golf course unless there's the chance to go on TV.'

'Have you ever met him?'

'A few times. Once or twice a year, they'll host these engagement things to make it look like we're a part of the community and so on. The thought's in the right place but no one seems to realise that the only people who come out and get involved are the ones who don't mind us anyway. We should concentrate on the teenagers and the kids – they're the ones who are going to grow into adults who can't stand us. We end up holding these dreadful events no one wants to go to, but if we did something like a football day, or if we hosted a BMX event, that kind of thing, we'd actually get a few of the lads down.' Jessica sighed – this was an argument she'd made before. 'Anyway, whenever we have one of these god-awful things, either the chief constable, his deputy, or one of the assistants turns up. They'll smile, wave, have their photo taken, and then sod back off to the house in the country. Pomeroy usually shows up if there's a free meal on the go.'

'He's *distinctive* then?'

'If by "distinctive", you mean "morbidly obese", then yes, he is.'

'Do you think whatever's going on around your station is down to him?'

DCI Cole had said it himself: *'Word has come down from above to get the Potter case sorted . . .'* Had Pomeroy given the call?

Before Jessica could reply, her phone began to ring. She apologised and took the call, then said sorry again after hanging up. 'I've got to go – another woman's gone missing.'

Everyone knew the drill with missing persons – make sure twenty-four hours had passed, ask if they'd checked the shed in case the person was hiding there. Was there any chance the absentee had simply had a night on the lash and fallen asleep on the bus home?

The reason Jessica drove across the city to the home of Joe Peters was that he lived with his girlfriend Leanne two streets away from the spot where it seemed likely Cassie and Grace had disappeared – and she hadn't been seen in almost sixteen hours. Joe had read about the other missing girls and persuaded the 999 operator to put him through to someone who would listen.

Joe's story was depressingly familiar and almost horrifyingly mundane. He and Leanne had argued over what to watch on television the previous night but, instead of compromising or turning the set off entirely, things had escalated into a full-blown barney and she'd stormed out of the house calling him every name under the sun. An hour later and Joe was regretting calling her a 'fat fucking bitch', which he insisted was in response to her branding him 'a small-cocked, weasel-faced wanker'. Joe insisted to Jessica that he wasn't 'small-cocked' but didn't seem to argue about being 'weasel-faced'. Either way, Leanne's mobile phone seemed to be switched off and she wasn't at any of her friends' houses, or her mother's, which meant that Joe had gone into a panic over the fate of the girl whose weight he had lovingly questioned less than a day ago.

It was precisely this kind of pettiness that was the reason why they didn't usually start to investigate missing people until an entire day had passed – often longer.

Joe sat in an armchair trying to rock their baby to sleep, cooing in the child's ear that 'Mummy will be home soon', while reeling off the list of insults he and Leanne had thrown at each other the previous night.

He placed the child on his lap and began massaging his shoulder with a pained groan, before adding: 'We've kicked off in the past but she always comes back.'

They took a photograph of the missing woman in case they needed to run an appeal – or if a body turned up.

As she left the house with Archie close behind, Jessica noticed a black woman leaning against the front door of the adjacent house, smoking a cigarette. With a side-flick of her head, she beckoned Jessica over. When Jessica and Archie were close enough, she broke into a knowing smile, showing an impressive array of bright white teeth. 'What is it this time?'

'Sorry?' Jessica replied.

'It's always something with those two – shouting at each other, swearing at the top of their voices, throwing things. Poor little baby has to sit through it all.'

'How long have they lived here?'

'Just over a year. I reckon your lot have been out half-a-dozen times since then.'

That was something someone probably should have checked before they'd decided to prioritise this as a missing persons case worthy of attention.

'How well do you know them?' Jessica asked.

The woman finished her cigarette and stubbed it out with her foot. 'As well as anyone knows their neighbours nowadays. He's Joe, she's Leanne – neither of them seem to work, that's about it.'

'Have you actually seen them arguing?'

A weary nod: 'Last summer – well, that one week in July – they were having a barbecue in the back garden. I went over for a sausage to be polite but couldn't get away quickly enough. They'd invited a bunch of their mates over and it was already rowdy by mid-afternoon. A few more beers and everyone was shouting at everyone else. I was in our back bedroom watching as she went for him with the big tong things they were using to turn the meat over. She was whacking him on the shoulder and calling him all sorts. Then she picked up a garden gnome and hurled that at him too. I was in half a mind to give your lot a call but didn't want the trouble in case either of them found out.'

With the alternative being that their killer had taken another woman, Jessica hoped this was another argument that had got out of hand.

Back at the station and they were making gentle inquiries into Leanne's whereabouts without definitively classing her as missing. A small team were checking number plates that had gone into the area the previous evening, with CCTV from the shops at the bottom of the road being looked at just in case Leanne had popped in. Both Joe and Leanne had a string of low-level convictions, mainly for breaches of the peace, and someone was examining their known associates too. All in all, it was quite the farce.

Jessica knew there would be a stack of paperwork waiting for her but didn't make it to her office before Fat Pat bellowed after her that DCI Cole wanted a word.

Despite apparently requesting her presence, he once again made her wait in the corridor, holding his hand up through the glass windows and then turning his back as he spoke on the phone. If he was deliberately trying to wind her up, then he certainly knew what he was doing. Jessica couldn't help but wonder if the person on the phone was Pomeroy.

After a few minutes of steaming in the corridor, she finally got the wave from Cole, calling her into his office. He didn't wait for her to sit before starting to speak: 'That was a phone call to say that the missing woman Leanne is no longer missing. Apparently she got on a train and didn't have the money to get back. She didn't realise anyone was looking for her. Apologies for sending you out there – but better to be safe.'

It wasn't a complete note of regret, nor had he used the word 'sorry' – but it was an apology of sorts, which was more than she'd had from him in months.

'We can't go chasing things up every time a couple have an argument.'

'I know, but there's something else . . .' Suddenly the apology didn't seem quite so charitable. 'I'm sending you home – it's late notice but there are all sorts of issues with staff and I need a senior officer to keep an eye on the area Cassie Edmonds and Grace Savage went missing from after dark.'

'You're putting me on nights?'

'For Friday and Saturday. Take the rest of today off and don't come in until late tomorrow evening. Take Sunday off too and then we'll look again at next week. I've checked things over with HR and Patrick, plus there's a bit of flexibility in the overtime budget if there's anyone in particular you want to take out with you.'

Jessica bit on her top lip, thinking of how best to reply. There was no polite way. 'Am I being picked on?'

Cole's face folded into a frown but his tone didn't soften. 'Why would you think that?'

Jessica wanted to ask him why he'd been off with her for months, plus who was putting pressure on him and why. Instead, she gave the only answer she could: 'No reason, Sir.'

28

Jessica sat in the small waiting area of the Indian restaurant trying to keep her temper. 'I just don't understand why you book a seat for half seven if you're here at half seven and all the tables are full. Doesn't that defeat the very purpose of making a booking?'

Adam sipped his pint of Cobra and patted her infuriatingly on the knee. 'They're just busy – it's fine. We'll get to eat.'

Jessica mumbled something about him backing her up for a change, going somewhere else, not wanting to be rushed, wondering why that waiter kept leaning against the doorframe not doing much, and then realising it was because he was trying to chat up the group of women in leather trousers.

All those things annoyed her, but none so much as the fact that she knew she *was* being picked on. It wasn't the first time she'd been switched to lates at short notice and likely wouldn't be the last – but the timing was fishy. Was it because they wanted a different officer to find something to pin on Holden Wyatt while she was off during the day, or were they trying to get her out of the way for another reason? The actual shifts wouldn't inconvenience her that much – she rarely slept for longer than a few hours at a time and being off during the day might give her a chance to get up to no good away from prying eyes. That still didn't stop her feeling marginalised – and even though she'd never met him properly, Graham Pomeroy's enormous frame was surely casting a shadow over her life.

In an attempt to put it all out of her mind, Jessica had told Adam she was taking him out for tea to wherever he wanted to go; the only proviso was that it had to be exactly where she wanted and if he could pretend that it was where he wanted to go as well, then she'd be really grateful.

Luckily, Adam was a good actor and a far more patient person than she was.

Jessica peered up at the clock again – quarter to eight. They should have sat down to eat fifteen minutes ago. She nudged Adam with her knee. 'Are you going to say something?'

'Of course I'm not.'

'Why?'

'Because we're in a restaurant. Do you really think the best thing to do is piss people off *before* they make your food?'

Fair point.

Fifteen minutes later and Jessica was working her way through a stack of poppadoms and tray of pickles as Adam leant back in his seat and watched her. 'It's nice to be out.'

'It's nice not to have to cook.'

'Since when do you cook?'

'I did you Pot Noodle on toast last week.'

'Find that one in a celebrity chef book, did you?'

Jessica dug a slice of poppadom deep into the mango

chutney, not daring to look up from the food because she didn't want to catch his eye. 'Sorry about, well, everything. Being late, sleeping on the sofa, being on nights . . .'

Adam sounded convincing, but then he'd had a lot of practice. 'It's fine – I'm going to pop over to Georgia's flat tomorrow.'

Jessica hadn't seen Adam's sister in months. 'How is she?'

'That's what I'm going to find out.'

'Oh, right . . .'

Adam reached forward and dipped his finger in the onion chutney. 'We should talk about Bex.'

'What about her?'

'Who is she?'

'I told you.'

'You said she'd stolen your purse and that you weren't sure why you invited her into our home. She's there now – it's fine, I trust you – but there has to be a point to all of this.'

Jessica finished off the final poppadom and drank some of her wine to give herself a few moments to think. Luckily, the waiter trotted over and began clearing the remains of the food away, giving her a few more seconds. Eventually, she gave her reply: 'I don't know what I'm doing.'

'She's seventeen, Jess.'

'I know.'

'Is it because of . . . ?'

Adam didn't want to say it outright – no one except Jessica's mother ever did – but it was clear what he meant. 'You think I'm trying to be Bex's mum?'

'I didn't say that – you're the one who said you don't know what you're doing. I just want to make sure you're not going to end up hurting yourself.'

'Why would I do that?'

Adam started to reply but had to pause as the waiter cheerfully brought over a tray with their starters on. It was all smiles and thank yous until they were alone again, then Adam leant in and whispered: 'You don't know who she is, Jess. I know you want to help and it's fine if you want her to stay at our house for a while – but you have to think about what you're getting yourself into. Are you going to help her get a job? Go to college? Find her own place? What about clothes, food and transport?'

'I don't know yet.'

'Can you at least try to think about things?'

Jessica took another mouthful of wine, holding it in her mouth, enjoying the slightly bitter taste. 'I *have* thought about them, I just don't know the answers yet.'

Adam tilted his head, smiling slightly. 'Okay.'

'Are you sure?'

'I want you to be happy, Jess.'

'What about us?'

'I'm happy if you are.'

She finished her drink. 'That's not an answer – what do *you* want?'

It was Adam's turn to become self-conscious, using a napkin to wipe something non-existent from his face and replying almost apologetically: 'I've already got everything I want.'

Jessica immersed herself in the food so that she didn't

have to respond, then changed the subject. She hated it when he said things like that because what was she supposed to say back?

The rest of the meal was terrific, the wine was smooth, the taxi drive back to the house was uneventful and the lights were off when they arrived home. Adam waved Jessica into the living room with a cheeky grin, asking if she fancied one more drink. Considering she planned, after seeing Adam off to work in the morning, to spend the rest of the day in bed, Jessica figured it couldn't do much harm.

They giggled their way into the room like a pair of teenagers left on their own for the first time. Adam took a pair of shot glasses and half-full vodka bottle out of the cabinet underneath the television and poured them each a glass. They flopped on the sofa and toasted their first meal out alone together for months. Jessica enjoyed the burn of the liquid on her throat and reached for the bottle, pouring another. Adam shook his head: 'I've got work tomorrow.'

Jessica didn't let that stop her, downing the second shot in one and slumping even deeper into the cushions of the sofa.

'Something's different,' Adam said, out of the blue.

'What?'

'I'm not sure – but something's not quite right in here.'

Jessica poured – and drank – a third shot. Perhaps moving onto lates wasn't a bad thing after all if it meant she had more evenings off in between times to hang around with Adam and go drinking. 'I think you've had too much to drink,' she said.

'You're the one slurring your words.'

'Am not.'

Adam sounded as if he was about to say something but then he paused, biting his lip. 'The candlesticks are missing.'

Jessica squinted towards the shelf they'd sat atop since they had partially unpacked but Adam was right – they had gone.

29

The alcohol helped Jessica sleep but Holden Wyatt, Damon Potter, Cassie Edmonds, Grace Savage, Bones, DCI Cole, Assistant Chief Constable Graham Pomeroy and strange curved symbols were haunting her.

Then there was Bex.

Jessica had checked through the gap between the door and the frame before she'd gone to bed but the teenager was in the same position she'd been in for the past few nights: curled into a ball under the bed covers, breathing deeply. Everything Adam had said at the restaurant was correct – but Jessica so wanted to help and knowing Bex had a roof over her head and food in her stomach was one of the few things that had got her through the week.

Although she knew she had to be up through the night, Jessica got up early and waited in the kitchen. She put some toast on for Adam, kissed him goodbye and then waited some more. She heard Bex moving around upstairs at twenty past nine and then the sound of the shower. Just before ten, the teenager emerged into the kitchen humming a song that Jessica didn't know. Her long black hair was wet and loose, the damp ends creating a wet patch on the oversized T-shirt Adam had given her; the angular tattoo on her arm was bold and bright. Her slim legs hardly seemed to have the width to support the rest of her frame as she padded barefoot into the room, stopping when she noticed Jessica.

'Oh, you're up,' she said. 'I thought you'd be sleeping most of the day.'

'I probably will be. Do you want something to eat?'

Bex grinned, chewing on the corners of her mouth hungrily. 'I shouldn't keep eating your food.'

'Maybe we should sit down one evening and have a talk about things?'

Jessica didn't know how Bex would take it but the teenager nodded and grinned again. Her face had started to fill out slightly over the past few days, which was perhaps no surprise seeing as she couldn't have got any thinner.

Jessica dropped a couple more slices of bread into the toaster and then started hunting through the cereal packets in the cupboard. That was the other thing about letting Adam do the food shopping by himself: he bought lots of cereal. If he could get away with eating it three times a day, he probably would.

Moments later and Bex was mashing a Shredded Wheat into a Weetabix while taking a bite of toast. Jessica took a strange pleasure in watching someone clearly so in need of food being able to wolf down the contents of her cupboards. That was until she felt self-conscious that she was turning into her mother. When Jessica had been a child, her mum constantly used to invite her primary school friends around after classes and then spend the evening trying to feed them as much as human beings could fit into themselves. Things hadn't changed by the time Jessica took Adam home for the first time. Her mother had frowned in disapproval at his slender frame and then spent an hour finding out exactly which foods he liked so she could shove them down his gullet over the course of an otherwise quiet Sunday afternoon. It must be a mumsy thing – and the fact that Jessica could happily keep making food for Bex, even though she rarely bothered to make anything for herself, was a worrying development.

That wasn't the only worrying thing.

'What did you get up to last night?' Jessica asked.

Munch, munch, munch.

'I had a walk to the end of your road and then carried on to the shops and back. It was nice to get some air but then it started getting cold again and I was convinced that I'd left the door unlocked. I'm not used to locking things.'

'Had you?'

'No, it's one of those things where you know you've done something but your mind won't switch off from it until you check. I sort of . . .'

Bex tailed off, delving into the mushy remains of her cereal and drawing her free hand across her chest protectively.

'It's okay.'

Scrape, scrape, scrape.

'I'm a bit like that with my bag,' Bex added. 'It's the only thing I have left from my mum's house. All my clothes gradually became too big so I . . . got some more.' She glanced away from the table guiltily. 'I know how to pack it so that I can reach anything I need and then it has this sort of balance to it. But you end up getting paranoid if it doesn't feel right. You think someone's been nicking off you while you've been asleep, so you're constantly on edge. Even though I know I've packed it right, I still get that urge to check it. I know it's mad.'

Jessica knew it wasn't. When you owned hardly anything, it made sense that you'd obsess over the things you did.

'How long were you out for last night?'

Bex lifted the bowl and drank the dregs of the milk at the bottom. 'I don't know – an hour? Should I have stayed in?'

'No, it's not that, it's just . . .' To compound the fact that Jessica didn't know which words to use, Bex took that moment to peer up from the table and smile at her. Whether she'd got her looks from her junkie mother or absent father, Bex really was naturally pretty, despite the slight hollowness she still had in her face. '. . . do you remember the candlesticks from the other room?'

'You said they'd survived a fire.'

'Right . . . it's just they're missing . . .'

Bex bit through the triangle of toast and then carefully put it back on the plate. She kept her eyes fixed on Jessica as she chewed, saying nothing. Jessica tried to read her face, her posture, anything; but there was only a darkness that hadn't been there before. Suddenly Jessica saw the Bex she didn't know – the street Bex, the girl who'd seen and survived things as a fourteen-year-old that Jessica didn't even want to guess about. Her pointed shoulders had angled forward, pressing into the material of the T-shirt, her eyebrows had turned into a V, with vertical crease lines in the centre of her forehead.

Bex's voice had dropped an octave into a forced calmness. 'What are you trying to say?'

'Nothing, I'm asking if you've seen them. Adam says he remembers them being there when he got home from work yesterday.'

'Are you asking if I nicked them?'

'No, I'm asking if you've seen them.'

Somewhere outside a pair of birds were singing to each other, probably complaining about the weather and wondering when it was time to go south. A car blazed along the street in front, wheels spinning as they weaved in and out of the parked cars in a rush to get to the next give way sign. Elsewhere, a lawnmower chugged its way into life, spluttering burnt fuel into the atmosphere as its owner took advantage of the temporary respite from the rain.

Inside, there was only silence as the two women stared at each other. Jessica was good at this game – she had played it enough times – but this was different because now she felt like the guilty one. Bex might have been thinner than she was, perhaps not as strong, as fast, or as experienced, but she was definitely better than Jessica at this.

Without a word, Bex stood, turned, and thundered her way out of the kitchen, up the stairs.

Jessica followed, halting at the bottom of the stairs: 'Bex, wait . . .'

Thump, thump, thump, slam!

Bex ran down the stairs so quickly that she stumbled on the bottom one, only just righting herself before falling. She was wearing a pair of jeans but hadn't done the button up and they were flapping loosely underneath the top she'd been wearing when she turned up on Jessica's doorstep. She was clasping her rucksack, glaring daggers at Jessica as she turned it upside down and emptied everything onto the hallway floor.

Thick socks, fingerless gloves, three identical long-sleeved cotton tops, a T-shirt, a pair of jeans, a rolled-up fleece, half-a-dozen pairs of knickers, bras, more socks, two pairs of balled-up thick dark tights, a metal spoon, a bobble hat, a scarf, a toothbrush, a fork, a knife, a tin opener.

Into the side pockets: a small pair of scissors, a handful of rubber bands, a much stabbier knife that clanged off the wall as Bex threw it in Jessica's general direction.

Jessica stood looking at the sharpness of the blade as Bex dropped the empty bag on the floor and began turning out her pockets, ignoring Jessica's protestations that it wasn't necessary.

A scrunched-up twenty-pound note, a ripped fiver, a handful of coins and a hair tie.

'There!' Bex shouted, fastening her trousers and straightening her coat. 'That's all I own. Most of it's nicked. If you want to take it back to the shops then fine – but I didn't take your stupid candlestick things.'

'I'm sorry, I was just asking.'

Bex began bundling the items back into her bag, far more haphazardly than the way she'd described before. Jessica crouched and picked up the blade: one single piece of metal with a thick handle that slotted all too comfortably into her palm. The blade wasn't particularly long but it was wide and ferociously sharp.

You don't know who she is, Jess.

Bex held her hand out, wanting the weapon.

'Why have you got this?' Jessica asked.

Bex spat the reply. 'Why do you think?' When Jessica didn't answer immediately, Bex snatched it away. 'You think I go around robbing people with it?'

Jessica tried to say no but she'd seen too many reports of knifepoint robberies to think differently and she'd only just finished dealing with Bones. Bex saw the hesitation and then the anger in her eyes was replaced by tears. 'That's what you think of me?'

'No, I . . .'

Bex finished cramming her belongings into her rucksack, stuffing the knife into its side pocket, and slinging the bag across her back. 'Forget it. What do you think it's like being a girl on the streets by yourself? Do you think you tell someone to piss off and they turn around and do it?'

'I know it's not like that!'

Bex pushed past Jessica with her shoulder and opened the front door but Jessica pushed against it, trying to force it closed again.

'Please don't go.'

If Jessica had been in any doubt about how Bex had managed to get away with picking people's pockets, then the teenager showed her once and for all, slipping underneath her arms and gliding through the door in a single fluid movement before Jessica could lay a finger on her. In a flash, she was outside.

Jessica began to follow but Bex was already halfway

along the path, reaching into her back pocket and pulling out the front-door key Jessica had given her. She stopped momentarily, throwing it as hard as she could in Jessica's direction before running away from the house and along the street.

30

Adam arrived home in the early afternoon, reminding Jessica that he'd told her the previous evening he was on a half-day. He knew instantly there was something wrong but Jessica could barely get the words out. She could deal with criminals, threats, bodies, horrendous interviews with witnesses and most other things the job threw at her – but knowing her big mouth had sent Bex back onto the streets to fend for herself was too much to take.

She'd tried to follow but Bex hadn't got by for the length of time she'd been on the streets by being careless. She had headed into the narrow alleyways that ran along the back of the houses opposite Jessica's and disappeared. Jessica knew a little about where Manchester's homeless community congregated but doubted Bex would be appearing there any time soon; not to mention the fact she had to work late that night.

Together, Adam and Jessica hunted through every room of the house but the silver candlesticks that had belonged to his grandmother had definitely gone. Adam asked if they could have been burgled but the more obvious things thieves would have taken – the television, the laptop – were exactly where they always had been. Jessica didn't own much jewellery, certainly nothing expensive, but they checked the bottom drawer of the dresser on Adam's side of the bed. As well as a pendant she'd had since she was a child, it was where they kept their passports and paper driving licences. Everything was there, but Adam insisted things weren't right, saying he'd left them stacked in a different order. Jessica didn't know either way, but he was anal about things like that so she had no reason to doubt him.

The obvious conclusion was that Bex had been through their things but Jessica didn't believe it. Why would she? As for the candlesticks, neither Jessica nor Adam knew if they were worth anything; they'd been kept as a reminder of everything they'd lost in the house fire and almost as a joke because they were so archaic and unlike anything they would otherwise own. Jessica had never lived on the streets but she knew the type of thing that would be sold for cash – and there were enough items around the house that Bex could have got money for if that's what she wanted.

All of that left the disturbing question of what exactly had gone on. Whoever had put the letter with the symbol on through her door knew where she lived – but Jessica had no idea who had left it, nor what they might have broken into the house for. Jessica knew she should tell Adam about it but it was another example of the job following her home and she was carrying too much guilt about that as it was.

The final part of the puzzle was revealed as they checked the doors and windows – the back door was unlocked, even though Adam insisted he'd locked it. That was something that couldn't be pinned on Bex because she'd only ever had a front-door key.

Someone, somewhere had it in for them. Or, perhaps more specifically, her.

Jessica twiddled the dial on the side of the passenger's seat and jolted the rear of the seat backwards until she was as horizontal as she could manage.

'Ow!' DC Archie Davey squealed from behind her, hastily trying to yank his legs out from underneath her seat.

'I told you I was going to have a quick kip.'

'You didn't say you were going to slam your fat arse into my legs.'

In the driver's seat, DC Rowlands sniggered childishly.

Jessica twisted around in the seat, tying herself up in the seatbelt and nearly strangling herself. '*Pardon?*'

Archie was still shuffling onto the other side of the back seat, rubbing his knees. 'Nothing.'

Their unmarked CID pool car was parked in the shadows of a side street leading away from the main road that was still blocked by roadworks in the area where Jessica suspected Cassie and Grace had disappeared. It didn't look as if the workmen digging up the road had done anything since the last time Jessica had been there.

Jessica closed her eyes but the glare of the constantly changing traffic lights from the other end of the street still burned through her eyelids.

A woman's voice crackled across the police radio. 'It's sodding freezing out there.'

Without opening her eyes, Jessica pressed the button to respond. 'It's November in Manchester, what do you bloody expect?'

A second woman's voice erupted from the speaker: 'I honestly think I might lose a nipple if I have to keep walking around in this. Can I borrow a coat?'

Jessica still didn't open her eyes. 'Will you all stop moaning?'

In fairness to the three constables chosen to walk along the main road, the mercury wouldn't have been bothering many, if any, numbers above zero. Each woman strutted along the quarter-of-a-mile stretch beside the area that was dug up, turning left into the next street and then looping back to the unmarked van at the beginning, where a cup of tea and a bloody huge coat awaited them. Then it was the next woman's turn. Between the three of them, they were wearing enough material to completely clothe one of Fat Pat's thighs.

Each of the three was wired up, primarily so their complaints could be piped directly back to the car containing Jessica, Archie and Dave, and to the backup van with two constables, a sergeant and the driver.

'Easy for you to say,' one of the constables shot back, 'you're not the one traipsing up and down with your arse hanging out of a skirt.'

Archie sat up straighter in the back seat, trying to peer around Jessica towards the deserted main road, knocking the back of her seat in the process.

Jessica shot him a dirty look. 'She only said the word "skirt" – it wasn't an invitation.' Dave's head had bobbed up like a startled meerkat's too. 'It's only Joy Bag,' Jessica added. 'You see her every day at work.'

'There's that new one too,' Dave replied, turning to Archie. 'What's her name?'

'All right,' Jessica interrupted. 'It's not a fashion show. We're supposed to be here looking for some nasty bastard, not gawping at anything female with a pulse.'

There was a short pause before Dave replied. 'If that's the case, then why are you trying to go to sleep?'

'What might appear to your untrained eye to be an attempt to sleep is in fact a careful refining of my thought process. Anyway, that's why we're a team – you do the looking out for nasty bastards, I do the careful planning.'

'With your eyes shut?'

'Exactly.'

A couple of minutes passed with only the merest complaint from Jane as she set off for her lap of the estate. Just as Jessica was beginning to relax, Archie cut the silence. 'You know what the problem is, don't you? Our lot aren't slutty enough. Northern girls are tough – they're not walking home in skirts and tops, half of them are out in their underwear. It's all the rage nowadays.'

'He's right,' Dave said.

Jessica hoiked her chair back into position and jabbed a finger in Dave's direction. 'As if you know what girls are wearing nowadays. When was the last time you went out on the pull and didn't end up home alone? The only crush you've got is on him.' She poked a thumb towards Archie in the back seat to prove her point. 'Now – can you please all stop talking because you're steaming up the windows and I can't see a bloody thing.'

Jessica wedged her head into the gap between the seat and the window and closed her eyes again but she could sense Archie and Dave exchanging a look.

She was trying to focus by thinking of anyone who wasn't Bex. Somewhere in the frozen city centre, the teenager was trying to find a safe spot to sleep. No wonder she kept a knife close to hand.

More complaining over the radio – this time because the heels were making Jane's feet hurt.

Jessica blinked her eyes open. 'What time is it?'

Dave's phone lit up the front seat. 'Twenty to ten.'

'Have you got any money on you?'

'Dunno, maybe a fiver?'

Jessica sat up straighter and held her palm out. 'Let's have it.'

Dave delved into his coat pocket and pulled out a scrunched-up note. 'What for?'

Jessica grabbed it and reached towards the back seat. 'Arch, you awake?'

'Aye.'

'I've got a really important job I'm going to trust you with – take this money, head directly down the road, second left, first right and keep going until you see the row of shops. Ignore the pizza place and first row of shutters, then follow your nose. I think I saw a chippy down there. I'm large chips, battered sausage and gravy, Dave's small chips, and get whatever you want.'

'With a fiver?'

'I'm sure you've got a few quid on you. Whatever you do, don't forget my sausage and don't let them scrimp on

257

the gravy. Now – chop, chop; most places around here close at ten so get a move on.'

Archie grumbled his way out of the back seat, complaining that he hadn't spent all the years in uniform and training just so he could end up on the chip run but Jessica told him to stop moaning, else she'd get him tarted up in a short skirt to patrol the estate and see how he liked it.

Icy air whooshed into the car as Archie opened the door, only for him to be shouted at for making Jessica cold.

When it was just the pair of them, Dave angled himself in the driver's seat until he was facing her. 'You're on one tonight . . .'

'It's been a week for it.'

'I've not had time to look at your symbol since we last spoke.'

'Don't worry about it – we'll get there. Izzy said the day crew have been snowed under today too. They've been interviewing everyone at the rowing club's party for a third time, making sure they've not missed anything. They've also had someone trying to sort out the number plate thing for this case but Hamish has been out in his taxi today, so every time he's out picking up a passenger, his number plate flashes up on our system. There are so many places you can buy a plate from nowadays that it's not as if we can narrow down when our guy might have cloned it.'

'Basically, we've got nowhere?'

'Precisely – that's why we're here.'

Over the radio, Jane announced that she was back in the van, as one of the other constables asked if she really had to go out in the cold. Jessica's reply was an unsympathetic 'stop whingeing'.

'Do you really think we're going to get anything doing this?' Dave asked.

'Of course not. It's probably the superintendent panicking that we've not made any progress so he needs us to look pro-active.'

The radio sparked to life again, the constable speaking quietly: 'Bloke in a hoody looking a bit weird on the other side of the road.'

'Probably Archie,' Dave mumbled.

They waited for a few seconds until she added: 'It's all right; he's just taking a piss in someone's garden.'

It really had come to something when that was considered 'all right', but it wasn't as if they could go charging in and arrest him for it when they were trying to remain in the shadows.

'How's it going with your granny?' Jessica asked.

'I told you before—'

'Yeah, yeah, she's not a granny. Anyway, how's it going?'

'She broke it off. It was probably for the best. With her further up north, neither of us fancied the travelling and it wasn't really worth it. We had a good time. Don't worry, I'm not going to jump you if that's what you're worried about.'

'I'd be more worried about you jumping Archie with the way you make eyes at him.'

At the other end of the street, the traffic lights flicked from green to amber back to red again, bathing the car in a bright chestnut glow.

Jessica closed her eyes again. 'Where is Archie with those chips?'

'He's only been gone a few minutes.'

'He could've run. I'm starving here.' Jessica expected a comeback regarding the size of her arse but it didn't happen. When she glanced sideways at Dave to make sure he was listening, his face was pressed against the misty glass. 'You're not licking the windows again, are you?'

Dave frantically rubbed the condensation away and pointed to the end of the street. 'Can you see that van?'

'I had my eyes fixed, remember?'

'Look at the logo on the side.'

Jessica leant across the handbrake, pressing her elbow into his thigh accidentally and squinting into the night. 'Is that . . . ?'

Jessica wasn't sure but Dave sounded certain: 'It's your logo.'

31

The traffic lights changed to green and the van surged forward, sending a cloud of exhaust fumes hurtling into the air.

'What are you waiting for?' Jessica shouted, trying to untangle herself from the seatbelt again. 'Follow that van.'

Dave was clumsily trying to turn the key. 'What about Archie?'

'He's going to have a lot of chips to eat. Go – quickly – they're getting away.'

Dave stalled the car, much to Jessica's annoyance, and then finally made the engine squawk to life, before bunny-hopping away from the kerb and accelerating to the end of the street, then turning onto the main road. In the distance, the van was racing away from them at a speed well above the 30 m.p.h. limit.

Jessica was straining against her seatbelt, trying to get a better view of the van. 'You do know the accelerator pedal's on the right?'

'I'm on it! It's not my fault the car's shite.'

'Do you need to swap seats?'

'God, no. I've not recovered from the last time.'

'So put your foot down then.'

Dave did just that, shutting Jessica up as the back of her head bounced off the headrest and he raced across a junction. Being Manchester, Jessica's agitation was entirely misplaced as the van quickly ground to a halt at another set of traffic lights. Dave eased off the pedal and Jessica radioed the backup vehicle to say they had been called away to follow up an alternative line of inquiry. She consoled them by saying that she had specifically asked Archie to treat them to sausage and chips and that they could thank her later.

Just as they eased in behind the van, the lights turned green and it accelerated again. Jessica reached forward and wiped the condensation away. The rear door of the van had once been white but the lower half was now covered in a grimy layer of filth. Someone had fingered the words 'Your mum's dirtier than this' into the muck but the top half was almost clean, the three-pronged logo stencilled clearly into the upper corner. In crisp, dark letters, a company's name was equally clear next to it: 'BUNCE 'N' BUILDERS', along with a website and a phone number.

Jessica picked up her phone and started tapping away, complaining about the reception, and telling Dave to make sure he followed the van without making it look like they were following it.

'It was only a minute ago you were telling me to floor it,' he complained.

Jessica ignored him, skim-reading the company's official website. 'It's just a normal building company with the usual "phone-this-number-if-you-want-us-to-rip-you-off" spiel. There's no address but there is a list of made-up awards. What type of people give out awards to building companies? "The winner of this year's best brick award goes to . . ."'

'They're out a bit late, aren't they?'

'They probably disappeared for lunch and got carried away.'

'I suppose they could be returning it to the depot?'

'How do you mean?'

'It's a Friday night. Some places have a fleet of vans that they leave in a central place for the weekend. It's still late to be out and about but it's only likely to be the company's owner working this late if it's a one-man operation.'

'How do you know so much about builders?'

'Not building; my dad was a plumber. He used to have to drop a van off every Friday night at his boss's house and then pick it up again on Monday morning.'

'Does that mean you could've been a plumber?'

'I suppose.'

'What happened? You turned up on time for the first day of training and they failed you on the spot?'

Dave burst out laughing but kept an eye on the road and followed the van around a corner, following a sign for Chadderton and the M62.

Jessica's phone burst to life, with Archie's name flashing up. As soon as Jessica pressed the button to answer, the DC's voice screeched through. 'What happened to you?'

'Important business.'

'I've got a giant bag of chips here.'

'So what are you complaining about? There's a van of underdressed constables who'll treat you like a conquering hero if you share with them.'

There was a pause as Archie digested her words before responding. 'Good point.'

The line went dead, with Jessica staring at the blank screen before repocketing it. 'He sounds happy.'

Dave continued to focus on the road, easing off the accelerator so that he didn't get too close to the van. 'Lucky sod.'

Just as Jessica thought the van was about to join the motorway, it took a turn, heading onto a country road with no street lights. Dave dropped back further, steering carefully along the tight turns as the rows of houses were replaced by trees and high bushes. They drove in silence, both unfamiliar with the area. After five more minutes, the van's brake lights glinted brightly in the dark as it slowed to a near halt. Dave had no option other than to keep driving past the address but Jessica managed a solid glance at the sprawling mansion set back from the road before it was gone. She continued to watch through the rear window as the van pulled off the road onto the driveway. Dave slowed and performed an impressive one-handed U-turn and then turned the headlights off as he eased the car back the way they had come, parking under the shadow of a tree on the opposite side of the road from the house.

The only light came from the faint glimmer of the moon trying to fight its way through the clouds and the glow from within the house. Jessica got out of the car, stepping into a muddy puddle and flinching as it squelched through her socks. She hauled her foot out of the sludge and crept across the road, sticking to the shadows until she was standing next to the gatepost.

Dave slotted in behind her. 'What are we doing?'

'Shhh. I don't know yet.'

The driver of the van had already climbed out and was using a remote control to raise the door of a wide garage on the right-hand side of the grounds. His feet crunched distractingly across the gravel as Jessica took in the scene.

The house was enormous – three storeys high and twenty windows wide. At the front were a fountain and a turning circle. Jessica couldn't look at properties this large without thinking of a different mansion . . . a different time. She blinked the drowning feeling away, pinching the webbing between the thumb and forefinger of her left hand, forcing herself to focus. This was a different house.

Dave must have noticed because he placed his hand in the small of Jessica's back and leant in closely. His voice was barely a whisper. 'You okay?'

'Yes. Thank you.'

She meant it.

There were no clues as to whether the house had a number or a name. Jessica could see neither in the grim light. From inside the garage, bright white lights illuminated three other vans parked side by side, exactly as Dave had predicted. Each of them had the three-pronged curved logo in the corner with 'BUNCE 'N' BUILDERS' and the contact details; the only difference was in the level of muck that was attached to the back doors. Parked next to the garage was an old Vauxhall that looked utterly out of place set against the splendour of the rest of the property.

After easing the van in front-first, the driver stepped back out, watching as the door hummed into place. Jessica could see only a silhouette of someone short with broad shoulders and heavy-looking boots. He stood for a few moments staring up at the house and then shrugged, walking briskly towards the front door, tossing the keys from one hand to the other and back again. Somehow, Jessica knew that it wasn't his house and she wasn't surprised to see him pushing the keys through the letterbox and then striding back towards the Vauxhall.

Jessica grabbed Dave's hand and pulled him away from the gatepost, back across the road. 'Quick,' she muttered, waiting for him to unlock the car. Behind them an engine growled to life, headlamps raging bright across the road, illuminating the side of the car and the hedges beyond.

Dave fumbled with the key fob, panicking as he plipped the doors open. 'Shite, he's going to see us.'

He started to head for the driver's side, but before he could move any further, Jessica already had the rear door open and shoved him inside. She launched herself after him, tugging the door closed with her foot. The lights from the Vauxhall dipped down and then up as it bumped over a grate at the front of the property, giving the driver an almost perfect view through their car window. Jessica put the palm of her hand over Dave's mouth and then leant forward, kissing the back of her hand and staring into Dave's eyes. He was so surprised that Jessica could see the red veins blistering out from the whites as the car lights hung on them for a few seconds before the vehicle turned and headed off along the road.

Jessica used the back of the front seat to heave herself up. 'What?' she said, scraping her hair out of her face.

'Was that really necessary?'

'I didn't want him to think we were watching the house.'

'So you'd rather he thought we were dogging?'

'You wish – I only had a second to think.'

'And your first thought was to make him think we were copping off by the side of the road in the middle of nowhere?'

'Well, I didn't hear you coming up with anything; you were too busy panicking.'

Jessica opened the door and climbed out, straightening her clothes. Dave followed sheepishly, brushing his hair forward with his hand.

'What's up with you?' Jessica asked.

'Nothing – apart from the elbow I got in the ribs.'

'Stop complaining and get a move on. If we're lucky there might be some chips left.'

'What are you going to do about the logo?'

'I don't know yet – but if you can haul your arse out of bed tomorrow morning, then I know a cracking place we can get breakfast.'

32

The rest of the night's operation had gone exactly as Jessica had expected: lots of moaning, no results and, perhaps more importantly, a closed chippy, no leftover chips and no one wanting to take the blame for eating the battered sausage. Jessica had no idea why anyone had thought their attacker would be prowling the area night after night after getting away with it twice, but that was far from the only thing going on at the station which she didn't have a grasp upon.

At a little after two in the morning, Jessica called a halt and they headed back to the station tired and cold. Jessica sent a text message to Garry Ashford, caught up on some of the paperwork that seemed to be breeding on her desk, and then snatched a few hours' sleep at home before attacking her alarm for doing what it was meant to and heading to the supermarket cafe.

Garry Ashford was already sitting at their usual table, empty mug stained by milk froth in front of him next to a well-scraped plate showing hints of baked bean juice. The relative calm of the weekday crowd had been replaced by weekend chaos, with children running in all directions shrieking as if possessed, pushchairs blocking every spare piece of floor where there might have once been space to walk, and plates, cups and cutlery stacked on every table.

Meanwhile, frantic, suicidal-looking members of staff tried to take orders, clean the tables, and not break their ankles on the various toys that had been dropped around their feet.

Jessica swayed around a double pram, stepped over a plastic keyboard, trod on a soft giraffe, almost kicked a lad who dashed across in front of her seemingly from nowhere, and finally fell into the chair next to Garry.

'We need a new meeting place,' she said as a baby started wailing just behind them.

Garry looked her up and down. 'You look like you've been sleeping in a bush.'

Jessica rubbed her eyes but didn't have the energy to stop herself yawning. 'I'm on lates, so spent most of the night in the passenger seat of a car.' She nodded over Garry's shoulder, to where Dave Rowlands was trying to extricate himself from the attention of two under-sevens, who were blocking the way into the cafe, demanding a toll. A boy had his hand out as Dave panicked, wondering whether he should give the kid a pound, or simply barge his way past.

Garry picked up his empty mug, clearly disappointed. 'How does it feel that one of your constables is in the process of being mugged by a primary school child?'

'I'm surprised it's taken this long. Twelve's the new sixteen – they're shooting up in the school toilets and impregnating each other, so seven's the new twelve. They're probably part of some international smuggling gang.'

Dave was saved by the children's mother finally noticing her little shites weren't peacefully sitting next to her. She limped across the cafe wearing light grey leggings that were so tight they were almost grafted to her skin, then grabbed her boys by the arms, dragging them away as Dave apologetically ran the gauntlet of the rest of the cafe. He finally took a seat next to Jessica and Garry, putting his elbows on the table and resting his chin on his hands. His hair was flat and unstyled, eyelids drooping heavily.

Garry puffed out a breath. 'You look worse than she does.'

'It's too early.'

'It's almost midday.'

'I didn't get to bed until six and I'm working again tonight.'

Garry held his empty mug up. 'This is a real day out, isn't it?'

Jessica couldn't stop yawning but took the not-so-subtle hint and stumbled her way across to the counter, ordering three cappuccinos, four espressos, two full English breakfasts, a caramel shortcake slice, a chocolate éclair and a scone. Her digestive system was going to hate her for it but after a pair of the espressos and half the breakfast, she was feeling almost human. Even Dave had perked up after working his way through his half of the food and his two espressos. Garry had wolfed down his scone in less time than it had taken Jessica to realise that there was a baby on the table next to them eyeballing her.

When they were finished, Dave shoved the empty plates to one side and wearily took a handful of printouts from his bag. Jessica placed the envelope that had been put through her door in the centre of the table, showing Garry the note inside: 'You've got the wrong man', and explaining that it could only relate to Holden Wyatt. Then she showed him the logo, saying that Damon Potter had been looking into getting a tattoo of it on the day he died, and that they'd spotted it on a builder's van the night before.

Garry took it all in his stride, saying the logo seemed familiar but he didn't know what it was, before taking a photo of it on his phone.

Knowing she was under scrutiny at the station, Jessica had to be careful about the type of searches she ran but Garry and Dave had done the work between them.

Dave was skim-reading the top sheet of paper on his pile, before catching Jessica's eye. 'You know you said last night that you didn't know why the website belonged to just a normal building company? That isn't quite true. Bunce 'N' Builders was only set up in the last two years and is owned by a guy named Freddy Bunce – except that he's also involved with at least three other building companies in the area. Triple-A Builders and One-Stop Builders are in the name of his wife, with him as a director, and FB Builders seems to be entirely owned by him.'

Dave fanned the pages out so that Jessica could see what he'd found.

'Is that some sort of tax thing?' she asked.

'Probably, but there's also a branding thing when you look at the four individual websites. The Bunce 'N' Builders name seems to be more down-to-earth. They advertise saying there's no job too small and I think it's mainly sub-contractors. That's not what's interesting, though.'

Dave nodded at Garry, who had his own pile of papers.

'Freddy Bunce is a name that's vaguely known in news circles,' he said, passing Jessica a printout of an article. She read the top few paragraphs and then snorted in surprise.

'I suppose that explains why he's got such a big house.'

'Exactly,' Garry replied. 'Nine months ago he was given a contract by the council to build a new housing estate for them. No one would reveal the exact amount but we know from freedom of information requests that the council have put in a seven-figure sum; then there's private financing and central government funding too. In all, it's going to be eight figures comfortably. That comes on the back of him building up the original company – FB Builders – from scratch. He was a self-made millionaire before this new money.'

'Do either of you actually know anything about him?'

Garry and Dave were both blank. 'I found his name in Companies House but that's it,' Dave said. 'That's when I called Gaz.'

Garry nodded. 'Apart from the obvious use of his name in the company's name, there's hardly anything about him to be found. The council made a big thing of their social housing push and so they had to use the builder's name on the press release but I couldn't find anything about him at all. That's not necessarily a surprise – there are all sorts of people with money around here who you wouldn't know the name of unless they made a big deal of it.'

'So we still don't know anything?'

Two shrugs. 'No.'

Jessica turned to Garry and raised her eyebrows. She didn't want to ask out loud but the journalist nodded anyway and told Dave everything about Graham Pomeroy and the phone calls he had made to the newspaper. They all agreed that it was unlikely that the *Herald* was the only place the assistant chief constable had contacted, trying to force the agenda over Holden Wyatt. Dave had never met him; the only scrap of knowledge he had was the fact that the man's nickname was Porky.

Spotting the logo on the van had left them with one more mystery – how did it connect a millionaire builder to a tattoo that a dead student wanted, to a letter put through Jessica's door? And what role, if any, did their assistant chief constable have in it?

Dave packed his papers away, adding Garry's to the stack, but there was a general sense of confusion. 'There is one thing you could do,' Dave said.

'What?'

'Ask.'

'How do you mean?'

'Phone up the number on the back of Freddy's van, say you like the logo and ask where it comes from.'

Sometimes the simplest solutions were the easiest to overlook.

Jessica took her phone out, checked the number on the website and then called it. A woman answered after one ring: 'Bunce 'N' Builders, how can I help you?'

Jessica cupped a hand around the mouthpiece, trying to drown out the sound of the screaming children. 'Can I speak to Freddy, please?'

'Freddy who?'

'The owner, Freddy Bunce.'

'Oh, Mr Bunce – he doesn't work Saturdays.'

'Do you know when he'll be back in?'

There was a pause and some tapping on a keyboard. 'Can I ask who's calling, please?'

'I'm from the council . . .' Jessica shrugged at the two men, who were clearly unimpressed at her feeble lie.

The female voice on the other end suddenly sounded more attentive. 'The council? Right, I . . . er, hang on.'

The line went dead, but Jessica covered the mouthpiece again just in case, whispering: 'It was the best I could think of.'

'Why didn't you say you were a customer?' Dave asked.

'I don't know – I wasn't thinking.'

There was a pop and then the woman's voice blurted out again: 'Sorry – I've just checked and he's going to be in the office on Monday. I can book you in for an appoint-ment, or perhaps there's something I can deal with?'

'I've got a really busy day on Monday. Perhaps if you can remind me of your office's address, then I'll see if there's a time I can drop round.'

The receptionist gave Jessica an address in Prestwich and then hung up.

Jessica turned to the two men. 'Did either of you know they had an office?'

Two head shakes. 'I assumed they worked from that house,' Dave said.

'At least it gives us somewhere to go on Monday.'

'Are you really going to ask him about the logo?'

Jessica smiled. 'If I can't think of anything else. It's not as if I can ask the DCI. If we're going to look into this, then it has to be us.'

They were interrupted as one of the boys who had tried to mug Dave screeched past their table, making a nee-nar siren sound before clattering into a chair and going flying elbows first across the polished floor. Before anyone else could move, the woman in the leggings was on her feet again.

'Kevin, what have I told you about running?!'

She shuffled from her seat towards her stricken son and helped him to stand. Jessica thought Kevin was upset at falling but there was a twisted fury in his face. As his mother brushed some dirt from his arm, he reeled back and punched her hard on the shoulder.

'Ow! What did you do that for?'

Kevin started to run off again but his mother held his wrist.

'What have I told you about hitting people?'

The boy was still snarling. 'What?'

She released him, wagging a finger in his face: 'Look at this.' She rolled the sleeve of her jumper up, revealing a mass of purple, blue and black on her shoulder. She was practically pleading with him. 'You don't realise how much you're hurting Mummy. It's painful when you hit people – do you understand?'

Kevin's brow was furrowed, body still tensed. 'Yes.'

'Really? Look at these.'

She pointed at her shoulder again and her son peered in, his stance softening a little. 'I'm sorry.'

His mum rolled her sleeve back down. 'Are you really?'

'Yes.'

'Okay, come here.' She pulled her squirming son towards

her and hugged him, before leading him back to the table.

Dave and Garry looked at Jessica blankly. 'What was all that about?' Garry asked.

Jessica was fairly sure she knew the answer: 'If you grow up seeing one person hit another person regularly, then you think that's normal.'

'You think she's got someone at home who beats her up?'

Jessica shrugged. 'She wouldn't be the first. There's not a lot we can do unless she comes to us, or something happens in public and it's reported.'

Garry was peering over Jessica's shoulder towards the woman, who was now going through the menu with her sons. 'I've never understood why people stay with someone who hits them. It's not love, is it?'

Jessica was about to reply that things were never that simple when she remembered visiting Joe Peters when his girlfriend Leanne was missing. He'd placed their baby in his lap and massaged his own upper arm. Their next-door neighbour had told Jessica that they fought physically as well as shouting at each other. Perhaps it hadn't been the baby that had taken the toll on his arms; maybe they hit each other too.

And then she remembered that he wasn't the only person she'd noticed nursing bruises recently.

33

Jessica walked into the maroon waiting room of Tim's Taxis and took a seat. The smell of the furniture and feel of the velvet was so vivid that she could've been back in that working men's club all those years ago, trying to figure out quite how people could become so angry over a piece of tape stuck to the floor. It was Saturday afternoon and raining, as ever, so a smattering of shoppers who had somehow figured out that the shop front with the lunchtime supplies sign was actually a taxi office were sitting around waiting for a lift home. In the back office, she could hear Tim talking into the radio. Jessica quietly showed her identification to the shoppers and asked them to leave.

Grumble-grumble-don't-you-know-it's-raining-out-there – and then the office was empty.

Jessica sat, running her hand across the tattered material of the chairs, listening to the rat-a-tat-tat of the instructions as Tim called them out to his drivers. In the background, there was commentary of a football match on the radio.

Tim's voice rang out from the office: 'Mrs Smith, your car's here.'

After a few moments with no reply, he repeated himself, before appearing in the doorway. He stopped mid-sentence, taking in the almost empty waiting room, before noticing Jessica.

'You're back.'

'Yep.'

Tim flicked his long hair behind him. He was wearing jeans, a checked shirt and a leather waistcoat, like a cowboy who'd taken a wrong turn somewhere in the middle of the Atlantic and lost his hat. 'Hamish is off today. I think he might be at the football.' He pointed a thumb over his shoulder. 'Bloody United are one down.'

Archie would be fuming.

'I'm not here for Hamish.'

'Oh.'

'Other half not around today?'

Tim's features twitched slightly. 'She has things to do on Saturday.'

'Tell me about her.'

'Why?'

Jessica stood and straightened her top, half-turning so he could see the earpiece she was wearing but deliberately not looking at him. 'Because I'm asking.'

'You heard us arguing the other day?'

'Yep.'

Tim sighed, sitting on the dark red bench and resting his head in his hands. 'I will never, *ever*, understand women. It's like you're a different species.' Jessica said nothing, waiting. 'I don't know the official terms but she is mental. You've seen her, right? She's stunning – I mean, what's someone like her doing with someone like me? When we met a few years ago, it was at this rock night in this place just off Canal Street. They host them once a month or so and my band was playing.'

'You were in a band?'

Tim looked up, half-smiling. 'Metal – I'm on drums. We broke up in the summer because our lead singer wanted to go out to LA and try his luck with some band who'd put an advert on the Internet. Anyway, a couple of years ago, we were doing our thing. It's just off the gay area, so you get a mixed crowd – straight, gay, old, young, queens, trannies, you name it. Normally you get your head down, bash away and hope for the best. It was a Sunday night and I noticed this blonde in the front row – just stunning. I say I noticed, but we all did – it's not like you could miss her. After we were done, we walked off and the first thing anyone said was, "What about that girl at the front?" You know what it's like with lads.'

He went quiet for a moment as the commentator on the radio went up an octave to describe a goal that would cheer Archie up wherever he was.

Tim undid his waistcoat. 'Okay, maybe you don't know what lads are like.'

'I do.'

'So you can guess the type of thing we were talking about. We were third on but it was a Sunday, so there wasn't anywhere we could head out to for a few more drinks because it was closing time. Plus we had to load all our gear back into the van. I wouldn't have minded heading down Canal Street – but one of the lads kept saying he didn't want to get bummed.'

He caught Jessica's eye, his lip curled upwards. 'I know, right? It's not the seventies any more – but that's the way he was. We ended up going back into the main area of the pub and propping up one end of the bar. We didn't have a big following or anything, but we wouldn't usually have done that because people get a bit crazy at the end of the night and you're just after a quiet beer with your mates.'

'But the blonde was there, right?'

Tim's slightly crooked features erupted into a full smile. He tucked his hair behind his ears and began fiddling with his waistcoat again. 'Aye, she was. Our singer – the guy that went off to LA – he was there ordering rounds for everyone, flashing the cash, thinking she was there for him. You couldn't talk to anyone because the final band was on and it was too noisy – but you could see it in the guy's eyes that he thought he was onto a winner, except that every time he turned around to talk to the barman, she squeezed my knee.'

A blast of wind rattled the windows at the front but Tim was back in the moment. 'After about an hour, the final band had finished and they called last orders. He held out his arm for her to cling onto as if he was going to take her home and she had no say in it – but she just smiled sweetly, gave him a wink and said, "I'm already sorted, thanks." His eyes almost popped out of his head when she turned around, grabbed my hand and marched me out of the pub. Mine too, if I'm honest.'

'What's her name?'

'Mandy. The thing is, the pretty ones are always the mental ones, aren't they? My ol' dad used to tell me that when I was at school – ignore the prettiest ones, they'll always fuck you up. Course, the only thing that fucked him up was the booze.'

Tim stood abruptly, making Jessica step back quickly, one hand close to her ear. Tim held his hands up to show he didn't mean anything by it, nodding towards a filing cabinet in the corner of his office.

'Do you wanna check out the top drawer? It should be unlocked.'

Slowly, Jessica crossed the room, not taking her eyes from him until she was at the cabinet. She slowly pulled the top drawer open, ready to leap back at any moment in case there was a nasty surprise in there. Instead, there were three bottles of vodka.

'Take your pick,' Tim called out.

Jessica took the one that had already been opened and returned to the office, handing it to Tim, who had sat again. He unscrewed the lid, took a breath, and then swigged heavily. 'Course, he may have had a problem with this stuff but he had a point – you go out with a normal girl and it doesn't take three hours to get ready to go out. You go out with a normal girl and she understands that money don't grow on trees. She gets that when you're in a band, it's mainly playing dingy small pubs for a couple of hundred quid that you've got to split between you.'

'Mandy's not a normal girl?'

Tim laughed and took another mouthful, holding the bottle close to his nose and breathing the fumes. 'How many girls do you know who look like that and are perfectly normal?'

Jessica shrugged – there was little point in arguing but she didn't think looks came into it. Tim took the gesture as an admission that he was right.

'Exactly, but that just meant she was the type of woman you couldn't say no to. After a year or so, she wanted to get married and I went with it. I've never wanted to be married, never wanted kids, a house, any of that stuff. I just wanted to go on the road and play drums. Suddenly, there I was in this two-up, two-down wondering what the hell I'd got myself into.'

'How long ago was that?'

Jessica already knew the answer – she'd done her home-work before coming anywhere near the office – but that didn't mean it wasn't worth hearing it from him.

Tim started counting on his fingers. 'A little over a year and a half.'

'But somehow you moved from playing in a band to owning a taxi company?'

'Stupid, right? We'd been playing all around the area and not really getting anywhere. There were a few hardcore fans who'd come along and make up the numbers but there was never going to be any money in it. When I was on my own, that would've been fine. I was happy living place to place, eating cold pizza and doing a gig every few nights. That was never going to suit Mandy. She liked the idea of going out with someone in a band, she just didn't want me actually being *in* the band – especially one that wasn't successful.'

'So it was her idea to start a business?'

Tim swigged his vodka again. 'Not exactly. It took me ages to realise but I did eventually figure out why she started seeing me – it was because she really thought the band was good. She thought we were playing local pubs at that point but then within a few months we'd be doing bigger clubs, then arenas. She thought she was buying into something that was going to be successful. When I realised that, I kept thinking I'd let her down. She thought she was marrying a soon-to-be rock god, but instead she got the hairy bloke at the back with drumsticks. None of that bothered me; I just wanted to play drums – if it was in front of a dozen people in some back room, that was fine. If it was in front of thousands of people at some festival, I would've treated it the exact same way.'

'I understand.'

Jessica really did. To an extent, on a different scale in a different line of work, she was the same. Big case or small case, there was a bad guy to catch. If you started prioritising one victim over another then you'd begin to see them as numbers, or targets, anything except people.

Tim took another drink, going silent as the commentator on the radio got excited again – United were two-one down.

'Bastard defence again,' Tim muttered, just as the internal radio rattled into life. One of the drivers was trying to get in contact but Tim ignored him.

'Anyway, when I realised I'd let her down, I was trying to come up with something else I could do that she'd appreciate. She was always watching these shows about these crazy parties that people have, where they hire out a zoo for the day and invite their mates; or they have pop stars arriving in a helicopter to serenade them for their birthday.'

'I once saw one where this girl dressed up as Snow

White,' Jessica said, 'and hired seven dwarves to do her bidding for the day. All her guests were dressed up as Disney characters.'

Tim laughed. 'Like I told you – girls are mental. What lad could ever come up with that?'

Jessica couldn't disagree.

Another drink, smaller this time, and Tim continued: 'On those shows, all the girls hire limos to get them to places. I told Mandy that we should start a limo hire business and I've never seen her so excited. I think she had visions of a fleet of pink cars chauffeuring her everywhere, and that we'd have a couple of others that would bring all the money in.'

'But it didn't work like that?'

'Did it bollocks. Do you know how expensive those things are? Then you've got to get insurance and everything else. It'd have been cheaper starting a helicopter company. The bank was having none of it – but the guy suggested that if we could run our own taxi company, the limos would become a natural extension if we were successful.'

No wonder they were both miserable.

'One thing led to another, and suddenly I'm here seven days a week trying to give directions to clueless drivers. Meanwhile, our lead singer's off in America, where I should be.'

Jessica held out a hand and took the vodka bottle from him. He didn't resist as she screwed the lid on and rested it under her seat.

'Who hit who first?'

Tim had hunched forward with his forearms resting on his knees but his head shot up, searching for Jessica. She held his gaze as he said: 'I've never touched her.'

'When did she first hit you?'

Likely without realising, Tim began scratching at his upper arm, returning his stare to his feet. 'Around a year ago.'

'Have you ever told anyone?'

'What do you think?'

'You know why I'm asking, don't you?' Tim didn't reply, tapping his foot and listening to the football commentary, so Jessica continued: 'You must realise there's a reason why no one's come through that door in the last twenty minutes – and it's not because you haven't sorted the sign out yet. We're trying to give you the chance to do things quietly. It will look better for you in the long run.'

'How many people have you got out there?'

'Enough.'

'But you came in by yourself?'

It could have sounded threatening but it didn't.

Jessica shrugged. 'I know this isn't the life you want – and I don't mean the band or the taxis, maybe even Mandy. The other stuff.'

No reply. Still two-one in the football.

'We're going to have to interview you properly at the station, take fingerprints, talk to your drivers to find out who was running the desk on the evenings you weren't – we'll put it all together with your help or without it.'

'What if I don't want to go quietly?'

Jessica tilted her head again, brushing her hair back to make the earpiece as clear as it could be.

'If I were you, I really wouldn't repeat that.'

34

Jessica was feeling smugger than Hamish Pendlebury and his scumbag solicitor. She sat in the chair across from DCI Cole's desk staring at the row of commendations and certificates pinned to the wall, listening to him on the phone waffling on about procedural stuff to someone she couldn't care less about.

Eventually, he hung up and spun around in his chair. He still wasn't looking *at* her, instead focusing on a spot just over her shoulder in a way that made Jessica so self-conscious she wanted to turn around and see if there was anything there.

'I did say you didn't have to come in today,' Cole said, still watching the spot.

'It's a Monday morning – what else am I going to do with my time?'

'Give me the rundown.'

This was the moment Jessica had been waiting for all weekend. Rarely did she gloat over her achievements, knowing that anything she was pleased about was tempered by other people's heartache, but here, for once, it felt good to stick a big middle finger up to whoever was making her life hard. From where she was sitting, it was the man across the desk.

Jessica began to read from her notes: 'On Saturday

afternoon, I arrested Timothy Stoddard for the murders of Cassie Edmonds and Grace Savage. The profile said . . .' Jessica paused, fumbling with her papers to find the right one, '. . . that our killer "had a deep-seated hatred of women", which is a fairly woolly and wide-ranging claim but at least had me thinking. I'm not actually certain it's the case here – but Tim Stoddard had a definite hatred of one woman: his wife Mandy, even if he loved her too. Neither of them have any history of abuse, no criminal record and nothing that could've naturally drawn us to them.'

That was a relief in itself – it was always a problem explaining to the media why you'd missed an obvious clue in the first place.

'Myself, DC Rowlands, DC Davey and PC Jamieson visited the taxi office when we were investigating Hamish Pendlebury and overheard Stoddard arguing with his wife. She ended up hitting him.'

'Did you do anything at the time?'

'Well, er, no – I mean—'

'Carry on . . .'

And so it continued: Jessica talked Cole through how they'd got to this point and he nit-picked at every detail where they could've done better.

Proving the case against Stoddard was not likely to be difficult. They had the motive that he felt emasculated by his wife and so had taken it out on other women; the physical evidence to show that he himself had been frequently beaten; they found the spare number plates he'd commissioned for his taxis, including a copy of Hamish's which he'd then used on another black cab; and the knife which had been wedged into a gap in the wall hidden behind the desk in his office.

Search teams were continuing to go through everything he owned but the only thing they lacked was either a full confession, or any evidence of the body parts he had cut from the women. Sooner or later, forensics would likely match something from his body to one of the victims. Given the size of his fingers and the way the women had been beaten, there was every chance they might find a partial fingerprint, or at least be able to match the shape of his digits to the wounds.

Under interview, the only thing he would talk about was Mandy. At first, his story about how they'd met had made Jessica feel slightly sorry for him. They had both had certain expectations from their relationship and neither had ended up happy. By the time he'd recycled it for the fifth time, Jessica was feeling less on his side, thinking that she had no desire to hear from either him or his slapper of a wife – in more than one sense – again.

DCI Cole was taking intermittent notes but still hadn't looked directly at Jessica, nor said well done. After a case was solved, everyone said well done – even those who hated you. Even Fat Pat from behind a cream bun. It was the done thing, like a reflex, or when a mate told you they were pregnant and you said 'congratulations', instead of 'oops, see you in sixteen years'.

Jessica waited for Cole to say something, even if it was to bring up Holden Wyatt again – not that she'd had much to do with that case in the past week. Without peering up from his papers, he dropped a different bombshell instead: 'The press conference is downstairs at eleven.'

'I don't want to be in it.'

'Tough – the assistant chief's coming over and if I've got to put up with Rosie, then so do you.'

'Who?'

'Rosie – the chief PR woman: you know her.'

'I know, I meant which assistant chief constable?'

Cole peered towards her, still not at her. 'Graham Pomeroy.'

'Oh, darling, you look fabulous!'

Jessica rolled her eyes and balled her fists tightly. This was not what she needed on any day, let alone when she was going to be in front of television cameras trying not to swear. She was sitting in an office off to the side of Long-sight Police Station's media room, away from the clatter as news crews bumbled their way inside, dripping wet, and began plugging in their cables into what definitely wasn't an electrical fire waiting to happen.

Rosie was the head of PR for the whole of Greater Manchester Police and, luckily for Jessica, they had very little contact with each other. It was probably a good thing for Rosie too, seeing as Jessica started to understand how the mind of a murderer worked on every occasion she spent any amount of time with the woman.

Rosie flicked a strand of Jessica's loose hair forward as Jessica tutted and nudged it back again. Rosie was some-where in her fifties but seemed to be the last person to realise, dressing at least half her age and wearing enough make-up to single-handedly put Debenhams in profit. 'Jessica, darling, it's *so* wonderful to be working with you again. You look *so* fabulous with your hair up or down, I just wonder if perhaps you could have it a little more down? The lights out there are going to be really bright and if it's down, it'll frame your face a little better.'

For God's sake.

'I'm not sure people will be worrying about what I look like quite so much as the fact we'll be telling them that we've caught someone who killed two women and they can go out to play bingo again.'

Rosie roared with laughter that even sounded genuine. 'Oh, "bingo", you're so funny. That's *so* fabulous. You're wasted here. Honestly, I've still got a few of my old showbiz contacts if you want a nudge.'

'You're all right.'

'Well, if you're sure. You've got one of those faces for it.'

'Faces for what?'

'Television, darling! What else? Look at the skin on you – and the hair. I know people who'd kill for hair like that. Well, not kill – perhaps maim.'

Rosie launched into guffaws of laughter, finishing with a huge coughing spurt that sounded as if a lung might come up. Meanwhile, Jessica tucked her hair back behind her ears and frowned at her own reflection in the mirror. This was humiliating. The only reason she hadn't sneaked away was that she was already in Cole's bad books for an unknown reason – that and because she wanted a glimpse of Porky Pomeroy in the flesh. Well, not exactly a glimpse, but she wanted to know if he'd recognise her.

When Rosie recovered, she stepped closer again and began holding various hair ties next to Jessica's ear, tutting and saying things like, 'No, that'll never do' and 'Hmm, maybe'.

Jessica glanced at her phone – five to eleven.

Rosie began humming to herself. When she caught Jessica's inadvertent scowl in the mirror, she broke into a sickly sweet smile. 'Oh, sorry, darling – you can't break old habits. When I was a performer, I'd be singing all the time. Some said I was destined for a career in the West End but one thing led to another . . .'

She clearly wanted the question to be asked but Jessica didn't trust herself to say anything. Rosie continued anyway: 'Young love intervened, of course. I suppose they say all things are meant to happen for a reason. I wouldn't have got my part on television if I'd gone to the West End.'

Jessica had met Rosie on four occasions – and every time she'd heard the story of how Rosie had 'starred' in a television soap. One of the constables had spent an afternoon phoning around to get the real truth – that she'd once been an extra for a dozen episodes and then killed off, but no one had the heart to break the myth.

'I still keep an eye on the trade papers, of course,' Rosie continued, oblivious to the fact that Jessica wasn't interested. 'Only last week I saw they were advertising for a new musical in Manchester. I'm a little too old now – but I could make a few calls if you wanted to audition?'

'I'm okay, thanks.'

'Are you sure? They say life begins at forty.'

Jessica had been in the middle of taking a sip from a

cup of water, but spluttered so badly that she sent the liquid sploshing over the side. 'Pardon?'

'I said life begins at forty – if ever you're going to switch careers, then it should probably be sooner rather than later.'

Jessica batted Rosie's hand away, untied her hair, ruffled it up and then retied it as messily as she could. 'I'm not forty.'

Rosie was frozen in position, hands hovering close to Jessica's head. 'You're not?'

'No.'

'Oh.'

'I'm not looking to change career either and I can't sing.'

'Oh darling, half the actors in musicals can't sing – they just pipe the lyrics in. It's all about having a pretty face.'

Jessica pushed herself up from the stool and headed towards the door, picking at her trousers and wondering how DCI Cole and Porky Pomeroy had got out of being annoyed by Rosie. 'I'm fine, thanks.'

As she headed along the corridor towards the entrance to the Longsight Press Pad, Rosie trailed behind, heels click-clacking on the floor. 'That's fabulous, sweetie, but I haven't briefed you about what to say yet.'

Jessica ignored her, fumbling her way across the mass of wet cables, waving a non-committal 'hello' to the handful of journalists she recognised and didn't want to throttle, and then taking her place on the end of the table that looked like it had been dipped in GMP branding. She poured herself a glass of water and then caught sight of herself in the monitor. Shite, she really should have let Rosie sort her hair out – she looked like she'd stepped off a rollercoaster. Her mum would definitely be watching this too.

Jessica turned her phone off.

Suddenly she was blinded as the dazzling white lights clinging to the gantry above fizzed to life with an ominous crackle. 'Fu . . .' Jessica disguised her surprise with a cough as she blinked ferociously, trying to see anything beyond the edge of the desk. From the side, DCI Cole emerged out of the heavenly glow, Rosie pinning a radio microphone to his jacket and telling him how fabulous he looked. Without a word, he edged past Jessica and took his seat in the seat farthest away.

Moments later, the bulbous figure of Porky Pomeroy stepped forward from the other side of the light, creating a near-eclipse as he waited for Rosie to clip a microphone to his lapel. He waddled up the three steps to the stage, puffing out his mighty bright red cheeks in exhaustion. His hair wasn't as thin or as grey as Cole's, but that wasn't saying much considering they barely had enough to weave a sock between them. Jessica focused on his blubbery face, wanting him to look at her to gauge the recognition. It was only when he got to the top of the steps and his head swivelled to face her that he gave Jessica the tiniest of glances and a minuscule nod, the type you might give to someone in the street if you thought you recognised them but had no idea who they actually were. Then he peered back up again and attempted to squeeze his way into the seat between her and Cole.

Jessica had been waiting for even the merest hint that he knew who she was but there was nothing. It was the kind of look he'd give to anyone who worked for GMP – 'Hello, do you know how important I am? Where are the biscuits?'

Rosie came up the stairs and attached a radio microphone to Jessica's collar and they were away. Despite any reservations about who Graham Pomeroy was and what his job entailed, Jessica had to admit that the assistant chief constable was the consummate pro during the press conference. She kept staring steadily at her glass of water, not wanting to catch anyone's eye just in case they asked her something ridiculous, but he relished the moment. First he blathered on about how proud he was of the people who'd worked on the case, then it was how their tireless efforts had got a dangerous man off the streets, how everyone's sympathies went out to the victims' families, how it proved GMP was in the 'painful process' of reforming following the Stretford Slasher scandal of a few months previously, and so on and so on.

After he'd finished speaking, it was time for the questions, which meant a race to ask the most moronic thing possible. Jessica tried to say as little as she could, doing the normal thing of praising everyone she'd ever worked with, met, spoken to, once glimpsed on a train platform in Cardiff and so on. Rule one of corporate PR bullshit: if in doubt, talk up other people, thereby making yourself seem not only like the genius that you are but humble at the same time. After that, pay tribute to the families of the victims, then pay tribute again, and – if you can – go for it a third time as well. Rule two: you can never pay enough tributes in press conferences. Because she had to, Jessica praised everything about the families, from their patience to their cooperation. She was one step away from eulogising their tea-making skills before realising that the teas had been made by the support officer.

Jessica knew she sounded like a recording of every other police press conference ever given, with the added complication – and skill – of simultaneously trying to ignore Rosie's thumbs-up and Tourette's-like nodding from the side.

It was everything that she hated about the job: the spin, the shite, the 'aren't-we-great' attitude. And now, here she was: one of them, nodding along and spouting the same old bollocks everyone else always did.

As soon as the conference was over, Jessica unclipped the microphone, dropped it on the floor, downed her water, and slipped through the side door into the corridor. She walked as quickly as she could through reception, telling Pat where he could shove his custard creams when he made some crack about her hair, and then bounding through to the area where the constables congregated, looking for the first familiar face.

As it was, DC Rowlands was at his desk, hammering away at his keyboard.

'Busy?' Jessica asked.

'Yes.'

'Tough, let's go for a ride.'

'Shall I take all the stuff we've got about you-know-who?'

'Yes.'

Dave picked up a thick wallet while Jessica signed out a marked pool car. She edged out of the car park, around the satellite vans and reporters' vehicles and then ambled along Stockport Road.

'You all right?' Dave asked.

'Why?'

'You're driving under the speed limit.'

Jessica ignored him, keeping the car steady. 'Did you see the press conference?'

'No.'

'Liar.'

'All right, I did. It was bloody horrendous – but that wasn't your fault.'

'That was Pomeroy next to me. I could practically hear his arteries bursting.'

'I saw the caption. Did he say anything to you?'

'Not a peep.'

Jessica headed towards Alan Turing Way, a personal favourite every time she saw the sign, not because she had any interest in mathematics or code-breaking, simply because it made her think of her father. As a child, he had taught her about the Second World War and how Britain had cracked the German Enigma code. She later found out that, despite his efforts for his nation, Turing had been prosecuted for being gay, which made her like him even more. Perhaps that was where her natural suspicion of anyone in authority came from? He was useful enough to help win a war but not allowed to love in the way he wanted.

'Are we going to Freddy Bunce's office?' Dave asked.

'Not yet.'

'Where are we going?'

'You'll see.'

Jessica followed the road out towards the motorway and then took the turn that led towards the country road they'd been on while tracking the builder's van. It was deserted, and when Jessica reached the large house, she parked the police car across the driveway, blocking it.

'What are you doing?' Dave asked, unclipping his seat-belt and looking over his shoulder.

Jessica had already opened her door. 'If they've got any neighbours, I want them to notice the car. Wait here, I'll be right back.'

Before he could protest, Jessica was out of the car, scrunching her way across the driveway towards the front door. She used her anger at the press conference to block out the claustrophobia the towering building evoked in her.

The doorbell offered an old-fashioned, satisfying 'ding-dong'. Jessica waited, pinching her own skin again, making herself focus, wondering if she would ever get over those feelings when she visited a large house.

After a minute, one of the large double doors swung open, revealing a perfect Barbie doll of a woman staring in confusion past Jessica towards the police car. 'Is there a problem?'

Jessica showed her identification, making sure the

woman had enough time to memorise it. 'Are you Janine Bunce?'

'Yes, there's not been a problem with Freddy, has there?'

'No . . . I was simply wondering where he is.'

After first seeming a little worried, Janine's posture changed entirely, a frown spreading across her otherwise smooth skin. 'Is there something wrong?'

'I'd rather speak to Mr Bunce.'

'He's working.'

'Can you tell me where?'

Janine bit her bottom lip, tilting her head to the side and peering over Jessica's shoulder again. With her bleached hair, long nails and slim waist, she didn't exactly seem the type to own two building companies. 'Gimme a minute.'

Janine pushed the door until it was almost closed and disappeared back into the house. Jessica turned towards the car, watching, feeling that buzz inside her. This was like the old days. One minute, two minutes, three minutes. There was no way Janine had simply popped inside to check an address.

After another thirty seconds, the door opened again. Janine hesitantly passed her a sheet of ripped-out notepad paper: 'I've written down his office address for you.'

Jessica read it and then put on an over-the-top performance worthy of Rosie. 'Wonderful, you've been just fabulous. Thank you so much for your help.'

She turned and strode back to the car, sitting in the driver's seat but not switching the engine on. She passed the address to Dave.

'Didn't you already have this?' he said.

'Yep.'

'So why didn't we just go there?'

Jessica stared through the side window towards the house where Janine was still standing in the doorway, watching them. 'Because sometimes, DC Rowlands, I just can't resist pissing people off.'

35

As plans went, it was ridiculous – but the lack of recognition from DCI Cole, the nit-picking, and the way she'd turned into everything she despised at the press conference, all coupled with the guilt that somewhere Bex was living on the street because of her, meant that Jessica didn't care.

Sometimes, getting on people's nerves was the only way to make herself feel better.

Jessica drove carefully towards Freddy's office, taking her time and expecting her phone to ring at any moment. The fact it didn't heartened her even further.

His office wasn't quite in keeping with the rest of Freddy's empire that Jessica had seen. Far from the sprawling driveway and enormous house surrounded by the greenery of Greater Manchester, the breeze-block building on the edge of an industrial estate not far from Prestwich wasn't exactly what Jessica had expected. It was only when she thought about it that it made sense: if you were looking to hire a tradesman, you'd pick a bloke with a phone number that had the same area code as yours and a local-sounding voice. If they could give you an address somewhere in the city limits, then all the better. People didn't want someone who lived in a giant mansion renovating their house; they wanted down-to-earth working-class types who'd come in, call them 'luv', and at least have the good grace to pretend they weren't ripping them off.

Jessica did a loop of the estate, driving slowly in the hope that people would notice and speculate about what was going on. Sometimes the image of a police car was far more powerful than anything an officer might actually have to say. As they passed the office a second time, Jessica could see a man standing in the now open doorway, watching them, arms folded. Jessica drove to the next roundabout, went the entire way around it, and then came to a halt next to the metal gates of Bunce 'N' Builders.

Although they'd seen four white vans at his house on the Friday evening, there was another here, plus one with the One-Stop Builders name on the side. Jessica got out of the car slowly, holding her phone to her ear, even though there was no one on the other end. She leant on the bonnet, watching Freddy watch her, having a conversation with an imaginary person. He was short, not fat but not thin either; he definitely didn't have the physique of a builder. It might have been something he'd done in the past but his arms were too thin for it now. Even though it was only fractionally above zero, he was wearing a T-shirt, trying to prove he wasn't cold. Dave had put his file on the back seat and was standing next to the passenger door looking between the two of them. Jessica felt a sudden pang of guilt for bringing him – he'd done more than enough for her in the past and yet she'd dragged him out to go along with something stupid again.

Jessica started walking towards Freddy, still having a conversation with nobody.

'. . . Well, if that's what he says, then that's what he says – I can't make all the decisions. Use some initiative. All right, see ya, bye.'

She hung up and continued walking, stretching her hand out to shake. 'Mr Bunce?'

Freddy nodded, not taking his eyes from her. They were narrow and calculating. It was easy to pigeonhole people but it wasn't the type of glare you'd get from someone who spent their time doing a day's work and then headed home. But then there weren't too many builders who owned huge mansions in the countryside. He gripped her hand tightly, squeezing in the way only a dickhead could. You could tell a lot from a handshake.

Jessica didn't grimace, instead handing him her identification and heading past him into the office without being invited. Freddy kept his cool, following, with Dave at the rear. The interior was smaller than it appeared from the outside but far less grim than she expected. Directly in front was a small desk with a young woman sitting behind it, connected up to a telephone headset; off to the right was an open doorway which Jessica made her way towards.

Through the side door, there was a tall leather chair behind another desk and rows of filing cabinets. A computer sat there, monitor off, while heat blazed from the radiator under the window. On the desk was a pad of headed notepaper, the company's name and the three-pronged logo clear at the top.

'I gather you visited my house,' Freddy said, returning her ID and perching in the leather chair, leaning forward.

Jessica went to sit opposite, in a seat that looked a lot less comfortable. 'Correct.'

'You could have called if you wanted me. My secretary can always get hold of me if necessary.'

Jessica looked to Dave and slapped herself on the head. 'I really should have thought of that.'

'What do you want?'

'It's a bit embarrassing, really.'

'What is?'

'It's more of a personal visit than anything official. I was going about my business in the centre at the weekend, doing a bit of shopping, getting wet, that sort of thing, when I saw one of your vans driving past. I was confused because it was a Saturday and I couldn't believe there was a builder actually working on a weekend.' Jessica paused, hoping for a reaction, but Freddy was unmoved. 'Anyway, the reason I'm here is because I was curious about your logo.'

She pointed to the notepaper on the desk. Freddy glanced at it and then scratched the back of his shoulder, still spikily leaning forward. His forehead appeared to have a permanent frown. 'You know my wife called me from the house, terrified. She thought I'd been in an accident, then she thought there was something else wrong when you insisted on talking to me.'

'Sorry.'

'And then you took that car of yours all around the estate before leaving it directly outside my business.'

'Sorry, I wasn't thinking.'

'No, you weren't.'

A hint of a smile crept across Jessica's face. It felt like being told off at school and finding it increasingly funny, no matter how many times the teacher said it was serious. Usually, she'd have the self-control to hide it but she allowed her lips to curl just long enough for Freddy to notice.

He sounded even more irritable when he spoke next: 'Why are you interested in that symbol?'

'Nothing in particular, I was just intrigued by it.'

'There must be a reason.'

'Nope: I'd just like to know where it came from.'

Jessica and Freddy stared at one another, each waiting for the other to break first. Unlike when she had been facing Bex, Jessica knew that this was a contest she'd win.

Freddy finally leant back in his seat, trying to appear relaxed, even though he clearly wasn't. 'It was just something I thought of.'

'When?'

'Why does it matter?'

'I'm curious.'

'Years ago, when I was at school.'

'So you were thinking about logos for your business while you were still a student?'

'I suppose.'

He was lying, which only made Jessica more curious about why he'd hide it. The forced relaxation looked even more awkward because his eyebrow was starting to twitch with anxiety.

'Does it mean anything in particular?'

Freddy began tugging at his T-shirt, pulling the shoulders

forward and then shrugging them back again. 'It was just a shape I fancied. Perhaps I saw it once?'

'Did you?'

'What?'

'See it once – or was it something you thought of?'

'I, er . . . I'm not sure why any of this matters. You said it wasn't official business . . .'

Jessica stood, exchanging a glance that she thought had a significant look about it with Dave, even though he clearly didn't know what she was thinking. 'No, no, that's everything. Sometimes we have to ask the odd question. You know what it's like with all the Eastern European tradesmen coming in and doing shoddy jobs; then there are all sorts of tax scams going on and rogue traders building these crumbling properties. I'm sure you don't have any problems with those types of thing.'

'Is there some sort of problem?' he asked.

'Not at all – I know what a busy time it must be for you with that juicy new social housing contract. What was it worth, eleven, twelve million?'

'I, um . . .'

'No matter, I'm sure you're a busy man.' Jessica took a business card from her pocket and placed it carefully on top of his desk. 'Never mind, if there's a problem, you can always call the station where I work. The number's on there.'

'Am I suspected of something?'

Jessica laughed again. 'Have you got something to hide?'

'Of course not.'

'There's your answer. Cheerio.'

Jessica hurried to the car as quickly as she could, muttering a 'come on' to Dave as they moved. She started the car and then handed him her phone, watching through the side window as Freddy stood in the doorway.

'What was all that about?' Dave asked, turning her phone over in his hand.

'Honestly? I'm not sure yet – but I bet you ten quid that my phone rings in the next five minutes.'

36

Jessica was grateful she didn't put any money on it, because it actually took six minutes for her phone to ring. 'Don't sit there looking at it, answer it,' she hissed.

Rowlands fumbled with the buttons before finally putting it to his ear. 'Hello.' Moments later, he held the phone out in Jessica's direction: 'It's for you.'

'Who is it?'

'The guv.'

'Tell him I'm driving.'

Dave went through the rigmarole of being the middle man in the conversation between DCI Cole and Jessica but she had known what the gist was going to be from the moment she'd walked out of Freddy's office.

'He wants us back then?' Jessica clarified when Dave hung up.

'"Now", apparently, as he shouted half-a-dozen times.'

'Interesting.'

'Aren't you worried?'

'No – because now I know for certain that there's a link between that logo and whatever it is that's going on at the station. As soon as we'd pulled away, Freddy was on the phone to someone complaining about us.'

'Porky Pomeroy?'

'Perhaps – but at least we know for certain it's not just me being paranoid.'

Jessica hadn't seen Detective Superintendent William Aylesbury for almost two years. He had been a DCI when she was first promoted to detective sergeant. At first, she'd not known what to make of him; he was more someone she'd tried to work around, rather than with. Gradually he had grown on her – and then he'd been promoted to DSI to oversee multiple stations. Over time, his appearances at Longsight had become less frequent and then he'd stopped coming at all, occasionally summoning DCI Cole to see him, or taking part in a conference call. In all that time, he'd never bothered to seek Jessica out – not that he had any reason to.

Which was why Jessica was so surprised to see DSI Aylesbury sitting in DCI Cole's office, legs crossed, cradling a cup of tea and laughing as if he was at a comedy gig. When he spotted her through the glass, he smiled and waved her inside.

He'd always had a presence, partly because of his height, but also because of his trim, athletic physique. He stood to shake her hand, reminding her of quite how imposing he was. Now in his late fifties, his hair was looking thicker than while he had been DCI and, if anything, he appeared fitter than she remembered, with a hint of a tan too – which definitely hadn't come from Manchester. If everything people said was true, then it was more likely a Portuguese golf course. He was surely only a year or two away from retirement – unless one of the assistant chief constable roles became available for any reason and then he'd be one of the first names on the list.

'Jessica, Jessica,' he said, over-pronouncing each syllable and being too familiar. 'It's so good to see you – and a DI now too.'

Jessica shook his hand: 'Sir . . .'

DCI Cole's face was blank as he watched from his side of the desk. Any hilarity that had been in the room moments before was gone.

'Sit, sit,' Aylesbury said, grinning too much. 'I figured it was about time we had something of a catch-up. I've been hearing good things.'

'Thank you, Sir.'

'You looked good on television this morning – I know what a ruck those things can be but you dealt with everything exceptionally. I know Graham was delighted with how everything turned out.'

'That's good to hear, Sir.'

Ugh. Jessica hated the sound of her own voice.

'I hear you were largely responsible for the arrest of Timothy Stoddard and that it was clean as well; no rough-housing, no shots fired.'

'It wasn't just me, Sir, there were other people involved – a true team operation.'

The two men exchanged a quick glance and Jessica thought she saw the I-told-you-so look from Cole. She was cooperating in an entirely non-cooperative kind of way, not quite giving the wanted answers. Aylesbury had a small hint of frustration in his voice when he continued. 'But it *was* you who talked him down, so to speak.' He swirled his hand around in front of his chest, stammering, before finally finding the right words. 'I suppose in old parlance, you made him come quietly.'

'I suppose so, *Sir*.'

Jessica knew he wanted details but she was also aware that he wasn't simply here for a cosy catch-up.

Another quick exasperated flicker between the two men: 'Would you care to say how you managed that?'

'Womanly charms? I've got a good range of pilfered jokes as well. Have you heard the one about the price of Velcro?'

Cole cut in: 'It's all on tape – she was wired in case Stoddard actually confessed.'

Aylesbury studied Jessica with a scratch of his chin and a considered nod. 'Aah, very good, very good. So you can speak with great diplomacy when required . . .'

Jessica allowed herself a grin. 'That's very kind of you to say, *Sir*.'

'Of course, this is only the latest in your run. I believe you brought a man into custody for the tattoo robberies?'

'That was DS Diamond, *Sir*.'

'And then there was the unfortunate incident with the, ahem, Stretford Slasher last spring . . . ?'

'That really wasn't much to do with me, *Sir*. I was just here.'

'I'm hearing all sorts of rumours about the outcome of Matthew Pratley's investigation into our district following that case. You know they're publishing early next year?'

'I don't really listen to station rumours, *Sir*.'

'Probably the best policy – but there could be all sorts of

shake-ups and redeployments. For some, it will be the end of the road but for others – people who get their heads down; those with good track records – this entire mess could turn out to be a blessing.'

'I'll bear that in mind, *Sir*.'

Aylesbury nodded, leaning forward and picking up his tea again. He took a swig, before returning the cup to the saucer, twisting the handle around until he was satisfied it was perpendicular to the edge of the table. So far, he'd been as subtle as a bloke shuffling his way into Sandra's: if she kept her head down and didn't cause too much trouble in the next couple of months, there could be all sorts of interesting opportunities come the new year.

Aylesbury sucked on the inside of his cheek, still watching Jessica. 'This all comes, of course, after what was an extended break . . .'

Jolts of ice prickled along the back of Jessica's neck. He couldn't use that against her: no one could. Cole knew as well as anyone what she'd been through. She angled slightly in her chair to look at the DCI behind his desk but he was deliberately avoiding her gaze.

She kept her eyes on Cole, even though it was Aylesbury she was talking to. 'As far as I'm aware, everything was cleared at the time with HR and anyone else it needed to be signed off by.'

Aylesbury adjusted his position until he was perched forward, diligently trying to catch her eye. 'Quite, quite – and you've been largely hitting your targets since returning, of course . . . so, with all of that in mind, can I ask where you've just been?'

Jessica could feel Aylesbury staring at her but didn't give him the satisfaction of acknowledging it. Finally, the buttering up and vague hints were over and they were getting to the point.

'I've had a busy weekend,' Jessica replied. 'I was moved to lates at short notice but then I had to come in yesterday to deal with Timothy Stoddard. I need a new pair of shoes, so I figured no one would mind if I nicked over to the Arndale for half an hour. My timesheets have been ridiculous this month anyway.'

Silence.

DCI Cole stared at his desk. DSI Aylesbury stared at Jessica. Jessica stared at the certificates on the wall behind the pair of them.

'You went shopping?'

'Not technically, *Sir*, I didn't buy anything.'

'But you're saying you were in the city centre?'

'I was in a few places – just a quick in-out. I didn't think anyone would mind; it's quiet around here.'

'Right . . .'

Aylesbury sounded as if he was about to launch into some sort of life lesson, so Jessica cut him off. 'Can I ask why you're interested, *Sir*?'

The question took him by surprise. 'Sorry?'

'It's just we've not seen you in months. Obviously that's none of my business – it's just curious that you're suddenly interested in what I'm up to. If you like, I can email you minute-by-minute updates of my whereabouts but I doubt there'll be a lot in there to interest you. If I'm not here, I'm usually at home. Sometimes I stop off at the supermarket on the way back. If you catch it at just the right time, there's a sweet spot for when they reduce the price of all the bakery items. It's an art form trying to get there at the right time.'

The DSI's eyes were narrow, piercing through Jessica. This was definitely not Grandpa Aylesbury; this was someone firmly on the greasy pole of corporate promotions. 'Perhaps your time would have been better spent trying to find the evidence needed to secure a conviction against the person who killed Damon Potter, instead of harassing innocent people?'

'If you ask DCI Cole, I'm sure he'll be able to tell you that I've been shuffled sideways in that case. Witnesses were brought in at times I wasn't here, Holden Wyatt was charged by someone else. I'm not omnipresent, *Sir* – and the whole point of what we do is that we don't know who's innocent or guilty until we've actually done the whole investigating thing.'

A pause for another sip of tea and then the rearrangement of the handle so it lined up with the desk.

'Are you saying you don't believe Holden Wyatt is guilty?' Aylesbury asked.

'I don't know, *Sir*, like I say – shuffled sideways.'

Aylesbury turned to face Cole and Jessica knew that this exact conversation had already been predicted.

'Wyatt has already admitted multiple assaults, including upon Damon Potter. We are going to look increasingly ridiculous if he is tried for an assault on someone, while we still don't have anyone for the actual death. The victim didn't put himself in that bin.'

'That's what I've been saying the entire time – but I fail to see how a group of students first saying they saw Holden at a party and then saying they didn't proves that *he* was the one responsible for dumping the body. We're not even certain whether Damon choked on his own vomit after drinking voluntarily, or if he was forced.'

'In that case, it's your job to get on with proving something and to stop messing around with other things – and that message comes down from on high. Do you understand?'

Jessica understood far better than he knew: Pomeroy.

'Yes, *Sir*.'

'Good – then I'm sure there's something you can find to be doing.'

Jessica stood and headed towards the door, turning at the last moment. 'Oh, by the way, it's a rip-off.'

Aylesbury and Cole exchanged a confused look. 'What is?' Aylesbury asked.

Jessica pulled the door until it was almost closed. 'The price of Velcro.'

Slam.

37

Jessica hurried down the stairs, ignored Fat Pat bleating about something or other, and went to find DC Rowlands. He was at his desk but barely visible behind a stack of ring binders, cardboard folders and printouts.

He acknowledged her with a nod but was clearly occupied.

'Got a minute?' Jessica asked.

'No – and I mean it this time.'

Jessica perched on the edge of his desk anyway but he continued working. She lowered her voice. 'We're definitely onto something – I've just been bollocked by Lord Aylesbury himself.'

Dave nodded but seemed nervous.

'What's up?' Jessica added.

'Nothing – be quick; I'm busy.'

'It sounds like Pomeroy's throwing his weight around – and given the size of him, that can never be a good thing. You're going to have to keep your head down—'

'What do you think I'm doing?'

Jessica glanced up from the desk, looking around the rest of the main floor. As she did, she felt a dozen pairs of eyes shoot down towards their desks, pretending they hadn't been watching. The only person who was still looking in her direction was DI Franks, who had moved to

Longsight recently. They had equal rank but Jessica had ended up with her own office largely by accident, while he had to share. They rarely worked together and, if anything, were in a constant silent competition over who had the most outstanding cases. Jessica wasn't overly competitive – but it was always better to be ahead of the other inspectors.

Franks was a greasy corporate type: all neat side-partings and crisp suits. He'd have been in his element at the press conference that morning and was exactly the kind of person who'd go far. If he ever left the station, then Jessica didn't know about it. He got on with his job, brown-nosed the right people and had the initiative of a plank of wood.

And he was smirking at her, half-pretending to be reading a document.

Dave was still tapping away on his keyboard and Jessica lowered her voice even further: 'What's going on?'

'I've been moved over to work for Franks. There was that raid on the post office van last week and—'

'Franks the Fanny?'

'Yes.'

'Funtime Frankie?'

'Yes.'

'Wanky Frankie?'

'Jess . . .'

'You've got to work for him to stop you working with me?'

'I didn't ask – I was *told* this was what I was doing, so I got on with it.'

Jessica stood. 'I think I'm going to—'

'Don't.' Dave's eyes were wide, pleading with her. 'Leave

it,' he hissed. 'It's not going to do any good if you get into some stand-up row with Franks in front of everyone. Why do you think everyone's watching you? That's what they're expecting. It's not as if this was his idea anyway; this has come from higher up.'

Jessica tapped him on the shoulder, acknowledging he was right – but she also had no doubt that her hastiness in taking him with her to visit Freddy Bunce had brought this on. Bunce had complained to someone, which had led to DSI Aylesbury turning up and laying down the law. There wasn't an awful lot they could do to her while she was still the golden girl from arresting Timothy Stoddard – so Dave was collateral damage.

She broke into a smile, gave a nod to Franks to show all was well and then whispered the word 'sorry', before heading to her office.

The final few hours of Jessica's shift were a waste of time. The one thing worse than getting to your office to find a pile of messages, memos and emails was getting to your office to find nothing. With Timothy Stoddard in custody, she found herself scratching around for work. Cases had been coming in as ever – it wasn't as if scroats stopped scroating and thieves stopped thieving – but, for whatever reason, they'd been picked up by, or assigned to, other people around the station. It wasn't paranoia any longer: Jessica was being marginalised and she knew it. Dave had been looking into the logo for her but there was no way he'd have time to do anything now, while Jessica's increasing anxiety about her position meant that she was wary of doing anything on her computer that wasn't one hundred per cent work-related.

For once, Jessica allowed herself to do nothing other than catch up on the paperwork that had been building over the past few weeks. She signed everything she had to, got her unread emails down to the hundreds, rather than thousands, and even risked a sandwich from the canteen. For many, it was the ideal shift; not for Jessica. She hated sitting around, detested doing nothing, bristled enough at the papers she had to file, let alone spending the best part of an afternoon doing it. But she did it anyway – because somewhere there was someone waiting for her to step out of line. The moment she did, they'd come down hard upon her, bringing up every previous transgression or questioning of authority. For now, she had to play their game and follow Dave's lead: keep her head down and smile.

She finished her shift exactly on time, a little after the sun had set. Mist had drifted in from the coast, hugging tight to the canal and river, bathing the city in its wintry, ghostly grip.

Jessica had spent so much time in pool cars that driving her own felt slightly alien. It was certainly a lot smoother than the clunky gearboxes and loose brakes that the shared cars offered. She waited at the traffic lights around the corner from the station as Manchester's usual rush-hour traffic hummed angrily back and forth.

She sat, watching in silence as the traffic lights across the four-way junction flicked back to orange before changing to red. Ahead of her, cars squealed as the lights for Jessica's direction changed. Hurry, hurry, hurry. All too quickly they were back to orange and Jessica did what everyone else did – accelerated through, getting across the line narrowly before the lights were red again. She heard car horns blaring behind, wondering who had beeped her, then she realised it wasn't her they were angry at. She had sneaked through the lights but so had the car behind.

As Jessica drove, she kept an eye on the car in her mirror. It was hard to identify the exact make and model; all Jessica knew was that it was a dark hatchback that appeared relatively new. For a reason that she wasn't quite sure of, Jessica turned off the main road, heading towards Eccles, rather than her own Swinton home.

The car followed.

As she reached another line of traffic, Jessica turned right without indicating, heading into a quiet housing estate.

The car followed.

Knowing something was up, Jessica eased off the accelerator, staying below the 20 m.p.h. speed limit, passing a closed primary school next to a church and then edging into a slow-moving line of traffic on the parallel main road. She watched her mirror as the hatchback moved into the row of cars two behind her. Cars stop-started along the main road, bright headlights puncturing the growing fog. Jessica turned up the heater to stop the windows from misting but the drop in temperature made her think of Bex, who was out somewhere in this.

Brake-clutch-accelerate.

Slowly, the vehicles moved forward, a car-length at a time, until Jessica reached a four-way junction. She turned right, heading in the direction she actually wanted to go, stamping on the accelerator and powering into the murk. Behind, she heard the roar of an engine. Conditions weren't overly hazardous but visibility was poor, so Jessica allowed herself only the briefest of glances in the mirror to see that the car had followed. In the gap she had given herself, Jessica could see the number plate, repeating it over and over to herself until it was almost chant-like.

Easing off the accelerator and back under the speed limit, Jessica used her car's Bluetooth to call Izzy's mobile.

'Jess?'

'Have you got a pen? Write this down.'

'Hello to you too. Hang on.' There was a muffled clattering of objects and then: 'Go on then.'

The car was now too close for Jessica to see the plate clearly but she had repeated it so often to herself that the letters and numbers had a rhythm to them anyway. She read the details out twice, making sure Izzy had them correctly.

'Is this a normal check?'

'No – don't put it through our system and definitely don't use your own name.'

'What do you want me to do then?'

'Don't get yourself in trouble but I know that you know people. If you can be creative . . .'

'I'll see what I can do.'

Jessica took the most direct route she could towards Swinton, trying and generally succeeding to avoid the Salford traffic and then taking the side streets until she was almost home. All the time, the car stuck close to her, the driver apparently unconcerned that it was obvious he was trailing her. Every now and then, Jessica would catch a brief glimpse of the driver as the street lights cut through the fog. It was definitely a male with a dark beard but aside from his hairy knuckles, the tinted glass and sun visor made it hard to see anything else.

She turned onto her street but kept driving past her house, taking a brief glance at the empty driveway that meant Adam wasn't yet home. On colder days, he usually drove. Sometimes he took the bus, and if he was feeling particularly unhinged, he'd even been known to walk.

Jessica wasn't sure what to do. She doubted the car was following her to find out where she lived – they could discover that if they *really* wanted – but, on the other hand, if it was someone trying to scare her, they were doing a bang-up job.

She reached the end of the street, turned left, then left again, and made her way along the road that ran parallel to hers. When her phone began to ring, she pulled over and answered it.

Izzy's voice sounded tired: 'I've got it.'

'You didn't do anything to get yourself in trouble, did you?'

The car that had been following glided past Jessica's, the driver not turning his head to look at her. She watched as the red tail lights disappeared into the fog.

'It's all fine,' Izzy replied. 'Have you got a pen?'

'Hang on.' Jessica dug into her door well and tugged out a pad and pen. 'Go on.'

'The car is registered to a company that deals with golf

course maintenance. The address is an actual course in Northenden.'

'Aren't there about five courses out there?'

'No idea but I've got the name.'

Jessica wrote 'Brooklands Golf Club', thanked Izzy and then spent five minutes on her phone looking up its details. Apart from using its website to declare the forward-thinking policy of allowing women to become members, and to advertise that the function room was available to hire, Brooklands seemed to be the same as any other golf club: boring and green.

With no sign of the car that had been following her, Jessica drove back around the estate and parked on her drive. Adam's Smart car was already there, so she blocked him in as she usually did. She turned off the headlights and spent a few more minutes sitting by herself in the dark, watching the mist swirl, breathing the cool air, all the time trying to ignore the relentless, overwhelming sensation that someone in the gloom was watching her.

38

The mist clung on through the night, eating into the fabric of the city until the streets resembled a Victorian postcard. Jessica slept in short spurts, waking every couple of hours and finding herself inexorably drawn to the window where she peered out towards the dim orange glow of the street lamps that were fighting a losing battle against the light-devouring clouds. Each time, she persuaded herself there was somebody close by, watching the house, watching her; each time she spotted nobody. One time she woke convinced there was somebody downstairs, waking Adam and asking if he could hear it too. As soon as he was awake and listening, the sound went away again – he said she must have imagined it but she couldn't have done.

She wasn't paranoid.

There really were things going on around her. The dark hatchback *had* followed her home. DCI Cole *had* been acting strangely and had isolated her. She *had* been put on nights at short notice and then the colleagues closest to her had been moved onto other cases.

But then there were reasons too. Perhaps he had isolated her *because* she'd gone off on her own one too many times. She *had* let Bones run, she *had* visited Tim and missed the significance of Mandy hitting him, she *had* dropped out of a late-night surveillance and gone off on a wild-goose chase after a van because it had a strange logo on it. Then she'd gone and harassed the company's owner and his wife about it. Those weren't the actions of someone completely in control of themselves, and especially not those of a competent police officer who was supposed to be supervising other people.

Then there was Holden Wyatt: DSI Aylesbury had a point, didn't he? How many times had Holden lied to her? He first failed to tell her about the party, then denied knowing Damon, then stayed quiet about all aspects of the initiation and abuse. By his own admission, he'd done awful things to Damon – so why wouldn't he be prime suspect? Perhaps it was one more piece of hazing that had got out of hand – a drinking game, or some sort of forfeit. Damon had drunk too much, taken drugs, and then Holden had panicked and got rid of the body in a bin that would have been emptied the next day if the bin men hadn't been on strike. It wasn't that far-fetched. Yet instead of getting to the bottom of it all, she'd gone off and done her own thing, convincing herself that DCI Cole was against her, despite everything he had done for her over the years.

And now, she couldn't sleep, climbing out of bed over and over to stare out of the window into the night where no right-minded person would be.

The only thing Jessica had to cling onto was the letter that had come through her door – 'You've got the wrong man' – and that symbol, whatever it meant. Anyone could have sent that, though. One of Holden's friends, his family. Even a colleague having a joke at her expense. She'd annoyed enough people over the years.

But what about the candlesticks? They were such stupid things that she and Adam had never used and likely never would. Who even owned candlesticks nowadays? Adam used to joke that if they bought some lead piping, rope and a pistol, then they could take a knife from the kitchen, plus a spanner from the toolkit, and have a real-life Cluedo set. They'd only kept them because there was so little left after the fire that it felt like they shouldn't be thrown away. Yet someone had moved or taken them – and Jessica didn't believe it was Bex.

She lay in bed, eyes open, listening as the wind whistled along the passage at the side of the house. She could hear the bins clattering into each other, perhaps tipping over and sending a sprawl of food packaging and other waste onto their driveway. She wasn't paranoid, was she? The letter and the missing objects proved it – someone was doing this to her. Weren't they?

Jessica felt the hand gripping her arm, squeezing gently, shaking her.

'Jess . . .'

Her eyes shot open in disorientation. Where was she? Who was touching her? In a flash, she grabbed the person's wrist, blinking quickly and trying to clear her vision.

'Ow, shite, Jess, it's me!'

'Wuh . . . Adam?'

'Who else?'

Jessica let him go, rubbing her eyes and trying to move her legs. It dawned on her that she was in bed – her bed –

but her eyes were so heavy that things didn't feel right at all. Somewhere there was a beeping noise too.

'What's going on?'

'Your alarm's going off but you slept through it.'

Jessica finally made her legs obey, hauling herself into a sitting position and picking up her phone from the nightstand before fumbling with the screen until the noise stopped.

'I never sleep through my alarm – not any more.'

'I know.'

Adam delicately pushed the hair away from her face; his hand was wonderfully warm against her skin. Jessica reached out to pull him towards her.

'Are you okay?' he whispered.

'I think so. What time is it?'

'It's only half seven. I was downstairs and heard the beeping. I thought you'd be up and about but it kept going on, then I realised you hadn't woken up.'

Jessica clung to him tightly. She constantly teased him about how thin he was but it wasn't because he under ate, it was simply his natural build. When he was beside her, it made no difference because he was still warm and could hold her the way she needed, her face slotting into the crook of his shoulder as if it was a missing puzzle piece.

The paranoia of the early hours had now dissipated but it was still there in the darkest parts of her mind, niggling away, making her question herself.

She couldn't believe she'd slept through the alarm. When she was at school, she'd needed her father to come and shout at her that it was time to get up. When she moved to Manchester and lived with Caroline, her sleeping patterns were all over the place – sometimes she'd sleep through an entire day without knowing she'd done it; other times she'd sleep for a couple of hours here and there. Caroline could sleep through anything but Jessica never had that blessing. More recently, she would always wake up exactly four minutes before her alarm went off, regardless of when she set it for. She even started playing around with the time, moving it forward and backwards by a single minute to see if it would affect her body. Instead, every time without fail she would wake up those four minutes early.

To go from that to not hearing her alarm at all was unfathomable.

Adam started patting Jessica's back gently, letting her know that he wanted to release her, but Jessica wasn't ready and began kissing his neck instead. She could feel his hands hesitating on her shoulders before tapping her again as he pulled himself away.

Jessica felt stung. 'Are you—?'

'I have to go into work early. Sorry.'

'Oh.'

'We've got time for a really quick breakfast together if you want.'

It wasn't what Jessica wanted but it was marginally better than nothing. She quickly got dressed, and then joined Adam in the kitchen. He had poured himself a giant bowl of Coco Pops and was shovelling heaped spoonfuls into his mouth. It was his usual pick-me-up but didn't exactly leave her tingling with affection, or particularly hungry.

Sod him if he didn't want to kiss her back.

Jessica made herself some toast in a huff and sat eating in silence until Adam broke it: 'Are you worried about her?'

The question took Jessica by surprise. 'Who?'

'Bex. I know you didn't want to talk about it, but . . .'

'It's fine.'

Adam stood, crossing to the sink and rinsing his bowl and spoon, before picking up the empty cereal box. 'Anything else for the recycling?'

'I don't know why you're so picky over it – everything ends up in the same landfill. It's just a giant council-run scam.'

'If it is a scam, then what do they get out of it? Surely it's more expense to pick everything up separately and then dump it in the same place?'

Jessica ignored him and his stupid logical reasoning, angrily biting into her toast. Bloody smart-arse.

Adam shrugged at her lack of reply and unlocked the back door. He'd only been outside for a few moments when Jessica heard him calling her name. Did he really need help putting the bins out? For crying out loud.

Jessica ate her final mouthful of toast and crossed to the back door, standing in the frame, stunned at the scene of utter carnage. All their bins were lying horizontally, plastic, paper and rotting food in a stinking heap on the ground. The dew had mashed the magazines she'd thrown out into the concrete. Jessica could see scraped remains of meals she'd eaten, bills she'd shredded and thrown out, a skirt she'd decided she was never going to wear again, tissues, some oranges that had gone off, a picture frame that had fallen off the wall and broken. Fragment after fragment of her life over the past fortnight sodden and left on the ground.

Adam was standing a little off to the side holding his hands out in confusion. 'What on earth caused this?'

'It was windy . . .'

'Not hurricane-windy.' He pointed towards the other side of the street where their neighbours had left their wheelie bins on the side of the road. 'It hasn't happened to anyone else's.'

'I don't know.'

'Could it be a fox?'

'I . . . suppose.'

Jessica had only ever seen one fox in Manchester and that was when she lived in a flat that backed onto a wooded area and a golf course. There was nothing like that around here.

'I'm going to need some gloves or something . . .'

It was only when Adam stepped back towards the house that Jessica saw the glint close to his feet. She pointed – 'look' – but Adam had seen them too. In among everything they had thrown away were their missing candlesticks.

Jessica and Adam exchanged a confused look. It was pretty much the only place they hadn't checked, but then why would they? Jessica had begun to believe that the unlocked back door was simply Adam's mistake but now it appeared as if someone had let themselves into the house while Bex had been out, picked up the two shiniest things, and put them in the bin. The only reasoning was that they had done it to mess with her mind – but who would do that?

Together, Jessica and Adam cleaned up the mess in virtual silence. If Adam suspected there was anything else amiss then he kept it to himself. Sometimes he understood her so well.

When they were finished, they had a quick wash-up and then Adam gave her a kiss goodbye and left through the front door.

'Jess . . .'

This time when Adam called her name, Jessica shivered. She could sense it in his voice: a confused, worried tone that wasn't usually there.

She made her way out of the front door, not wanting to see what was waiting for her. When she got over the doorstep, all she could do was stare. It should have made her angry but Jessica felt only justification because this confirmed she wasn't imagining things.

Adam knew exactly what to say again: 'I suppose this proves it was done by someone who knows you.'

Jessica laughed, feeling a single tear run down her cheek at the same time. She reached out and took his hand, pulling him to her as they both stared. If anyone else had said it in any other context then she would have been hurt, angry, or both.

'Is someone out to get us?' Adam whispered, seriously this time.

'I don't know.'

'Bex?'

'No.'

'At least they know how to spell.'

Jessica smiled but there was a lump in the back of her throat and another tear. She hadn't imagined everything: the proof was in front of her, spray-painted along the side of her car in capital letters.

'BITCH'.

39

Adam said he would take the car to a garage to have it resprayed but Jessica didn't want to let him do that for her. Instead, she drove just over a mile to the workshop closest to them and sat in the car by the side of the road waiting for the mechanic to turn up while passing pedestrians stared at her. A few cars even beeped their horns in recognition – 'wahey, there's a bitch we can taunt'.

Jessica called the station and told Pat she was going to be late due to 'car trouble', which wasn't even a lie – even if he did cough to show how suspicious it sounded. Either that, or he choked on a piece of pastry.

Shortly after half past eight, the mechanic turned up, rubbing his chin with a wry grin. He was younger than her, stubbly, cute. Jessica got out of the vehicle knowing she looked a mess: she'd not had time to sort herself out properly before getting in the car, while there had been a mixture of tears and self-said pull-yourself-togethers. Jessica wasn't even sure why she was upset; she'd been called far worse and had terrible things happen to her but somehow this felt more targeted.

The mechanic glanced from Jessica to the car, and back to Jessica again. He had dark eyes matching his hair and a grin that she guessed he usually kept for casual lean-ins on the bar when he was trying to chat a girl up. Ten years ago Jessica might even have gone for it.

He finally settled on Jessica, lopsided smirk on his face. 'So, whose boyfriend did you shag?'

It was so inappropriate that Jessica couldn't stop herself from laughing. That inevitably brought more tears, which the handsome mechanic with the rough hands was only too happy to indulge with a friendly grin.

Sometimes it was nice to feel wanted, even if it was by a too-young man who likely thought you were a total slapper.

After a bit of what she assured herself was most definitely not flirting, Jessica caught the bus to the city centre and then a second bus out to Longsight. Pat made a point of checking his watch as Jessica finally arrived at the station; her only comfort was that it wasn't raining. She was about to head past reception towards her office when he got to the point: 'You're wanted upstairs.'

Jessica had half-expected it and refused to give Pat the satisfaction of scowling in front of him as she headed up the steps.

This time, Cole didn't make her wait, waving her in while somehow managing to be utterly dismissive at the same time. 'Car problems?' he said, not getting up from behind his desk.

'I had to take it to the garage.'

He nodded but she couldn't work out if he believed her. 'After yesterday's . . . events . . . Superintendent Aylesbury and myself have decided that your talents would be better used away from looking into Damon Potter's death. We've brought an inspector in from the North district to start all over again. It was thought that a fresh set of eyes might bring a fresh perspective.'

He paused, waiting for Jessica's reaction, but it was only an official confirmation of what had been going on unofficially for days. 'Since when?'

Cole didn't even look up as he replied tersely, 'About an hour ago – when your shift started.'

When she said nothing, he picked up a printout of an email: 'We've had something come in overnight which you can work on.'

He handed the sheet across and then turned away and began typing. Jessica read through the details of the case – something menial that a DC could do with their shoelaces tied together.

'Any problems?' Cole asked, not looking up.

'Of course not, Sir.'

'Excellent – then we'll talk again later in the day. You can let yourself out.'

Jessica said nothing, spinning and walking out of the room. Her first thought was to tell Dave or Izzy what had happened overnight but she knew Rowlands would be under Wanky Frankie's thumb – hopefully only his thumb – and that Izzy would be busy. Too many people around the station knew they were friends and she didn't trust anyone other than Izzy, Dave and . . .

'Archie, my old pal – how are you doing?'

Jessica accidentally slapped him on the back harder than she meant, making the constable partially regurgitate a bit of sausage. Given he had bought it in the station's canteen, that could only be a good thing.

He coughed up a bit more and then struggled to down a mouthful of water in between splutters. 'Give over, Jess.'

She had a quick glance around to make sure there was no one nearby and then crouched to whisper in his ear: 'My office, five minutes.'

Four and a half minutes later and Archie peered around Jessica's door, eyebrows raised in curiosity.

'Shut the door,' she said. 'And lock it.'

Archie did as he was told. 'Yaright?'

'Did you just ask if I was all right?'

'Yeah.'

'Only a Manc could turn four words into one – "Are you all right?" Anyway, I've got a job for you.'

'Okay.'

'But it needs to be between you and me.'

'I won't say owt.'

'How's your memory?'

'I can tell you who scored the goals at any United match I've ever been to. Go on, test me.'

'No, thanks. I'm going to give you a couple of names but I don't want to write them down, email them, text them or anything. They also can't be connected back to me. Are you still up for it?'

Archie was rocking on his heels again in the way he had been when he was ready to square up to Holden. He was excited, thinking it was proper police work for once. 'Aye, it's sound.'

'First one is a person – Freddy Bunce. He owns some

building companies, so does his wife. There's next to nothing about him in our system or in any news archives but I want you to try to find something that links him to Brooklands Golf Club in Northenden. Perhaps he's a silent partner somewhere, or whoever owns the course used to be a neighbour. Something like that.'

'Freddy Bunce and Brooklands Golf Club – no worries.'

He turned to leave.

'Don't you want to know why?'

Archie turned back, looking surprised. 'Sorry?'

'Don't you want to know why I'm asking you to look into things for me?'

He shrugged. 'Don't matter, does it? If you're asking then there's a good reason. If you want me to do it quietly, then fair enough. I'm chuffed you've asked, to be honest.'

'It's because other people might be keeping a close eye on Dave and Izzy. It had to be you.'

Archie sniggered, knowing Jessica had said too much – she could've just let him think it was because he was the chosen one but that wasn't the style of either of them. 'You don't have to explain. I'll sort it. Shall I call you?'

'No . . . I just . . . I'm probably overreacting but best not. Come and find me if you need to.'

'Sound – but if you could not go around slapping me in public, it'd be appreciated.' He rolled his shoulders forward. 'Gotta reputation to uphold an' all that.'

Jessica skimmed through her notes, trying not to feel as if this was a job someone else should be doing. 'Right, Mr, er,

337

Naismith, I'd just like to go back over what you've told me, if that's okay?'

The man lying face down in the hospital twisted his head to face her and mumbled something that sounded a bit like 'yeah', although it could have been 'ow'. Given what had happened to him Jessica didn't know which, but she carried on anyway – more to double-check that she could read her own handwriting.

'So you were at home last night with your girlfriend, er, Kylie.'

'Right.'

'And you own a house together?'

'Yes.'

Jessica made an extra note, before continuing. 'You were watching television and having tea together when, and I'm quoting here, "she went mental with the fork".'

A grunt.

'I know you've already told me once but I do think I should probably ask you to confirm for a second time exactly why she, ahem, "went mental".'

Michael Naismith propped himself up slightly, until he was in a yoga-like position: on his front, legs and hips flat against the bed, chest thrusting upwards, neck arched. 'We were watching this midweek singing show thing – it's like a preview to the weekend, so you catch up with who's singing what and how rehearsals are going; that kind of thing.'

'Right.'

'Do you watch them?'

'Er, no . . .'

Liar.

'Okay, well anyway, there's this girl on there – Jenga or something like that—'

'She's called Jenga?'

'Something like that. She was singing this Boyzone song and I was like, "Oh, for fuck's sake. Not Boyzone."'

'Right.'

'Anyway, like I said, we were eating spaghetti bolognaise and Kylie dropped her plate.'

'Why?'

'I dunno – probably because she was so surprised.'

'At the fact you don't like Boyzone?'

'I suppose – she's always been a fan but I thought they were shite first time around. Every time the key changes they're up out of their stools like they've just shat themselves. Whenever she goes on about them, I keep it quiet but it just sort of popped out.'

Jessica peered back at her notes. Michael's opinion about the Boyzone members' arses was ironic considering what his girlfriend had done with the fork and the reason he was lying on his front.

'Okay, so anyway – in essence, and correct me if I'm wrong, but you made a comment about Boyzone which she didn't take too well and that's when the incident with the fork and your, er, body happened.'

'Right.' Michael plopped himself back down onto the bed. 'I know I called you and you had to come out but you're not going to press charges, are you? It was only a misunderstanding – a bit of a tiff. All couples have them, don't they?'

He was right that all couples had tiffs but Jessica wasn't convinced this was a regular outcome.

'We'll have to come back to you,' Jessica said. 'The CPS will take into account likely cooperation of a witness, and seeing as you're the only witness that might mean they don't take things any further. It's not for me to say.'

'It was just a mix-up.'

'She was aiming for somewhere else? Either way, like I said, someone will be in contact. If it's any consolation, Kylie did say she was sorry.'

Jessica made her way back through the hospital corridors trying to figure out if Michael and Kylie's story would make the top five strangest things she'd investigated. When she'd interviewed Kylie, she had given more or less the same story, except that in her version she really did sound like the aggrieved party:

Kylie: 'It's just I really love 'em.'

Jessica (mishearing ''em' as ''im'): 'Michael?'

Kylie: 'Oh yeah, I love 'im too – but I meant Ronan and the boys.'

Jessica had gone from investigating murders and serial thieves to interviewing a couple who'd fallen out over a boy band while eating spaghetti.

As she crossed reception, Jessica spotted the payphone on the wall. She slotted in 50p and called Archie. 'Who is it?' asked his gruff Mancunian voice.

'It's Jess. I'm on a payphone, so be quick. If you've got something for me then I've got a funny story about a man's arse for you.'

'Why would I want to hear about another man's arse?'

'Trust me; you'll want to hear this. Have you got anything?'

'Aye.'

'If there's no one around, you can tell me now. Better than keep sneaking off to my office.'

'Two ticks.' Jessica heard Archie shuffling and then he was back: 'I didn't find much. Brooklands Golf Club is owned by a fella named Logan Walkden. I couldn't find much about your mate Bunce, except for the obvious.'

'What's that?'

'It seemed so simple that I didn't think to write it down at first, then I thought you might want to know anyway. Walkden and Bunce are both local lads, both born in the same hospital a couple of months apart. I've got their birthdays if you want them – they both turned fifty this year.'

The phone began to beep, telling Jessica her time was up. 'Thanks – I owe you an arse story.'

Archie had time for one word before the line cut out – well, four if he came from pretty much anywhere else: 'Yalright'.

40

Jessica drove back to the station trying to think of what it all meant. She was pretty sure that Freddy Bunce had complained about her, while a car probably owned by Logan Walkden had followed her home that very evening. They were both the same age – but so what? It was still a long string of unconnected things: the symbol on the letter through her door, the tattoo that Damon Potter wanted to get, Bunce, Pomeroy and now Walkden; no one thing connected to another.

The traffic was light and Jessica completed the journey all too quickly, with no particular plan of what to do next. She coasted through the station and returned to her office to begin typing everything up. It really was like the old days.

And then she had a thought.

Jessica loaded the Greater Manchester Police website, which was full of the same old nonsense – a top five most-wanted that no one would look at, reported crime statistics that no one – including those who worked for GMP – believed, a map of the city, an open letter from the chief constable banging on about the community, a timetable of events people wouldn't attend, and a list of the senior staff. Jessica clicked through to the Longsight officers' page and stared at her own face. The picture had been taken years ago and barely seemed like her any longer. She had slightly spottier skin, shorter, darker hair and a bizarre glimmer of optimism. She thought that it had probably been taken not long after she met Adam, before what happened with her colleague, Carrie – before everything else. She wasn't that person any longer.

With a click, Jessica got rid of the photograph and moved on to the command team – the chief constable, his deputy and the assistant chief constables. Graham Pomeroy's photo had definitely been taken a few years – and about five stone – ago. In the picture, his cheeks only slightly overhung his jawline and Jessica could only count three chins instead of the five he had now. She clicked on his face and skipped the top part, concentrating on his biography instead:

Assistant Chief Constable Graham Pomeroy

Graham joined GMP twenty-one years ago after a spell with the Royal Air Force and training as an engineer. He has worked in many roles through constable, sergeant, inspector in Bury, Salford and Manchester (Metropolitan). After deployments with strategic command and tactical firearms, Graham was asked to oversee the implementation of a new community policing policy in Salford.

A successful spell there saw him promoted to chief inspector, where he worked in Bolton and Wigan before being promoted to superintendent.

After another fruitful deployment to corporate assistance, Graham was promoted to assistant chief constable, where he currently oversees territorial outsourcing.

No wonder the public thought they were all wankers – anyone who sounded that boring in a profile they'd approved deserved everything coming to them. Jessica had no idea what 'territorial outsourcing' involved – presumably something to do with having police officers in various territories. How hard could that be? And what was 'corporate assistance'? Nowhere in his profile did it mention that he'd seemingly spent a large number of those twenty-one years eating.

Jessica scanned to the bottom where it listed the awards, commendations and qualifications he had. There was no date of birth but it was easy enough to work out the year because of the date he got his O-levels. She had to use her fingers to count and then wrote it down on a pad just to be sure. After checking it four times, Jessica was certain: Pomeroy had been born in the same year as Bunce and Walkden.

She tried to remember what Garry Ashford had told her about Freddy Bunce.

Nine months ago he was given a contract by the council to build a new housing estate for them.

He'd printed off an article about it and Dave had packed the information they had into a cardboard wallet. Where had it gone?

Jessica didn't want to be seen around the station potentially conspiring with anyone, let alone Dave, but she didn't have much choice. She headed through the corridors to the main area in which the constables worked. In the front corner was DI Franks' office, which he shared with one of the detective sergeants, whom they hadn't managed to cram into the sergeants' station a few doors down. Jessica had been concerned for a while that they were going to force her to share offices with Wanky Frankie but had so far been lucky.

Keeping her head down, Jessica hurried past his office door and glided swiftly towards Dave's desk. The stack of binders and folders had shrunk somewhat, but he was still slumped in his seat, typing. It looked like he had barely moved since she last saw him.

As she approached his head shot up, peering over the folders towards Franks' office. 'Jess, I, er . . .'

Jessica didn't waste any time, but she did lower her voice: 'What happened to the printouts about Bunce?'

Dave frowned and then started sorting through the folders on his desk. 'I don't know. I can't remember when I last had them.'

'You had them when we went to Bunce's house and office yesterday.'

His face fell: 'They're probably still in the car. Sorry – we were rushing around and then I was busy answering your phone.'

Jessica gave him a wink. 'Missing me yet?'

Before he could answer, she snatched a pad of Post-it notes from his desk, turned and headed back off the floor as quickly as she had arrived, thrusting the pad in the air and hoping that 'borrowing' stationery was enough of a reason for her to be walking past her friend's desk if anyone wondered.

Claiming she'd left a jacket in the car, Jessica was

relieved to discover the vehicle she'd taken the previous day was still on the premises. She signed the keys out and hurried to the car park, dreading the thought of hunting around the back of the patrol car.

The first thing she noticed as she climbed in was the stench. When she'd been in it yesterday with Dave it had seemed fine – but now it smelled like someone had emptied a takeaway Chinese over the steering wheel. The front and back seats were clear, leaving Jessica to crouch on all fours and go digging underneath. As her fingers slipped into something sloppy, Jessica realised that someone had indeed been eating Chinese food. A foil tub of what had once been noodles had congealed into a cold, mushy, stinking tray of goo. Jessica tried not to gag but took the tub out and dumped it in a nearby drain, wiping her fingers on the material of the back seat and hoping she was able to check out a different car the next time she needed one.

Some of her colleagues really were disgusting.

Deeper under the seat was a small pizza box, folded over and over, then wedged in place. The grease stains may have been dry, but they were still foul.

The first offering from underneath the passenger seat was a well-worn, partially torn beacon of respectability: *Asian Jugs*. Jessica flicked through the first few pages of the magazine and had to admit that the material did at least live up to what the title promised.

Dirty bastards.

Just as she was beginning to think she had covered her hand in day-old Chinese slime for no reason, Jessica's fingers finally closed around the cardboard folder.

346

Wash hands, sign the keys back in, wash hands again, leave the porn mag in Archie's cubby hole, back to the office.

Jessica locked her door and spread the printouts across the spare desk that had once belonged to DS Louise Cornish. She felt that familiar prickle of anticipation at the back of her neck after reading the first five paragraphs about Freddy Bunce's contract to build social housing for the council – the deal that had cost an eight-figure sum.

'. . . the council's head of planning, Declan Grainger, 49, said: "This is a momentous day for the city of Manchester . . ."'

The article had been written nine months ago, which meant the council's head of planning and the person to whom he'd awarded a ten-million-plus contract were the same age. So was the owner of a golf club whose car had followed her. So was Assistant Chief Constable Graham Pomeroy.

Hmm.

Jessica kept reading. There were a lot of boring details about the number of houses that would be built and the new roads that would be needed, something from the Housing Secretary, a quote from the chamber of commerce – and then the line that made Jessica's eyes nearly pop out of her head:

'. . . Mr Bunce, who has worked on projects across the region, said this development would have a special meaning for him because it would involve converting the site of his old school. He said: "St Flora's is where I spent my formative years . . ."'

Hmm.

Not wanting to use her computer just in case, Jessica took out her phone and searched for St Flora. There was a bit about being the patron saint of the abandoned, that she was born in France, lived in Jerusalem, and that she was a virgin. Jessica wondered how many other people through history would have that as part of their epitaph. Was it really something to gloat about? She knew a few kids at her old school who could likely claim that all these years later, but it was unlikely to be through choice.

Jessica kept digging and found out that 'Flora' was originally a Latin word, relating to the Roman goddess of flowers. Those pesky Italians had a god and goddess for everything, though that didn't particularly help until she began searching for other translations of the word 'flower'.

Blomst, virág, fiore, gėlė, kwiat, cvet, flor, something . . . Japanese. Jessica even checked the Welsh translation: *blodeuyn* – as if anyone pretended it was a real language.

And then she saw the French word: *fleur*. For a reason she didn't know, Jessica clicked on the image search. There were a dozen images of flowers and then the one that was on the corner of the envelope put through her door.

The fleur-de-lis was a symbol that had three prongs; one curled to the left, one went straight up, one curled to the right. At the bottom was a small loop holding the strands together, making it look like some sort of sheaf.

As Archie might say: bingo.

41

Jessica continued staring at the logo. It was no wonder it seemed vaguely familiar to Dave – it was apparently a team badge for an American football team, originally coming from the French royal family. She knew nothing about either of those things and assumed he had seen it on the jerseys of the glorified rugby players, as opposed to having an in-depth knowledge of the French aristocracy.

Knowing that doing her job with the minimum of fuss was the best way to not be noticed, Jessica put through the paperwork relating to Kylie's attack on Michael. Despite what she'd told Michael, the CPS would likely prosecute anyway – they had the medical evidence and a pair of statements, so witness or no witness there was little chance they were going to lose the case. Start flashing around photographs to a jury or magistrate of Michael's hairy arse with a fork impaled in it and you were going to ensure two things:

1) Laughter, definitely in private, perhaps in public.

2) Sympathy for the victim and a conviction.

Everyone could empathise with that type of injury because everyone knew what sitting down entailed. Kylie had been bailed to appear back at the station later in the afternoon where she'd be told her fate.

For now, Jessica had at least ninety minutes to kill. She

hurried out of the side door of the station in an effort to avoid Fat Pat knowing where she was, and then looped around to the front gate, onto Stockport Road, walking across the street and into Ali's News.

Jessica whipped her identification out of her pocket and handed it to the young Asian man behind the counter. 'Do you have a phone?'

He examined the card, turning it upside down and over, before handing it back. 'You wanna buy a mobile?'

'No – have you got a payphone?'

'No one has payphones nowadays, lady. What year do you think it is?'

'Do you have a phone at all in the back?'

'Yeah.'

'Can I use that?'

The lad scratched his head uncertainly. 'The manager's told me not to use it.'

'Yes, but I'm not you.'

'Don't you have a mobile?'

'Out of battery. It's an emergency.'

'Er, I don't know, lady . . .'

Jessica took a five-pound note out of her pocket. 'I won't tell if you don't.'

He looked at the cash, then Jessica, then the cash again before snatching it. 'Cheers, I was only expecting a quid.'

He lifted the counter for Jessica to duck underneath and then led her into a back room packed with boxes of chocolate bars, crisps and fizzy drinks. When she had been eight, this was her dream. It pretty much still was.

The young man pointed at a light brown phone attached the wall. 'You have to dial nine first.'

When she was alone, Jessica fished out her mobile, found Garry Ashford's number, and then pressed it into the phone on the wall.

'Hello.'

'Garry, it's Jess.'

'What happened to your number?'

'I'm being careful – listen, I've got some names for you. Have you got a pen?'

'We meet one time when I don't have a pen and you spend the rest of eternity banging on about it.'

Jessica smiled. 'All right, fine: Graham Pomeroy, Freddy Bunce, Logan Walkden and Declan Grainger. Can you see if you've got anything in your archive connecting them to a school named St Flora's?'

'Our archive's awful.'

'I know, I've seen it, remember – but you'll still have more chance than me. You might be able to find something online but I've been struggling.'

'I'll see what I can do but I am actually busy.'

'We all are. Just one thing – if you need to call me, don't go direct. Figure something else out.'

'Are you going to tell me why?'

'Not yet – trust me, if you spot a link, you'll see it yourself.'

Jessica hung up, thought about nicking a bar of chocolate, reminded herself how old she was – and what job she did – then headed back into the main part of the shop.

The young man had a set of earbuds in and was merrily

drumming away on the counter top until he spotted her. 'All sorted?'

'Yep.'

At that moment, Jessica's mobile sprang to life. She delved into her pocket, removing it with an apologetic look of fake confusion. 'Sorry, it must have had some charge after all.'

The call was from a local number she didn't know and Jessica answered it as she headed through the door back out onto the dank, grey street.

It was a woman's voice: 'Hello, is that Ms, er, Jessica Daniels?'

'Daniel. No "s". Loads of people get it wrong.'

'Right – and you're a police officer?'

'Allegedly.'

'Right, it's just that I work at City Magistrates' Court and there's someone here who's given us your name and number.'

42

Jessica took a CID car from the station and headed across the city to the magistrates' court at the back of Deansgate. The person who had called didn't seem to know too many details, simply that Jessica's name had been mentioned in court and that the members of the bench had requested her presence if it was at all convenient.

If an officer was due to give evidence, it would be worked into their rota – often a half-day, no less. If your case was up first, you could get in, read from your note-book, try not to sound like too much of a prat, and then sit at the back of court hoping the thieving/abusive/stupid criminal you'd nicked actually got done for it. If you were *really* lucky, you'd get a quick turnaround and then you were left with a couple of hours to slowly make your way back to the station via the nearest all-day breakfast place. If you weren't so blessed, your case would be on last and you'd spend six hours sitting in a court foyer twiddling your thumbs while being eyed by a parade of scroats waiting for their moment of justice.

Jessica hadn't been notified of any court dates, but the reason soon became apparent as she entered the foyer and showed her identification. The usher led Jessica along a corridor.

He seemed particularly giddy: 'To be honest, none of us thought you were a real person.'

'Sorry?'

'We all thought it was a ploy to keep herself out of protective custody. You see it all the time.'

'I'm sorry; I have no idea what you're talking about.'

'Didn't anyone tell you?'

'Tell me what?'

'Oh, right, well I suppose we're here now anyway.'

The usher indicated a wood-panelled door in front of them, knocking twice before opening it for Jessica. As he retreated, she stood in the doorway looking at the two people sitting at a table. One was clearly a duty solicitor: smartish suit that wasn't as expensive as anything the defence lawyers wore, slightly crooked tie, gently scuffed shoes.

The other was Bex.

She was hugging her knees into herself, backpack on the floor next to her, dark hair scraped away from her face into a ponytail. 'Hello,' Bex said quietly, not quite meeting Jessica's eye.

The previous evening, Bex had been arrested in the city centre after trying to pick the wrong pocket. The former head of inner-city policing for London's Met police was in town to visit his daughter at university and Bex had been caught trying to lift his wallet on the street outside Victoria Station. He frogmarched her to a nearby police officer on duty at the Manchester Arena, gave his statement, and then carried on his business.

Miraculously, Bex had no criminal record. The youth

court magistrates were happy to release her with little more than a slap on the wrist – except that she was unable to provide an address of where she could stay. After speculating that they would send her to what amounted to a children's home for her own good, Bex had coughed up Jessica's details.

And so it was that Jessica was called into the court to say that she would be only too happy to give Bex a roof to sleep under. Given her position within the force, they hadn't thought twice before releasing the teenager.

The journey back to Jessica's house was a quiet affair. The only thing Jessica said was that she wouldn't allow the knife into her house. Bex said she'd ditched it while the policeman who'd arrested her was looking the other way – which was probably sensible given that she would have received a proper sentence had that been discovered in her bag.

Inside the house Jessica took Bex up to the spare bedroom. The girl dropped her bag on the floor and lay on the bed. 'Thank you,' she said quietly.

Jessica thought about being angry, asking where she'd been and lecturing her on how close she'd come to being locked up – but it wasn't the time. 'It's fine,' she replied. 'I'm sorry for bringing up the missing candlesticks.'

'I didn't take them.'

'I know. I knew that then – we found them.'

'Where?'

'In the bins outside.'

'Why were they there?'

'We don't know.'

Bex pushed herself up on the bed until she was sitting. She was wearing three or four layers of clothing but still seemed tiny. 'I don't understand.'

'Neither do I – there's been something going on. Someone went through our rubbish and graffitied my car. We think they might have broken in and gone through our things. We don't know.'

'What did they write on your car?'

It might not have been most people's first question, but it would have been Jessica's and she quite liked the fact it was Bex's too.

'It said that I was a bitch. Don't worry, Adam's already said it – at least it proves it was someone who knows me.'

Jessica forced a smile but it felt rawer now.

'I don't think you're a bitch.'

Jessica shrugged and smiled wearily – what else could she do? 'Thanks.'

'Do you know who did it?'

'No – sometimes when you do this job, you piss off certain people.'

Bex took off the outermost top and dropped it on the bed. 'I'm sorry.'

'You don't have to apologise – it wasn't you.'

'Not for that. I didn't want to steal from that guy but it's been so cold – there was all that fog last night and I thought it'd be safer in the hostel, only I didn't have eight quid.'

'You don't have to explain.'

'You'd been so nice to me and I know you were only

356

asking about your things because you had to. I shouldn't have gone, I was just—'

'I get it – people don't like being accused of things they haven't done. I see it every day.'

'You don't have to let me stay, I just didn't want—'

Jessica stretched across to the dressing table and opened the top drawer, taking out the front-door key Bex had thrown at her and lobbing it – gently – in the girl's direction. 'I've got to go back to work but we'll talk later. I need you to promise me something.'

'What?'

'Don't leave the house – I don't want you running away and—'

'I won't.'

Jessica hadn't planned it but there was suddenly an urge she hadn't felt before. She sat on the bed and opened her arms, motioning Bex towards her. The teenager bit her bottom lip for a moment but then made her decision, leaning forward and hugging her back.

Before Jessica knew what was happening, it was too late: the weeks of mistrust, suspicion and paranoia came pouring out in a flood of tears. Bex pressed her bony arms into Jessica's back, clinging tight and perhaps understanding that Jessica needed her as much as she needed Jessica.

43

Jessica didn't have long to pull herself together before she had to head back to the station. Quite what had come over her in the bedroom with Bex, she didn't know – but then there was a lot she hadn't understood about the past couple of weeks.

To show how far her status had slipped, it turned out that apparently no one had noticed she'd even left. Jessica checked in with the CPS and then went to wait in reception for Kylie, ready to give her the bad news that her fork of doom was going to see her heading to court on a section thirty-nine assault charge. The only consolation was that she'd likely get off with a minor fine or a supervision order – but she was still going to be in the papers as the girl who shoved a fork up her boyfriend's arse.

Kylie seemed to take the news well, although her main defence seemed to be that she hated it when Michael didn't support her interests. How that translated into falling out over Boyzone, Jessica didn't know – but who was she to judge?

Jessica was about to head back to her office when Pat waved her to one side. She thought it was going to be for a crack about anything ranging from her driving to the state of her office to the fact they were still running her television appearance on the twenty-four-hour stations. Instead he had a Post-it note for her.

'Your cousin called. I don't know why he's phoning here – but if you could tell him to try your own phone in future, then it would save me having to act as everyone's personal answering service.'

Jessica had been a fraction of a second away from blurting out that she didn't have a cousin, before catching herself. 'What was the message?'

He thrust the note under her nose. 'Why don't you have a look at the note before asking? Not. Your. Answering. Service.' He wagged a finger so close to her face that she had visions of biting it off. He might even lose a third of a pound.

Jessica snatched the note away and read the words, knowing exactly what it meant: 'Usual place. ASAP.'

The late-afternoon crowd in the supermarket cafe was slightly different from the morning lot. Gone were the single mums nursing quiet cappuccinos; now there was a scattering of parents stopping off with their children on the way home from school for a cheap tea. There was also a curious number of teenagers, who must not have realised that popping in for a can of Coke and a chocolate bar on the way home from school wasn't exactly cool. In the far corner an emo-looking girl with a lifetime's worth of make-up crammed onto her face sipped at a strawberry milkshake while listening to something through her headphones, as her emaciated boyfriend stared at his shoes. Not far from them three lads still in their PE kits, mud streaks and all, were each on their phones, giggling conspiratorially.

Jessica slid in opposite Garry feeling tired, thinking that it seemed a lot later than the clock claimed it was. Conspiracies everywhere. Garry had a can of drink in front of him, straw poking from the top, along with two newspapers.

'We've got to stop meeting like this,' Jessica said. 'We'll soon be on first-name terms with the staff. Then we'll be able to ask for "the usual", then we'll get a booth named after us. Before you know it, we'll have relatives wanting our bodies to be buried in the car park, saying "It's what they would have wanted."'

Garry glanced over his shoulder towards the window. 'I think you've made me paranoid. I spent the whole journey here checking my mirrors to make sure I wasn't being followed.'

Jessica thought she'd cheer him up by telling him that she was pretty sure she *had* been followed the previous evening – hence the reason for giving him Logan Walkden's name – and that someone had been through her rubbish, possibly broken into her house, and definitely graffitied her car. '. . . and yes, before you say it, at least it proves it was someone I know,' she concluded, stealing Adam's joke again because it was the only thing that stopped her from getting upset. She really had lost it with age.

Garry must have sensed that, because he nodded gently and smiled. He unfolded the top newspaper. 'Our news archive is dreadful – but our announcements, births, deaths and marriages section has been digitised for years. Apart from the advertising, it's the only bit that makes any profit, so the owners spent some money getting the archiving up to date.'

'I've never looked at that part of a paper.'

'It's a big deal online – plus it's one of the few times people actually buy the paper itself. They still like seeing their name in print when it's their birthday, or they're getting married. It gives them something to cut out and keep. There's no way I would've been able to check the news sections for those individual names, but in the end it only took one search to get a day and date. This is from three and a bit years ago.'

He flicked a third of the way through the paper to a large page showing face after face with a long list of names and congratulation notices. He didn't say anything, passing the page to Jessica and pointing to the bottom.

Thirty-year reunion

Pupils of the former St Flora's all-boys grammar school held a reunion this week to mark thirty years since taking their O-levels. The school, which closed eleven years ago, is on a site scheduled for development.

Underneath the caption was a photograph that ran the width of the page; around a hundred men all decked out in dinner suits were toasting the camera. Jessica recognised Graham Pomeroy instantly in the bottom right-hand corner, just about making it into the frame. He had a full glass of champagne and a grin that was almost lost to his blubbering chin. Four along from him was Freddy Bunce, looking unassuming. He had a little bit more of a builder's physique, with larger arms than when Jessica had met him, and seemed uncomfortable in the suit, his smile unnatural. On the far end of the line at the other side was James Jefferies in his wheelchair, not smiling, not even looking at the camera. He was wearing his bronze medal and a suit that didn't quite fit.

Along the bottom of the picture, everyone's name had been painstakingly listed, so Jessica had no problem finding Logan Walkden in the back row, standing tall and proud, hands behind his back, neck pushed forward like a strutting turkey; or Declan Grainger standing next to him, shorter and looking a little like a beaver with big front teeth. Partially hidden behind them was a flag that showed the school crest: something in Latin that Jessica couldn't make out over the top of a fleur-de-lis.

Jessica glanced across the cafe at the three students still wearing their PE kits. One of them was showing something on his phone to the others and all three nudged each other with their elbows and howled with laughter.

Suddenly things began to make sense. No one would make the connection, because why would they?

Jessica could see in Garry's face that he wasn't quite there yet. 'Are they working together?' he asked.

'How many people do you still know from school?'

Garry shrugged. 'Hardly anyone – one or two from university.'

Jessica allowed herself a small smile. She also knew at least two of the people he knew from university. 'Remember when Dave Rowlands was giving you stories on the quiet and no one could figure out where you were getting them from?' Garry started to protest but Jessica cut across him. 'All right, been there and done that. Let's just say you operated on a nod and a wink. Nobody ever looked into the fact that you could know each other because no one ever does. The only reason somebody might realise that a person is an old school friend is if you introduce them that way – especially if you come from a big city.'

'So these people are all friends . . . ?'

'Grammar schools were before our time – but we both know it's where young people went after passing the eleven-plus exam. You had to have something about you to go in the first place, so let's assume everyone in this photo was relatively clever. Now let's guess that the names of the people we know were somewhere near the top of the class: look at what they've achieved – business owners, an Olympian, an assistant chief constable and so on. You must remember being at school and there were always a few kids everyone knew were going to go on and do something half-decent?'

'Yeah, then there were the other kids you knew would be serving you at the local Spar for the next ten years.'

Jessica laughed softly: 'Exactly. It's the ninety per cent in the middle you don't know about. When I found out they were all the same age, it reminded me of something Holden said – "Everyone wants to be wanted, don't they? It's about feeling a part of something."'

'So you think this lot were part of a club?'

'Perhaps. It might not be as formal as any of that. You don't need a grand meeting house, or some secret cigar lounge; all you need is a nod and a wink. There's no need to ever acknowledge each other publicly – I'd bet this is the only photo you'll ever find of them together, unless there was a twenty-year reunion and so on. Don't invite each other to weddings, don't have them as godparents to your children, and why would anyone ever suspect?'

Garry was beginning to get excited, sensing a story that Jessica knew he'd never be able to write. He just didn't know it yet.

He pointed at Declan Grainger. 'So this guy is on the council and has a large say in planning – and he gave a big project worth millions to this guy?' He pointed at Freddy Bunce.

'Exactly. I'll bet if you work your way around the names, you'll find others too.'

Garry pointed to a face Jessica didn't recognise. 'He's a lawyer. He owns a firm in the city.'

'Think of the chain: you only need a few key people. Perhaps Logan Walkden decides he wants to build a golf course. He needs someone who could give planning permission, a lawyer to sort all the paperwork out, someone who owns a building company, a landscaper for the course, and so on. At the end of all that, there's an awful lot of money swilling around, but unless you make a big deal over the fact the person you're shaking hands with is someone you once went to school with, then why would anyone ever know? How many things like that have happened over the years? When you throw councillors into the mix with public money, you could be talking a fortune. It's like when you're looking for a builder or a plumber –

you always ask a friend and they'll say: "Oh, I know a guy . . ."'

'And if you've got a high-up police officer in there, then if ever there's a problem with a person asking questions, you have someone to put a bit of pressure on . . .'

Jessica suddenly felt vulnerable, hoping that wasn't true but acknowledging that Garry was only confirming her own theory.

Perhaps sensing that, Garry tried to shoot it down: 'It's a bit limited, isn't it? Not everyone in this picture is going to be successful?'

'That's why you would occasionally need to bring new people in. You wouldn't need that many – just a select few in key positions.'

Finally, Garry got it: '. . . Like Damon Potter?'

'His dad is local, which would be important too. It would all be about keeping wealth among yourselves, so you don't want someone that's going to disappear off to London to build a property empire. I met Damon's father – he's called Francis and runs a haulage firm in the city. After university, Francis was going to help his son set up any business that he wanted. He'd have been the perfect person for the St Flora people to bring in. You want those who are young, rich and have a promising future.'

'So you think the Olympic rowing guy tried to recruit Damon and then . . . ?'

Jessica shook her head. 'James Jefferies is in a wheel-chair and doesn't even seem to like students. He might have been the one that made the phone calls to try to get the members to change their stories about what Holden

Wyatt was doing on the night Damon died – he even told us he had students' phone numbers – but I wouldn't have thought he was otherwise involved.'

'Why would he want them to change their stories?'

Jessica took a deep breath. She didn't know for certain but the small amount of evidence she did have was staring out of the picture at her in grainy black and white. She pressed an index finger to his face. 'To protect this guy.'

44

Jessica knew she had only one way of getting justice for Damon Potter – and it involved her doing something she'd spent the past few weeks avoiding.

She knocked on DCI Cole's office door and waited as he held a hand up. He was on the phone again, facing the wall, avoiding accidental eye contact. Eventually, he waved her in, making a point of checking his watch: it was time for them to go home.

'I need to talk to you about something, Sir.'

'Can it wait until tomorrow?'

'No.'

Cole yawned, making no effort to hide it, and turned to face his computer screen. 'Go on then.'

Jessica sat opposite him but didn't know where to start. Then she thought about the messing around she'd had to endure through the day: borrowing cars, taking buses, the back and forth.

She told him about her car and her bins and before she knew it, everything was flooding out: how she felt marginalised, bullied and paranoid. She told him about the past fortnight and gave him a photocopy of the reunion picture, pointing out Pomeroy and everyone else. Then she showed him the final face and told him why she thought

Damon Potter had died. It might have been an accident but someone should still take responsibility for it.

Cole listened without interrupting, glancing at the photograph as Jessica talked him through it. When she was finally finished, breathless, he stared at her. For a moment, it felt like the Cole of a few years ago, not long after they had both been promoted and they worked together all the time; when he put his trust in her to go out and do stupid things that got results.

Then he peered away again, leaning back in his seat and yawning once more. His eyes were closed and there was an uncomfortable silence. He looked old. Defeated. When he finally opened them, he was staring over Jessica's shoulder, pinching the bridge of his nose. His voice was croaky and low: 'Have you ever felt so tired that you don't know what day it is?'

'A few times.'

'I'm just so sick of all of this: I lost my wife, I hardly ever see my kids – and even when it's my days with them, they'd rather be out with their mates. Not that I blame them; I'd have been the same. Then I come here and sit in this office and the phone never stops ringing.'

He glared at the phone on his desk, as if willing it to prove his point. It remained silent.

'The meetings, the emails, the paperwork. Then I have requests from upper management.' His eyes flickered to Jessica's and away again. 'People I need to keep an eye on. I used to be a young man: fit, happy, with a life to look forward to and now . . .'

Jessica didn't know what to say and could rarely remember feeling so uncomfortable.

Eventually, he finished the thought: '. . . now I'm resorting to sending capable people out on fool's errands. I don't even know why I bother coming in.'

Jessica assumed he was speaking about giving her Kylie and Michael to deal with but didn't push it. 'What would you like me to do, Sir?'

Cole's eyes snapped open. He pointed to the face in the photograph that Jessica had identified. 'I'll make the necessary arrangements. We'll get a warrant for his house and office and we'll go in early tomorrow morning.'

'Me too?'

He nodded wearily. 'You too.'

45

There might have been a certain satisfaction in getting the tactical entry team to smash their way through a door at five in the morning but Cole had told her to keep it low key and Jessica wasn't about to disobey him now.

If there were any residents of the quiet cul de sac awake at this ungodly hour, Jessica thought it would be a good time for them to look out of their windows because they were about to get a show. She rang the doorbell and knocked three times – not too hard but enough to wake anyone up, even her. A few seconds later, a light came on somewhere inside. Officers had gone to the back of the house just in case but Jessica doubted there would be any trouble. There was the sound of footsteps on stairs and then a weary-sounding male voice: 'Who is it?'

'Detective Inspector Jessica Daniel.'

'Oh . . .'

There was a rattle of a chain and the sound of a bolt being pulled across until the door was opened, revealing a man in stripy pyjamas, a long felt-looking dressing gown and hair that seemed to have been styled by electroshock treatment.

Professor Robert 'Call Me Bob' Harper stared on wide-eyed as Jessica shoved the warrant under his nose, waved her fellow officers inside, told him that his university office was being turned upside at that very moment – then informed him that he didn't have to say anything but that if there was something he was later going to rely on in court then he should probably spit it out.

His face was blank: 'Can I at least get changed?'

Six hours later and that was still the only thing Call Me Bob had said. He had been taken to the cells underneath the station, phoned his solicitor, and then spent the rest of the time apparently going over his story with him.

Jessica had risked breakfast in the canteen and then gone to see Cole in his office. He looked even more tired than the night before but offered a small smile when he told her that his phone hadn't rung all morning. Jessica didn't know if that was a good or bad thing – but she could guess. After that, she had gone to keep her head down until Bob – and his solicitor – were ready. Whatever they were talking about seemed to be taking a long time for someone who was ostensibly just a lecturer.

As she was re-reading every piece of evidence they had, there was a knock on her office door. Archie sauntered in, hands in pockets. 'I always knew it was him. The dodgy hair gave it away. I told you he was iffy.'

'Saying someone's a bit "iffy" rarely leads to a conviction. If you were so sure, why didn't you point it out properly a week ago?'

'I figured I'd let you get the credit. No one likes a smart-arse marching in and saving the day, do they?'

Jessica waved him in and he wheeled across the spare office chair, legs splayed wide, nodding knowingly. 'Is everything all right with the other thing you had me looking at?'

Jessica had almost forgotten that it was Archie who had first pointed out that Freddy and Logan were the same age. It seemed like such a long time ago. 'Yes, forget it – all sorted. Anyway, why are you in a good mood?'

'Someone left a little present in my cubby hole last night.'

Jessica suppressed a giggle – *Asian Jugs* had gone down well.

'Anyway,' Archie added. 'I know how *I* figured out it was Call Me Bob but how did you finally work it out?'

Jessica didn't want to talk about the photograph – it was never going to be part of any case they had and, aside from Garry, her and Cole, no one else knew about it. Seeing Bob in the middle of the photo alongside all the other names had put her onto him in the first place but they had more than that now.

'It was you, actually,' Jessica said. 'When you knocked those papers off his desk to show his hip flask, it had me thinking all along that perhaps he was hiding something. When we hit a wall, I started to run a few further checks on him.'

As a white lie went, it at least served its purpose. Archie rolled his shoulders forward and sat up straighter, embarrassed by the praise. 'Aye, well, I didn't do that much . . .'

'His office is in that huge building that overlooks the park. Last night we checked his swipe-card access and found out he left around fifteen minutes after the final confirmed sighting of Damon at the rowing club's party.

Assuming Damon had left to go home, there's a very strong chance they would have seen each other in the car park.'

'That's not much on its own.'

'We found cocaine at his house and the alcohol at his office, plus remember how he kept going on about Damon? He was obviously fond of him.'

'Is he . . . ?'

'I don't know. He's still a bachelor, not that it necessarily means anything.'

Archie stared at Jessica, lips pursed. He must have known that the things she'd listed so far didn't mean much other than they'd have him on a drugs possession charge. It was a jump from that to murder or manslaughter but he also didn't know what she did about Bob's connection to Pomeroy and everyone else. She'd told Garry the grammar school clique would need promising, rich youngsters, so who better to recruit them than a business professor? Something told her that there was more going on than she suspected too – no angry phone calls to Cole, and the length of time Bob had been with a solicitor, made Jessica think that this wasn't going to be a standard interview. The first rule of any successful group was to protect itself above any individual.

Perhaps sensing that there was more to it than he realised, Archie nodded with a fake knowingness. 'So what's he doing?'

'Downstairs with his solicitor.'

'Definitely guilty then.'

'I want you to be in the interview room with me.'

Archie couldn't stop the surprise from spreading on his face. 'You sure?'

'Yes.'

'And it's all right with—'

'Let me worry about other people.'

Soon after, word came through that Bob was finally ready. Just Bob – no solicitor.

When Jessica had let him get changed earlier, Bob had opted for his teaching wear – cords and elbow patches. His hair had been flattened at some point since then but the past few hours had clearly taken a toll – his skin seemed saggier, eyelids droopier.

With the tape and camera running in the interview room, Jessica reminded him that there was no need to be there by himself.

'I can speak for myself,' Bob said.

Jessica felt confused: 'But you've just spent the past few hours downstairs with your solicitor . . . ?'

'I decided to dispense with his services.'

'Right . . . the first thing we need to discuss is—'

'I did it.'

'Did what?'

'It was me who left Damon's body in that bin.'

Jessica had thought something unexpected might happen but not this. She started searching through the papers on the desk in front of her. Even Archie sucked in a small gasp.

Bob was facing the video camera in the top corner of the room, talking to Jessica but not looking at her. 'Shall I start at the beginning?'

'Okay.'

'I was looking into starting an after-hours club at the university – something for the brightest and best. Damon fitted the bill, obviously. I'd spoken to him briefly about it around the university and he seemed willing. That night, I had been working late at the university. I swiped out and saw Damon walking out of the park.'

Jessica suspected that part was true – although the 'after-hours club' sounded unlikely given what she knew.

'He was, let's say, a little worse for wear. Perhaps not drunk as such but a little giddy and giggly. I asked if he wanted a lift home.'

'You didn't take him back to his flat though . . .'

'No – we went to my house. I said we could talk a little more about my idea for the club and he was fine.'

'What happened at your house?'

Bob's voice cracked slightly. 'He said he didn't really like beer, so we were drinking whisky. Then I asked if he wanted to try something a little stronger.'

'What?'

'I suppose you've already found it by now – but I usually have a small amount of cocaine around the house. It helps at the end of a week.'

'Damon's flatmate said he wasn't into drugs.'

Bob shrugged. 'What can I say? I didn't force him.'

'Did anything else happen between you?'

Bob looked away from the camera, facing Jessica. 'Like what?'

'Do you want me to spell it out?'

'If you're asking if we had sex, then no. It wasn't his thing.'

'But you asked?'

'Does it matter?'

Jessica decided not to push it while he was talking freely anyway. 'What happened after that?'

Bob turned back to the camera. 'I really don't know. One minute he was fine, the next he was convulsing on the floor. He started coughing and I didn't know what to do. The next thing I knew, well . . .'

Jessica had a sense that the story was true – except that Bob had taken him back to his house to talk about the St Flora's group and not an after-hours club. Damon wouldn't be the last student to overindulge in booze and drugs and Bob wasn't struggling to tell a made-up story, plus it fitted with the forensic evidence they did have.

'You know that Damon choked to death on his own vomit?'

'Yes.'

'You could have saved him, possibly by altering the angle his body was at – definitely by calling an ambulance.'

'I know.'

'Why didn't you?'

'I'd been drinking too. I didn't quite realise what was happening until it was too late. I tried shaking him but he was gone.'

'What about an ambulance? They could have talked you through resuscitating him.'

'I don't know . . . it happened really quickly.'

'You were thinking about yourself, knowing that if a

student was found dead in your house with drink and drugs in his system, then it'd be the end of your career.'

Bob shrugged. He did seem genuinely devastated, head bowed, arms under the table. 'What do you want me to say?'

'Tell me what you did with his body.'

'You can probably figure it out. I got a sheet, wrapped him up, put him in the back of the car and drove back to the university.'

'Drunk?'

'I'm guessing you've never been in a situation like that but it's amazing how sober you feel.'

Jessica was pretty sure that breath tests and blood-alcohol levels didn't take that into account, but then drink-driving was the least of his worries.

'How did you lift him by yourself?'

For the first time, Bob seemed unsure of himself. 'Sorry?'

'He was a rower – I've seen the photos and he had a lot of muscle on him. He was taller than you as well.'

'I . . . didn't really think about it.'

'So you're saying you carried him by yourself?'

Bob glanced to the camera, then Jessica, then back again. 'Of course.'

That was something she very much doubted – but there was no evidence to the contrary.

'Why did you return to the university?'

He spoke without a pause, the story perfectly drilled. 'Familiarity? I'm not sure. A few years ago, there was a man fished out of the river who'd fallen in and drowned. I suppose I thought it would be easy enough to make it seem like that. It was late . . . well, early, I suppose. At the back of the university buildings, there are these lanes that run down to the park and the river but there were a few small groups of people around wearing suits and dresses.'

'What did you do?'

'I waited. There was a party on, so when it went quiet I took Damon down towards the front.' He caught Jessica's eye. 'I had to drag him some of the way on the path but I had the sheet. When I got down there, I spotted the metal bin and thought it'd cause fewer problems if I left him there.'

'Why?'

'I'm not sure . . . I wasn't thinking properly. I suppose I thought that if his body ended up in the river then it could have floated anywhere.'

It wasn't the best of reasons but given the rest of his story, it almost made sense: she didn't believe he actually wanted to hurt Damon and he likely wouldn't have known that the bin was going to be emptied hours later. In a strange, warped way, being left to be found in a bin offered a minuscule amount of dignity compared to floating miles in a river and perhaps never being found. Of course, the truth could be that Bob left the body there knowing the blame would be thrown elsewhere. Either way, he had a story that he was sticking to.

Jessica nudged Archie with her knee under the desk and he was instantly the jack-the-lad Manc, as much at home selling dodgy TVs as he was in an interview room. He pressed both forearms onto the table, looked at Jessica, then back across the desk again.

378

'What a load of old bollocks. You expect us to believe that you carried the body of a strapping young athlete out to your car, down a ramp, then lifted him into a bin all by yourself? Give over, mate. I've heard more convincing stories off Scousers.'

Bob didn't flinch, staring at the table. 'Believe what you want – I've told you the truth.'

'And what about this after-hours club of yours? There must have been something else going on – Damon was a smart kid: rich, athletic, bright future. What were you offering him that made him so keen to go back to your house?'

He'd asked the exact question Jessica wanted him to without even knowing it.

'I don't know. He was very academic – I can only imagine he enjoyed interacting with others who were up to his level.'

'What a load of shite.'

'I don't have anything else to say.'

And he didn't. Archie kept pushing and pointing out the inconsistencies in Bob's story but he would only repeat that he'd told them all he knew.

Eventually, Jessica tapped Archie on the knee again and he backed off, still staring ferociously across the room. 'I just have one final question,' Jessica said. 'Who are you scared of?'

'Sorry?'

'I've seen enough people who are scared of other people over the years. It gives off a scent. I can smell the fear in here. Constable?'

Archie joined in: 'Aye – fear and bullshit. The room stinks.'

'Who is it?' Jessica asked.

Bob's eyes flickered up at the camera again but he didn't flinch, shaking his head instead. 'Who have I got to be scared of?'

Jessica ended the interview and called the uniformed officer stationed outside to take Bob back to the cells. As the professor stood, Jessica slotted behind him as Archie moved in front. Archie apologised to the officer for messing up protocol but it gave Jessica the moment she wanted. She reached up and pulled down the collar of Bob's shirt. He spun and tried to tug it back up but she had already seen the tattoo just above his shoulderblade embedded on his wrinkled skin: a black and white fleur-de-lis.

46

Jessica sat in the chair opposite DCI Cole's desk, telling him everything that had happened with Robert Harper. He nodded, asked her if that was all, and then said he'd deal with the CPS. Jessica was already on her feet in the doorway when the red mist hit. It had been building for so long that she was pointing a finger and shouting before she knew what she was doing.

'No, that's not all. You *do* realise he almost got away with it because of you? Whether it was Pomeroy or whoever else, you let them do this and you almost let some kid get the blame for it.'

Cole peered past her along the length of glass where the corridor was empty. 'If you're going to raise your voice, can you at least do so when the door's closed?'

Jessica slammed it. 'That's your answer?'

Cole remained sitting, voice calm. 'I was asked to do something by a member of the command team. I did as I was told.'

'You did as you were told without asking questions!'

'Perhaps that's something you need to learn? We got there in the end, didn't we?'

Jessica couldn't believe what she was hearing. Getting there in the end shouldn't be the way they did things. She spat the reply. 'I know what you did.'

Cole's lip were sealed but he snorted ever so slightly through his nose, nodding. 'Do you?'

'Yes.'

Without a word, he dug into his pocket and took out a set of keys. He turned and unlocked a black metal filing cabinet behind him, reaching into the bottom drawer and taking out a shoebox. He locked everything back up before turning towards Jessica and offering her the box. 'Go on.'

Jessica took it hesitantly, lifting the lid and pulling out tightly packed folded newspapers. At the bottom was something she recognised. Something she hadn't seen since a cold evening in a cobbled alleyway.

'These are my glasses,' she whispered, barely believing they were there.

'I know.'

She glanced up. 'Where did you find them?'

'I think you know.'

Suddenly, the fact that Cole had been cold with her for months made sense. 'I—'

'I don't want to hear what you have to say. I'm still a police officer. Sometimes it's better not to know.'

'But—'

Cole spun and grabbed her wrist. '*Stop*, Jessica. They were found at a crime scene where someone was shot dead. No witnesses and a gunman that apparently had no connection to him. I don't want to know the rest.'

'I didn't—'

'*STOP!*'

Cole's voice thundered around the room and he gripped Jessica's wrist so tightly that she dropped the box.

'I don't want to know,' he added, still shouting. 'Just take those and do whatever you want with them – but if you want to lecture anyone else about what they get up to, then perhaps you should look at yourself.'

Jessica picked the box up and began to put the news-paper back in.

Cole's voice was almost back to normal when he spoke again: 'You should know that I've already put my notice in. I finish officially on December the thirty-first. There's going to be an announcement soon. Pratley's review is due on January the second but Greater Manchester Police's past behaviour is going to be branded "institutionally corrupt". It won't affect anything from the past ten years or so – but it will still recommend a top-down reshuffle. It's going to be a very different place to work from next year.'

'How do you know that?'

He snorted again. 'Because when you mix with others and don't spend all your time working against them, believe it or not, some people are more willing to talk to you.'

'I'm sorry, I—'

'I don't want to talk about it. We've got a few more weeks and then we go our separate ways – but if you think I'm such a bad guy after everything that's happened, then perhaps you should ask yourself who put that letter through your door.'

Jessica stared at him, searching for the truth, even though his eyes were still fixed on his desk. '*You?*' She paused, still not believing it. 'Why wouldn't you just tell me?'

'You forget that we've worked together for a long time.'

'I don't understand.'

'Since when did you listen to me? Or anyone? You were happy to go away thinking I was whoever you wanted me to be. I told you that I had to listen to – and obey – what I was being told by other people. I could hardly endorse you running around poking your nose into things officially.'

Jessica almost whispered the word 'Pomeroy' again but Cole had confirmed it without needing to say the name. He was far better at this game than she was.

'How did you know about the logo?' she asked.

'How did you find out about the connections between everyone in your photograph?'

'They were all the same age.'

'Do you know how old I am?'

'You're not—?'

'I wasn't in their year – I'm a little older. It was my school crest.'

Jessica stopped to consider it. Asking someone which school they went to thirty or so years ago was not something people did. 'So you knew about them?'

'Not really – there were a couple of lads in my year who called themselves Florians. No one thought anything of it but they used the symbol. When the pressure was being put on me from above, it was mentioned that perhaps I should remember where I came from.'

'Pomeroy knew that about you?'

Cole nodded but wouldn't say the name. 'It didn't take much to put two and two together once I knew that,' he replied. 'I didn't know anything about Damon Potter getting it tattooed – that was news to me – I just thought I'd give you enough of a nudge to figure it out yourself.'

'Freddy Bunce's van?'

'I have no idea – you found that.'

Jessica still hadn't worked it all out but she had a few theories. She wasn't going to find out any more from sitting around with a shoebox in her lap.

'I should go,' she said.

Cole didn't reply but then he'd already said it – she needed to look at herself.

47

Jessica sat in the supermarket cafe nursing a cup of tea. It wasn't so long ago that she would have been drowning her sorrows in a pub but this felt more appropriate.

Dave had piled through lasagne and chips, while Garry had eaten a salad, saying that he had to look after himself. Jessica had simply drunk her tea. It was dark outside, time for them all to go home, time for the staff to start thinking about closing.

After telling the pair of them about Bob's confession, which would be common knowledge soon enough anyway, they still had the same questions she did. All Jessica could offer was speculation.

'I checked the name of the solicitor Bob was in with on our sign-in sheet,' she told them. 'He's a junior partner at a practice in the city centre.' Jessica pointed at a figure in the middle row of the class photo which Garry had placed on the table. 'Guess who owns the firm.'

It was one more person from the picture to add to the assistant chief constable Graham Pomeroy, builder Freddy Bunce, golf club owner Logan Walkden, council planning officer Declan Grainger, professor Robert 'Call Me Bob' Harper – and possibly Olympic medallist James Jefferies.

'Why would Bob take the fall?' Dave asked.

'In many ways, he didn't. I think he was pretty much

telling the truth. Either he'd invited Damon to his house to recruit him to the Florians, or—'

Gary interrupted: 'Where did that name come from?'

Jessica hadn't told them about DCI Cole's role. She cursed herself for being careless and quickly moved on. 'I think it's some sort of old school nickname. Anyway, either that was the reason Damon was at the house, or it was because Bob was trying it on as Archie thinks. He won't tell us either way, so it's almost irrelevant. I suppose he took the blame because it was his fault. If you assume there are powerful people in the group, would you rather admit to perverting the course of justice and risk a man-slaughter charge, or would you rather face them? Even if he goes down for the greater charge, Bob will probably be out in three or four years. His career's over but that would've happened just from us finding the drugs.'

The two men nodded before Dave replied. 'Do you think he acted alone?'

'I doubt it – Damon would have been heavy. Archie hammered Bob on it in the interview but he kept denying everything. There's only so much you can do. We looked at phone records but there was nothing. He could have used a payphone or a different mobile if he called someone to ask for help.'

'What about Holden?' Garry asked.

'He's still on remand for the assault charges.'

'I meant do you think they were trying to recruit him?'

'No chance – he didn't have the academic side to him, or the big money. Holden wanted to be the student presi-dent at the rowing club because it was the only thing he

387

had in his life. He was convenient. I suspect our Olympian friend knew a little more about the hazing and initiations than he ever let on. When word came around that one of his old school friends could be in trouble, he put a call into Holden knowing that the kid looked up to him. He encouraged him to tell the police what he knew, knowing full well he'd tell us about the initiation rituals. Meanwhile, he called the other club members and asked them if they could *really* remember seeing Holden later in the evening when Damon died. He would have said that Holden was looking at implicating them all in the hazing and suddenly the stories started changing. It's funny what people can and can't remember when there's a chance they could be dragged into something. We'll check James' phone records – but it won't prove anything. He'll say he was phoning them all to urge them to go forward with what they knew. Holden's already told us that.'

Dave wanted to finish the thought process, so Jessica let him: 'Holden thought he was doing the best thing by confessing to us, where really he was doing exactly what James and the rest of the Florians wanted him to. He didn't expect the other club members to turn on him or change their stories, but when they did, it was already too late.'

'Exactly.'

'What about the logo?' Garry asked.

Jessica paused for a drink. She wasn't entirely sure. 'I guess the tattoos are some sort of badge of honour, like a secret handshake. Perhaps they all have them, perhaps only a few. I remembered that when we went to see Freddy that he kept scratching his shoulderblade—'

'I noticed that too,' Dave said.

'It was the same with Bob in his office, like a subconscious thing. Bones told us that Damon had been looking for a tattoo and I tried Bob's collar on a whim in the interview room. It was a bit stupid really.'

Garry didn't seem convinced. 'If it's such a secret – a nod and a wink, the odd phone call, don't be seen together, that kind of thing – then why would Freddy Bunce set up a building company with that as its logo?'

Jessica puffed a breath through her teeth. 'Who knows? We were at his house and it was this huge extravagant place, then he was wearing a T-shirt in the cold just to show that it didn't affect him. He's probably a bit of a show-off, but I guess the other thing is that you can hide in plain sight. If anyone questions anything, it's an innocent builder's logo – or an old school badge.'

Dave seemed nervous. '*You* questioned him about it.'

'I think that's what started the chain – he called Porky Pomeroy to complain, he told Cole to shut me down.'

'But you got there anyway?'

'Yes . . .' Dave and Garry exchanged a nervy look.

'What?' Jessica asked, confused.

'What do you think they're going to do?' Dave said.

'About what?'

'About *you*.'

Her eyes narrowed. For whatever reason, it hadn't crossed her mind. 'All I did was my job – they'll be more annoyed at Call Me Bob for being careless.' Jessica looked at the clock high on the wall. The assistants had cleared the other tables and were leaning on the counter at the front glaring at them. 'We should go.'

Garry started packing his papers away, as Dave downed the rest of his drink. 'There's only one thing we don't have a clue about,' Garry said.

'What?'

'Who sent you that letter?'

Jessica shrugged. 'I guess we'll never know.'

ONE WEEK LATER

Jessica sat on the sofa with Adam's arm draped around her. In comparison to all too many that had gone before, it had been a quiet week.

'Ready to talk about it yet?' he asked.

On the television, the adverts came on, so Jessica switched it off. Anything was better than watching some shiny-faced dick try to sell you a loan on daytime television. The mornings were the worst. 'Our DCI is leaving at the end of the year. They announced it yesterday.'

Jessica hadn't spoken to Cole since he'd told her, but with everyone else knowing, it now seemed real.

'What does that mean for you?'

'I don't know.'

'Promotion?'

'Definitely not.'

'More time off?'

Jessica laughed and wedged herself further into his shoulder. She'd just watched him eat two bowls overflowing with Coco Pops – yet he was still desperately skinny. What with Bex upstairs, it meant she was the fat one of the house. 'I've been thinking a lot about time off recently.'

'What about it?'

'What if I wanted more?'

'I thought you said you were owed a few days. Perhaps

they'll let you take time instead of money? We could have a weekend away?'

'I didn't mean that – I meant taking lots of time off. Perhaps when Jack goes, I should too. It's like the end of our era anyway – Jason left, now Jack. There's that Pratley report due in the new year and it looks like there'll be another reshuffle. New chief inspector, possibly a new super, and so on. It would be a good time.'

'You know I'll support whatever you want to do. It's never been about the money – after my grandmother and your dad, plus the insurance money after the fire, it's not as if we're scraping around for pennies.'

Everything Jessica had been thinking came flooding out: 'We can look into all we talked about . . . we couldn't adopt while carrying on as we were. Someone like Iz can balance everything but I'm not like that. I have to be as good as I can be at one thing at a time.'

Adam kissed the top of her hair. 'I know.'

'And that's still what you want – the meetings, the appointments . . . ?'

'Jess – we were going to have a son together and I was delighted with that. I think that would have given us a bit more work than having to visit a few social workers. I've been waiting for you to say this the whole time; I just didn't want to force anything. We're going to do it together.'

'Sure?'

'Yes!' He dug his fingers underneath her ribs and began tickling but Jessica bucked so violently that she ended up headbutting him in the chin.

'Ow,' they said together, rubbing their various injuries.

'What about Bex?' Adam whispered.

'I want her to stay as long as she wants . . . if you're okay with that.'

Adam grinned. 'We got a big house because we wanted to fill it with people. Babies didn't work, so if you want to start collecting people from the street, then fair enough.'

Jessica returned his smile and wrapped her arms around him again. 'There's something about her. I don't know what. I just get this sense that she's going to do something with her life. I like it.'

'It's nice spending a morning with you,' Adam said. 'Your late shift and my half-day Wednesdays work out well. Perhaps I'll get used to it if you really are going to give your notice.'

'I am.'

'You don't have to.'

'I want to. I'm going to do it later.'

Adam fought to get his feet out from under her. 'I still have to be at work for twelve, so if you can move your car from the drive to let mine out . . .'

He stood but Jessica pointed down at her pyjama bottoms and fluffy white boots. 'I'm not dressed to go out-side.'

'I can't drive your car – you have the seat too far for-ward.'

'So move it back.'

'Why can't you do it?'

Jessica stuck out her bottom lip. 'If you *really* loved me, you'd move my car first, then come back for yours.'

'Or, I could just sit in my car, wait for you to move yours, then go to work . . .'

'Addddddaaaaaaaaammmmmmmmmmmm . . .'

He rolled his eyes. 'Fine. Where are your keys?'

'I don't know – in the kitchen somewhere. I can never find them.'

Grumble, grumble.

As Adam clattered around the kitchen shouting about all the places he *hadn't* found them, Bex crept into the room. She was wearing a set of thick pyjamas and dressing gown that Jessica had insisted on giving her the money for. Bex promised to get a job, or else find another way that didn't involve stealing to pay her back. She seemed confused. 'What's up with him?'

'He's lost some keys.'

Adam's voice called 'found them' from the kitchen and then his footsteps echoed their way up the stairs.

'You look happy,' Bex said.

'I think we've just made the decision to adopt.'

Bex grinned, reaching out and touching Jessica's knee. 'That's lovely.'

'I'm going to quit the police.'

'Oh . . . why?'

'I can't do both and I don't want to do that any more. I've done too much.'

'You're only young.'

Jessica shrugged. 'Better to go now than wait until I'm forty or fifty.'

Bex nodded, taking a breath and turning away. 'I've been thinking too. You said you wanted to help me figure

394

out what I should do with my life. I think I want to go to college. I was always okay at school but other things kind of took over and—'

'That's really good. There are lots around here. I can help you go through prospectuses – unless you already know what you want to do?'

Bex shook her head but grinned. 'I'll get a part-time job and I can pay you rent. I don't want to stay forever – not because of you or Adam, just because—'

'I understand.'

Adam clumped his way back down the stairs and peered around the living-room door at Jessica, thrusting her keys in the air. 'I hope you appreciate this.'

He was trying to stop himself laughing but Jessica played along. 'I'm sure I'll find a way to say thank you.'

'There are cars parked all the way up and down the street too, so I'm going to have to go all the way to the bottom, then walk back and get my car.'

'Wow – my hero.'

Bex dissolved into laughter, which set Jessica off. Adam was stifling a smile as he headed to the door.

'Oi! Are you going to give me a goodbye kiss?'

'I'll bring your keys back in and do it then.'

The front door slammed and Jessica shifted to the edge of the sofa to watch him try to move her car seat. He had forgotten where the mechanism was, leaving Jessica to giggle as he stood with his hands on his hips, arms in the air.

'He's lovely,' Bex said.

'He really is. Just don't get him going about the *Star Wars* sequels. Or cartoons from his childhood.'

Finally Adam found the lever, heaved Jessica's chair back and climbed into the car.

'Where did you find him?' Bex asked.

'On a case. I think he's been in my head ever since, even when we weren't together.'

The engine rumbled to life and Adam edged it towards the road, waiting for a passing car.

'Are you really looking forward to giving up the job?' Bex asked. 'I thought you were the type who would end up running yourself into the ground before you'd even realised.'

Jessica leant closer to the window. 'I probably was. I think a combination of you and Adam especially made me realise that other things are important.'

'I suppose you only get one chance at life.'

Jessica peered at Bex and grinned. 'Exactly – and I can't wait.'

She turned back to the window just as Adam pulled out, turning right onto the road. For some reason the car didn't surge ahead as Jessica would have expected, almost as if his foot had slipped off the accelerator. It came to a halt in the centre of the road outside the house next door. Jessica could only just see the top over the parked vehicles but had a perfect side view of Adam's confused face. He looked both ways and then checked the mirror.

Jessica stood just as the explosion shredded its way out of the bonnet with a ferocious roar. She didn't have time to speak, to breathe, before the car was engulfed by an inferno that erupted sideways, tearing through the metal and popping like a tin can in a microwave. The fire leapt to one of the parked vehicles but Jessica only had eyes for one: hers, where another boom signalled a second explosion that made the car bounce half a metre into the air before landing in a crackling, simmering shard of flames.

AFTERWORD

Um. Sorry about that ending. I had plenty of angry emails after I broke Jessica and Adam up in an earlier book, so lordy knows what this will bring.

I just want to make it clear that this ending wasn't written without plenty of thought beforehand. You'll have to trust me . . .

It goes without saying that the story here is fictional but I wanted to make that extra clear, simply because the University of Salford really does have a rowing team. Partly to avoid any confusion with reality but also to give the story a marginally better setting from my point of view, I have given them a made-up headquarters in the real Peel Park. It's not there, so don't go looking for it.

On a slightly similar note, the explanation of GMP's structure is also a deliberate blend of truth and fiction.

Other than that, any other mistakes you didn't notice are entirely mine, as ever. The ones you did spot were added in by a person or persons unknown. Honestly.

There are, as always, lots of people to thank, primarily: Nicola, Trisha, Natasha, Jodie, Susan, Sam, Stuart and Tom – they know why. These books don't write themselves – I really wish they did – but it takes those people to take my meanderings and make them better.

Finally, a disclaimer: Jessica's views on workmen,

builders, plumbers, golfers and taxi drivers are all hers and definitely not mine. This is especially true if I need the services of a workman, builder, plumber, taxi driver or, erm, golfer.

COMING SOON

FOR RICHER, FOR POORER

The tenth book in the Jessica Daniel series

Three houses have been burgled in five weeks. The robbers barge in through the back, disable any way to contact the outside world, and then ransack everything – before distributing the stolen cash to local charities.

It might be robbing from the rich to give to the poor – but Detective Inspector Jessica Daniel is not a happy bunny. The new DCI has a whiteboard with far too many things on the 'unsolved' side and he wants the burglars found. Doesn't he know Jessica has other things to do?

There's a lottery winner who's gone bankrupt, the homeless teenager Jessica's taken in, a botched drugs raid, a trip to London with DC Archie Davey, and a man-mountain Serbian with a missing wife who's been pimping out young women.

All the while, someone's watching from the wings and waiting for Jessica to mess up. Officers are being pensioned off and booted out – with a certain DI Daniel firmly in sight.

COMING SOON

DOWN AMONG THE DEAD MEN

The new Manchester-set crime novel from
Kerry Wilkinson

'I'm going to do you a favour: I'm going to tell you my name and then I'm going to give you thirty seconds to turn and run. If any of you are still here after those thirty seconds, then we're going to have a problem.'

Jason Green's life is changed for good after he is saved from a mugging by crime boss, Harry Irwell. He is then drawn into Manchester's notorious underworld, where smash-and-grab is as normal as making a cup of tea.

But Jason isn't a casual thug. He has a life plan that doesn't involve blowing his money on the usual trappings. That is until a woman walks into his life offering the one thing that money can't buy – salvation.

extracts reading groups
competitions books new
discounts extracts extracts
competitions discounts
books new events
events extracts books reading groups
new books
new titles reading groups
interviews events
books events extracts
discounts interviews new
new books events books
events new extracts
discounts extracts discounts
www.panmacmillan.com
extracts events reading groups
competitions books extracts new